THE WAY

THE
WAY

CARY GRONER

Spiegel
and Grau

S&G

Spiegel & Grau, New York
www.spiegelandgrau.com
Copyright © 2024 by Cary Groner

This book is a work of fiction. All characters, names, incidents, and places are products of the author's imagination or are used fictitiously.

Interior design by Meighan Cavanaugh

Library of Congress Cataloging-in-Publication Data Available Upon Request

ISBN 978-1-954118-42-3 (hardcover)
ISBN 978-1-954118-43-0 (eBook)

Printed in the United States

First Edition
10 9 8 7 6 5 4 3 2 1

There's a world behind the world we see that is the same world but more open, more transparent, without blocks. Like inside a big mind, the animals and humans all can talk, and those who pass through here get power to heal and help.

—Gary Snyder, *The Practice of the Wild*

When we remember we are all mad, the mysteries disappear, and life stands explained.

—Mark Twain, *Mark Twain's Notebook*

Well shit, people, which is it?

—Anonymous

THE WAY

1

That afternoon, as we made our way through the ruins of Santa Fe, the high desert sky cleared to brilliant blue and I thought we might be safe, at least for a while. The rubble of the city lay quiet under its soft, muffling blanket of dust and sand. There were tentative peeps and calls from a few scattered birds, but of human noise I heard not a whit. Mainly what I noticed as we passed through, Cassie and Peau and me, was the ringing of flagpoles as hanging chains blew into them.

There seemed to be just the one tone—a low, resonant *ting*—each *ting* separated from the next by a pause of five or six seconds, piercing peaks of sound that emphasized the emptiness of the silent valleys that lay between them. Elementary school, high school, post office; buildings long fallen to rebar and broken cinderblock, but each with a steel pole outside, each staff with its spousal chain, so that as you slogged through town on the weedy roads, roads bordered by the charred piles of buildings they once gridded, you moved from one chiming sphere of sound to the next. It brought to mind some ancient feudal world, where cloistered territories of power and safety were defined by the peals of bronze church bells. In those days they sometimes had distinct melodies for weddings or funerals, or for fires and invasions. There were church bells in Santa Fe too, of course, but the elegant mission towers that once hefted them skyward had fallen, so the bells squatted off-kilter on the ground, silent and vaguely sullen. As often as not, some critter had taken shelter underneath. A good use of them, I couldn't help thinking. Who needed to hear about weddings anymore?

I had no clue, but what I *did* know was that I was too old for this. At fifty-two, which practically made me a Methuselah, both my prognosis and my prospects were increasingly dire. Everyone was younger than me, often by decades, but of course "everyone" is a deceptive term, implying bounteous humanity when in fact almost no one was still alive. The few wandering strays that caught sight of me—lice-ridden, straw-haired urchins with hollow eyes; starving, desperate teenagers; the occasional feral twentysomething—tended to start and stare, gob-smacked by the grizzled old beast, poised on the blade's edge of whether to attack or sprint for the hills.

I did my best to find a middle path. If I had any food, I'd offer them some, and this typically had a propitiating effect. I couldn't afford to lead them into dependency, though; too much ground to cover and too little time to do it in. Nor did I dare suggest that I owned more provisions than I showed, which would have painted a target on my back. I had to act tougher than I felt, in other words, but this was the story of my life. And, of course, there were the reasons for my urgency, nine mounted men doing their monomaniacal best to hunt me down.

Places like Santa Fe made it harder to forget everything we'd lost, and remembering gave me a hollow flutter of anxiety in the pit of my stomach. We all lived on the precipice of annihilation now; there were no doctors, no vaccines or medicines, and formerly minor injuries like sprained ankles could quickly doom you.

To the south, Albuquerque still stood, albeit empty of people. This was a little better but not much. Its few skyscrapers had settled off plumb, as if emulating Pisa, and all their windows had been broken out, though by bird strikes or hammers or the compressive effects of time and desiccation and gravity, who knew? They gave the city its most unsettling and beautiful characteristic, though, for even in gentle breezes it began to whistle and moan like a collection of giant wind instruments. High flutelike trills, the baritone of oboes, human-sounding wails and cries of despair, all this resonated through the streets depending on the direction and velocity of moving air, so that the place exhaled a full-throated symphony of lamentation and downfall. The buildings bled long vertical streamers of rust from the summer monsoons, and many were bearded with verdant vines like ancient Mayan temples. On the bright side, they hosted millions of pigeons and doves and songbirds—and, of course, peregrines, who happily devoured the other birds at every chance. In Santa Fe, there were no such reassuring signs of life. I could still imagine cities out there full of fine, healthy men and women, young and old, gleaming in the night with the full galactic bounty of electric light. I'd yet to see one, though.

One good thing about Santa Fe was the money. It was ubiquitous, fast-drying, and tough, so it was excellent for starting fires. As we neared the western edge of town, I collected fistfuls of tens and twenties from the grate over a storm drain and stuffed them in my kindling sack. There was more everywhere, but I didn't have room for it all.

We started up into the mountains, and I was overjoyed to be out and away from the city. There in the southern Rockies it was a perfect evening. We rode west on an old state highway, as nearly as I could tell, though my ancient map had been folded and refolded so many times it appeared to have been dredged up from oceanic submersion and dried in a pitiless sandstorm. I had what I needed, though: two solid mules and a hitch rigged up so they could pull the old rusted-out F-150. The truck sported a fiberglass camper shell, bedding for me and Cassie (though it was her habit to crawl into mine), a nest for Peau in the front seat, food and cooking gear, and a .22 long rifle with a scope and a handful of bullets. Without the engine, transmission, drive shaft, and gas tank, the truck sat high and light on its squeaky springs. It was an easy haul for the big, tough mules, and with a bottom welded in, the engine compartment made fine storage space. So we bounced along through the rocks and weeds, vaguely westward on the abandoned road, overgrown and overhung and wild, partially blocked here and there by boulders or landslides. The truck never would have made it on engine power, given its balding, senescent tires. The mules were splendid, if not excessively speedy, with the further advantage that they found their own way perfectly well and I didn't really need to steer. I just held the reins in my left hand, out the open window, and gave them an occasional flick when needed.

The sun set and the moon slid its big hungry face up over the ridge behind us in the east. The air cooled, turning to a kind of blue crystal. We were snug enough in the truck's cab, even without a heater. Cassie was curled up on the bench seat next to me, blended well into her blanket by all the fur she'd shed, her whiskers twitching in mouse-dreams. Peau soared out over us somewhere, reconnoitering a likely place to stop for the night, seeking intelligence and company from whatever others of his kind he could scare up. It wasn't difficult; people were scarce, but ravens were everywhere, hundreds of tribes with their own dialects. He did his best to communicate to me what he gleaned, and usually he succeeded.

The old snow in the crevices between the trees took on a hard cobalt shine from the moon, and dampness rose from the ground, hovering in a low layer of mist. The sky deepened into a soothing, fathomless ultramarine. Venus gleamed ahead of us in the west. Stars were blinking awake, though there was still enough soft, diffused light to see by. I felt stupendously lucky to be alive. Of course it was perilous, wandering alone through mountains that had been aggressively reclaimed by pumas, grizzlies, wolves, and such. With people gone, even coyotes had expanded their ranges and become confidently militant. There were worse things out there than bear and cougar, too, but it wasn't worth dwelling on. The mule deer were more plentiful than ever, there were millions of jackrabbits, and even elk and bison were spreading, all of it a bounty to their carnivorous brothers and sisters up the food chain. The secret lay in all the abandoned corn farms, vast fields of barley and alfalfa and other grains, stunted and uncultivated now, mixed in with weeds, but perfectly acceptable to your average doe or cow elk. Nutrition leading to fecundity, followed by predation. Hence the need for a good, hard camper shell; in a tent we would have been dinner for whatever toothy thing wandered by. I took some solace knowing that the plentiful four-leggeds drew attention away from soft marks like me, but I never got careless.

Cool wind pushed the pines around, and they whispered among themselves, spilling all their piney secrets along with cones and nuts. It pleased me to anticipate the rituals of evening. Zagging in the rising wind, Peau sailed in and landed on the flank of Mule One, as was his wont. Mule One, the girl, and Mule Two, the guy, halted. I hit the brake so the truck didn't bump them in the butt, which they found irritating, and life improved when the mules weren't irritated. Peau hopped over to the hood, then to the mirror, as I rolled down the window.

He carried a small, stringy mass in his beak and dropped it into my outstretched palm. Horsehair. He indicated a direction with his head and emitted a series of staccato clacks and little caws. If you can learn Morse, you can theoretically learn Raven, though the latter contains a lot of body language, a variety of subtle vowels, and a range of meaningful inflections that take time to master. I usually got a sense of what he *meant*, anyway, and this was one of the most confounding aspects of the world's metamorphosis. Had the animals changed, or had I? Why were we now able to understand one another in ways that we couldn't before?

I knew it was entirely possible I was losing my mind, but such matters are notoriously difficult to judge from the inside. Insanity, it seems to me, is just another kind of betrayal, and the lunatic often ends up in the same position as the deceived lover, by which I mean the last to know. You can try to console yourself with Laing's First Pablum—insanity as the rational response to a deranged world, etc.— but seriously? Does anybody who's ever had a crazy friend really believe that?

In any case, I knew roughly where Peau was suggesting we go, even though I was confused by the horsehair. I thanked him, and he took off.

"Yo, mules," I said, and One and Two sighed in their martyred mulish fashion and leaned into their harnesses. We followed a spur road to a little clearing, where I smelled the horse before I saw it. So *that* was it.

The stallion lay by a granite outcrop with a black streak down it, and he smelled like burned flesh. He'd probably been struck by lightning during the storm that had drenched us in town the previous day. He was stiff and a little bloated, but not too badly, and the meat would be fine when cooked. It was a lucky find, though we'd have to camp both uphill and upwind.

The upwind was obvious. The uphill was so we could settle in quietly behind some sort of obstruction and keep an eye on the horse without being seen (or smelled) by whoever else got interested in it in the course of the night. Every hungry beast within five miles would want a piece, and they'd all be lifting wet noses into the tattletale breeze just about now, calculating direction, travel time, and potential for conflict. I was also thinking about our pursuers, who, because they were on horseback, might be overtaking us soon if their tracking was halfway decent.

I got out of the truck to look around. I loved the reassuring bang of a truck door closing. It spoke of the security of manufacturing, all the things we'd squandered. If you had to, you could always jump back inside and be safe, even in a thunderstorm. About the only thing that could get to you was a grizzly, which could hook its claws into the crack between the door and the frame and yank the door right off the cab. I'd seen the aftermath of this once, and it was extremely unappetizing, though evidently not to the bear. Jesus, those things can eat.

Oh, and the ants, of course. We have hunting ants now, apparently from somewhere in South America, and they sow terror wherever they appear. Weather stripping doesn't stop them, and there are enough holes in the front of the truck, under the dash, where various hoses and wires and cables used to be, that they'd come pouring in like water. You're okay if you stay out of their way—despite their name, they're mostly scavengers, like the native ants—but they're three-quarters of an inch long, a russet color, and if they catch you sleeping or wounded and unable to run, you're finished. They paralyze you with venom, swarm to the attack, and can skeletonize a person in about an hour. Unlike, say, pumas, they don't bother to kill you before they start eating, so it's an extremely unpleasant demise. Ants can smell, and I was worried that the horse might attract them, along with everything else.

I gave the stallion a nudge with my foot and he emitted a long, ghastly fart. Not the usual grassy, amiable fart of a horse but something much ranker and deader. I gagged a little, but some of the bloating went down. It was nearly dark now, and I'd have to get to it right away.

I found a place where we could park, nestled in a clearing with rocks all around, a kind of natural little fortress, just the sort of snug haven I had in mind. It lay thirty or forty feet upwind and slightly uphill, in fact, so I could look down onto the horse without having to smell him, unless the wind changed. A tall cliff behind us made ambush unlikely.

Once we were parked, I hauled the poke nest off the roof and set it up. This consisted of a portable perimeter of pine poles, six feet tall and spaced four feet apart; I pounded the sharp ends into the ground with a hand sledge. The poles were connected with interwoven barbed wire that I'd attached with U-nails. The thing rolled up for storage on the truck, then unfurled for deployment in a tidy circle at night. "Poke nest" is a rough translation of a term Peau used, because, as a bird, it looked like a nest to him, and he had to be careful where he landed on it lest he get pricked by barbs. It was essentially the same as the thornbush barricades that surrounded huts in Africa to keep out lions and hyenas.

I gathered wood, built a little stone hearth, got the fire going, then took my knife and trotted down to the horse. It was solidly dark now, with just a little light from the moon shafting through the trees, but I had a headlamp I could recharge with a thing I'd rigged up. The mules pulled the truck, which turned the wheels, which fed the battery, which connected to a little universal charger. It was a mule-powered flashlight, essentially, not fancy but good enough to let me see what I was doing.

I took a few seconds to sharpen the knife on a rock, then sawed off the horse's back leg—the one he wasn't lying on—and tried to get as much of the good thick muscle up in the thigh and flank as I could. The whole piece must have weighed a hundred pounds. I threw it over my shoulder, humped it back up to the truck, and dropped it on the ground. Peau swooped in, black from the black sky, suddenly materializing in the firelight as if the tips of his feathers were ablaze. He landed on the truck with a little click of claws.

What ho, he said—a ravenism of hearty greeting that translates quite well this way, I think. Cassie hopped out of the truck, looking sleepy and vaguely disgruntled. They glared at each other, as was their habit.

I led the mules into the poke nest, then put a bucket of water and one of oats between the truck and the cliff face, so the mules would follow and be hard to see back there.

Ravens are wary of large, fresh carcasses, as if they're worried the animal might still be alive and trying to trick them. This may explain why in some places they collaborate with wolves on a hunt. Certain flight maneuvers and vocalizations help the wolves find prey, and once the pack has made the kill and begun eating, the ravens drop in and take a share. Peau, like others of his kind, preferred his dinner tartare and alfresco, so now that I'd cut open the horse's flank, he flapped over, landed, and began enthusiastically plucking away. I wasn't a hunter, but in situations like this it was an easy enough symbiosis.

Over by the fire, I skinned the flank, sliced off thin steaks, and started grilling them. Cassie and I ate together, and as soon as the rest of the steaks were mostly done, I tossed them, still hot, into an old perforated ammo case we kept for such things. They'd finish cooking in there, then dry out and keep for three or four days. We'd be well provisioned.

We were almost done with the cooking when three coyotes showed up. They saw the fire and hesitated, but their hunger quickly overcame their inhibitions. Peau left the horse and flapped into a little tree beside the truck. I'm often impressed by the graciousness with which smart animals cede ground—none of the aggressive displays you got with humans, just practicality. *Wow, you're big. So long!* No blame, no shame.

Coyotes, I'd learned, often like to start in the nether regions, and true to form they plunged their greedy mouths into the horse's anus, tore off his balls, and proceeded from there.

I turned away to finish the cooking. When the meat was safely stowed, I stretched out the horse's long Achilles tendon, which I'd saved. Horse tendon is strong and springy and useful for all kinds of things, so I wanted to cure it and have it available. I pulled the hot steel grill off the fire, leaned it against the rocks, and tossed on more wood. An ostentatious display of thermal technology never hurts when you want to impress substantial, hungry beasts. We were reasonably safe in the poke nest, though, and if push came to shove there was always the truck.

The coyotes had quickly opened a gaping hole at the back end of the horse and were gorging themselves, snarling and snapping at each other as they ate. The horse expelled great blasts of fetid gas, and I was glad we were upwind, but the coyotes didn't seem to notice. Then, after about ten minutes, all three suddenly looked up at once, came to full alert, and scampered away into the darkness.

We heard the bear snuffling and mewling its way in. It emerged from between trees into the far edges of the firelight. A black sow without cubs; I didn't think there'd be much danger. She studied us briefly, arrived at her apparently disparaging conclusions, then found her way to the horse and went to work. She was practical and efficient, almost humdrum, tearing off long strips of bright-red meat and scarfing them down. Once she glanced up at us again, more or less as a formality, then returned to feeding.

After half an hour of this, she looked up, peered into the darkness, then turned and shot from the clearing like a furry black cannonball. Bears always look ponderous and slow until suddenly they're not. It's sobering to remember that a grizzly can overtake a Thoroughbred, at least in the first hundred yards, and the black bear appeared nearly that fast.

We heard a sound off in the woods. I'd encountered something similar before and hoped I was mistaken, but then it came again, and I knew I wasn't. It was a tiger chuffing, and my heartbeat kicked up a notch.

"Into the truck, everyone," I said, and we all hopped into the cab together. I closed the door as quietly as I could, but I didn't stop pulling until I heard the reassuring click of the latch. Then I locked both doors. I rolled the window down a couple of inches so I could hear, and we sat there, watching and listening. The mules got nervous, pawing at the earth and clearly wanting to run. I wished I could talk to them the way I talked to the others, because I wanted them to shut the hell up.

Soon a movement caught my eye, stripes moving among stripes. The big cat slunk between blue moonbeams and tree shadows as it cautiously entered the clearing. No more chuffing; it proceeded with

utter silence, its shoulders rolling like ocean waves, smooth and powerful beneath its skin. Then, as a cloud passed over the moon, the cat
vanished completely into the shadow of a little cliff, and the whole
world darkened, as if the tiger had come to me upon my death and
gently closed my eyes.

The cloud passed. The tiger slipped from the shadows and cautiously approached the horse. Then, much as the bear had, it looked
up. The fire had burned low, but the tiger smelled smoke, it smelled
mule, and it probably smelled me. But unlike the bear, which had
merely peered in our direction and registered nothing interesting, the
tiger looked me right in the eye, through the glass of the window. I
could barely see the cat, but I could certainly see its eyes, which seemed
to gather the moonlight and starlight reflected off of everything
around us and concentrate it all into that glowering stare. It held my
gaze while I held my breath, a good five seconds, and then in one fluid
motion the tiger leapt over the horse and swept up through the rocks
as smooth and ghostish as fog crossing a ridge—but fog with a purpose, fog with vision and focus. It halted noiselessly at the edge of the
poke nest, a trace of steam curling from its nostrils in the cool air, its
eyes like moons. In the cab of the truck, fur, feathers, and the hackles
on the back of my neck all stood on end. The tiger raised a huge paw
tentatively, batted at the barbed wire, then rubbed its head against the
nearest pole, leaving scent from the glands at the corners of its mouth
just like a house cat. A male, and we were apparently in his territory.

The mules started screaming and running back and forth in our little barbed corral, three paces then halt-and-turn, three paces, halt-and-
turn. The tiger watched them and began to stalk the perimeter, looking
for a way through.

I knew that the tiger could jump the top of the poke nest if he
wanted to. He had a nice, tidy dinner waiting for him in the form of a
dead stallion, of course, but some big cats just like to kill. The more
agitated the mules got, the more excited he became, until he was

pacing back and forth, drooling in the moonlight, tracking the mules'
every move, and making little tentative lunges that panicked them
even more. For a second I thought they were going to try to run right
up the cliff face, and if they'd been goats they might have succeeded. I
didn't want to think about what we were going to do if they got
killed—we'd be stranded and utterly screwed. This possibility made
me angry, because I was not exactly on vacation. I had commitments,
miles to go before I slept.

I opened the door and got out. The tiger turned, lunged into the
barbed wire, then gave a startled snarl of pain and backed away, disen-
tangling himself and furiously shaking his paws.

"Leave them and eat your goddamned horse!" I yelled, pointing at
the stallion, as if this should clarify everything.

I half expected him to jump the wire, tear me to pieces, then slaughter the mules. Instead, he stopped cold, sat down on his haunches,
panted a bit, then lolled out his tongue. It was the weirdest thing ever,
as if he'd been playing a terrifically fun game, and now he was disappointed to be scolded. He shifted his gaze between me and the mules,
as the mules backed right up into the rock wall, almost falling over
their own haunches trying to get as far from him as possible.

The tiger got up and turned away. He sauntered casually back
down to the horse, pausing for a second to spray another one of the
poke-nest poles. He grabbed the horse by the neck and dragged it off
into the shadows under the rock overhang. Six-hundred-pound cat,
twelve-hundred-pound horse, dragged twenty yards using mainly jaw
and neck muscles. It made an impression.

I suspected I reminded the tiger of someone, presumably someone who could inflict punishment and had been used to ordering
him around. Even more amazing he hadn't killed me, if so. I got back
into the truck. It took me a while to slow my breath and calm my
shaky hands.

An hour later, I dragged out my battered, scratched-up old night-vision goggles and peered into the darkness under the overhang. I could barely make out the horse's white ribs. The tiger, gorged, lay on its side asleep, breathing steadily. I figured he would sleep three or four hours at least, and it occurred to me that he might turn out to be the best possible thing to come along under the circumstances.

In any case, nothing would unfold soon. Peau cleared the cat hair away from his spot in the cab while Cassie and I climbed into the bed in back. I lay there a while, watching the stars through the plexi roof, and finally felt calm again. I remembered seeing time-lapse video, in the old days, of the stars as they turned through the sky and ultimately fell below the horizon of the nighttime earth. It created the most astonishing effect of the planet moving through space. Without the special photography, though, everything felt less sensational. The stars I saw existed only as light, really, for the photons that found my retinas had left their various suns thousands or millions of years before. Those stars would now be in different places, or possibly even be extinct. What I saw was just a kind of mashup of reality, the legacy of different times and places that had all found their way to earth at this same moment. I'd often wanted to go back in time—to move backward over the cemetery of spent hours, as Italo Calvino once wrote—in order to undo miscellaneous blunders or stupidities of mine. But, of course, time travel was impossible except in the way I was experiencing it now. I had all the ordinary thoughts people have when they watch a night sky, reflections that nevertheless feel profound and original because they arise in the intermingling of contemplation and emotion and lived experience. Space was incredibly vast; we were impossibly small; what did it all mean?

It was more than that, though. I was thinking about people I'd loved and lost, and there were so many of them it had become hard to keep track. This filled me with melancholy, for I knew that just as their lives had ended, my own death was long overdue. And what then, when it did come? Where would I be, how much time did I have? There was no way to know, naturally. But the vastness of the night sky, the knowledge that eventually all those stars would wink out and the universe would plunge into eternal lifeless darkness, made me profoundly sorrowful. We human beings had had our chance, and we'd blown it.

I finally managed to drift off a little but woke up again soon enough. I'd been grinding my teeth, and my bad molar had begun to throb. I got up, crawled out of the back of the truck, put on my boots, grabbed my pad and pen, and shuffled sleepily over to the camp chair I'd placed by the fire. I laid a couple of branches on the coals, blew a little flame to life, then fed in bigger pieces as the fire resurrected itself. Cassie hopped down from the truck bed, came over, and curled up next to me. She never liked sleeping alone. I uncapped the pen and began to write.

Dear Eva,

We're in the mountains tonight, and as usual, when the moon is up and the stars are clear and the air is cold, I think of you. I can so easily imagine something you might say—something smart and funny and cutting in that way you have—as if you were here and whispering in my ear. I think of the warmth of your body and your breath, the feel of your skin against mine.

I've been traveling the past three weeks with a raven and an old cat, and it's lovely to have the company after so much time by myself. Five months ago, the raven showed up at the meditation center, where I'd been living as caretaker because everyone else was long dead. The cat wandered in, half-starved, a few weeks later. Cassie's an enormous tabby, part Maine coon, I think. She had a collar and a name tag, so somebody had owned her once, and she's reasonably tame for a cat that's had to fend for herself. She's changeable, sometimes sweet and sort of a goofball, sometimes bitchy. You'd like her.

When the raven first sailed in, I was sitting outside, finishing lunch.
I'd never liked eating alone, but alone was the only way I ate anymore,
and I was feeling a little more glum about this than usual. Suddenly
there he was, perched in a tree, saying, "Grawk!" which might as well
have been "Nevermore!" Nevermore was pretty close to how I felt about
humanity in general, and of course this brought to mind the poet. It
seemed too obvious to call him Poe, though, and I'd had enough French
in high school to remember that "peau" meant "skin," so I settled on
that. It's just one of those embarrassing, stupid pet names, not that he's
actually a pet, or that it makes any difference to him.

He was curious about me, watching from nearby branches and
emitting soft chucklings and little gurgles as I did my chores. One day
I shared my lunch with him—he especially liked the homemade potato
chips—and after that we were pals. He and Cass maintain an uneasy
détente, given long and regrettable interspecies history (in the
Latinate terms you favor, Corvus corax + Felis catus = Animus
maximus). They don't completely relax around each other yet, but I
hope that will change. In any case, with time we've all begun to
understand one another, and that may help.

It's hard to explain this since I don't completely understand it
myself. The longer we kept company, the more I began to pick up their
words—much as a child would, through some combination of
repetition and context and maybe even telepathy. Once you get used to
Raven, it's actually quite musical, as if you've interspersed a variety
of resonant vowels with castanets for consonants. My comprehension
is still primitive; I speak English to them, but in the same way, it
appears they've begun to get it. Sort of like good sheepdogs, except
that Peau is smarter than any dog who ever lived, and Cassie, while
not quite in his league, is certainly no slouch.

I know what you're thinking, dear Eva. Animals who speak are for
myths, for fables, for children's stories. Well, we're all children now,
doing our best to navigate a world transformed, too wild for

comprehending. Of course, in most of the old legends, humans and animals conversed as if it were the most natural thing in the world, and I like to think this represents a kind of world-healing. They're excellent companions for me, in any case. I have no way of keeping Peau, but he seems content to stay. We encounter flocks of ravens everywhere we go, and he appreciates the opportunity for sociability and reconnaissance. But ultimately he seems to prefer my company, and his keen interest and evident joy in everyday things are a tonic for me.

To matters more dire: a splinter group of the American Revolutionary Militia (known generally to nonmembers as the Asshole Reactionary Meatheads—hereafter the ARMs) continues its pursuit. I've learned something of their leader, a brute named Flynn, and I gather he's not only strong and durable but also reasonably shrewd. All the things I'm not, in other words, including heavily armed.

And speaking of myths, I suppose we're not so unlike Orpheus and Eurydice, you and me, in all our catastrophic failure and grim aftermath. So bear with me, if you will—you have nothing now if not time, after all—while I unfurl the story's sails and see where the wind propels it, this fearful voyage of my life without you.

—Will

Cassie woke up and watched me as I finished writing. I fed the pages into the fire in the order I'd written them. When the first page had spun itself into flame, then floated upward in blue smoke, I added the second. Soon it was gone too, and then the third.

Cass's eyes were large and inquiring.

"It's a little like mail," I explained. I told her that people used to communicate with letters, phones, and computers, but that all stopped when there were no more electrical grids or post offices. This was simply my idea of another way to do it.

Admittedly, I didn't know how Eva would read my letters. It just felt to me that the smoke somehow represented the essence of the intention, and that under the circumstances, that would have to be good enough.

I PUT ON MY COAT, got a blanket for Cassie, let the fire die down again, and then we waited. Eventually I heard them coming. The moon glowed overhead, cutting through the glade with shimmering blades of light. The men were trying to be quiet, but they weren't especially good at it. Twigs snapped, misjudged steps kicked rocks, a stubbed toe led to a quiet curse.

I picked up the night goggles and counted two men in front, one hanging back. None of them had goggles, and only the one in back carried a rifle; the others held machetes.

The wind had shifted, and the stench of the horse was assailing us, but this also meant we were downwind of the men and they wouldn't be able to smell the last of the smoke from the embers.

I could barely see what happened next, but I could hear plenty. The tiger awoke and slunk around behind the first two men, then took them out quickly, methodically, and enthusiastically. A sudden lethal pounce, a vicious bite to the neck, an eviscerating swipe from a massive paw, then another leap, all with great snarlings from the cat and shouts of surprise from the men, who had no idea what was going on or where to run. The slaughter took less than half a minute, and when the first two men had been dispatched, the tiger turned to the third. By then the guy had climbed up into a pine and begun to fire his rifle more or less at random. This was stupid for all kinds of reasons, not least of which was that bullets were now worth about a million bucks apiece, though of course a million dollars was actually worth nothing. When one of these valuable little commodities ricocheted off the rock behind us, I lay down on the ground and tucked Cassie in safely between me and the rocks, just in case. The tiger, who seemed to know something about guns, crept behind another tree and crouched down, waiting. Soon enough, the man had emptied his treasury and the rifle fell silent.

"Collins!" he yelled.

I couldn't decide whether to answer or not. It would reveal where we were, and he might have more bullets tucked away. But we were safe enough behind the rocks, and I wanted information.

"Who's asking?" I replied. The cool night air carried sound so well that we didn't need to shout.

"Name's Redding. I work for Buck Flynn. Is this your cat?"

"He's one of them," I answered, bluffing. "I'd hoped Flynn would come meet him himself."

"Can you call him off?"

"Not really," I said. "Mind of his own. You know tigers climb trees just as well as cougars, right?"

"That thing's a *tiger*?"

I sighed. "You could save yourself a lot of trouble by telling Flynn to find another hobby and leave me alone."

"Nobody tells Flynn what to do but Flynn," he groused.

"But I've got nothing he wants."

"The way I hear it, you've got *everything* he wants."

"Mules, you mean?"

"Get serious."

"Even if I did have something, I'd never give it to Flynn," I said. "He'd have to kill me, and then he wouldn't be able to find it anyway. So this whole thing is pointless. Tell him that."

"You're a human being," Redding said.

"So?"

"So you feel pain."

"You're out of bullets and you've been treed," I pointed out, perhaps a bit sharply. "You're not really in a position to be issuing threats."

Redding grumbled something in response, but I couldn't make it out.

Cassie batted at me. The tiger had snuck to the bottom of the tree. It leapt up and started climbing.

There was a scrabbling of claws on bark, a tiger's roar, a strangled cry of surprise from Redding, a crashing of limbs, and then a sickening *thunk* at the base of the tree, the sort of sound you might get if you dropped a watermelon onto pavement. It was soon clear I wouldn't be getting any messages to Buck Flynn that night, except perhaps the message he'd get when he came to collect what was left of his posse.

I felt a little guilty now. The tiger had done my dirty work for me as well as any soldier or assassin. I was grateful to him, but that didn't mean I wanted to run into him the next morning.

2

We surveyed the scene cautiously after the sun rose. The tiger had decamped, fortunately, and it appeared that the coyotes had returned at some point and picked the men down to gristle. The hunter ants were carting off what little remained of them.

The men had a few things I wanted, so I carefully stepped around the ants and picked up the machetes, which had been dropped in the general havoc. I took Redding's rifle, as much to keep it from Flynn as to have it myself, then gave him a once-over. No more bullets, but a decent hunting knife at least. I'd hoped for a good pair of boots—real manufactured boots with molded synthetic rubber soles, one of the great underappreciated creations of civilization—but nobody here had anything better than mine, which was a sad commentary on the state of affairs in the footwear department.

It was hard to know how long it would take Flynn to locate them, but even if it was within the day, the ants would leave only polished skeletons in shredded clothes. He'd have no way of knowing if the men had ever caught up with us, or if we had anything to do with their demise. That was fine by me.

I rolled up the poke nest, secured it to the rack on the camper top, scattered the ashes of the fire, then let the mules pull the truck out while I followed with a long pine branch and swept away our tracks. I continued this until we were back on the broken asphalt of the road, then tossed the branch away and got into the truck. The tiger had bought us some time, and it was a fine morning.

Then, about two hours later, it occurred to me that by taking the gun and the machetes, I might as well have left a calling card. Stupid, stupid, stupid. Flynn wouldn't know for sure it was me, but who else was out here?

I wasn't going back, though. He knew the road I was on, so it would be best to put as much distance between us as possible. We were making a solid four miles an hour, twelve hours a day, and if I could get a daylong head start, they'd have a hard time making up the gap, fast horses or not. For one thing, they'd kill their mounts without a rest day here and there—yet another advantage of mules, who could pretty much slog away forever.

Anyway, the two machetes made me a wealthy man. The rifle was good too—an old Marlin .30-30 saddle gun with a smooth lever and a scope. I doubted I'd ever use it even if I had the right ammunition, but I'd be able to trade it for two months' worth of provisions if I found the right person, and two months of food security was about as good as life got these days.

AFTER A COUPLE MORE HOURS, when the morning had warmed up and we'd put fifteen miles or so between ourselves and the carnage, I found a wide, flat spot and pulled over. I hobbled the mules and let them graze, then built a fire and dragged out the ammo can. The horsemeat had finished cooking in there, and it was tender and juicy; all it required was a little heating. I'd stopped along the way to pick a couple of wild onions and some mushrooms, so I put the steel grate

over the flame, got out the cast-iron skillet, and dropped in some horse
fat to get things going. It smelled wonderful. I cut up the onions and
fried them, then added the shrooms, and finally sliced up a flank steak
and dropped in the strips. My mouth was watering at the smell of it all,
and Cassie was hungry too, so I dropped some steak into her battered
steel bowl and she set to, making little satisfied growling noises. Peau
wasn't around; I figured he'd flown off to explore.

Such good, basic food, onions and horse. I felt replenished and
stronger after eating, and it was easy to be out in the light and clear
morning air. My mind was still on those men, though. How had Buck
Flynn found out about me, anyway? Who *was* he? The whole situation
was full of unanswered questions, and I hated unanswered questions.

Redding hadn't seemed like a bad fellow, and how can you not be
touched by someone who's come to take you prisoner and ends up
pleading for you to call off your tiger? Haplessness, lack of adequate
resources, failure to plan—just the kind of errors I was prone to. If it
weren't for the poke nest, those men might have found us all dead.
Well, not Peau, and maybe not Cassie, but certainly the mules and me.
A few straight poles and 260 feet of barbed wire salvaged from an old
fence, giving us sixty-five feet at four strands down, which translated
into an open shelter roughly twenty feet across, enough for the truck
and the mules and a little moving-around space. Old rusty wire with
little stabbers. Precious as gold, but if you had fencing pliers and decent gloves, there was plenty to be harvested.

Cassie, sated, lolled on her back in the sun. I rubbed her belly a tad
too aggressively; predictable retribution, but she was gentle enough
about it. Soon Peau fluttered down and landed on the hood of the
truck, carrying a flowering sprig of rabbitbrush in his beak. He carefully set it down, then cocked his head back and forth to admire it.

"What ho, my lord," I said. "Adding to your collection?"

He bobbed and croaked in a way that signified *Yes*, so I told him what
folks called it. I added that the Native people had made the roots into

medicinal tea for coughs and colds, and that they'd used the bright-yellow flowers to dye things. He seemed satisfied and carried the plant into the truck bed to put it with a couple of other little bundles he kept there, one of sage and one of something I didn't recognize.

RIDING IN A HOLLOWED-OUT PICKUP at four miles an hour, studying two sweaty mule asses all day, you begin to appreciate how big the world really is. Years ago, when I had a car, fifty miles was nothing, a forty-minute drive on the freeway. Now it was a hard day's work, at least for the animals.

We were on what was still more or less a road, and the mules knew what to do. Even so, resting my hands on the wheel from time to time made me feel useful. It was April, according to my beat-up old watch, which also helpfully informed me that it was 72° outside. And although I'd always loved spring, for its flowers and its storms and its promises of hope, the question that pounded my poor head was how anyone, in good weather or bad, was supposed to live a harmless life.

Once, at the Colorado dharma center where I lived (*gonpa*, in the Tibetan), I was walking outside when two insects flew by me in a big aerial tumble. One was a yellow jacket, the other a bald-faced hornet, and they were all wrapped up in a yellow-and-black ball, in mortal combat. The hornet was chewing the legs off the yellow jacket, and they were stinging each other, over and over. The hornet was bigger, and I figured he'd eventually prevail. After a few seconds, they careened off, and I lost them in the trees. But *that*, I thought, perfectly exemplified samsara, the suffering of cyclic existence. Me and Flynn, in other words. Everybody and everybody.

THAT AFTERNOON, after we'd crossed over a gorgeous mountain pass, one of those high saddles that looks like the Swiss Alps, complete with boulders and snowfields and soughing pines, Peau took off for one of his occasional aerial rambles. He never had any trouble finding us again, and I was glad that he got so much enjoyment out of it. In my twenties and thirties, I'd made my living as a science writer, and I was thrilled when the old shibboleth about anthropomorphism finally took a stake through its dark, blood-sucking, vampire heart. For centuries, scientists in Descartes's mold had sneered at any suggestion that animals could feel emotions—we were projecting, they were really just soulless meat machines, and so forth. Of course, maintaining this brittle belief meant ignoring anything that didn't fit the paradigm, as if none of the arrogant jerks had ever bothered to look their own pet beagle in the eye. It was all a desperate attempt to cling to the crumbling precipice of sapiens superiority, in other words, which made everyone feel better when it came time to slaughter animals, or enslave them, or otherwise treat them like shit.

Eventually we developed fMRI with AI vectoring and learned that lots of animals have roughly the same emotional centers in their brains that we have, show similar electrical activity in those centers, and hence presumably feel most of the things we feel. Fear, love, rage, devotion, jealousy, all of it—even ennui on hot, muggy days—with any differences so insignificant as to be meaningless. Jane Goodall and a handful of others had been trying to tell us this for decades, of course. Researchers found that corvids generally (ravens, crows, magpies, and others) are at least as intelligent as chimpanzees and possibly more so. A ravenmaster for the Tower of London—and what a job *that* must have been!—once wrote, "It didn't take me long to learn that ravens really do speak to us," and he was presumably in a position to know.

This isn't to say that animals' minds are exactly the same as ours; in many cases they're very different. We seem to be better at abstract thought, including the crucial understanding that someday we will die. But the emotional foundations of our experience turn out to be very much alike, and there are things they do routinely that we manage rarely or not at all.

I once read an article about a family of elephants in Africa who had a human benefactor. The elephants were free, but for many years this fellow had created sanctuaries for them and intervened when there was trouble with local farmers. The man was getting old, though, and eventually he died. Soon afterward, all the elephants stopped what they were doing and walked ten or fifteen miles to his home. They solemnly circumambulated the house for an hour or so, then returned that night to where they'd been.

How did they know the man had died? What did they feel that compelled them to make the journey? Humans, too, sometimes report knowing when a faraway loved one has died, and all this makes it clear that our comprehension of the fabric of reality is primitive at best.

So when Peau took his afternoon free-flights—and especially when we'd come across a flock of other ravens—I could see he was exhilarated. More than once I'd walked out to the edge of a bluff, so I could watch them playing at eye level. They weren't food-gathering, they weren't establishing social hierarchies, they weren't enticing mates. Ravens did all those things and more, of course, but for many hours a day, all they did was fly around, ride updrafts, swoop between cliffs and trees, chase each other like puppies, shriek and caw back and forth, and generally have a kick-ass time. When they were free-floating, riding thermals or otherwise taking it easy on a warm afternoon, they often checked in with one another using a vocalization that sounded like *quark*, as if they were a flock of particle physicists at a conference.

Though every group had a different dialect, there was enough commonality in the lingo that Peau could communicate. Once I tried to mimic what I'd heard, but I didn't get any response, so I just shut up and let the ravens have their rave.

As for my own relations with animals, I felt a lot of guilt. Without the mules, I would have no chance of finishing the journey I was on. They were so stubborn that they sometimes drove me crazy, but every day I worked them like—well, like friggin' *mules*. I never believed that they didn't feel or understand what was happening to them, though. It didn't take a friendship with a brilliant bird to eviscerate *that* pathetic fallacy.

SOON PEAU CAME ZOOMING in a little faster, and at a steeper angle of descent, than I was used to seeing. He landed on the hood and quickly hopped over to my window, his throat hackles bristling and his "feather pants" flared out, sure signs of agitation or fear. He then emitted a few staccato little caws, confirming the impression, and I caught the terms for "big," "strange," "sky," and "coming."

I halted the mules. At first I thought he'd seen some kind of aircraft, but I couldn't imagine how such a thing was possible. Even if someone had found a working plane, they'd never get it started because the fuel would have been unusable for years.

I got out of the truck and peered across the valley to the south. There was definitely something weird approaching; it had crossed the nearest range of mountains and was closing in on us. It covered the sky, and at first I thought it must be some kind of unusual storm. But there wasn't any lightning or thunder—just a low, dull roar. I had no idea what it was.

We got into the truck and I shut the door. "Yo, mules!" I yelled, and they took off at a brisk trot.

We found shelter under some trees as the thing began to pass overhead and the mountain fell into shadow. The sky roared like the engine of a distant jet, something I hadn't heard in fourteen years. The mules pranced, skittery in their traces. Cassie slunk down to the floor of the cab under the dash on the rider's side, and Peau flattened himself into the seat, retracting his neck, so that he looked almost like roadkill. From the sky descended a putrid white deluge, which spattered everything that wasn't under cover.

I suddenly had an idea of what might be going on, much to my relief. I got out of the truck with my binoculars and scanned the sky from beneath the branches, trying not to get hit.

Passenger pigeons—millions of them! In the late 2020s, a San Diego biotech company had brought them back from extinction using old DNA samples. At first there were only a few dozen, protected in aviaries, but apparently they'd gotten free and were regaining their status as the greatest flocks ever to fill the North American skies.

Lars's friends at Scripps might have been involved in this, it occurred to me. Lars, who had initiated the whole desperate misadventure we were on.

Despite the tree cover, I was starting to get pelted, so I got back into the truck. After ten or fifteen minutes, the flock thinned out and moved on. I flicked the reins and we continued on our way, but now Lars was on my mind.

THE JOURNEY HAD BEGUN several weeks previously, when I made the mistake of checking my email. The Colorado dharma center had solar panels, so I could still use a laptop from time to time, and I'd learned it was possible to maintain an account through the server at a public library in Saskatchewan, of all places. There was never anything in my inbox, though, so I'd gotten out of the habit of checking. Then one day, when I was feeling especially isolated and hungry for contact, I did, and there was a message from my old friend and mentor. We were floored to find each other still alive.

He had an urgent request, he said, though you could never be sure with Lars because he considered everything urgent. He asked me to travel to a small hospital in the little town of Crestone, a half day's ride. He didn't want to explain further in an email, and I had misgivings, but I got my kit together, saddled up, and headed out.

I found the hospital easily enough. It had been abandoned years before, like the rest of the town. Deadfall pine branches littered the roof, and the windows were streaked and filthy. Outside, two people were watering their horses as I rode up. They introduced themselves as Robert and Jasmine; they had a key and led me inside.

We walked down a shiny linoleum hallway and entered an old operating room, which was dusty but otherwise reasonably well-preserved: a table, high windows, counters and cabinets. Big, round surgical lights hung overhead, though there was no electricity to run them.

I was unused to the company of other people and felt a little awkward, so I just sat down on the operating table and said, "Well?"

It was a substantial ask, as it turned out. They reassured me that it was a safe, simple procedure. They would implant a tiny ampoule somewhere inside me, though they wouldn't tell me where. This was for my own safety, so that I couldn't divulge its location even under duress. That got my attention, obviously, and not in a good way.

I asked what would be in the ampoule, and they told me.

I was skeptical. "A cure? Seriously?"

"We're not completely sure," said Jasmine.

"It has to get to California," Robert explained. "Lars will know what to do with it."

I almost laughed. "You might as well ask me to shoot myself in the head," I said. "No one could survive a trip to California."

"Really?" asked Jasmine. She looked to be in her mid-thirties, with sandy blond hair and a calm, frank gaze. "Lars gave us the impression that if anyone could manage it, you could."

I wasn't keen on flattery, especially when its apparent aim was to put my life in danger. But then I thought about that life, such as it was. The cat, the raven, assorted mice, and me, all shacked up together at the gonpa. I tended the gardens, I cleaned as best as I could, I ate sparingly, I swept the graves.

"Are you really doctors?" I asked.

Robert cleared his throat. "She is, sort of."

"*Sort of?*"

"I'm a veterinarian," Jasmine said. "But this isn't complicated."

"You're not making a super-compelling case, here."

She shifted her weight. "If we don't find a cure for this, I'll be dead in a few years, and so will Robert."

"If I try to make it to California, I'll be dead in *weeks*, not years."

"It's no small thing, for sure," said Robert. He was a polite fellow with a bushy beard, a ponytail, and large, round glasses held together at the bridge by electrical tape. Glasses were rare and precious now, and they gave him a thoughtful, owlish look. "If you can't, you can't," he went on. "Sorry if we've dragged you into town for nothing."

"It's all right," I said. "It's kind of nice to see other people for a change."

Robert nodded, and they exchanged a brief glance. They picked up their coats and walked down the hallway, then turned back to me when they got to the front door. "We'll need to lock up," he said quietly.

They looked so fucking sad. It was overstating matters to say that by saving my own skin I'd likely be sacrificing theirs, but it wasn't over-stating matters by much. And never mind how many others needed saving.

It occurred to me, then, that a journey to California might not be a completely terrible idea, perilous or not. Lars lived there, and he likely had answers to my old, troubling questions about Eva's fate—answers that might help me finally understand what had happened to her and then, ideally, let her go. I wanted very much to ask those questions, and I was pretty sure I needed to ask them in person if I expected an honest response.

I stood, then sat down again. I really wasn't sure I could manage this.

"I expect I'd need a few things," I said at last.

They walked back down the hall and reentered the room. They asked me what I wanted, and I told them: two healthy mules, food, and, if they could find an old surplus store, a pair of night goggles. Oh, and a tattoo. I was thinking of something I'd read about, a way ancient Greek spies had hidden messages during one of their many wars.

"A tattoo?"

"Per my instructions, and not to be divulged to anyone, including Lars," I said. There was a deserted tattoo parlor down the street that I thought might still have needles and ink on a shelf somewhere, so Robert went to see what he could discover.

Jasmine told me about her veterinary practice as we waited. Apparently, a few people were still alive on scattered ranches, and they had horses and cattle that needed tending. There were goats and sheep too, and the occasional domestic dog or cat. She often had to travel for a day or two in harsh weather to these places, so Robert went with her, and they both carried rifles. They knew Lars through a mutual friend in Boulder.

"You live a hard life," I said.

"I don't know if there's any other kind anymore," she replied. "Anyway, it's not so different than it was a hundred and fifty years ago. Those people had to be tough."

"They were."

Robert returned a few minutes later, having found what he needed at the parlor. They had a little propofol to sedate me with, and they told me they'd use surgical glue so I wouldn't have to deal with stitches. I'd never know where they put it, they said, and then they sent me off to sleep.

I awakened, woozy, sometime later. I wasn't noticeably sore anywhere, but the ampoule was tiny, a tenth of the size of my smallest fingernail. I figured they'd hidden it in my back, where I couldn't see, and they'd evidently done a good job. When my land legs returned, I got dressed and we left together. They locked the door and thanked me.

Outside, an afternoon thunderstorm was blowing in from the southwest. As I climbed onto my horse under that wide, unsettled sky, I noticed someone off in the distance, partly hidden by trees, watching us. I asked them who it was.

"No idea," Jasmine said.

"Maybe we should give you one of our rifles," said Robert.

I shook my head. "I'm one of those kooks who don't even kill spiders, even though spiders freak me out," I said. "It would be wasted on me."

Robert smiled a bit skeptically, and then we rode off in different directions.

A couple of weeks later they brought the mules and the other stuff to the gonpa. I thanked them and fed them; then, after they left, I inspected the animals and sorted everything out. I discovered that they'd hidden a rifle under the bags of rice, but by then it was too late to do anything about it, so into the truck it went.

3

Two mornings after we saw the pigeons, we crossed the Continental Divide. Beautiful, dun-colored canyon country spread out to the west as far as we could see, and the air was fragrant with juniper and piñon pine. Iridescent green dragonflies buzzed about with astonishing acceleration, pale snowfields gleamed miragelike on the highest peaks, and the light shimmered in cool morning air.

The old road switchbacked downward, zigzagging back and forth across the western face of the mountain range. As the day progressed, the temperature rose sharply. By late morning I was sweating and realized I had only a couple of gallons of water left. A stupid oversight, the kind of mistake I was making more and more. I suspected that in the nearest canyon I could see, down at the bottom of this long declination, we would most likely come to a river. But my map was worn, and it was hard to tell exactly where we were. As best I could guess, the river would be the old San Juan, and depending on where we crossed it, we'd find ourselves in what used to be either Utah or Arizona. I'd heard rumors of small regional fiefdoms, feudal areas centered around walled towns, and most of these would be near rivers because it was the only way to irrigate and grow crops.

But who knew if such places actually existed or, even if they did, whether the river would have any water in it? Most of the upstream dams were long gone—blown up or silted, overtopped, and failed—so that the rivers had returned to the natural state of things in the high canyon country, floods followed by moderate flows for a while, succeeded by dry gravel beds that held an occasional stubborn pool full of desperate, gasping fish. Easy pickings for coyotes and bobcats and raccoons. But if the river levels were up, there was no telling what state the bridges would be in, or if any of them still stood. We could take our chances finding a ford, but one misstep into deep water and we'd be done.

Peau flew on ahead and found us again in late afternoon. It was hot, and we'd already gone through most of the remaining water, given that the mules needed much more than I did. Cassie lay in the bedding in the back of the truck, making herself as long as possible to dissipate the heat. I steered us into the shade, halted the mules, and got out my binoculars.

With a little magnification I could see the river, brown and flowing full. The canyon rose sharply on the other side, and there was fenced cropland in the floodplain, terraced and fed by some kind of irrigation system. So it wasn't just a rumor; there were people here.

The town was perched on the opposite bluff, a hundred feet up a switchbacked road. High walls, barbed wire, people keeping watch. This was good and bad, I knew; good that they could defend themselves, bad wondering what they had to defend themselves *against*.

Three or four of them had rifles; the others held crossbows. By the river grew a large stand of willow, strong and light and straight, perfect for arrow shafts. There were always plenty of feathers around, and any sort of scrap steel or even obsidian could be made into heads. They'd be well-armed.

I couldn't see a bridge anywhere, but there was some sort of mechanical arrangement below the town—a couple of cables crossing the river with a flatboat attached to them. A ferry. I thought it might be big enough to transport us. Of course, this presumed that they wouldn't shoot us when we came down the road.

THE SUN SET QUICKLY as we descended the mountain. The pines at altitude gave way to juniper, then oak, then to riparian cottonwood and willow as we reached the canyon floor. Cool air flowed through the trees, a relief after the afternoon heat. By the time we reached the water's edge, night had fallen.

The situation worried me for all the obvious reasons. It wasn't impossible that these people immediately killed outsiders and confiscated their goods. I tried to concoct a plan to talk myself out of trouble should I run afoul of some local tin-pot despot, but it was hard to come up with anything without knowing more.

There was no moon yet, though millions of stars drifted overhead, confined to a bright band between the looming rock walls. As my eyes adjusted, I could perceive the outlines of trees in starlight, and then I heard the low, smooth rumble of the river somewhere before us. I slackened the reins and let the mules have their heads. They brought us to the water, stopped, and began to drink.

Across the channel, perhaps fifty yards away, two bonfires blazed. Their gleaming orange reflections snaked over the water, and I could see figures silhouetted near the flames. A gust of air blew downriver and burst across us, rippling the reflected stars and stirring the cotton-woods to life.

Cassie was wide-eyed in the seat beside me. She seemed entranced by the water, and I assumed she was wondering about fish. "Strong current," I said to her. "Don't get too curious."

I summoned my courage and called out to the people, but it seemed they couldn't hear me over the noise of the wind and water.

There was something strange off to our right. I walked over and found a thick post with an old school bell set atop it. I rang it a few times, startled by how loud it was.

Two of the people on the far shore looked in my direction, which made my heart kick up a notch. But we had to take our chances. They walked toward the boat carrying torches, then fixed the torches to the bow and started across the current. The ferry was primitive but apparently reliable enough. As they approached, I realized that it was actually a decent-sized barge, maybe twenty feet long, with railings around the edges. If we took the mules out of harness and put them beside the truck, we'd fit nicely.

When they finally beached the barge, I saw that they were teenage boys, maybe sixteen and seventeen. The older one held a rifle and stayed aboard, training it on me. The younger pulled the torch from its holding bracket and came over. He was well-muscled and obviously wary, so I raised my hands to show I wasn't carrying anything.

"I'm Mateo," he said. "You here for the ceremony?"

I didn't know what he meant, so I explained our situation, doing my best to sound harmless.

"Where are you trying to get to?"

"California, or whatever they call it now."

He smiled. "Good luck with *that*."

"Can we stop here for the night?"

"What can you pay for the ride?"

I told him I had horsemeat. I wasn't sure how fresh it was, given the afternoon heat, but since we'd cooked it halfway to jerky, I hoped it would serve. I brought it out for his inspection, and he sniffed it.

"Not too bad," he said. "Mind if I have a bite?"

"Help yourself."

He pulled a knife from his belt and sliced off a piece, then bit into it. "That's good," he said. "I haven't had horse in a couple of years."

We negotiated a price—roughly ten pounds of meat for the ferry ride, which seemed fair—then the mules pulled the truck partway onto the barge. We unhitched them, led them to the side, then pushed the truck forward until the boat was balanced. The other boy, named Tule (after the reed, apparently), closed the chained gate behind us and we set off.

I'd wondered how two kids could pull such a big craft across the water, but now I saw how ingeniously they'd set it up. The barge was able to pivot a bit relative to the current, secured in place by smaller cables that attached to the hull and set the angle. This allowed the boys to turn it slightly so that the river did the heavy work; the current pushed it across, and the ferrymen just needed to keep it stable and on track.

I noticed, in the torchlight, that they were trying not to stare at me.

"I'm the oldest person you've seen in a while, I'll bet."

They laughed a little shyly. "Like, in years," said Mateo. "How come you're still alive?"

"I don't know," I said. "Kind of wish I did."

I asked them what the ceremony was about.

"You'll see," Tule said. He seemed a little less friendly, and it crossed my mind that the ceremony might possibly include a human sacrifice that included me. I could see that his teeth were rotten—a common affliction, now, in anyone over the age of ten, given the lack of dentists—and I thought maybe he was simply in pain. My one bad molar was enough; it was hard to imagine a mouthful of yellow and brown teeth, like a cob of flint corn. In any case, I wanted to keep things congenial. They could easily shoot me and dump me overboard, and they'd have two mules and a truck full of useful goods if they did.

In mid-channel, I noticed huge, streamlined shapes moving under the water around the boat. They were twelve or fifteen feet long and seemed to glow. The boys didn't pay much attention to them. I was leaning on the swaying chain railing when one of the glowing things suddenly turned, accelerated toward the barge, and rammed it with such force I was almost pitched into the river. Mateo caught me by the shirt and pulled me back.

"What the *fuck*?" I yelled, my heart pounding.

They laughed. "Freshwater crocs," said Mateo. "You want to stay away from the side."

"*Here*?" I panted. "What are they doing here?"

"Nobody knows where they came from," he said. "They started showing up after Mayhem. We figured out pretty quick that we had to keep our goats away from the water, because they liked them even more than fish."

I shuddered, recalling that the mules had had their snouts in this water only minutes before. "What about the glow?" I asked.

Mateo shrugged. "At first, some people wanted to believe they were sacred," he said. "They dropped that idea when the crocs started eating kids. Human kids, not goat kids."

"Jesus."

I could make a guess about what was going on, though. Whoever bred the crocs' forebears might have been doing CRISPR work on them—say, giving them jellyfish genes that would help them adapt to colder water, and which might also impart bioluminescence. The breeders were supposed to render them infertile, too, so this kind of spread didn't happen, but nature had an uncanny way of circumventing barriers to fertility. Of course, the special genes might also have been just for fun, the usual tendency of tinkerers to think that because they *could* do something, they *should*. But watching the creatures in the water, I realized that making them glow would have had a practical application too, given how easy they were to see at night.

"Ever hunt them?" I asked.

"Sometimes," said Tule. "It's dangerous, but we use the ferry and homemade harpoons, and that helps. Good meat and good hides."

"How many people live here?"

"Three hundred or so."

I whistled. That was a lot of mouths to feed in this day and age. I hadn't seen three hundred people in one place in over a decade. Since Mayhem, as the ferrymen so eloquently put it. Mayhem hadn't been a single event but rather a string of calamities spread out over a few years, but the name fit nicely anyway.

"I noticed as we were coming down the mountain that you had some pretty good-looking fields," I said.

"Yeah, we terraced it all so it's easy to irrigate," Mateo replied. His dark hair was tied back in a long ponytail, and he had a calm, explanatory way of talking that I liked. Soothing, like a good science teacher, with a soft Hispanic accent. "We had to build fences so the deer don't destroy everything."

"Keeping everybody in corn?"

He smiled. "Pretty well," he said. "Beans, wheat, barley. Hops. You probably saw the fruit trees."

"Apple and lemon?"

He nodded, with a little modest smile of pride. "Underneath them we grow cabbage, carrots, cantaloupes, and squash," he said. "Hemp over in the sunny part, for cordage and the occasional smoke. Potatoes, of course. The river floods every spring, so we wait to plant until afterward, when the soil's strong again."

"There used to be two or three dams upriver from here, I think."

"Maybe," he said, as if the idea were entirely speculative. "The river runs free now. If there were dams, there'd be no silt in the floodwater, and we'd be screwed. The big upstream farms are abandoned, so when all the fertilizing stopped, the algae died and the fish came back. We think maybe the crocs followed them in."

This conversation did a lot to put me at ease. The boys and I seemed to understand each other. We were members of the same lost civilization who spoke the same language. They were farmers and hunters; I was a traveler. Roles established for millennia.

Now that I was calmer, I noticed how tired I was and wondered where we'd stay. I figured we could set up the poke nest and spend the night by the river. But as the ferry came up against a crude wooden dock and Tule jumped off to tie it up, I saw light at the top of the switchback road that led up from the riverbank.

"You're just in time," said Mateo. "Welcome to Cottonwood."

He and Tule walked off to find friends. I could see people walking past the top of the bluff and starting down the road, carrying candles in some sort of translucent containers. First there were ten, then twenty, then the whole road was full, as the long, illuminated line wound slowly down the switchbacks. I got the mules back in harness and led them over to the base of the cliff, under a stand of trees. Soon people began to collect on the sandy beach by the river and to light new bonfires.

Peau had flown off somewhere. Cassie was in the front seat, so I put her out of sight in the back, from an abundance of caution. "Lie low until you see me again, okay?" I said.

She yawned and curled up amid the sleeping bag, blankets, and general clutter. I locked up the truck and walked back to the river.

The beach was long and broad, almost more like an ocean beach than a riverbank, and soon there were five bonfires spaced roughly thirty feet apart. The smoke smelled of juniper as it drifted along the riverbank, then wafted up into the sky. Guards stood near the water's edge, watching for crocs.

More people kept strolling down the trail, illuminated by the candles they carried, talking quietly to one another, occasionally laughing or coughing. There seemed to be a lot of coughing, though I wondered if it was maybe from all the smoke. Everyone was young—lots of kids and teenagers, people in their twenties, then a few who appeared to be in their thirties, and that was it. There was a nice blend too: white and Latino and Black kids, and a bunch of tweeners that evidently came from mixed marriages. It was astonishing to see so many people in one place, and I had to wrestle down an urge to rush up and start hugging them all.

As the last of the townspeople descended the hill, someone played a flourish on a horn, and a couple appeared at the top, surrounded by men carrying torches. Some version of a feudal lord and lady, I supposed. They started down, and by the time they arrived at the bottom, everyone else had taken up positions three and four deep on the sand at the edge of the river. Two folding chairs were set up on a small wooden platform—I admired the earnest attempt at pomp and circumstance—and the couple smiled and sat. They appeared to be in their late twenties and were easy to see in the firelight. He was tall and broad-shouldered, with long, dark hair, an impressive beard, and slightly mischievous eyes. She was slender, red-haired, and strikingly pretty. A perfect alpha couple, in other words. Two kids, apparently theirs, darted into the firelight and chased each other around the chairs, until the woman spoke quietly to them, and they sat down in the sand next to each other.

The king—or duke, or whatever sort of potentate he was—raised a hand and everyone quieted down. "Lucia will officiate," he said.

Queen Lucia stood. "Thanks, Alejandro," she said. "I know we're all eager to start the party."

Had they actually managed to create a benevolent monarchy here? Given everyone's ages, I began to wonder if the whole pageant was intended ironically, like a sort of post-Mayhem homecoming bash.

Lucia began to speak, then, and quickly shamed me for my skepticism.

"Before we break out the beer, let's remember why we've gathered," she said. "Every one of the candles you hold represents someone we've lost in the past year. Parents, siblings, lovers, in some cases your children. We don't know where their souls go; we only know that their bodies have been taken from us. We do our best not to feel angry about this, but I know sometimes it's hard not to."

One of her kids came over to her and put his arms around her legs. She paused to touch his head. Alejandro picked up the boy and held him in his lap as Lucia continued.

"When you put your candle on the water, think of that person you loved and wish them well in their travels," she said. She spoke simply, without histrionics or affectation, just stating things as she saw them. "Think of your candle as lighting their way, and pray that they find happiness there. What we always want, I know, is to bring them back to life, but in spite of all the old stories, we can't. We hope we'll see them again when we die, but we don't really know if we will do that either. The only place we know for sure where they continue to live is in our hearts, so the best we can do is hold them there if we can. The deepest blessing they leave you is that you loved each other while they were alive—not just that you were loved, but that you had the good fortune to love them in return."

There was a fair amount of sniffling and dabbing at eyes by now. Given what I'd been worried I'd find here—maybe a bunch of dangerous hicks of the Buck Flynn variety eking out a medieval living—the heartfelt humility of this brief speech took me aback.

Several young men with torches and spears still stood in the shallows at intervals of a dozen feet or so, presumably to discourage the crocs, and now a few of the townspeople made their way to the edge and carefully put their candles on the water. The candles were stuck to wooden bases and encircled by translucent paper, so the effect was of a flotilla of small, lighted sailboats. The current began to carry them away.

The dozens of lights now illuminating the water glowed almost like a mirror of the bright Milky Way overhead. People were sobbing, and the king and queen stood together as their children nestled, big-eyed, in front of them. It seemed as if all those lost souls had been momentarily embodied, so we could feel again our affection for them, our sorrow at losing them, and then relinquish them and see them gracefully depart.

How could I not think of Eva, in the firelight, with the smoke drifting? I briefly felt a warmth around me, as if she were there. A few unclaimed candles sat in the sand by one of the bonfires, so I walked over and picked one up. I lit it, then took it down and placed it on the river.

It took five or ten minutes before all the lights disappeared downstream. When the water remained illuminated only by stars and firelight, people turned to each other, speaking quietly and exchanging embraces. King Alejandro coughed, and it seemed to me that, strong and robust as he appeared, he was nevertheless a little unsteady on his feet. Soon the torchbearers escorted him and his family back up the hill.

What finally occurred to me, then, was that nearly everyone who lived here had lost someone they loved in the previous year. These people may not have been medieval, but their *lives* had reverted to something similar, and even if those lives weren't necessarily nasty or brutish, they were pretty much guaranteed to be short.

Three guys were rolling out a big oaken cask, which reminded me that Mateo had included hops and barley among the town's crops, and that Lucia had mentioned beer. The cask was tapped, glasses were produced and filled, and everyone started to drink.

I thought about how sorrow and loss, particularly when mixed with alcohol, almost invariably nudge people toward hedonism and lust. The baby boom after every major war, for example. Or a wild party by a river after a ceremony to honor the dead, for another. It isn't hard to understand, really: when a species' natural response to the decimation of its population is to go out and fuck like bunnies, you have a successful species. We had always been one until we weren't, but those deep engines still drove us.

Which was a stupidly overanalytical response to a beach bash, or a wake, or whatever it was. I decided to get myself a drink. The cups were old white ceramic things with chips and dings that looked like they'd been scavenged from a defunct school cafeteria, which they probably were. But they shared one crucial quality: they held beer.

I hadn't tasted beer in a decade; it was thick and yeasty and bitter, almost more of an Irish ale, and good lord what a revelation. A group of drummers had set up congas of various sizes and pitches, built from wood and hide. They clustered near one of the fires and began with a few tentative syncopated rhythms, but it didn't take long before they were really rolling. All those beautiful young people soon began to do what beautiful young people do in the presence of sand and beer and drums: they danced wildly, heads and arms and breasts and legs flying every which way.

I joined them, doing my best to keep up with their joyous abandon, trying not to think about how my joints would feel when I tried to unfold them and walk around in the morning. I got a few glances—I was a stranger, and an old one at that—but mostly I was ignored by the unbridled teens and twentysomethings who leapt and bounded and twirled all around me.

Then, in the firelight, I noticed a woman who was a little older, maybe in her late thirties. Large brown eyes, dark hair in a ponytail, pale linen blouse with delicate embroidered flowers. She was fit and she could move, and she was watching me too. We looked away, we looked back, feigned nonchalance, revealed interest. It had been so long since I'd been in a situation like this that I was startled to find myself still capable of it. The gonpa hadn't been that strict; my friends would occasionally gather on a Saturday night to put on some music and dance. When Eva was there, she loved it, and that was the last time I'd danced with anyone. The woman and I found ourselves inching closer to each other as we circled the flames. After a minute of this cat and mouse, a minute in which it wasn't always clear who was playing predator and who prey, we were dancing together. Not touching, exactly, but not *not* touching either. Fingertips grazed shoulders and arms and waists, then pulled back. There was a lot of drumming and whooping all around us, so we worked our way a little farther from the racket, and it struck me as so hilariously, wonderfully human that we'd accomplished this entire choreography, from noticing each other twenty feet across a bonfire to standing close together, tentatively exploring each other's skin, without needing to say a single word.

"Who the hell are *you?*" she finally asked.

I switched my beer to my left hand, stuck out my right, and told her my name. She took my hand in hers and said, "Isabella." And even though we should have let go of each other's hands at that point, we didn't, and this led to an awkward sort of one-handed dance that made us both laugh. I drained the last of my beer, put the cup down in the sand, and grabbed her other hand. The conversation had to be kept simple, since the noise from the drums necessitated yelling in each other's faces.

"*How did you get here?*" she asked.

"*Mule and truck!*"

"*Where from?*"

"*What used to be Colorado!*"

"*How did you get to be so old?*"

"*I failed to die!*"

She laughed. I almost asked her the same question but was saved by an uncharacteristic moment of good sense. I could tell that my back was going to be a locked-up, pain-charged slab of rigid meat the next morning, but I figured that maybe if I had more beer it wouldn't be as bad, or at least I wouldn't care as much. So I got us more beer.

After another half hour or so, when I was beginning to wonder which would come first, the hangover or the heart attack, the drummers mercifully decided to take a break. Isabella and I were soaked and gleaming with sweat. She looked better sweaty than just about any creature I'd ever seen, except maybe a racehorse.

We wandered across the sand until we found a place under a tree, apart from the others, and sat down together. She leaned into me, and I put my arm around her. She shivered a little.

"Cold?" I asked.

"A bit. I've got a sweater somewhere; I just have to go find it."

"I'll help, if you like."

"It's nice to be able to talk without shouting," she said, and then suddenly she kissed me. Her lips were soft and slippery, and her tongue darted into my mouth, and in a few seconds I had to reach down and adjust my pants, a furtive maneuver at which I was completely out of practice.

A shadow fell across us then, and we quickly disentangled ourselves. A large, broad-shouldered man stood between us and the fire. I couldn't see his face or judge his expression, but Isabella looked up at him and smiled.

"Hi, honey," she said. "You ready to go home?"

"Nah," he said. "Everybody's taking tomorrow off, so a few of us are going to stay up and see the sunrise."

"Is Beth by any chance part of the few of you?" Isabella asked.

"Well, yeah . . ."

She considered this. "Okay," she said then. "It's probably time you two started a family anyway."

"*Mom.*"

"Just saying."

He bent down and kissed her cheek, then turned to me.

"Hi," I said and stuck out my hand.

"Hey," he said. He smiled and shook my hand, then turned and sauntered gracefully away.

"I thought I was about to get killed," I said.

"You're good with him as long as you treat me well," she answered, smiling. "Where are you staying tonight?"

I wasn't sure if this was a question or an invitation, but I didn't want to presume.

"My truck, probably, unless I get a better offer," I said. "How come?"

She shrugged. "I happen to know a nice woman who just found out she's got the house to herself, that's all."

"Sounds all right."

"Of course, if you're attached to your truck . . ."

"It's the mules I'm attached to, but not *that* attached."

Soon the drums started in again, and all the kids fell into wild motion, as if they'd suddenly been plugged back in. Isabella found her sweater and put it on. We got into the truck, then the mules hauled us up the switchback road, past the iron gate through the town's high walls. The walls were impressive, I noticed, twelve or fifteen feet tall, smooth adobe with barbed wire at the top, the sort of walls that told you everything you needed to know about what lay outside of them.

Others were returning home by now, but there were no more candles, so we all did our best to avoid one another in the dark. The mules, of course, were well-suited to this, and a little light spilled out to the road from lanterns inside a few of the houses. I could feel the night's energy, the force of mountains and river and stars, the way they sometimes open you up to the wild fullness of the world.

"Who was your candle for?" I asked, as we bumped along.

"Sam, my husband," Isabella said simply. "How about yours?"

"I didn't know you'd seen me."

"I'd been scoping you out for a while. It's rare to have strangers here, especially anyone over thirty."

"Mine was for someone named Eva."

"Is there a story?"

"I may never know all of it, so I'm not sure."

"I think I understand that," she said, and I could tell that she *did* understand. I liked her more and more. It was good to discover these things about each other; the absence of illusions brought with it a kind of sweetness.

"Anyway," I said, "it was a long time ago." And it occurred to me then that, yes, in fact, it *was* a long time ago. I'd been living like a monk for years because the outside world had become a terrifying wilderness, and I preferred my circumscribed life at the gonpa. But I didn't really *have* to live that way, did I?

The houses here stood in neat little rows—a onetime company town, I guessed. After another block, she pointed. "Here we are."

"Whoa, mules," I called. Just then, Cassie jumped through the window dividing the cab from the truck bed.

Isabella yelped in surprise, then laughed. Cassie immediately tried to commandeer her lap.

"Don't get comfortable, Cass, we're going inside," I said.

"Everyone here has rodent problems, including me," said Isabella. "Okay if we bring her in for the night?"

"She'd be delighted."

We got out and approached the house. The moon was full and I could see that it was actually quite cozy, a small bungalow with rosebushes out front. Isabella opened the door and led me into the living room, where she lit a kerosene lantern. The floors were made of dark, broad-planked, dinged-up wood; old photos hung on the wall; and amazingly, in the corner, stood an upright piano. I hadn't seen anything as sweetly domestic as this in years.

"Do you play?" I asked.

"Of course."

"*Will* you play?"

"Sure."

Cassie scurried off into the kitchen. She could hear things that were totally out of my range, the little ultrasonic squeaking of mice.

Isabella went to wash up; apparently the river-fed tank on the hill behind the town provided enough water for necessities, but there was no electricity and otherwise things were spartan. While she was gone, I checked out the living room. The photos were of her as a child and a teenager, and of their son, and presumably of Sam, a handsome Black guy with kind eyes and a warm smile. They looked happy together.

Isabella returned in a few minutes wearing fresh clothes, so I excused myself and went to the bathroom to clean up. There was only cold water, so I did my best with a washcloth and a towel. When I came back out, she was building a fire in the kitchen cookstove.

"Hungry?" I asked. "I have horse steak in the truck."

"Twist my arm."

I got the steaks and put on a clean shirt while I was at it. When I came back inside, the fire was going and Isabella was playing the piano. I put the steaks in a big cast-iron skillet; they were getting past their prime, and I wanted to kill anything that might have been growing in them. There would be enough for her son when he came home, and probably for breakfast too. I still hadn't seen Peau, but I figured he was off with new friends.

Soon Cass had killed three mice and was stalking a fourth. Isabella played Bach, she played Chopin, she played jazz. She'd clearly trained, and she was good. The piano was even in tune, or at least so little out of tune that my ignorant ears didn't know the difference. It was exalting to hear a piano played well in a snug house with a warm stove.

She told me her story as we ate dinner. She had been the village piano teacher. Sam was a geologist, and this had once been a mining town, as I'd suspected from the housing stock. He did the planning rather than the dirty work, and they'd had a good life until shortly after their son, Nicolas, was born. When everything came crashing down, they realized that they were living in one of the few places that could realistically become self-supporting. It had been difficult nevertheless.

"Once so many people were dead, the wildlife came back faster than anybody expected," she told me. "We had hungry bears breaking into houses within a year. There were cougars and wolves. But worst of all were the people."

"Who?"

"The preppers, the thugs from ARM who never seem to go away. The Alliance of Racist Motherfuckers, we call them."

I smiled. "There seem to be a few translations of that acronym."

"Well, Mayhem would make a prepper out of anyone," she went on. "We thought maybe we could coexist with them, but they were impossible; they kept trying to put themselves in charge and take over the town. They wanted the teenage girls basically as sex slaves, and they didn't much like Blacks or Latinos, which meant they *really* didn't like a blended family like ours. But the town is over half Latino, and finally we all got together and threw them out."

"And they went?"

"Sometimes it took unpleasant encouragement," she admitted. "It's sobering, what you learn about yourself when the shit goes down."

"Ever hear of Buck Flynn?" I asked.

"I think so. Some sort of exceptional badass?"

"By reputation, anyway. I haven't had the pleasure yet."

"Is he after you?"

"You could say so."

"Well, you're safe inside the walls for now."

In the kitchen, Cassie pounced again, and there was a louder-than-usual squeal.

"I think she got a rat," said Isabella. "That's a princess of a kitty you've got there."

We ate in appreciative silence for a little while. "What happened to your husband?" I asked at last. "Was it ARM?"

She shook her head, looking somber. "Sam died of appendicitis," she said. "That's how it is now—infections, injuries, whatever. Six people have died in the last year of infected *teeth*, which never used to happen. You probably noticed all the coughing."

"What is it?"

She said it was TB, that it had been roaring back in the past few years. There weren't any antibiotics, of course.

I asked if people there had had Disease X.

"The thing that makes you crazy for about nine months and then kills you?"

"Yeah."

"We don't have much of it," she said. "Mostly people die before they get it. I'm the oldest person here, and I'm thirty-eight."

"You seem healthy, though."

She admitted that she wasn't, in fact. It had started a couple of months before, and although she'd tried to keep her son from noticing, she was pretty sure he was figuring it out.

"What's going on?"

"Little stuff, so far," she said. "I can't keep track of what day it is, and half the time I forget to feed us until Nicolas reminds me or goes ahead and cooks something himself. My sense of smell is almost gone. Oh, and the other day this dog started making these whining noises at me, and I swear they sounded almost like words. You could say it's depression, but I've never been depressed, so I'm pretty sure that isn't it. Do you know anything about it? I'm not just worried for myself but for Nicolas too."

I'd learned enough to know it didn't sound good, and the possibility of a talking dog troubled me for all the obvious reasons. I tried to think of something reassuring to say.

"Well, even if it is Disease X, it doesn't seem easily transmissible," I said. "If Nicolas gets it, it probably won't be for another twenty years or so."

"Well, he needs to get Beth pregnant soon, anyway," she said. "Most of his friends already have kids, and he'll be lucky to live as long as I have."

We'd come to this—the mother of a teenager actually wishing he'd hurry things along. Morality was marvelously flexible, of course. In Britain after World War I, when a whole generation of young men had been wiped out, the church tacitly encouraged practical philandering so the population could be rebuilt from the few remaining males. The paperwork was managed so that the single mothers weren't shamed, and society forged ahead.

Isabella reached across the table and took my hand. "So you don't have any qualms about . . . ?"

I smiled, relieved at the chance to reclaim the evening from all this grim talk. "I can't think of anything I'd rather do."

It had been a very long time for both of us, and there was nearly as much nervous laughter as there were sighs of pleasure, but we found our way. Afterward, when we'd caught our breath, we lay beside each other, talking about her son, and the town, and our lives. It was cozy under the covers, she was warm and kind, and we both enjoyed the chance to let our hands roam freely over another person's skin after so many years. I began to wonder, should I manage to survive this journey, whether I might find my way back here. It didn't seem a bad idea to settle in what appeared to be one of the few functioning villages left in the country, even if it did have a king and a queen and a considerable caseload of TB. But Isabella was likely in the early stages of a relentless and fatal deterioration, and I knew that even if I *could* return, by the time I got here she'd either be well past recognizing me or dead.

She spoke quietly, then, nudging me out of my ruminations. "There's enough horse left that we can have steak and eggs for breakfast, if Nicolas doesn't inhale it all when he comes home," she said.

"You have eggs? Actual chicken eggs?"

They'd turned the abandoned shack next door into a coop, she said. Several people in town had the same idea, so eggs were where folks got most of their protein. All the chicken shit went onto the fields, and they had a little open market where everyone brought eggs and vegetables and even some meat to sell.

"I'd love steak and eggs," I said. I asked, then, how they managed trade here. "Doesn't bartering everything get ungainly?" As soon as I brought it up, I felt stupid: the pillow talk of the middle-aged.

She didn't seem to mind, though. "We tried barter for a long time, but finally it became impossible," she said. "Every transaction became a haggle. Everyone always felt that someone else was getting the better of them. So we finally broke into the old bank, blew the vault, and distributed the cash. We know it's worthless anywhere but here, but so what? It's not like anybody's planning a vacation, and if you *decide* it has value, then it has value."

"You're talking about plain old American money?" I asked. "Greenbacks?"

"Sure, what else?"

"Isabella, you just hit the jackpot."

She eyed me skeptically. "How so?"

"There's money everywhere out there," I said. "In Santa Fe it blows down the streets, collects in the tumbleweeds, clogs the old storm drains. It dries fast and doesn't deteriorate into pulp, so it's great for starting fires."

"Are you saying you have some?"

"I have seven or eight thousand dollars in the truck. I'd like to keep a little in case I come across anyplace else that uses it, but you can have some if you want."

She grinned and pulled me to her—and then, to my amazement, uplifted by this news, we actually managed another go-round. I wasn't convinced my sad old heart could take it, but it endured. When it was over, we held each other a while, then drifted off and slept like rocks.

· · ·

WE AWOKE LATE THE NEXT MORNING as sunlight streamed in through the dusty blinds. A wonderment, luxuriating in a real bed with a beautiful woman. We stirred and muttered, sleepily touched and nuzzled each other, then finally got up and pulled on our clothes.

Cass appeared from wherever she'd crashed, so I let her out and tidied up the kitchen floor, on which were scattered assorted mouse tails, a few random feet, and the bottom half of a rat. I threw them all into the tall weeds in back as Isabella lit a fire in the stove and got the horse steaks going. She scrambled eggs while I cut a few slices off a dense loaf of barley bread, then we sat down together and feasted.

"I liked what the queen had to say last night," I said, as we ate.

She stared at me. "The *what?*"

"Lucia, whatever her title is."

Isabella laughed. "She's the *mayor*," she said. "She was elected. We're not *that* far gone."

Soon Cass scratched at the front door, so I got up and let her back in. She trotted over to Isabella and rubbed her face against the chair, purring. Isabella reached down and petted her.

"She's a valuable item around here," she said. "After Mayhem, the cats started having trouble breeding, but whatever afflicted them unfortunately didn't slow down the rats and mice."

"Any left?"

"Cats? Three or four," she said. "Their owners rent them out for exorbitant fees and live in the best houses in town. We have to send one into the granary twice a week to keep the mice under control. I don't suppose you'd want to part with her?"

"She's family. Sorry."

"I understand," she said. "Just had to ask."

After breakfast we cleaned up. She wanted to go to the market, and I needed provisions, so we walked over, pushing the old yellow wheelbarrow she kept for such errands.

It was sobering, seeing the town in daylight. A small grid, roughly six blocks by four, maybe two hundred houses in all, many of them empty and falling to ruin. A handful of larger, two-story homes stood among the trees; I figured they'd once belonged to company managers and were now occupied by the commercial feline oligarchy. The wall surrounding the town, topped in barbed wire, made the place appear a little less like a fortress and a little more like a prison. And yet roosters crowed, dogs barked, goats bleated, parents called to children who shrieked with laughter and ignored them. The sounds of every settlement in the world.

In the town square we passed a modest church, a tavern, and the abandoned, vault-blown bank. Finally we arrived at the market, a compact cinderblock building with a veranda and vegetable bins out front. A dozen people wandered in and out, examining produce and catching up on gossip.

I bought barley flour, cornmeal, a hundred-pound burlap sack of oats (breakfasts for me, two squares a day for the mules), carrots, onions, potatoes, even some rice—anything that would keep. When Isabella had finished shopping, we loaded everything into the wheelbarrow and pushed it down the bumpy road back home.

I stowed my groceries in the back of the truck while she put hers in the pantry. As we were finishing, Nicolas showed up, looking sleepless and disheveled.

"Something's happening at the river," he said. "You may want to go see."

WE HEARD THE RIFLE SHOTS when we were still a few blocks away. Isabella and I climbed the stairs to the parapet and surveyed the scene below. The boys who'd been tending the ferry had retreated behind the walls beneath us and slammed the iron gates shut, after which the firing from across the river stopped. The ferry was safely tied up on our side, and to our left and right at the top of the wall, four guys held rifles, waiting.

Across the water, six men on horseback trotted back and forth. I couldn't imagine how they'd gotten here so fast. They must have picked up our trail within a few hours of our departure, then ridden with little or no rest ever since. The men sagged in their saddles, covered in dust, hollow-eyed and exhausted, and their horses didn't appear to have fared much better.

One of the men was presumably Buck Flynn, but I didn't know which one. I had the impression from the previous encounter that he was careful in his plans and might tend to hang back and observe while his underlings advanced to test the waters. Which was literally what they proceeded to do.

Two of them waded their horses into the river and started swimming them across. The guy next to me on the wall, a kid named Forest, spoke quietly to the others. "Save your bullets," he said. "I don't think we'll need them."

It quickly became clear why not. In daylight, with the reflections on the water, the crocs would have been invisible from the riverbank. But from up where we stood, they were obvious. The horses were about halfway across when four long, dark torpedoes closed swiftly on their targets. Suddenly one horse screamed and was pulled under. It resurfaced briefly, without its rider, then was pulled back down again, and the water where it had been turned crimson. The other horse was quickly attacked as well, and both of them, along with their riders, disappeared into the bloody current.

One of the men across the river was yelling orders to the others. Flynn was, indeed, hanging back in the shadows of the cottonwoods. I borrowed a pair of binoculars from Forest.

Flynn was hard to make out, but what I *could* see startled me. He was big and powerfully built, but I'd expected that; he was commanding the type of men who'd cut his throat the instant they scented weakness. What I hadn't foreseen was that, in a world where men like him lived all day in the sun and were covered in tan, leathery skin, Flynn was deathly pallid, white as a bleached carp. At first I thought he might be an albino, but his hair and eyebrows were dark. I had no idea how to account for this freakish appearance, for there in the shade he seemed almost translucent, like some kind of animated hologram.

Then he rode forward out of the shadows, and in the sunlight he seemed to materialize more fully. I thought he looked vaguely familiar, and then I understood why; this was the man I'd seen watching us in the distance as I left the Crestone hospital.

He ordered his men away from the water. His vaguely fishlike eyes were large and pale and wet-looking, and as I watched him, he suddenly glanced up at the wall. His eyes found mine, and I felt a kind of pressure wave move through my head, as if he'd somehow forced his way into my brain and begun rooting around for useful information. It was a startling sensation, and I immediately lowered the binoculars and looked away.

Forest fired his rifle, and I jumped at the report, just as a chunk of bark flew off a tree behind Flynn. Forest had missed his head by inches, and without thinking I pushed down the rifle barrel before he could fire again. Flynn quickly spurred his horse back into the trees, then collected his last three men and led them upriver at a gallop.

Forest looked about eighteen, young by my standards but old enough for soldiering. He rested his rifle on the parapet. "Can't imagine why you'd want to do that SOB any favors," he said.

How could I explain the terrifying karma of this situation in a way that didn't make me sound like a lunatic? "It's not him I'm doing the favor," I said. "It's you."

He made a *tch* sound. "Won't help me much if they come back and find a way in."

I knew he was right. Everything had happened so quickly, but after years of having it impressed on me that about the worst thing you could do was kill another human being, I'd reacted reflexively.

Isabella touched my shoulder. "The nearest bridge is a good thirty miles upriver," she said. "That should buy you some time."

We started for home, but I was shaky, haunted by Flynn's eyes. I could see why his men put themselves in harm's way for him, now. Those eyes radiated ferocity, but there was more to it than that. Somehow, simply by staring at you, Flynn could communicate how deeply he was disappointed, how he held you responsible for that disappointment, and how profoundly you were going to suffer as a result.

WHEN WE GOT BACK TO THE HOUSE, Peau flew in and landed on my shoulder. Isabella startled back a step.

"Also family," I explained, petting his head. It always surprised me, how light he was for such a big animal. Hollow feathers, hollow bones.

Isabella moved forward and carefully ran her fingers down his back. He bobbed and emitted a soft *grawk* of pleasure. "Quite a menagerie," she said. "Any others I should know about?"

"Just us three and the mules."

We were feeling a little awkward now, I could tell. We both knew it was time for me to go. "Look . . . ," I began, but she put a hand on my chest.

"Don't. It will make it harder."

I nodded, then went to the truck and got my kindling sack. "I haven't forgotten about the money," I said. "You're not offended?"

She smiled. "I can't afford to be."

I counted out the crumpled bills on the truck hood. It was mostly tens, twenties, and fifties, so it took a while. Peau flew off, but I knew he'd find us later. "Four grand for you, three for me?"

"It's generous of you," she said. "Thanks." She glanced around and carried the wad inside.

I loaded the rest of my stuff and called Cassie, who came out and hopped into the truck. I put the mules into harness, then Isabella came back out and took me in her arms. We held each other for a good long while.

4

I went northwest, away from Flynn, up out of the river valley and onto a high desert plateau. According to the map, it looked like we'd be proceeding on a haphazard series of state highways and BLM roads. We'd also be going through Navajo and Hopi land—or possibly skirting it, depending on which route we ended up taking. I'd heard rumors that a few people were still alive on the rez but that the standard greeting for white strangers was likely to be a bullet to the heart. Given that we'd shot and starved and infected them with deadly pathogens for four hundred years, stolen their land, kidnapped their children, and then destroyed the world for an encore, this wasn't hard to comprehend. I was eager to avoid trespass but wasn't sure we could.

It was a calm morning, even so. Rock doves cooed in the arroyos, and once, in the distance, I thought I saw another great flock of passenger pigeons, flowing swiftly over the landscape like a shape-shifting, polychrome cloud. Gray-blue mountains rose up on the western horizon.

It had been sweet, sleeping with Isabella, but also a little unsettling. She was the first woman I'd been with since Eva, fifteen years before. Sex, I'd found, didn't seem drastically different from person to person.

We adapted to what our partner enjoyed, of course, but mainly our bodies did what human bodies do.

What varied was intimacy. Maybe because Eva and I had been so much younger then, everything felt like effortless, profound communion, whether we were making love or hanging out, talking about our interests and our lives. Our senses of humor were similarly dorky, but more generally she *got* me in a way nobody ever had before, and vice versa. Being with her was like rediscovering some long-buried aspect of myself, a shy child who emerged from shadows into light with just a little kind coaxing. For the first time in my life, I genuinely liked who I became in someone else's company. So even though I'd enjoyed my time with Isabella, it did accentuate the contrast between what I'd once had and what was available to me now, and this made me a little sad.

We were traversing arid country with big, striated rock formations and dry canyons. I was glad it was still early spring, for the freshness of the air and the manageable heat. We traveled all afternoon, then stopped in the evening to make camp in a wide meadow between tall redrock palisades. I set up the poke nest and built a fire.

We ate, but I was troubled. I kept seeing Flynn's eyes, seeing his men and their horses pulled under by the crocs, seeing all that blood in the water. I'd always feared drowning; the thought of struggling for air and being unable to get to it was horrifying, and the prospect of drowning while being dragged to the bottom in the jaws of a giant reptile stirred my deepest atavistic dread.

I rested by the fire awhile, then decided to send a letter.

Dear Eva,

There's been a lot of death since I wrote you last, and I'm responsible for some of it. Indirectly, but still. Violent, bloody death, as if there hadn't been enough of it in the past fourteen years. The world is so transformed that in many ways you wouldn't recognize it, but in this it hasn't changed at all.

At the gonpa, I was taught that dying involves a transition of consciousness analogous to falling asleep and dreaming. Where you end up next depends on how you've lived—a proposition that isn't unique to Buddhism, of course—but even if the next life turns out to be hellish or otherwise unpleasant, it's still temporary. This seems preferable to the possibility that this brain and body are really all we have, and that at death our universe ends in eternal black oblivion.

Here's what troubles me, though: I've had a couple of surgeries in my life, and it seems to me that general anesthesia is actually the closest we get to death, a better analogy than falling asleep. Under anesthesia, you can cut someone open and root around in their innards as if they were dead. Good luck with that if they're crashed on the couch for an afternoon nap.

Each time I awoke from anesthesia, though, I remembered nothing. From the moment they started the drip until I groggily regained consciousness in the recovery room, there was no awareness, no sense of time passing, just complete blankness. If that's the closest we get to death in life, what does that suggest about the real thing afterward? What if all this talk about reincarnation is only wishful thinking, and we're really nothing more than animals who die?

This is a bleak prospect, obviously, which I suppose is why most people prefer not to think about it. But I think about it all the time, I can't help myself.

And yet, here I am writing a letter to a woman I love—a woman who is, in fact, dead—and hoping she'll somehow get it, or at least get the feeling of it, and she'll send me a sign that she has. Does this make me a hypocrite? Once I could talk to you about such things, and even when we disagreed, there was pleasure in the pushback.

I miss that, and you.

—Will

I burned the pages, per my custom, and watched the smoke rise and dissipate. Then, in the darkness outside the poke nest, I was surprised to see our firelight reflected in a dozen pairs of eyes. They were a couple dozen feet away, and I had the sense that they were more curious than aggressive. Had they ever seen a fire before? Coyotes probably, or maybe large raccoons, but who knew what lived out here these days? They could have been wallabies or meerkats or hyenas, whatever had once inhabited some zoo or preserve. The poke nest was solid and would do its job, so this was merely unnerving rather than scary. We sat watching each other for a few minutes, and it was almost as if they carried glowing coals in their skulls instead of eyes. I briefly wondered if they might be imaginary, a product of fear and exhaustion, so I closed my eyes and visualized them gone. After half a minute I opened my eyes again. They were not imaginary.

Then, gradually, a little at a time, there arose from them a high keening sound, almost a ululation, the sort of quavering wail you might once have heard from mourners at a fireside funeral in a desert oasis, under date palms and stars. I was mesmerized, as if I were hearing an elegy for an entire lost world. For all I knew, I was. I wondered if, whatever these animals were, they might be the last of their kind, and if they understood this and were mourning their imminent extinction. As the sound reached a crescendo, a large meteor fell burning across the sky and disappeared behind the cliffs.

Soon the keening subsided, then eventually it stopped. The eyes remained, however, so finally I went to the truck and crawled into the back with Cassie. Outside, as the fire faded, so did the eyes, though I suspected they were still there, waiting, regardless of whether I could see them.

IN THE MORNING, I took down the poke nest and stowed it on the truck, then wandered out to check tracks. It was hard to tell what I was seeing; they might have been canine or feline or even mustelid, or possibly something else entirely. Cats and weasels didn't travel in groups, though—lions excepted—so ultimately I just didn't know. I walked back to the truck and made breakfast, hoping that whatever they were, they weren't planning to follow us.

While the oats were cooking, I looked over the map again. I could triangulate roughly where we were, and I decided on a detour. Because they'd gone south, Flynn and company would have to travel eighty or ninety miles to catch up to us forty miles west of here, where the roads would converge, and they'd already looked half-dead with exhaustion at the river. Soon Flynn was going to have to rest the horses or he'd be stuck someplace with a few thousand pounds of meat and nothing to ride.

I could afford a little time, and I was feeling the need for spiritual counsel. The last I'd heard from an old friend of mine, David Marsh, he lived in a mountain hermitage somewhere north of where we were camped. This had been over fifteen years ago, and I had no idea if he was still alive. I'd never been to his place, but I still had an old, crumpled, hand-drawn map he'd once sent me, in with my other papers.

David and I had first become acquainted in the writing program at Irvine, oddly enough. We'd both hoped to become novelists, and we hit it off right away. Our friendship eventually became complicated, though, because he turned out to be a lot more talented than I was, and we both knew it. He went on to become successful—briefly, anyway—while I segued into science writing and eked out an existence that way. In school, we'd had long conversations about our feelings of spiritual destitution and general existential angst, and then one day out of the blue, when we were in our early thirties, he got back in touch and told me about the meditation center he'd moved to. There was a Tibetan lama there he liked and thought I should meet. So a few weeks later, after some polite badgering from him—pointing out, among other things, that it was only a four-hour drive from Denver, where I was living at the time—I went.

I was hesitant and easily distracted, though, about what you'd expect from a young journalist, whose credibility and job security hinged on being interested in a lot of stuff and professionally skeptical about all of it. I'd ended up contributing as best I could: helping in the kitchen, weeding and watering the large vegetable garden, doing carpentry or whatever needed to be done, and folding in meditation time when I could. I found that I enjoyed it, but in those early days, an hour a day was as much as I could manage before I got sore and distracted.

David, by contrast, was focused, dedicated, and indefatigable. Lama Sonam saw his potential early on and started sending him into long retreats. Weeks, then months, then years. He was always modest and unassuming about his progress, however, and even though I was jealous of his trajectory, we'd remained friends.

He was about my age, and it was a long shot that he'd still be alive. But he had been at the hermitage since before Mayhem, so it was possible he'd avoided its worst ravages. In any case, my heart was heavy—remembering Eva, baffled by how to live ethically in a violent world—and I had to try.

He'd sent me the map all those years ago, in case I ever happened to be in the area and wanted to drop in. I wasn't sure how useful it would be after so much time and destruction, but the map turned out to be surprisingly accurate. Late in the morning we passed through the town of Sage Springs (deserted and fallen to ruin); went out the old highway (full of tall weeds, and how can anyone not admire weeds, pushing up through concrete year after year, tearing it apart with nothing more than soft stems and leaves?); passed the gas station (no electricity for the pumps, anything left in the tanks would have been unusable for years, and pigeons were roosting in the broken plastic sign atop its steel post). And then . . . nothing. There was supposed to be a turnoff onto a dirt road that ran down through a dry wash, then up the other side. It went around the back of a hill, then up to his place on the mountainside. I found the turnoff, but instead of crossing the arroyo, the road came to the edge of the wash and disappeared.

Peau was flying around, talking to the local ravens, and I was, as usual, in awe of his sociability. From what I could tell, there were now about a thousand ravens for every human in North America, a substantial improvement in the state of affairs, by my lights. He seemed happy to try to get to know them all.

I halted the mules, got out, and called him.

I'd always loved the smell of a high desert morning. Sagebrush; creosote; cool, dry air. Peau seesawed down through the sky and landed on Mule One. Her flank gave a little quiver, and she stamped a foot, but that was the extent of the protest. She was used to it by now.

"Want to try an experiment?" I asked him, holding out David's map.

He hopped over and peered at it.

"Scientists say that only human beings can look at a landscape on a piece of paper like this and relate it to the real thing," I explained. "Well, they said that until they figured out that a border collie could do it, but that was the only exception."

He made a soft *awk* noise that I'd come to understand was analogous to an indulgent sigh. I pointed to the map. "Here's where we've been," I said, indicating the landmarks we'd passed. "Here's where we are now, and here's where we're supposed to go."

He looked around, surveying the landscape, then studied the map. I asked him if he saw the problem. He bobbed in assent, though he didn't look particularly pleased. I was, after all, trying to goad him into action by comparing his brain to that of a dog, and I sensed a trace of resentment.

Just then I felt a rumbling in the earth. At first, I thought it was a quake, but this wasn't really temblor country, and then there was a different, pounding sound. I looked off to the right and saw dust rising.

"Fly!" I said to Peau. He took off, and I quickly slipped back into the truck. The mules pranced nervously in their harnesses, and Cassie sat up and looked out. The dust cloud rolled closer, and then I saw a herd of animals stampeding down the dry wash. A hundred, two hundred of them—there was so much dust I couldn't tell—but as they approached, I was astonished to see that they were camels. Luckily, they were concentrated enough that they'd miss us, poised as we were up on the arroyo's lip.

They thundered by like a brown blizzard with legs. Dust seeped through the weather sealing and the holes in the floor of the truck, and Cassie started to sneeze. It took them a minute or two to pass, which they did in their odd, loping gait without a glance at us. Then they quickly disappeared around a downstream bend. I didn't move right away because I figured something must be chasing them, and I shuddered to think what it was—a pride of lions or a pack of huge dire wolves, maybe. But after a few minutes, there was nothing. It seemed they were just on their way somewhere.

When the dust settled, Peau drifted back down and landed on the hood, looking ruffled and uneasy. I explained about the old game farms and refuges. Tigers, crocs, bison, camels, and maybe whatever had been staring at us last night. If I were a captive tiger or a camel, and people stopped coming to feed me, would I be deterred by a little wire fencing? I would not.

"There were six or seven thousand tigers in the old U.S. before Mayhem, and it turns out they feel pretty much at home here," I said. "I guess the same goes for camels. Anyway, now we know what happened to the road."

Cass shivered in evident revulsion and chittered the feline term for "ugly."

Peau took off and flew over the dry wash, then gained altitude in a thermal, crossed over the hill, and disappeared.

He returned a few minutes later and told me what he'd found. He was better than any surveillance drone. As usual, I had to do some filling in, but it was getting easier to piece the phrases together.

We could get to the spot marked on the map, he suggested, pecking at it with his beak for emphasis. The road picked up on the other side of the arroyo, behind an outcrop of rock. The place was where the map said it was; there were trees and a couple of dwellings, though he hadn't seen any people. I thanked him and got back into the truck.

Peau took off and led us to where the road reappeared. It was rough going; there were washouts every fifty feet or so that the truck could barely pass. The mules pressed on, though, and we wound around behind the hill and started up the mountainside. There was nothing but sage and bitterbrush, but as we got higher, the air cooled a bit and smelled moister. After about a half hour I saw the trees, sure evidence of a spring. Then two little shacks came into view, in the shade. We turned up the dusty drive that led to them.

When we got closer, six or seven dogs charged down the drive and quickly surrounded the truck as the mules halted nervously, their skin shivering. The dogs barked furiously and snapped at the windows, and Cassie, big-eyed, crept closer to me on the seat.

I heard a sharp whistle from up near the cabins. The dogs stopped barking but stayed where they were, and then a young woman came strolling down. She was maybe twenty-five, dark-haired and willowy, with intelligent eyes and a skeptical set to her mouth. She wore an old flannel work shirt, jeans, and leather hiking boots, and she carried a sawed-off shotgun.

She approached the truck and said, "Back off," and the dogs slunk away. I rolled down the window. She kept the shotgun leveled as she cautiously appraised me, then glanced at Cassie. The presence of a cat seemed to reassure her, and she soon appeared less fearful and more annoyed at the intrusion.

"David Marsh still live here?" I asked, hesitantly.

The hardness left her stare. "Jesus Christ," she said, breaking into a smile. "Is that you, Will?"

We'd met? How could I possibly know who she was?

She put the sawed-off on the hood, opened my door, and leaned in to give me a hug.

"You don't recognize me, do you?"

"I'm sorry . . ."

"I'm Pela, Will. From the gonpa."

Pelageya! The last time I'd seen her she was ten years old. Her parents had fled Russia when Putin invaded Ukraine, then had her the following year in Latvia. They'd come to the U.S. on a religious visa to study with Lama Sonam in 2030, when Pela was seven. I remembered her as a curious, rambunctious kid, and we'd hit it off because she wanted to improve her English and was interested in science, and I could actually help her with both of those things.

"Don't cry," she said softly, and I realized that tears were running down my cheeks. Then I saw that she was crying too. I got out of the truck so I could get my arms around her better, and we stood there, holding each other, two old soldiers seeing each other for the first time since the long-lost war.

"I thought you must have died ages ago," she said.

"Your parents?"

She shook her head. "Everyone's gone except David and me. And now you."

We walked to David's house, my arm around her shoulders and hers around my waist, wiping futilely at our tears. She told me that as soon as the pandemic started, her parents had brought her here, but that they'd become sick on the way. They were buried up the hill.

"I've thought of you," she said. "You were kind to me back then."

"You were a great kid. You made it fun."

She smiled. "I'm pretty sure my father would have begged to differ."

"It's always easier to be the outside man," I said, and she laughed.

It was cool under the trees, and soon I heard the burbling of the spring and smelled the water. On a hot desert mountainside, you can smell water deep in the back of your pharynx, the way a shark smells blood. Live-saving, delicious ambrosia.

"It's sweet here," I said. "Can you grow enough food?"

"Not really," she answered. "There's no fat on us. Every few months I take a horse into Princely and trade for a couple of fifty-pound bags of rice. That, with the garden and the hens and the goats, keeps us in our bodies for now."

Chickens skittered around the yard, pecking. We came to David's cabin, which had a covered front porch with prayer flags strung across it. We walked up the stairs, which caused the whole rickety place to shudder, then Pelageya knocked on the door.

I heard David's voice from inside. "Come," he said.

So odd, how all experience to the contrary, our default is still to expect people to look the way we saw them last. David sat cross-legged on a cushion against the opposite wall, a dozen feet from us. He had aged so much I barely recognized him.

Two tall windows flanked him, one on each side, and to his right was his shrine. He'd hung traditional *thangka* paintings around the walls— Shakyamuni Buddha, Padmasambhava, Red Tara, Longchenpa—and paintings of a couple of protectors, Ekadzati and another one I didn't recognize. On the shrine stood water bowls and a burning row of butter lamps, as well as framed photos of several lamas, including Lama Sonam, our teacher. There was even a photo of several of us who'd been in hundred-day retreat together once, looking happy and relaxed and much younger. I noticed that Pelageya was in it too, still a child, sitting pixielike between her beaming parents. Next to the photo, a couple of sticks of incense burned slowly in a brass holder, the smoke curling upward toward the ceiling.

David was thinner than I'd ever seen him, really just skin and bones. His salt-and-pepper hair flowed down past his shoulders, and his beard was scraggly and untrimmed. He sat perfectly still, quite at ease, and as we came into the cabin, his eyes found me and twinkled in recognition.

"Where'd you find this old buzzard?" he asked Pela, and she smiled.

"He found *us*."

I went to him and kneeled down so we were at eye level, then placed my forehead against his, per the Tibetan custom. We stayed that way a few moments, then segued into a plain old Western-style hug. He was so bony I didn't want to squeeze too hard. Pelageya quietly brought me a spare cushion, then, and I sat down near him.

"You two want some tea?" she asked.

"Please," said David. "Bring a cup for yourself too."

Noiselessly, she left.

"Gooseberries," said David.

At first I thought this was some sort of koan. "Sorry?"

"Her parents named her after a character in a Chekhov story, 'Gooseberries,'" he said. His speech was even softer and more measured than when I'd known him before, as if it now emerged from a place of utter peace. "The story emphasizes how beautiful and quiet the young woman Pelageya is. I always think it's funny, because you'd expect the real girl to turn out just the opposite, right? But in fact she's exactly like that. As if Chekhov's story had some magical power to impart character to anyone with that name."

"You're forgetting 'About Love,'" I said. "She reappears in that story, and it turns out one reason she's so quiet is that she's terrified of her alcoholic, abusive boyfriend."

"I *had* forgotten," he said, chuckling. "That's Chekhov for you."

Part of our ease with each other had been a sense of shared professional territory, an appreciation of the knowledge we had in common. We got each other's obscure jokes and had never had to do a lot of explaining. But now, sitting here with him, I also remembered how being in the presence of people like him—people palpably calmer than I was—tended to bring my own faults into greater relief and make me feel even more anxious than usual. I was curious, too, about how the relationship between him and Pela had evolved.

"She keeps me alive, in case you're wondering," David said, as if I'd just come out and asked him. "There's nothing going on; she has her cabin, I have mine. She does most of the work, though I help with the garden and the animals. I do make sure she gets twice as much food as me. She's young and she needs it."

"Of course."

We sat quietly for a minute or two, and it was a relief that neither of us felt a need to fill the silence.

Then he asked, "How come you're still alive, anyway?"

"Beats me; it defies all odds. How come you are, other than Pela's help?"

He shrugged. "Not a clue. Do I stink as bad as you do?"

"It's hard to tell," I said, and we laughed. "Next time I cross a river maybe I'll spend a little time in it."

He asked how I'd spent the intervening years, so I filled him in, describing how I'd stayed on at the gonpa as a caretaker after everyone else had died. There was water and plenty of stored food, and I wanted to protect the place if I could. Besides, where would I go?

"I've lost track," David said. "What year is it, anyway?"

"Twenty forty-eight."

He was genuinely astonished by this. "So much time," he said. "So many people gone." He trailed off, shaking his head sadly.

Soon Pelageya knocked lightly on the door and appeared with a teapot and three cups. She sat down with us and poured it out. It had been years since I'd tasted Tibetan-style tea with salt and butter, and it seemed a marvelous indulgence.

"We don't have a yak, so we have to use goat butter," she said apologetically.

It was definitely a little goaty, but I didn't mind.

"It's excellent," I said. "Thanks, Pela."

David sipped his tea, then set down the cup. His eyebrows had become quite bushy with age, and this seemed to give his eyes even more intensity than they already had.

"As best I remember, I sent you that map years ago," he said mildly. "Took you long enough."

"I've always been a procrastinator."

He smiled. "I suppose you saw the camel herd."

"If we'd been fifty feet farther on, they would have trampled us."

"They go thundering up and down that dry wash all the time," he said. "I have no idea why. You'd think they'd pick a direction and stick to it. *Migrate* somewhere, you know?"

He laughed, then asked me why I'd finally come after all this time. I explained about my journey, about Buck Flynn, how it seemed impossible to live without causing harm. He considered this, sipping his tea. After half a minute, Pelageya leaned over and poured him more.

"This journey of yours is important?" he asked.

"It could mean the difference between someone Pela's age living another ten or fifteen years, the way it is now, or living another sixty or seventy, the way it used to be."

Pelageya smiled. "Sounds important to *me*," she said.

"And these forces have arrayed themselves against you," said David pensively. "Why?"

"I can't imagine," I said. "But I keep having to choose between my principles and my life. If you have no principles, you live like an animal. But if you're dead, it's pretty hard to maintain your principles. So it isn't always clear to me what I should do."

He contemplated this conundrum.

"Every time you take a breath, you inhale millions of airborne microorganisms," he said then. "They would infect you if they could, but the mucous linings of your nose and lungs catch them and kill them. You know all this, Mr. Science Writer."

I smiled. "Sure."

"So when you breathe, you kill. The only way to stop killing is to stop breathing, but then you kill yourself. There's no way around it."

"Mmm . . ."

"From what you've told me, it's their pursuit of you that leads them into trouble," he continued. "Should you surrender and let them have what they want? Which means that humanity in general is denied what you're carrying? Does that strike you as a wise and compassionate course?"

"Not especially."

"Of course it isn't, Will, don't be obtuse," he said a little sharply, then.

"But my vow to do no harm wasn't only when it was convenient. It was even at the cost of my own life."

"Ah, I see," he said. He sipped his tea, considering this. "Some texts say that, and I would never diminish the importance of your *samaya*. But other sources say that if you're attacked, you're perfectly justified in defending yourself. The Shaolin monks made a sort of franchise out of it, after all, and who are we to tell them otherwise?"

"Well, which is it?" I asked, frustrated. "You can't have it both ways."

"Welcome to organized religion!" David said, laughing softly. "The last Dalai Lama once said that if someone is doing harmful things, you should stop them, because they're harming themselves as well as others. Your compassionate motivation is what matters; that's the karma of it."

"But other beings keep taking on my karma *for* me," I said. "Tigers, crocodiles, whatever. It's not fair to them."

"Will, it seems you're getting a lot of help on your journey. Are you oblivious to this?"

"Of course not, but it still raises questions," I said. "Yesterday morning, on the parapet, a teenage kid had a chance to shoot Flynn, but I stopped him."

David considered this. "That was likely the right course," he said reflectively. "But tigers and crocodiles are just doing what tigers and crocodiles *do*. If they or some other natural forces show up to help you, you might consider them protectors and feel gratitude instead of tormenting yourself."

"I don't want to torment myself," I answered. "What I *want* is to airmail the ampoule and be done with it."

He smiled. "It's just like dharma practice," he said. "What's that old saying—'The only way out is through'? I always liked that, at least until they turned it into an advertisement for something."

"Laxatives, probably," said Pela, and we laughed.

"But we have all these elevated aspirations," I went on. "Then circumstances force us to act like barbarians."

"Look, Will, until we're awakened, we *are* barbarians," David said. "So every day we suffer the *fate* of barbarians. It's called samsara; maybe you've heard of it."

I grumbled something in the affirmative.

He studied me. "Would you say you had pure motivation for this journey?" he asked. "Is your aim to benefit other beings?"

"My motivation is *never* pure," I confessed. "There's always a little subterranean whisper: *I want this, I want that. Me, me, me.*"

"Based on what you've told me, though, it's best overall for the people pursuing you if they fail," he pointed out. "If so, your job is to be sure they do."

"And if they're harmed?"

"It's best if they're not harmed by your actions. But if something happens because of *their* actions . . ."

"For example?"

"Suppose they're chasing you, and you hide in a grizzly's den. If they follow you in and the bear wakes up and sees them first, that's kind of their problem, isn't it?"

"This is a metaphorical grizzly's den, I take it?"

"I'm talking in terms of general strategy, but when things get ugly, I guarantee you it won't *feel* metaphorical."

We laughed quietly then, the three of us together, and I felt a particular, special contentment wash through me for the first time in years, the satisfaction of being with the people of my tribe, with my sangha, of being known and understood and accepted, regardless of how screwed up and batshit I felt on the inside. Jung wrote that once you feel summoned to a spiritual path, you find yourself set apart from all your old family and friends, because you've become aware of a problem they don't see or understand. You may even feel that you'll betray them if you follow that path. But a far greater betrayal occurs if you chicken out, because then you fail to realize the deepest meaning of your own life. And as difficult as it could sometimes be to get along with other people at the gonpa, we shared a bedrock foundation. We were all walking the same road, and we would help one another despite all obstacles. It was among the most powerful bonds I'd ever experienced, possibly even stronger than my bond with Eva, and it was so wonderful to rediscover the feeling that I was suddenly near tears.

"Know what I wish?" I asked, my voice wavering a little. The two of them shook their heads in perfect unison, in the way people sometimes do when they've lived together a long time. "I wish we were Zen students, so you could give me a koan, and then I'd get it, and my head would explode into enlightenment, and then we could all relax."

David grinned. "You know, Zen and our way are like brothers," he said. "If you want a koan, I'll give you my idea of one. It relates to the nature of self."

The nature of self was one of my many torments, of course. Even the Buddha taught different things to different people about it, based on what he perceived to be their needs and ability to comprehend.

"Okay," I said.

"This koan comes in a very special form known in America as the knock-knock joke," said David.

"Seriously?"

"Of course," he said. "But again, it's a special form. You have to start."

Pela and I glanced at each other. This was quintessential David.

"Okay," I said. "Knock knock."

He grinned back at me a little fiercely. *"Who's there?"* he demanded.

The wind went out of me, almost as if he'd punched me in the chest. I realized I had no answer—had no clue *how* to answer, even—and for a moment it felt exactly like my head exploded, that my awareness no longer had a scrap of boundaries around it. Watching whatever my expression was, David just sat back and roared with laughter.

SINCE I HAD so much food in the truck, we decided to offer *tsok* that evening. David and Pela still did this practice regularly, but I'd stopped long ago since I didn't have anyone to share it with, and it felt particularly lonely to do something by myself that I used to do with a roomful of friends.

We prepared the food as beautifully as we could, roasting potatoes and cutting them into long slices, arranging carrots in an elegant mandala on a plate, sautéing onions in a pan and piling them into a graceful mound in a terra-cotta bowl. Pela used some barley flour to make *tormas*, symbolic offering figures that we painted and set on dishes.

We decided on a Longchenpa sadhana we all loved, and David led us through it. He was really in his element leading a puja like this, calm and clear and forceful, glowing in the energy of his decades of training. And in the hours it took us to do the practice, I felt an old self emerge, the Will who used to meditate every day, before and after his other tasks at the gonpa. It was reassuring to know that I could still find that calm, spacious mind, or at least a taste of it. It was dispiriting that I didn't spend more time in that state than I did, in my daily life. But it felt so wonderful—paradoxically full and empty at the same time, like standing in a strong, warm wind at the edge of a cliff—that I was glad to breathe in whatever I could.

It was well after dark before we got to the part where we shared the food, and I was famished. As we ate quietly, offering our food to the benefit of all beings, David turned and regarded me, his eyes like deep, warm seas.

"Tell me," he asked quietly. "Who have you been writing to?"

I suddenly felt self-conscious. "How can you possibly know about that?"

"You don't have to talk about it if you don't want to."

It took me a moment. "Do you remember Eva?"

"Sure," he said.

"She was *intense*," said Pela.

I tried to decide how much to say. Eva had stayed with me at the gonpa for fourteen months, but ultimately things had become difficult between us, and she'd moved to L.A.

"A year after she left, early in the pandemic, I got a call that she'd died," I said quietly.

"So why do you write to her?" Pela asked quietly, avoiding my eyes, as if she were afraid she'd hurt my feelings.

"It's hard to explain," I said. "Sometimes I feel her with me, that's all. My skeptical self tells me that I'm refusing to accept her death. It's hard for me to sort out what's real and what's just something I want to believe."

David smiled. "And what does your non-skeptical self tell you?"

"That her consciousness continues," I said. "I know it doesn't make any sense; she should have moved on into another body long ago. But it seems to me she hasn't, and I have no idea why not. I suppose I write because I miss her, and because I *can*."

"Mmm," said David, and then we all ate in silence for a bit, until he spoke again. "Look, I don't really understand this myself," he said finally. "But wherever she is, I have a feeling she's getting your letters."

He spoke with such calm assurance that it was impossible not to take him seriously. The thought that my letters weren't merely a futile, self-indulgent exercise brought my heart right into my throat. I tried to fight it down but couldn't, so he and Pela waited for me as I wept.

When I'd calmed down a little, we finished eating and got ready to do the final stages of the puja. Before we started, though, he spoke to me once again.

"This issue that concerns you about general anesthesia," he began, with that little smile of his.

"David, you're freaking me out."

"Sorry," he said. "I just want to put your mind at ease a bit. There's a level of awareness that transcends that blank nothingness. Keep going, maybe try some dream yoga. You'll figure it out."

IN DREAM YOGA, the goal is to achieve lucidity, so that dream consciousness is recognized as essentially the same as waking consciousness. Once that continuity of awareness is established, it can ideally be carried across the threshold of death into the bardo that lies beyond, and ultimately to enlightenment. I'd tried the practice from time to time but had never been any good at it, though I did notice that my dreams became more vivid.

I sometimes had a recurring dream about a place where there were two mountain lakes, with a powdery gravel path leading from the lower lake to the upper one among smooth, pale boulders. Tall granite spires stood behind the lakes, illuminated in a kind of golden light, as if it were always morning there. Big pines grew among the rocks, and the lake water was limpid, pure, and cold.

This place always looked the same, as if it had an independent existence and I was visiting it in my real body. The dreams seemed more like memories that way, and often, upon awakening, I wondered if the lakes *were* real, a place I'd been to once and forgotten. But I could never place them. Their repeated appearance made me wonder how such a dream world could seem every bit as constant and consistent as this one did.

I felt convinced that Eva existed in that territory, somehow. I felt her presence when I had those dreams, and once or twice I thought I'd caught a fleeting glimpse of her, reflected in the water. It was almost as if she were answering my letters by appearing there. I couldn't tell what her answers were, but when I woke up I felt happier about things for a while. As if her death had been a simple mistake, a rectifiable error, and in the dreams I realized she was there with me, conscious and loving, still available for wry commentary and larking about and lovemaking.

Of course, it isn't easy to practice dream yoga if you can't get to sleep in the first place. As I'd often found in my life at the gonpa, *tsok* had a way of energizing me to the point of insomnia. So I lay in the truck that night, listening to the crickets and recalling my life there. I thought back to the first time I'd met Eva.

One afternoon I'd been out hoeing in the garden when an old green Subaru came bouncing up the drive. People wandered into the place out of curiosity several times a week, so I didn't take much notice. But then she got out of the car. Hair like flax, deep blue-green eyes, a fluidity of movement that suggested athleticism and easy physical capability. She glanced at me with an expression that conveyed experience and intelligence and humor. I unbent myself from my toil and stood straight, suddenly conscious that I probably looked like a dirt farmer, and that a dirt farmer wasn't going to be good enough for this girl, whoever she was.

There was no one else around, so she came over and we introduced ourselves to each other. It took me a moment to realize that we'd met the previous year, when she'd accompanied Lars to a conference. She was his daughter; she'd seemed warm and funny over lunch, but we were both preoccupied with work and hadn't spent much time together.

That afternoon at the gonpa she explained that she was on her way back from visiting a friend in Boulder. She'd heard where I was living from her father and thought she'd stop by to say hello.

We took a stroll so I could show her around. I asked about Lars and about her work. She'd recently finished a postdoc at UCLA, studying some arcane aspect of bacterial immunology related to phages.

"Similar to your dad's field?" I asked.

"Not really," she said. "Sometimes it's best to keep a little distance from my father, as I gather you've discovered."

When I was in my early thirties, failing as a novelist but making my bones in journalism, Lars had been a renowned researcher in La Jolla. We'd met at a couple of conferences, and for whatever reason he took a liking to me. He brought me along and taught me the basics and sent exclusive stories my way.

"Your dad was kind to me, and I don't think he's ever understood why I dropped out of that world so suddenly."

"He was definitely pissed," she said. "I think he wanted you to run communications at Scripps and help them with grants."

"He talked to you about it?"

"Sure," she said. "Anyway, I decided to take a year off before I look for a job, so I've just started knocking around."

It occurred to me that she might possibly want to spend part of that year here. I felt a little surge of adrenaline.

I helped carry her stuff into one of the guest rooms, then went to finish my work while she had a shower and changed. We met later in the dining hall and staked out some territory by ourselves in the corner. A few of my friends trickled over to say hello, but the vibe was clear, and mostly we were left alone.

"It's beautiful here," she said. "I've never spent any time in this part of the country, but I think I could get used to it."

I explained that it had been a kind of homecoming for me, that after grad school in Irvine I'd returned to live near the old family ranch where I'd grown up.

"I had a great-grandmother with the odd name of Jinx," I told her. "She came out here from the Ozarks in the 1930s to marry a guy and became a ranch wife."

"How did she meet him?"

"The ranch in question was actually the place she'd spent the first six years of her life, and the guy she married was her stepbrother. I'm named after him."

"So that ranch is still in the family?"

I nodded. "Turns out that spending your teenage summers bucking hay bales and laying irrigation pipe is the perfect way to prepare yourself for white-collar work, because you *never* want to go back."

"And yet here you find yourself, hoeing in the garden."

"Higher-purpose hoeing, in this case."

"Which sucks the worst, I'll bet."

"It does, in fact."

We laughed. She wanted to know if the food was always this good, and, hoping my answer might tempt her to stay longer, I assured her it was. This was a lie, but generally the food wasn't bad, depending on who had kitchen duty in a given week.

She tied on an apron and joined me on the dish crew, which I took to be a good sign. People who showed up with precious ideas about the idyllic, contemplative life usually didn't last long. She joked around with the others and seemed to get along with everyone. I thought I might disintegrate from happiness.

After we'd finished the dishes, we went for a walk to watch the moonrise.

"Is it sage I'm smelling?" she asked.

"It is," I said. "*Artemisia tridentata*."

"Three-toothed? What does that refer to?"

I picked a leaf and held it up so she could see the way the end was formed. "Probably there's something insufferable about science nerds discussing Latin names in the moonlight," I said.

"I like being insufferable, don't you? I wish I could make a living at it."

"I don't even know how you *do* make a living," I said. "What are phages, anyway?"

She explained that they attack bacteria in roughly the same way viruses attack our cells, injecting genetic material into them as a vehicle of reproduction. "They're the creepiest things ever," she said. "They look like a cross between a spider and a lunar lander, and there are a trillion of them for every grain of sand on the planet."

I shivered a little. "So what's attractive about studying them?"

"There's so much resistance to antibiotics now that we're running out of ways to kill bacteria," she explained. "They're really good at it, so if we understood them better . . ."

"Ah," I said.

We walked on, inquiring about each other's lives in an earnest and vaguely industrious way. Her parents had divorced when she was ten, it turned out, and her mother returned to Sweden without her. Lars had put a lot of pressure on Eva to succeed, possibly in response to what he referred to as "the abandonment," and this often caused friction between them.

"Did he push you to go into the sciences?"

She shook her head. "I was interested anyway," she told me. "Though when I was a teenager I tried to find something else, because I *didn't* want to be like him. He was ambitious in an aggressive way that I found revolting."

"How so?"

"Publications, prestige, grant money," she said. "It all put me off; to me, science was supposed to be pure. But by my junior year of college,

I had to admit that science was the only thing I was naturally good at. At a certain point I just wanted the path of least resistance, you know?"

"Sure," I said. "Except that so far I haven't found *any*thing that's easy for me."

She laughed kindly and surprised me by slipping her arm through mine. We strolled down the dirt road as if we were on an evening promenade in a Paris park. She asked if there was anything I *was* passionate about, that I might like to do even if it was difficult.

"Right now I'm just doing this," I said. "It doesn't exactly have career prospects, but it's plenty difficult. Does that make me sound like a schlub?"

"Of course not."

"I mean, I always wanted to be a big success of some kind when I was younger, because I assumed otherwise nobody would love me," I said. "But lately I've begun to wonder if love is mainly for people who are afraid of being alone."

"You have it backward," she said. "I think love only really works for people who *are* comfortable alone. Otherwise, it's a big codependent mess, complicated by maddening offspring."

I smiled. "You don't want kids?"

"Maybe not *never*, but certainly not now. What about you?"

"I don't know," I said. "I always figured I'd have them. I'd probably be a terrible father, though."

"Why?"

"I'm selfish. I only want to do what *I* want to do. You can't be like that and have kids."

"My parents were like that, and here I am," she said. "My existence disproves your theory."

"Well good," I said. "If all I have to give up is a stupid little theory for you to exist, I'll take it."

"Heavens, a romantic," she said. "I thought you'd all gone extinct."

"The last of the Sentimentosaurs, dying in a tar pit," I said. "Goodbye, cruel world."

We managed to delay hitting the sack for an entire two weeks after that evening. Eva turned out to be a little awkward and self-conscious in bed, which came as a pleasant surprise, because I was pretty much the same way. And so our first few months together became a project of leading each other out of that inhibited discomfort into a kind of relaxed, joyous abandon that neither of us had experienced with anyone else. We weren't virgins *in corpore*, but we almost were *in spiritus*, and what we experienced together wasn't so much deflowering as efflorescence.

I'd had a nickname at the gonpa: Eeyore, because I tended to be as dour as Pooh's donkey pal. Within a few weeks of Eva's arrival, though, my friends had started calling me Mr. Happy. This was gently derogatory, of course—it referred to my utter lack of equanimity—but I didn't care. And anyway, there's no insufferability like the insufferability of new lovers, especially at a meditation center.

THE NEXT MORNING I awoke, sleepily, to find Cassie stretched out to her full, impressive length beside me. We were hurkle-durkling—luxuriating in wakefulness beneath warm covers for a while before we had to get up. I petted her. She purred and yawned. We were a little postapocalyptic diorama of domestic contentment.

The mules grazed nearby, enjoying the lush grass that grew in the shade close to the spring. Peau flapped to the tailgate carefully carrying another prize he'd found, a bunch of spiky aloe vera leaves. He'd heard about the plants from some local ravens but said he didn't know what humans used them for. I told him aloe was good for burns, including sunburn, and even some rashes. He emitted a satisfied little *awk* and added the leaves to his other plants in back.

"If you were human, you'd make a good ethnobotanist," I said. He didn't know what that was, so I explained. He seemed pleased with the idea.

It was briefly possible to forget that we had to pack up and keep moving. I wanted to stay; it was idyllic here, and my memories of past happiness made it all the more alluring.

I dressed and went off into the trees to piss. How lovely, to stand in cool desert morning and water the sage. When I came back, Pelageya was standing by the truck, staring in.

"That's the most gigantous cat I've ever seen," she said. My initial impulse was to correct her English, as in the old days. My better impulse was to shut up, because, in fact, "gigantous" was a lovely word, at least coming from her.

Pelageya reached in and scratched Cassie behind the ears. Cassie purred, then Peau flapped over and landed on my shoulder.

"They're beautiful," Pelageya said. "They seem unusual, somehow."
I like this one, said Cass, and Peau concurred.

Pela went off to collect eggs for breakfast. "My," said David, who'd quietly ambled up behind us. "Talking animals. What will they think of next?"

"How did you get that so fast?" I asked. "It took me a couple of months before I even started to notice." David shrugged, then petted Peau gently on the head. "In the Himalayas they call you guys *gorawks*, because that's what you sound like to them," he said.

Peau said he didn't know that word—*Him-something*.

"The Himalayas?" David said. "Big mountains, the tallest on earth."

Peau perked up and asked if there were really ravens there, and David told him there were tens of thousands. Peau made his happy little cooing noise and said he liked knowing that.

"Well, that's a relief, anyway," I said. "I was beginning to wonder if I was losing my mind."

"Ah," said David, waving it away. "In a bunch of traditions this kind of thing is associated with wisdom."

"Really?"

"Sure. When Athena gave Tiresias the gift of prophecy, he realized he could understand the language of birds. There are lots of other examples: Solomon and David in the Quran, Albertus Magnus. Oh, and Odin!"

"*Odin?*"

"Odin supposedly kept a couple of special ravens. They had these insane Nordic names I can't remember but that translated as 'Thought' and 'Memory.' They flew all around the world and kept him apprised of what people were up to."

Peau strutted a little, said that sounded kind of like what he did, and David smiled. I confessed that in my case, though, the madness theory might be closer to the truth than the one about wisdom.

"Well, there's overlap, after all," he pointed out. "Both lunacy and enlightenment can demolish our ordinary reality. It's what you do with that experience that makes the difference between the yogi's hut and the madhouse."

I SPREAD SOME OATS out on the grass for the mules, then fetched more potatoes and onions from the truck. Pelageya and I prepared the meal over the wood cookstove in the outdoor kitchen by her shack. David sat in the shade at the nearby table.

"David, you really are emaciated," I said. He shrugged, as if there were nothing to be done, hence no reason to worry about it.

"Look," I continued. "I've still got a truck full of food. I'll leave most of it with you, and I have a way for you to get more."

"How?" Pelageya asked.

"There's a walled town called Cottonwood south of here," I said. "I'll tell you how to get there. Believe it or not, they still use money."

David laughed. "What good is that? We don't have any."

I went to the truck, brought back my kindling bag, and handed it to Pelageya. "Three thousand, give or take," I said. "There's a market, and you can buy decent supplies instead of just trading for rice."

Her eyes gleamed. "Is this all you have? We couldn't—"

"You *could*, in fact," I said. "That's the only place I've been that still uses the stuff. I'll give you the address of a friend, so you'll have a place to stay."

"Is it a dangerous trip?" she asked. "When I go to Princely, I take the dogs and the shotgun and keep a knife under my shirt."

"So you see," David interjected. "This sane young woman has no qualms whatsoever about defending herself. Watch and learn."

I cautioned her about the keening creatures that had sat near our camp at night and warned her to stay out of the river because of the crocs. Then we served up the food and sat down to eat. I told them I was headed to Princely that day, as it happened, and wondered if there was anything I should know. Pelageya told me that it had become something of a trading center, though they didn't use money. People bartered or used gold.

"You'll want your head on a swivel," said David. "Pela has a boy-friend she stays with, and he always escorts her home in case some-body follows her out of town."

I grinned at her. "You didn't say anything about a *boyfriend*."

"Stop," she said, blushing. "It's very casual. I don't like talking about it."

"She doesn't like talking about it because the dude in question is extremely hot," said David, chuckling. "She's afraid we'll think she's shallow."

She threw a potato slice at him. He caught it and ate it greedily.

We chowed down in earnest for a while, all of us having seconds and then thirds. When we were finished, we carried the plates over to the sink, and Pela and I did the dishes. Afterward I hitched up the mules, and Peau flew on ahead to scout. We all hugged, then David gave me the name of a woman in Princely, someone named Serena.

"She'll give you a safe place to stay," he said. "Also, she may have something you need."

I thought he was kidding around. "Well, I'm always happy to get something I want," I said, perhaps too flippantly.

He eyed me, just a bit fiercely, and then I realized his tone had changed. "I didn't say *want*," he replied. "I said *need*."

"Uh-oh," said Pela. "When he says that, you know you're in the shit."

5

It was a long haul to Princely across a hot, sun-blasted plateau. If Pela crossed this on horseback every few months, she was even tougher than she looked.

Peau flew back to the truck after about an hour, so we took a break to rest and water the mules at an old cattle tank under a forlorn paloverde tree. He'd seen almost nothing out there, he said; it was a salt flat and empty of birds.

When the mules were refreshed, we went on. Cassie snoozed in her little nest of rags on the seat, and Peau settled in beside her. I was thinking about the photo on David's shrine—all the people at the gonpa who were gone now. Lama Sonam, of course, who could be funny and impish or surprisingly wrathful depending on what he thought was required in a given situation. He'd mainly been patient and kind with me, but I suspected this was partly because he didn't consider my prospects so brilliant that it was worth driving me too hard. I'd been deeply saddened by his death, knowing that from then on, I'd have to navigate sometimes scary and unpredictable terrain with only my own unreliable wits.

But it wasn't just Sonam, of course. A slew of people were gone forever, friends I'd been close to during what were, in retrospect, some of the happiest and most fulfilling years of my life. Even the last of us—David, Pela, and me—were lying on the tracks and the train was coming, and to pretend otherwise was foolish.

We had a long day's ride ahead, so Peau, perhaps sensing my despondency, started telling me about the various words he'd heard for "wind" in the dialects he'd encountered on our trip. It was the most he'd ever spoken to me, and I appreciated how he'd been bringing me along slowly, from words to phrases to what were now, for all intents and purposes, sentences.

It's difficult to translate the terms themselves, as they consisted of the usual clacks and gutturals and soft cawing sounds, but, loosely described, there was the kind of zephyr that blows gently over flatlands on a mild day; wind that blows toward a mountain and will lift you up as it rises to cross over; conversely, wind descending from the top of a mountain, which can knock you flat if you're not ready for the downdraft. There were terms for different kinds of thermals: the easy, gentle ones in warm weather; the violent ones that can turn into dust devils; even the kind that arise in cities, that often start in the corner of a tall building when the sun shines on it. Peau said you could ride those right up past the top of the building like a little elevator if you wanted to.

I realized midway through this minor disquisition that I wouldn't retain any of it; the terms all sounded too much alike to me. It seemed rude to stop him, though, so I kept quiet.

Cassie woke up toward the end and listened. When Peau was finished, she yawned and said that someone on earth might actually find it all interesting. Peau, his feathers ruffled, replied that she'd find it interesting enough if she needed to fly somewhere without getting killed. But of course, he added, the only way she'd ever fly was if someone threw her off a cliff.

Cass narrowed her eyes and replied that that someone certainly wouldn't be a lightweight like him, would it?

"Knock it off, you two," I said.

IN THE AFTERNOON we followed the road down into a narrow canyon with steep sandstone walls. Boulders littered the old asphalt, some as small as bowling balls, some bigger than the truck, and the mules had to do a lot of weaving to pick a way through. I'd seen enough Hollywood Westerns when I was young to recognize this as a classic place for an ambush, but it seemed unlikely that anyone else was out here.

Soon I started seeing trash by the side of the road. All sorts of once-useful items had been abandoned—carts and wooden wagons, baby carriers, blankets, plastic coolers, rotten cardboard boxes full of clothes, jerricans, kitchenware, empty jugs and bottles, hoes and rakes and splitting mauls, worn-out boots and moldy shoes, then still *more* shoes, as if everyone had suddenly been possessed by an irresistible urge to go barefoot. It looked like Godzilla had picked up a department store, inverted it and shaken it out, then left everything to rust and rot in the sun and desiccating air.

After a half mile of this we came to the bones. Ten or fifteen human skeletons, the ribcages and spines of dogs, even the skulls and pelvises of a few cattle. The human skeletons still wore clothes, though they'd deteriorated to almost nothing, leaving bleached skulls and arm bones sticking out of sun-wrecked rags.

What on earth had happened here? It wasn't so different from the destruction in the cities I'd passed through, except that in those places, the bones had been scattered by scavengers, whereas here they'd remained as intact skeletons. The arrangement suggested that the people had been fleeing *toward* the town, which made me curious about what had been chasing them. I'd wondered this about the camels, too, but it had turned out that nothing at all was chasing them. The whole scene was baffling.

And then, as I saw the pattern in the collection of skeletons, I began to understand. We were in a slot canyon, one of several that fell out from the eastern mountains like toes from a high-arched foot. When the people came through here a few years earlier, there must have been a rainstorm in those mountains. They had indeed been trying to get to town, I felt sure. They would have been aware of the danger, they would have felt the vibration in the earth and heard the roaring behind them, low at first but gaining volume as the flash flood closed in. The walls were too steep to climb, so they'd dropped their belongings and tried to run. When the water caught them and quickly rose to their thighs, some of them would have kicked off their shoes to swim for it. And then the roaring liquid wall would have caught them, carrying with it a load of dense and suffocating silt. It would have bashed them into boulders and broken their bones and drowned them, then washed them into an eddy. There, the bodies had sunk and remained long after the canyon had drained again.

I was eager to get out, but there hadn't been any rain in the mountains, so there was really no danger. And then, as if the place had read my thoughts and decided to prove me wrong, I felt a deep rumbling in the earth.

It wasn't a flash flood, and it wasn't my next fear—a rampaging stampede of large mammals—either. A smallish boulder had simply dislodged itself from the sandstone above us and come careening down the slope. Colossally bad timing, yes, but obviously not uncommon: How else would all the other rocks have gotten here? I looked out the window just in time to see the thing come barreling toward us, then bounce once before it leapt up and collided with the truck. It was only a couple of feet in diameter, but it weighed plenty and it was moving fast. It slammed into us behind the rear wheel, shoving the truck sideways in the road, then tumbled on for another few yards before crashing into the opposite canyon wall and coming to rest.

Cassie shrieked, more or less overlapping Peau's croaked *awk!* The mules halted, swaying to get their balance and stamping nervously.

"It's okay," I said, reflexively trying to reassure everyone, but it pretty clearly wasn't okay. Peau hopped past Cassie to the window and took off without a word, though I wasn't sure if this was for reconnaissance or escape.

I got out and walked around back. The right rear quarter panel of the truck was bashed in, and the frame was bent. I went to the mules and led them forward a few steps. The truck rolled, but with a horrible squeal.

I was pissed at Pelageya, who could have mentioned this canyon of bones and boulders. But I had no choice but to get back into the truck, turn the mules, and drive us on. The metallic shriek was unbearable, so I tore off little pieces from Cassie's rags and shoved them into my ears. It didn't help much.

Soon enough we came out of the canyon and the road climbed a rise. The sun was getting low in the west, and I still didn't see any sign of Princely. I pulled my map off the dash to get a sense of how much farther we had to go, then saw a little note on it. It turned out that Pelageya had circled the canyon in pencil, then written, "Careful here. You'll see why."

Finally, around sunset, we came to the edge of a bluff that overlooked a broad, flat valley. A narrow river meandered through it, and in the middle of the valley, by the river, stood what I took to be the town. I was surprised to see what appeared to be electric lights down there, the first I'd encountered in fourteen years. I checked the map again to see if Pelageya had noted this, but evidently she hadn't wanted to spoil it for me. Or maybe she hadn't realized how rare electricity was.

Cassie gazed at the town a few moments, her eyes wide. *Land stars,* she said.

· · ·

PEAU REJOINED US just before we got to town. *What ho*, he said, fluttering in to land on Mule One's flank.

"What ho, my good lord."

He cocked his head disapprovingly at the noisy truck, then hopped into the cab. Three highways converged here: the one we'd been on, plus one from the southeast, then another heading out northwest, which we'd take when we departed. I saw no walls, no fences; anybody could come through if they could manage to get here, and I remembered David's advice about keeping my head on a swivel.

As we entered the town, we saw other travelers on the street and another dozen rigs of varying configurations. Mostly there were wooden wagons with rubber car tires, and dirty plastic tarps for cover, that were pulled by teams of horses or mules. I saw one other setup like ours, though, an old rusted Tacoma driven by a blond guy with a ponytail. He'd harnessed two big gelded mustangs to it. These drivers were teamsters in the original sense, and the long-dead members of the long-busted union would have been proud to see them returned to their equine roots: truckers hauling food and grain and lumber and alcohol, through heat and dust storms and the ubiquitous threat of banditry, at something like our rate of fifty miles a day. We also saw what appeared to be the occasional family, traveling to find lost relatives or better land or just to leave something ugly and heartbreaking behind. Civilization on the hoof.

The town was only a few square blocks, but a fair number of people were out. As usual, almost everyone looked under thirty. Their occasional smiles revealed the expected rotten teeth, too, but it was the same as anything else—when everybody stank, nobody stank.

The air was cool and dusty, and old Christmas lights had been strung along the storefronts and even raised high over the road, casting buildings and people in reds and greens and yellows. Peau and Cassie watched, rapt, through the windshield. There were no actual streetlights, but there were lights inside houses and shops, and the place felt festive. We passed a restaurant and a café, two more things I hadn't seen in years, and I swooned at the smells that wafted out—of meat roasting and potatoes frying, and warm, yeasty bread, and coffee. *Coffee!* Where and how did anybody get coffee anymore, especially out here?

Gangs of men wandered around, loud and loose from alcohol, peering into shop windows, making demeaning and insinuating remarks to other gangs of men. There was a fair amount of coughing; TB had evidently found its way here too.

Then, as we went by a saloon, I heard a guitar and a banjo, and stamping, dancing feet—so much life so full of the past that it was possible for a moment to forget. A burly bouncer dragged out a skinny fellow by the collar. He crossed the planked wooden sidewalk and tossed him, not without a familiar tenderness, into the road. The thin man lay there, and as we passed, I heard him mumble something about the goddamn riffraff.

"Timmy boy, the riffraff is *you*," said the bouncer amiably. He turned to go back inside.

A huge juniper stood in the middle of the next block, surrounded by a ridiculous miniature picket fence. The tree posed no threat; traffic here moved at walking speed, and horses were a lot smarter than people when it came to avoiding obstacles. But there was a fence anyway, one that might have slightly retarded the advance of a lame chihuahua. The tree, too, was strung with lights. Three kids had climbed into the branches and were pelting passersby with hard little berries. The adults successfully feigned surprise and occasional outrage. "Throw me some more and I'll make gin," called one man, and the kids obliged and blasted him. He laughed. "Little bastards," he said, ambling on his way.

I followed David's instructions and soon found his friend's place, half a block down a side street. It was a big old house with a driveway along the side and an open courtyard in back, where I parked the truck. I went around to the front entrance to find Serena.

The door was ajar, so I let myself in. The living room was crammed with old furniture, including a garish red couch and a low coffee table holding ancient movie magazines, their pages as yellowed and crackly as desiccated skin. There were a couple of brown faux-leather chairs and two lamps with tinted, fake Tiffany shades. Five young women lounged about, chatting in low and vaguely sarcastic tones. They took one look at me, then turned away. Substantial makeup and insubstantial clothing; it was pretty clear what was going on here. The trucker trade, of course. What was David thinking? That what I needed was a teenage hooker?

I was, by then, expecting Serena to be a hardened pile driver of a madame, someone straight out of Dickens. But she turned out to be a slender woman of about thirty, with dark hair tied back, calm, clear eyes, and a floral-print dress. She looked as if she'd just returned from her day job at the library.

She welcomed me and I explained the situation. She smiled, appearing relieved.

"Of course," she said. I gave her a small sack of potatoes for the privilege of sleeping in the truck in her courtyard, where I'd be able to keep an eye on the mules.

I got them out of harness, then led them into a little carport that had been refashioned as a stable. I fed and watered them, then ditto for Cassie. Peau, as usual, was fine fending for himself and flew off to see what he could discover.

I was hungry and thinking about the restaurant, so I went back inside to see if Serena had eaten. She couldn't leave, though; it was a quiet night, but even so she had to mind the place and keep an eye on the girls. She said the restaurant had takeout if I wanted to go pick up dinner. You just had to bring something to carry it home in, and she had an old stainless container with a handle and a strap-down lid that worked.

"How do you pay for things here?" I asked.

"There's a blacksmith who makes coins for us," she answered. "You take in your gold or silver, he melts it and casts it, then keeps a pinch. Easier than bartering, and he gets rich."

"I'll bet."

"Anyway, in this case, the restaurant owner is a client," she continued. "I have an account there, and he has an account here, and things generally balance out. So order what you want."

"What can I get you?"

"I'll have a steak, medium, and plank fries," she said. "Tell Jim to send some for the girls too. I hope you're not a vegetarian, because you'll starve out here if so."

"Steak sounds fine, actually. By the way, how in hell do they get coffee?"

"Oh, it's sort of the new cocaine," she said. "All brought in from Central America. Four armed men for every wagonload, and even that's not enough sometimes. We have three or four coffee widows in town already."

THE GIRLS, NOT SURPRISINGLY, exhibited little interest in hanging out with an old guy who wasn't paying for their time, so they took their food upstairs. I must have looked like something unearthed from the Cretaceous era. But it meant Serena and I had the kitchen table to ourselves.

"How do you know David?" I asked.

"He's my dad's cousin," she replied. "I knew him growing up in Saint Louis. He and I are the last people from our family still alive."

"How did you end up here?"

"Oh, long story," she answered. "A man who turned into a rat."

I smiled. "I think I've heard that story."

"Yeah, the details vary but the gist is always the same."

She'd visited David at his hermitage a few years before, she said. She didn't want to live there, though, so she went on to Princely. That was where she met the rat, but after a few months he took off with another woman and she was on her own.

"Around here it's sort of like Alaska a hundred years ago," she went on. "There are five or ten men for every woman, and people live hard lives. There are ARM cells too, so you have to be careful what you say."

"How do you translate ARM around here?" I asked. It was getting to be a kind of survey.

"I call them the Antediluvian Reptilian Monsters," she said.

"I like that."

Anyway, she continued, there were no schools or libraries or law practices or police departments or hospitals or real estate offices anymore, most of the places women used to work had vanished, as if we were in Afghanistan under the Taliban. You could leave, but where would you go, and how would you safely travel there? You might get married, given the abundance of single men, but quantity didn't equal quality. The odds were good, but the goods were odd.

A year previously, she heard that the woman who ran this place had gotten sick with something and died. The girls were going hungry and didn't know what to do, so she stepped in and got things organized. She tried to get enough food for everyone and did her best to keep them from getting beaten up or killed by their johns. The girls were mostly orphans, good kids with few options, and now she felt responsible for them. The best they could hope for was to keep from getting syphilis or the clap or herpes or HIV or TB, and never mind the specter of pregnancy, which meant death in childbirth about one time in eight, given how young they were. A competing house had opened on the other side of town, too, offering significant discounts. Business here had dropped off drastically as a result.

"Any way for the girls to get out?" I asked.

"Once in a while some lonely, moony fellow will allow himself to fall in love," Serena said. "Then the girl can move into his house or his trailer or whatever. Sometimes they start families and stay on fairly happily, and sometimes they're back a week later, all bruised up."

We ate as we talked, which seemed oddly casual, given the bleakness of the subject. The steak was a little tough, but it was still a restaurant meal, something I thought I'd never have again.

"Where do the girls come from?" I asked. "How do they end up here?"

"A few are locals," she said. "Others get picked up by truckers somewhere else, with great promises of paradise on the open road. The drivers get tired of them after a few weeks, and if the girls are lucky they get dumped here instead of the middle of the desert, where depending on the time of year, they're killed by heat, cold, dehydration, wolves, or God knows what. A few of them came up together from an orphanage in Flagstaff when it shut down. They had a wagon made out of an old trailer, and their mule died here, so here they were. It's like that."

"Good lord."

"Yeah, as David used to say, welcome to samsara," she said. "Which reminds me, you never told me how *you* know David."

So I told her our history, including my time at the gonpa.

"How was *that*?" she asked. "David once told me the hardest thing was getting used to ineffability. I didn't even know what he was talking about."

I laughed and said I thought he meant that in the Old World we'd grown up in, there was an acknowledged path to success: you studied, applied your knowledge, met mentors, worked or published, then eventually mentored others. Training at the gonpa had turned out to be an entirely different animal. Yes, you had to read the texts and try to understand what they really meant underneath all the cultural context and symbolism. But eventually you had to apply what you'd learned in the most fundamental way, which meant sitting there on your aching butt, month after month, as you simply waited for certain things to happen. You couldn't *make* those things happen, though, and it was far and away the most difficult thing I'd ever done.

"But David managed okay, didn't he?"

"David was pretty much a prodigy at everything he tried," I said. "He was oblivious to the physical pain of sitting all the time, and largely immune to distraction of any kind. He just went for it."

"Sounds like him."

"Yeah, I get envious," I admitted. "But then I compare my problems to those of your girls, and I mainly feel like a dick."

We finished eating, then she said it had been a long day and she still had work to do. We carried the plates to the sink, and she filled one side of it with hot water. Such a luxury—in Cottonwood they'd had water, but here they had *hot* water. When we were done with the dishes, I said good night and went out to the truck.

WHEN I WOKE UP, my bad molar was throbbing, probably from chewing the steak. I lay there a few minutes, contemplating what still lay before us. Mainly, I had to get the truck fixed and get out of here before Flynn & Co. appeared. I figured I had a day or two, but even so, I felt a little surge of anxiety.

Serena had made breakfast. The girls were still asleep upstairs.

"Any hope of a dentist here?" I asked.

"None, I'm afraid."

"Anybody who can weld, then?"

"Your *teeth?*"

"My truck."

"Ah," she said. It turned out there was—Miguel's, three blocks away. As for the tooth, she suggested I try the old Rexall. There were no commercial drugs, but there was a chemist named Bruce who could concoct a fair amount of stuff from whatever was around. "He's a bit of a wizard," she said. "And yes, he has an account here."

After breakfast I brought Cassie inside and introduced her to Serena.

"God, she's huge," said Serena, petting her. "Maine coon?"

I smiled. "Part," I said. "You're the only person I've met who even knows what a Maine coon is."

"Well, of *course* I do," Serena said, more to Cassie than to me, in that cute talking-to-the-cat falsetto some people get. She kept petting. "Yes, yes, yes, we know what a Maine coon is, don't we?" she went on, as Cassie purred.

I thanked her for breakfast, got the mules hitched up, and drove over to Miguel's, doing my best to ignore the truck's god-awful squeal.

Miguel had a bad leg and made his way around his dusty old shop with an air of patiently accommodated pain. This, combined with the set of his jaw and a certain look of besieged determination in his eyes, contributed to the feeling that he was considerably more seasoned than his relative youth suggested. He lay down on the creeper and scooted under the back of the truck to survey the damage.

"Boulder, huh?"

"With an actual engine I might have gotten out of the way."

"Yeah, mules' zero-to-sixty isn't much to write home about. Have to admire the mileage, though."

He banged on a couple of things with a hammer, peered around some more, then rolled himself back out. The frame was cracked, which had pushed the axle mount slightly askew, which was putting torque on everything from the wheel bearings to the differential and causing the noise. He just had to straighten and weld the frame and the rest would take care of itself. He said he couldn't do anything about the body damage, which included a cracked fill pipe, but since there was no gas tank connected to it, it didn't matter.

"What will I owe you?" I asked.

"What have you got?"

Something occurred to me. If he had welding gear, he probably had acetylene, which I'd been thinking might come in handy. I noticed that there were nine or ten three-gallon tanks against the wall and asked if that was what was in them. It was, and as far as he knew it was the last to be found for hundreds of miles in any direction.

"If you were to do the job, would you be willing to throw in a tank of acetylene and a torch?"

"It took me a while to collect all that, and when it's gone there won't be any more," he said. "Anyway, if you want to use acetylene, you'll need a tank of oxygen to go with it."

"What would all that be worth in dollars? The job and the gas, I mean."

"I barely remember dollars, 'cause I was a kid," he said. "Maybe four or five hundred?"

I considered this. "I've got a Marlin .30-30 short-barrel saddle rifle with a scope," I said. "I think it's worth a little more than that, but I don't have any ammo for it."

"Well, I can *make* ammo," Miguel said, his eyes brightening. "I've got a crate of empty shell casings, and lead and powder and a press. Can I see?"

I got the rifle out for him, and he held it, aimed it, worked the lever, and whistled appreciatively. "Look, mister, I'm an honest man," he said then. "This is worth a hell of a lot more than a little welding job and some hot juice. Is there anything else I can throw in?"

I told him that my other rifle was a .22 and asked if he had any ammunition for that. He had three boxes of the stuff, it turned out, and would happily give me one. A king's ransom, as far as I was concerned, but no big deal to him. We shook on it, and he said to come back after lunch.

Princely felt more like a real town than Cottonwood, mainly because it had once been one, rather than a cheap company shantyville for miners. The houses were nicer—old one- and two-story clapboard places with front porches and decent detailing—and the roads were paved instead of dirt. Junipers and cottonwoods and oaks grew along the streets, and there was even a city park with green grass and children playing in it. All this seemed even more miraculous since it was sitting in the middle of a desert and made possible only by proximity to the river. The kids in the park chased each other around and screeched happily. Mind-boggling normality, except that these children couldn't begin to conceive that the world had once had so many people in it. To them, Princely might as well have been New York.

The houses were mostly weathered down to wood, though, since there was no paint to be had. Someone had made whitewash from what must have been a local lime deposit, though, so in the course of a few blocks I passed three crews laying it on, doing their best to stave off decay. Which meant there was an actual economy here, which meant that sooner or later they were going to have to reinvent some sort of money that didn't require the involvement of a blacksmith.

I walked downtown. The morning was quiet. What you get when nobody's over thirty, I figured—late nights and a day that doesn't start till after ten.

A block down Main there was a flatbed wagon, maybe twenty feet long, with truck tires, a seat, and four mules in harness. Half a dozen rough-looking men were unloading huge bundles of steel cable, the hoops five or six feet in diameter, onto a series of smaller wagons. I stopped to watch. One of the men turned to look at me, and an expression of scorn passed over his face.

"We don't need any help," he said. "You're too old anyway. You'd drop dead the first day."

He was a rangy guy, early thirties, with a scraggly beard and greasy blond hair that hung past broad shoulders. I had to wrestle down my younger self's impulse to tell him to fuck off.

"Probably right," I said. "I was just curious what you're doing."

"What are you, a cop?" There *were* no cops, of course.

"He might arrest us," said one of the others jauntily.

"The only arrest *he's* going to get is cardiac," said the first man, and they all had a good laugh at that.

I was utterly at a loss for a retort, so I just turned away and kept walking. By then I'd realized what was happening, anyway: the cable was steel from long-dead power lines. These crews went out and pulled them down. Some would be used in the local grid, probably, the rest sold and transported elsewhere. Strong, high-quality stuff that nobody made anymore.

Humility was good, I reminded myself as I walked. Unfortunately, this didn't change the fact that at the moment I basically wanted to shoot them. It was frustrating, after all those years of meditation, to find myself still getting lost in the murderous machinations of my own lousy temper.

I found the Rexall on the next block. It had a little sign in the window that read "Bruce Hannock, D.Chem."

I pushed through the door, which had a little bell over it. Hannock was busy doing something behind the counter. He was about forty, balding and bespectacled, with a paunch and a tattered white coat. He probably didn't have long to live, given his age, and he didn't look much like a wizard, but I wasn't in a position to quibble. The shelves behind him held forty or fifty large plastic bottles with formulas written on them. The stuff must have been old, but there was a fair amount of it even so.

"Help you?" he asked, friendly enough.

"Toothache."

He put a small bottle in front of me. I opened it and saw pale-brown powder.

"What is it?"

"Aspirin, basically," he replied. "Salicylic acid made from willow bark."

Peau would like to know about this, I thought. I asked Hannock how much I should take.

"A pinch three or four times a day," he said. "It's the straight stuff, though, no buffering. Take it with food so your stomach doesn't bleed."

"Thanks," I said. "It's on Serena's account."

He made a quick note. "She's a good one," he said. "Those girls would be in deep shit without her." I appreciated the sentiment, but I was trying to push away the image of this pudgy, balding guy getting sucked off by a fifteen-year-old. I was eager to be on my way.

Halfway down the street, then, a couple of scruffy-looking fellows wandered into my path. Drifters, I guessed, passing through on the highway and between rides. Their clothes were in shreds, their shoes worn almost to nothing. One wore a long, filthy overcoat full of holes. I veered to get out of their way, and they veered with me.

"Get us some food, man," said the one with the overcoat. A command, not a request.

"Sorry," I replied, and tried to ease past them. He grabbed at my arm, and before I knew it, I'd turned and given him a shove. He tripped over the other guy, and they both toppled onto the planked sidewalk.

"Jesus, take it easy!"

"*You* take it easy," I shot back. Displaced rage, I knew; it was the guys on the truck I wanted to knock down, not a couple of starving bums.

Anyway, so much for my generous, spacious mind. Anger followed by shame; the best thing was to keep moving. I passed the restaurant, trying to calm down, then turned the corner and halted in my tracks. I wasn't quite sure whether to believe my eyes. There was another little café, which was amazing enough in itself, but a hand-lettered sign in the window said, "Internet."

I took a moment to collect myself, then went inside. To my amazement, they had muffins too, and the combination was too much to resist. I got my courage up and told the barista, whose cardboard name tag said Molly, that Serena had told me to charge everything to her account. A guy washing dishes in the kitchen overheard me and waved his assent. Serena was clearly a good person to know around here. I wondered if coffee and a muffin would be like a madeleine to Proust, bringing back vivid sensations of an earlier life.

"You really have web access?" I asked.

"Sure," Molly said.

"Where does the town get electricity, anyway?"

She explained that Princely had salvaged a few hundred solar panels from various installations in the surrounding counties fourteen years earlier, when things were falling to pieces and all the main grids went down.

"We got it arrayed on the hill overlooking town," she said. "Our electrician was still alive then, and he helped us wire it up. We can't run anything heavy-duty like a laundromat, but we've got a handful of computers, and Main Street's pretty at night. People can have a few lights in their houses, as long as they're LEDs."

"Good thing they last. Nobody's made them in years."

"After that it will be candles again, I guess."

"Where are your servers?"

"It varies," she said. "Last I looked, they were in New Zealand. I don't even know where New Zealand is."

I hadn't checked my email since I'd left the gonpa. That day, the servers were in Iceland. Presumably the connections got routed to whatever was available, but data moved slowly because it now depended on deep-sea cables. All those nimble little satellite uplinks had been hobbled by lasers—some Chinese, some Russian, some ours—during Mayhem. It was like trying to cook on a camp stove in a windstorm; as soon as you got rolling, the flames blew out and you had to start over.

The coffee was incredibly good, and it did indeed resurrect a sense of my younger self, when my body felt strong and fluid, my mind clear, and all kinds of things were still possible in the world. My hands trembled as I sat down at the keyboard. Gmail had been snuffed years before, along with Palo Alto and the Bay Area more generally, but thanks to the Saskatchewan library, I hoped I'd still be able to connect. I typed in my login and my password and waited. After half a minute, astonishingly, everything came up. My spam folder contained six thousand messages. All that shit was on autopilot, and it kept coming even though all the boiler-room trolls had long since vanished under their bridges and turned to dust. The grift that keeps on grifting.

My inbox held one message, sent the week before.

"Will," it read. "CA border closed. Nation-state now. Take old UPac tracks Opal–Bakersfield, stay on for tunnel to SLO. No trains, no guards. Sooner better, running out of time. Trust escort will help. Lars."

I hit Reply: "Lars. You can type normally, you know. Remember email? We're all out of practice, but it's not a fucking telegraph."

I was about to tell him where I was, but then it occurred to me that Buck Flynn might have resources. If he found a way to hack my account—though could anyone hack anything anymore, at least without a hacksaw?—he'd know just where to find me. Of course, he might also be able to track my IP address, and there weren't too many places I could log on in the first place, but the point was that I'd underestimated him before. It was an *Art of War* sort of thing.

"I won't be taking that route," I wrote, knowing full well I would be and congratulating myself on this crafty misdirection. "If all goes well—which is to say, better than it's going now—look for me in a couple of weeks. The Mojave is an issue. It takes more than one night when traveling via mule, and I don't want to be caught out during the day. I don't know what escort you mean, but don't send me any more emails as I won't get them. I'm doing this because you said it was urgent, but it's also dangerous and a pain in the ass, so if I'm not there in a month, assume I'm dead. —Will."

I hit Send, logged out of my account, ate my muffin, and washed down some aspirin powder with the last of the coffee. Then, out of curiosity, for old times' sake, I went to the search bar of the browser and typed in "Google." It took a second, but then the message came up: "404: Not found." Nothing had changed, in other words, though I appreciated the irony that you couldn't google Google because Google was gone. One more lost window on the world.

A young couple came in and took a table. The place had big front windows that let in the light, and it felt so incredibly normal to just sit there, having checked my email, sipping a hot drink. After she'd served the others, Molly came over and stood by the table, watching me a little awkwardly.

"You want to sit?" I asked.

"Thanks," she said, but she stayed where she was. She was a raw-boned strawberry blond, with strong shoulders and those dry, reddish cheeks that suggest an upbringing on a high, windy ranch with cold winters. I asked what was on her mind.

"I know this is rude . . . ," she began, tentatively.

I smiled. "I'm fifty-two," I said. "It's okay, it's natural to be curious."

She relaxed a little. "What I mean is, how did you do it? Both my parents died in their early forties last year. I've never seen anyone like you. I'm just wondering if there's some kind of secret."

"If I knew, I'd tell you."

"Oh, okay," she answered, deflated. I asked how old she was. "Nineteen next month," she said. "My boyfriend's twenty-three, so I'm trying to get preggers as soon as I can. There's so many orphans now, I don't want my kids to end up like that."

"Well, have fun trying."

She blushed a little and suppressed a grin. "Thanks. We are."

IT WAS ONLY ABOUT ELEVEN O'CLOCK, so I walked up the hill to have a look at the solar array. It was impressive, all that angled blue glass baking in the morning sun—the kind of technology we could only dream about producing now.

I felt a little lightheaded, probably from the coffee, so I sat down in the dirt. There was a moist breeze from the west, and I noticed clouds piling up over the mountains. The air felt wonderful; it had probably been months since it last rained here. The roads would be muddy, but mules were the original ATVs. We'd get through.

I stopped by Miguel's on the way to Serena's. He was finishing up, so he brought the mules in from behind the shop and hitched them up. They walked forward a few paces. No wailing metal.

Then Mule One took a huge shit on the floor. I wanted to intervene, somehow, but of course there wasn't anything to be done except stand there and wait for her to finish. She dropped quite a pile.

I apologized to Miguel and found a shovel.

"I put fresh grease in your differential, which should help too," he said, as I transferred the dung into a big old galvy bucket. "There's one more thing I want to do."

Acetylene was actually pretty explosive, he explained; it wasn't nitroglycerine, but it wasn't all that safe, either. He wasn't thrilled at the idea of having even a small tank of it rolling around in the back of the truck as we headed out into hot desert on bad roads. So he lifted the hood and rearranged my storage shelves, then took a couple of measurements and fashioned a holder out of an old metal bracket. He welded it in behind the wheel well with deft precision, padded it with some felt, then set the acetylene tank in it. The oxygen fit snugly beside it.

"You're good," I said.

"Practice." I took the bucket of mule shit outside while he found an old bungee and strapped down the tanks. "If it gets over a hundred and ten outside, turn the knob and vent it so you don't get blown up," he said, when I'd come back in.

We shook hands. I gave him the Marlin, he handed me the .22 bullets along with the torch and a pair of welding goggles, and we were off.

A skilled mechanic and an honest guy, I reflected. That should have made more of an impression on me than the jerkwad cable harvesters, and for some reason it hadn't. We tended to fixate on the thing to be avoided, though. An evolutionary advantage, but regrettable nevertheless, because all too often we failed to appreciate the stuff we should, like Miguel. Or, for that matter, Serena.

EVERYWHERE I WENT, I ended up wanting to stick around. I was tired and dirty, and not particularly enjoying the role of questing hero. I liked Serena, and after Princely, it was going to be all wilderness all the time until I crossed the Central Valley and reached the coastal mountains in California. If I reached them. But Buck Flynn was on my mind, and there was no way I could stay here.

Since I'd given most of my food to David and Pelageya, I went to the store and traded for a fifty-pound bag of rice. When I got back to the house, Serena came out.

"Can we talk?" she asked, and I nodded.

She led me out back, where we sat in a couple of old plastic chairs in the shade of a grape arbor.

"There's someone I want you to meet," she said.

"Okay . . . ," I answered, puzzled now.

"She's younger than the other girls, and she doesn't particularly get along with them," she said. "She's very angry, and I don't know what to do with her."

I was trying to process what this was about. She wanted me to counsel her somehow? I was completely unqualified, and mainly I'd counsel her to get out of here any way she could.

"I'm not sure what you want me to do."

"I was thinking maybe you could take her off my hands," she said.

"Wait, *what?*"

"Hear me out," she said. "She's fourteen, she's bright, and she'll work. For now she just helps me with the place, but she'll be fifteen soon, and then she's got to start taking on johns. The other girls have toughened up; they know how to survive. It won't be like that with her."

"She's not tough?"

"She's tough enough, but not that way. I worry it will break her, that she'll end up hurting herself. I can't have that on my conscience."

"Can't you just let her keep doing the stuff she already does?"

She shook her head. "It wouldn't be fair to the others," she said. "Money's getting tight, and she can't stay if she doesn't start bringing some in. Would you meet her, at least?"

"Look," I said. "There's a whole band of ARM crazies after me. She wouldn't be safe. They'd only kill me, but we both know what they'd do to her."

I thought this would end the matter, but it didn't. "It's bad either way," she said. "I trust you have plans to evade these people?"

I smiled at how she'd put this—the sweet librarian talking. "Of course I do," I said. "But there are a lot of them and one of me, and plans don't always work out."

She sighed. "I understand," she said, sounding resigned.

And then I reflected on what I'd just been thinking: that if asked, I'd tell this girl to get out of here however possible. Which made me, once again, a hypocrite. I also wondered, briefly, what it might be like to have the company of an actual human being for a change.

I sighed. "Look," I said. "Suppose we meet. If she doesn't mind putting herself in harm's way, and if I feel comfortable enough, then I'll consider it. But we both have veto power. If either of us says no, it's no."

She smiled. "There's one thing you'd better do before you meet her, though."

"What's that?"

"You smell like a dead goat. Would you mind taking a shower?"

I laughed. "I'd *love* a shower, whether I meet this girl or not."

I TURNED ON THE WATER and stepped under the warm spray. The tub beneath me soon turned brown with all the grime.

It felt wonderful. I washed my hair, scrubbed my body a second time and then a third, and finally felt clean. I'd brought in my extra set of clothes, so I put them on and handed the dirty ones to Serena, who was so eager to bribe me that she offered to wash them and hang them up.

When I went outside, the girl was sitting on the tailgate of the truck, playing with Cassie. Cassie would attack her hand, then the girl would subdue her, at which point Cassie would loll on her back for a moment before attacking the hand again.

I walked over. She looked up at me, then back at the cat. "I'm Sophie," she said, as if this wasn't particularly good news.

"Will."

A smirk played at the corner of her lips. "As in free, or o' the wisp?"

Well, okay, I thought: The word play was encouraging. Not getting that it's rude to play around with the names of people you've just met, less encouraging.

"As in last and testament," I said.

I hoped she might laugh, but instead she studied me dolefully. "I guess it fits, then."

I noticed that she looked a little like Eva and wondered if this might put her at ease.

"Don't take it personally," I said. "But you remind me of someone I used to know."

"I don't take it personally," she answered. "Some guy says that to me about three times a week. You need a better line."

My face suddenly felt so warm I thought I might be blushing. "I didn't mean it like that."

"Good to know," she said, then nodded at the truck. "Nice ride," she said. "Two mulepower, huh?"

"That's about the size of it."

"Where do you sleep?"

"In the back."

"Where would I sleep?"

"Well, in the back."

"Would there be something between us, Will?"

"About forty years, I figure."

"That ought to do, along with my shiv."

Shiv? Had she been watching old prison movies? "I've got machetes," I said. "I'll give you one."

"Not nearly as handy in close quarters, but thanks."

It was hard to tell when she was kidding and when she wasn't. This criticism had often been applied to me when I was growing up, as I recalled. I wondered if there was some way to defuse the tension.

"I'm guessing we'll also end up with this gigantous cat between us," I said, remembering Pela's word.

"I *hate* cats," she said, and Cassie looked up, startled. "The only thing I hate worse than cats is birds. Probably you have a bird too."

It took me a second. Serena must have told her. "No reason you can't sleep on the roof, I guess," I said. "Like that dog Snoopy in the old cartoons."

"I hate dogs and I hate cartoons too. Plus, the bird would probably shit on me."

"There's always the ground, then. Unless you also hate scorpions and spiders and rattlesnakes and mud."

"No, those I love," she said. She hummed a few bars from "My Favorite Things," probably thinking I wouldn't get the reference. How could she know anything about old musicals?

"Raindrops on roses and whiskers on kittens," I said. "Julie Andrews."

"Brown paper packages tied up with strings," she replied. "The Unabomber."

I laughed; I couldn't help it. "Goddamn, girl. Where'd you get all this ancient history?"

"Goddamn, dude," she answered, eyeing me. "A man of culture with a double-mule pickup? How can I say no to that?"

She smiled for the first time then. Amazingly enough, she had decent teeth.

While she was inside packing, I took a look at the map. I followed the river upstream to the bridge where Flynn and his riders would have crossed. I hadn't noticed before, but there was a road leading straight from that bridge to Princely. It must have been the southeastern one I'd seen when we came down the grade into town. I did the math and felt the hair stand up on the back of my neck. I'd had the two sides; they had the hypotenuse. I knew they needed a rest day. Allowing for that, and the distance, they would likely be here . . . today.

Shit! I was on my feet, gathering my things and throwing them into the truck. I called for Serena, and she came out.

"I miscalculated," I said. "We have to go *now*."

"She's going with you?"

"Evidently."

We dragged my still-wet clothes off the line; then she ran upstairs to hustle Sophie along and get her out the door. In another ten minutes, the mules were in harness and we were packed.

And then I realized that Peau was off somewhere. I couldn't wait for him. He'd have to find us on his own.

Serena and I embraced hurriedly. "Thank you for this," she said. "I'll remember."

"If I were you, I'd lock up this afternoon, pull the blinds, and leave the lights off tonight," I said. "You don't want those guys here."

6

Over the western mountains, dark thunderheads had gathered with lightning flashing inside them. We were headed right into the building storm, and I was worried about Peau. I was behind the wheel, Cassie beside me on the ratty old bench seat, Sophie by the window.

Thinking about *The Art of War* had gotten me thinking about, well, the art of war. Sun Tzu put a lot of emphasis on using weather and terrain to your advantage, especially if you were outnumbered. Of course, he didn't have things like warplanes and artillery, but neither did we, so his advice had become more relevant than ever. If you were cornered, your options were limited. Less so if you did the cornering.

We were coming into the canyon country that fell out away from those western mountains. I knew the area a little; in my twenties, before everything went to shit, I'd taken a semester off from college to explore. I'd gone backpacking and climbing in southern Utah and then down here, in the country closer to the Colorado River. I'd rambled down miles of slot canyons, sometimes climbing out if they came to dead ends, or wading through cold, chest-deep water after rains. There was a particular place I remembered, so I found an old trail map among the pile in the back. I was pretty sure I knew how to get there.

Cass asked where Peau was. I didn't want to freak Sophie out by talking back, so I gave Cass a meaningful look and she seemed to understand. Then it apparently occurred to her that this presented unprecedented opportunities. She'd rarely uttered more than a few words at a time before, but suddenly she became alarmingly loquacious. I was able to follow most of what she said, for better or worse, and when I missed the details, I still got the gist.

She'd watched me, she said. Everywhere I went, I wanted to stick around. I'd meet some woman or a couple of old friends, and it was like I'd forgotten what I was supposed to be doing. She'd had no idea how lazy I was!

Sophie reached over and scratched Cass behind the ears. "She sure makes a lot of little noises," she said. Then she glanced at me. "Why is your face so red?"

Mainly I didn't like being lectured about indolence by a friggin' *cat*, but I couldn't say that.

"Look," I said to Sophie, "things around here aren't quite the way they seem."

She sighed. "You're a perv. I knew you had to be a perv."

Cass observed drily that the girl was perceptive.

"Stop it!"

"Stop what?" asked Sophie.

"I'm talking to the cat."

"Oh dear God," said Sophie. "Just let me out. I'll get rained on, I don't care."

"You can't get out, it's dangerous."

"What are we doing, four miles an hour? I'm pretty sure I'll survive the deceleration."

"That's not what I meant."

"Maybe you could explain what you *did* mean, Will."

She sounded so much like my fifth-grade teacher, the gigantic, tanklike Mrs. Farnsworth, that I shivered with a sudden somatic memory of terror and oppression. I started in about Flynn & Co., but she stopped me.

"Serena told me all this," she said. "I'm more worried about *you* right now."

"Here's the thing," I said. "It's just that a few months ago, I realized that the cat and the bird and I could sort of communicate."

"Did Serena know about this?"

"No."

"Kind of a big thing to conceal, don't you think?"

"I knew her for a *day*, Sophie."

"So you're what, like Dr. Dolittle in that movie?"

I sighed with frustration. "Yes, I'm exactly like Rex Harrison in every way."

"Didn't he have about ten wives?"

"Six, I think, but not all at once."

What did I tell you? said Cass.

"Okay, so what did she say right then?" asked Sophie.

"She was being snotty. She's pretty much always snotty."

"Cass," said Sophie. "Repeat what you said, slowly."

Cass emitted the same series of mewls, *adagissimo.*

"It's only little noises, Will. You're a lunatic."

"I'd like to point out that you asked her to repeat what she'd said, and she repeated it. So she understood *you*, even if you didn't understand her."

"How would I know she repeated it if I can't understand?"

"Hmm . . . good point."

Just then Peau sailed in and landed on the rump of Mule One. "Peau!" said Cass and I together—one word, one meow, synchronized.

Sophie stared at us. "Now *that* was weird."

"That's what I'm trying to tell you," I said.

Peau fluttered back to the window and hopped into the cab. He turned around and his tail feathers slapped Sophie in the face.

"Jesus!" she said.

Peau asked with irritation who the girl was and why she was taking his spot on the seat. Cass replied that the girl was getting used to the idea. *What idea?* Peau asked, and Cass answered, *Us.*

Peau gave a little croak of comprehension: *Oh.*

"Okay, so this is really starting to freak me out," said Sophie. "I mean, it *sounds* like those two are having a conversation. Are those two having a conversation?"

"The good news is that, as usual, you're not missing much."

"Oh hell," said Sophie. She'd turned pale, even greenish. "I feel a little sick to my stomach."

"Whoa, mules."

She got out of the truck, kneeled down by the ditch, and noisily threw up.

Charming, said Peau.

Sophie rested there a while, her head down, evidently contemplating her abysmal fate. Eventually she got up, wiped her mouth on her sleeve, and came back to the truck. I handed her a canteen through the window, so she took a swig. I wondered for a second if she'd gotten all the puke off her lips. She returned it to me, and I wiped the spout on my shirt before screwing down the cap.

"This is really pretty upsetting," she said. She put a hand on the truck but stayed outside. "I mean, things aren't bizarre enough?"

"It helps to think of it as one way the world is becoming whole again," I offered.

"Right, whatever," she said a little sharply. "Now that I think about it, what mainly bothers me, aside from the obvious insanity, is that I don't like feeling left out of conversations."

"I'm like that too," I said. "We're insecure in the same ways."

"Well, yay." She stood back and looked around her, as if considering escape routes. "If it's like this all the time, I'm not sure I can stay. I'll just feel freaked and sad and pissed off."

"Might be better than dead," I said.

"It also might not be." She gazed back toward town. "I can still walk back to Princely, so those aren't the only options."

I told Peau and Cass that I'd like them to speak slowly so Sophie could get used to the sounds and the rhythms. I also told Sophie that it was entirely possible that she'd never understand, that you might have to be old and a little crazy for it to happen.

Cass said that young and crazy might be good enough, and Peau cawed out a laugh.

Sophie pounced, glaring in at them. "Okay, right then, what did she say?"

I told her.

"Well, you little *bitch*," Sophie said. "I petted you for half the morning and I get *this?*"

Cass's ears went flat, and she backed away with a hissy little mewl.

"She's remorseful," I told Sophie.

"She doesn't sound remorseful. She sounds like a little bitch-ass prom queen if you ask me."

"Wow," I said. "You'll pick this up in no time."

Sophie finally slid back into the cab and shut the door. Cass hopped into the back. I snapped the reins; the mules leaned their shoulders into the harnesses and trudged onward.

Peau gave me the lowdown. He'd waited around until he saw Flynn and his men. Flynn had started asking around, and perhaps predictably, almost everyone knew about the old fart with the F-150. He also discovered where we'd stayed, so he rode there and banged on the door. As Peau watched, flitting between windows, Serena collected the girls and hustled them upstairs, where there was a ladder to an attic hatch. They climbed into the attic, pulled the ladder up behind them, then shut the hatch just as Flynn's men kicked in the front door. The men never found them, but they did destroy the place. They took axes to the furniture, broke most of the windows, kicked holes in the walls, and tore out what little plumbing there was. Then they headed across town to the other whorehouse, talking on the way about how they planned to ride us down in the morning.

I was angry about the house but relieved Serena and the girls were safe. "You're good, Peau."

He simply found a convenient branch wherever they were, he said. Apparently, it hadn't occurred to them that he might be anything other than a dumb bird. Cass, from the back, said it hadn't occurred to her either. Peau swiveled his head around and was about to retort when I headed him off.

"Business before pleasure, you two," I said. "Anything else?"

Peau turned reluctantly from Cass and told me they had a couple of hounds now. Flynn had picked up two more men in Princely and now had five.

Sophie watched this exchange, looking baffled and spent. Finally, though, she exhaled with a sort of sorrowful resignation and asked what she'd missed. I took this to be a good sign and filled her in.

When she heard the number of men, she perked up a little. "Only six total?" she said. "A decent ambush spot and a couple of AKs ought to deal with *that*."

"Pardon me?" I said, and Peau eyed her in surprise.

"Let me guess. You don't have a single firearm in this whole rig?"

"There's a .22 semiautomatic, but I wouldn't use it on them anyway."

Which prompted other questions, most of which were themed, albeit politely, along the lines of what particular kind of nut I was.

"Ever hear of a guy named Bruce Lee?" I asked.

"Sure. Nineteen-seventies wayback machine, right? I saw one of those flicks."

"He called it the art of fighting without fighting."

"Yeah, but Bruce Lee could *fight*, dude."

"I'd rather let them drive themselves over the cliff. If they get enough momentum, they won't need a push."

"Like jujitsu, you're saying."

"I've managed so far."

"You've been *lucky* so far."

"Partly, sure."

"My experience is that luck tends to run out," she said. "In fact, I'm pretty sure my luck *has* run out. So what about me? If they catch us, you're just going to hand me over?"

"Well, no, I . . ." I hesitated, trying to figure out what to say.

"For fuck's sake," she said. "Where's the goddamn rifle?"

IT WOULD BE DARK in a couple of hours, so I turned off the highway and followed the old BLM road back into the canyons. Since Flynn had dogs now, he wouldn't have any trouble tracking us down.

We were hopping between sky islands of lush vegetation amid the desolate, dry seabeds. The piñon pine and juniper forests were a relief from the flat sagebrush plain, and after an hour I found the spot I was looking for, near the beginning of a slot canyon. I was pretty sure I recognized this place, and even if I was wrong, it would serve well enough. We took the mules out of harness and hobbled them, then brought them oats and water. Sophie helped me gather firewood, and we set up the poke nest around us. Peau was already in the air, checking the place out, so I called him back.

"Can you follow this canyon downstream?" I asked. "See if it stays wide enough for the truck to fit. There should be a natural ramp that heads up from the canyon floor and meets a dirt road."

After he flew off, I collected some stones and built my usual U-shaped hearth, with rocks all around to block the wind and an open front so it would draw. I laid the fire and showed Sophie how I'd rigged the truck wiring. Not only would it charge a flashlight, but the cigarette lighter still worked. All I had to do was push it in, then take it when it popped and hold it to a little tinder. As soon as the tinder started smoking, I moved it under the wood, and then things took care of themselves.

"You don't have flint and steel?"

"Sure, but this is easier."

I dropped my old grill across the rocks and put on the rice pot. Sophie dragged the .22 out of the truck to check it out. She found the box of bullets and slid them in one after another until the magazine was full.

"It only holds five?"

"It's for small game, not storming Normandy."

Cassie appeared at the back of the truck and hopped down, then trotted off for evening mousing.

Sophie lifted the gun and aimed it. "Nice balance," she said.

"You know about these things?"

"The guy who ran the orphanage in Flagstaff was a gun fiend," she said. "He tried to teach all us kids, but I was the only one who gave a shit. He and I went to the range all the time."

A cool breeze came pushing down through the pines. A few minutes later, Peau sailed in and landed on a rock near the fire. *What ho*, he said.

"What ho, my good lord. Find any dinner?"

He'd found a lizard, some pine nuts, and something I didn't know the raven term for.

"Pine nuts?" I said. "I wish you'd brought some back."

He asked what pockets, exactly, I proposed that he use. I smiled. The more I got used to his sentences, the more variety and tone I heard in them. He could actually be quite droll.

"It's extremely weird listening to half of these conversations," Sophie said.

"Sorry," I said. "I'll try to keep you filled in."

Peau said that the canyon was wide enough for the truck all the way, and about a quarter mile down there was a natural ramp out. So this was Little Creek Canyon; we were exactly where I thought we were. I brought Sophie up to speed, then we sat back awhile, in companionable silence, to contemplate the fire.

I'd been a vital young man the last time I'd come here, a member of a functioning society in a world with almost nine billion people in it. It seemed like a dream of someone else's life on another planet, now. I knew that in some sense I still was that person, but in another way, he was long gone, sloughed off as dead cells and scattered to the winds.

So what was this continuity, this illusory sense of self? Memories that weren't anything real at all, just coded chemicals occasionally activated by a little electrical charge firing through neurotransmitters. A past that didn't exist in any concrete sense, other than those unreal memories. A personal history built on a foundation of sand, in other words, prone to shifting and collapse.

Knock knock. Who's there?

Forty minutes later, when the rice was cooked, I got the cast-iron skillet, greased it with lard, then sliced and fried carrots and wild onions to go with the rice.

"Those onions smell good," said Sophie.

It was the first thing she'd said that indicated some slight proximity to good cheer instead of misery or confusion. "Yeah, I was glad to find them," I answered.

Sophie laid the rifle aside, then sat cross-legged near me. The fire danced orange in her eyes as if the inside of her head were alight.

Peau was starting to get that signature sag in the feathers that signaled he was ready for bed. He flew over to the truck and hopped into the cab. I dished out the food, then Sophie and I started eating. It had been a long day, and it felt wonderful to get a little nourishment, there in the cool air as the smoke drifted up toward the stars.

"It's good, Will. Thanks."

"Sure."

Our eyes met for a second, and she smiled. Well, I thought. Goodness me.

Cass appeared at the edge of the firelight, carrying a dead wood rat. She brought it over, settled down, and started gnawing on it. There were the usual sounds of gristle popping and bones snapping, the shearing noise of teeth cutting muscle. In a moment, the head fell off.

"Well, that's appetizing," Sophie said.

Cass asked who the prom queen was *now.*

"Probably I don't want a translation of that, do I?" said Sophie.

"Nope."

When Cass was finished, she hopped back up into the back of the truck and disappeared into the bedding. Sophie and I sat a while longer, feeding the fire. Now that my stomach was full, I put a little of the aspirin powder in my water and drank it.

"What's that for?"

"Bad tooth. I keep the bottle in the glove box, if something's ever hurting you."

"Thanks," she said. "What did you do that pissed off the ARM guys so much, anyway?"

"I'm carrying something they want."

"What?"

I explained the situation—the email from Lars, the brief surgery. "Anyway, he asked me to go to California," I said. "Which, these days, is sort of like asking someone to soak themselves in gasoline and crawl through a minefield holding a lit match."

"Adventure travel," she said, and I laughed.

We were quiet awhile, then. Lightning was still flashing over the mountains, followed by low booms of thunder. We could smell the moisture in the air.

"What's going to happen tomorrow?" Sophie asked.

"Bad things, most likely."

She stared thoughtfully at the fire. "These men don't know I exist, do they?"

I told her that it might keep her safe. "Let's make sure you get through the day in one piece," I said. I banked the fire so we could re-start it early in the morning, then stood up to go crash.

"Look, I have to know," she said. "I'll be safe with you in there to-night, right?"

I patted her shoulder as I passed by. "You've got plenty of things to worry about in the next twenty-four hours," I said. "That's not one of them."

I could tell she was still hesitant, but a few minutes later we squeezed in—Sophie on one side of Cass, me on the other. I unzipped the big sleeping bag and spread it over the three of us. Cassie put all four paws up against me and they were so cold I jumped.

I lay awake a long time, then, worrying about what I was planning and the manifold ways it could go wrong. It would require precise tim-ing and far too much luck, but Sophie's fears to the contrary, I hoped mine hadn't yet run out. I remembered David's advice about the bear's den, how if something bad happened to those men, it should result from their actions rather than mine. Perhaps this was sophistry, per-haps not. Anyway, if Sun Tzu had heard the scheme he would likely have laughed, then kindly offered me some version of Confucian last rites and bid me farewell.

I WOKE UP TO GRAY SKIES just after dawn. A cool, damp chill blew from the mountains; I could see the storm still unleashing its rain up there. It had poured half the night and would likely continue for an hour or two before the morning sun broke it up and warm updrafts drove out the front.

I got up, dressed, gathered fresh kindling, and blew the fire back to life. I laid on some bigger branches, then, and started heating water. I was stiff and a little sore, the usual vicissitudes of age, and my boots felt too small until I walked around in them a little and stretched them out. I was nervous, which tended to scatter my concentration and make me miss things.

I fetched oatmeal from the big burlap sack and poured it into the pot when the water was boiling. I stirred it, then moved it to a cooler part of the grate so it could simmer. Overhead, the birds were stirring, filling the morning with song, tentatively at first, then in full throat. Peau hopped out of the cab and flapped over to me. I asked how he'd slept. *Tolerably*, he croaked; he'd find some breakfast and see what was happening on the road.

I explained what I had planned, if you could even call something so dependent on good fortune "planned." I wanted to stow him and Cass and Sophie up in the rocks, in case it didn't go well. He listened carefully, but his head kept dipping lower and lower, which meant he was concerned. He asked hesitantly what they should do if afterward I was, as he tactfully put it, no longer airworthy.

"See if you can get Sophie back to Princely," I said. "There's nothing in the other direction for a long way, and without the truck and the mules, she and Cass will die out there."

When the oatmeal was ready, I went to roust Sophie out. She and the cat were all bundled up together in a decent imitation of domestic harmony.

"Ladies," I said. Sophie stirred. Soon she crawled out, and I handed her breakfast.

"Sleep okay?"

"Mmm," she said. "That cat's actually a pretty good bag warmer."

"One reason I keep her."

When she'd eaten, we took down the poke nest and stowed it on the truck, then got the mules in harness. I handed Sophie a rucksack with food in it, a canteen, the .22, and the bullets. We found a place higher up in the rocks overlooking the canyon, where she could hide out with Cass and Peau. I explained what I hoped was about to happen and said she was absolutely not to shoot anybody unless it was obvious they were about to kill me. She nodded.

I clambered back down, took the mules by the bridles, and led them down the slope into the canyon. It wasn't that deep, about ten feet from bottom to top, but it would serve. We went downstream until I found a spot under a couple of overhanging cottonwoods, where I piled up a little brush to camouflage the truck, then got in and waited. The mules sensed my anxiety and stamped their feet, eager to run from whatever was coming.

Peau fluttered in soon afterward. Flynn and his men were already close. They'd be here in a few minutes, he said, and he reminded me that there were dogs too.

I was nursing increasingly serious doubts about this. We were a good five miles from the mountains that drained into this canyon system. I had no idea how much it had rained last night, or how long it would take the water to get here. If it came too soon, I'd be dead. If it didn't come at all, I'd be dead. If it came but there wasn't enough of it, I'd be dead. There was far too little margin for error.

But what to do? They would have overtaken us this morning anyway. Sophie didn't approve of the idea any more than Sun Tzu would have; it required not only timing and luck but also a leap of faith, and when you'd lived a life as hard as Sophie's, faith was in short supply. She had romantic ideas about hiding in the rocks with the .22 and picking them off, but they were agile young men and would quickly outflank us. I did my best to calm the butterflies in the pit of my stomach and wait. As for a leap of faith, I remembered what David had said to me about an array of natural forces that seemed to be assisting me. So I did what I often did; I put out a general request to the universe that this would somehow turn out all right—a request at which my skeptical self scoffed.

I pointed up to where Sophie and Cass were hiding and told Peau to go stay with them. And then I thought I felt a little tremble in the rock under the truck. Half a minute later there was another one. And then another. I heard hoofbeats and voices, and Flynn and his men appeared at the edge of the canyon. They were thirty or forty yards upstream, and they hadn't seen me yet, but the hounds were baying and straining at their leashes, and I knew they'd find me soon.

Another rumble in the rock, almost a little earthquake this time. All the birds fell silent. Lizards went skittering up out of the wash, climbing the slickrock as if jet-propelled. The mules' heads went up, their nostrils flaring and their flanks rippling with tension. It was coming at least. I thought briefly of those poor souls I'd passed on the way to Princely, washed-up skeletons and abandoned shoes and the lingering vibe of surprise and horror. I hoped to hell I wouldn't end up like them, a skeleton chest-deep in silt in a sandblasted truck.

Another quake, bigger this time. I didn't think the men would feel it on horseback, but in a few seconds they'd hear it. I wanted them down in the canyon *before* they heard it.

"Yo, mules!" I cried, and the beasts, already jittery in their traces, exploded into motion. The brush flew off us, and we were suddenly blasting all out. I heard a yell from Flynn and watched in the rearview as the riders plunged down the slope after us.

Okay, David, I thought. Sophistry or not, that was *their* choice.

The mules were galloping so hard that the truck, dragged behind them, kept slamming into the rock walls, and I actually had to steer for a change. I briefly remembered the canister of acetylene, too, and worried that I might be blown to pieces before I had a chance to finish what I'd started.

The riders were gaining on us—thirty yards, then twenty—and I heard their gleeful whoops. I'd always thought of the mules as draft animals, plodding and reliable, but now they were sprinting like a couple of doped-up Thoroughbreds, barreling down the canyon so fast I worried they'd tear themselves right out of their harnesses.

I checked the rearview again—ten yards. Nobody was pulling out a rifle, because they needed both hands to control the horses. And then I saw it behind them—tall and brown and fast, roaring down the canyon carrying logs and mud, slapping over the lip at every corner, a wall of what was basically liquid cement as fast as a fucking Ferrari. Where was the goddamn ramp?

The flood overtook the hindmost with arresting velocity—they were there, riding, and then suddenly they weren't, as if they'd fallen back into a big, dark mouth that slammed shut. The leading wave was about to crash over another one when I looked ahead and saw the ramp.

"Mules, right! Mules, right!" I yelled, suddenly unsure if they could hear me over the roar of the flood, and I yanked hard on the reins and turned the steering wheel with my right hand. There was a sudden lurch, a veering upward and away so violent that for a second I thought the truck would roll over. And then we were out, just as the water blasted the last of the riders and bulldozed him under, a mere second or two before it would have taken us. I was aflame with adrenaline, gasping for breath, and I thought for a moment I might prove the Princely cable thieves right and have a coronary right there. I'd lain awake half the night wondering if I was crazy to try it, and then the whole thing was over in less than a minute.

The mules slackened to a gallop, breathing hard, then downshifted to a trot. The flood roared by, the full channel bounding in standing waves. We came up the ramp into sunlight, and now the mules became their old stolid selves, walking, wasting not a calorie. I was practically weeping with relief, and I made a promise that whatever else happened, I'd find those mules an excellent home when we were done with this journey, a place of tall green grass and sea breezes, of snug stables with ample straw to lie down in at night.

I looked up. There, on the old road in front of us, sat Buck Flynn astride his heaving horse, and two of his men on theirs, and both of his hounds, panting with their tongues hanging out. The canyon was crooked but the road ran straight, and the flood had taken only three of them.

Flynn leveled his rifle at me. "Kindly step out of the vehicle, sir," he said, and his two rowdies grinned like hungry demons, their teeth weirdly sharp and their eyes, maybe because of the night carousing, so vividly bloodshot they seemed to glow.

7

I sat tied to a tree, up in the rocks twenty feet from the creek, just in case there was a second surge. But the water started to drop after a few minutes. Flynn and his men paced and conferred. We were a quarter mile downstream from where I'd stashed Sophie, but I saw Peau circling overhead, reconnoitering. After a minute he flew off again.

The men sat down with the dogs a few yards away and pulled some food from their saddlebags. They looked vaguely familiar, but it took me a minute to realize that they were from the gang of cable thieves in Princely. One, I noticed, was the fellow who'd given me so much shit about my age.

Flynn turned to me and for the first time, at close range, we had a chance to size each other up. He was huge, as I'd noticed before. Late thirties, six-four, probably 250. Would have made a good linebacker if he'd been younger and there were still football leagues. And weirdly, he remained white as chalk, as if his veins ran with some concoction of milky sap rather than blood. His eyes were wolf's eyes, pale blue and shimmery and penetrating, and as before, I had the queasy feeling that his gaze somehow pushed through my own eyes into my brain and read my thoughts. It made me look away. Part of my discomfort, though, was that it wasn't a one-way street; he might be feeling out my mind, but in the process, I also got a strong sense of his, and I didn't like what I found there.

"You might be less of an idiot than I thought you were," he said then.

"I'm tied up and you're not, so I doubt it."

Flynn allowed himself a smug, victorious smile, and in that moment I understood him better. He was one of those men who considered every other man in the world a fool. And not just men; women and children and animals too. He was the only wise, intelligent soul in his universe, and it was his great act of magnanimity, every day, simply to tolerate the rest of us in our fathomless imbecility.

I knew that such men tended to end up badly, but I'd never believed there was such a thing as genuine evil in the world. Arrogance and savagery, sure: Hitler, Mussolini, Stalin, Mao, Pot, Habyarimana, Karadžić, Kim, al-Assad, Putin, Trump, Xi, Bolsonaro, Vermacher, Sokolov, Smythe—all the haughty, self-satisfied monsters of modern times, architects of hate and repression, each of them repelled by weakness because weakness was what they feared most in themselves. It didn't take a shrink to parse it out: their cruel, hard fathers would have adored one another. The strong were courted, the vulnerable crushed—human history, in other words. Such men were driven by the things that have always driven us: greed, fear, anger, and, at the root of it all, the sort of ignorance that drove people to seemingly inhuman deeds. But evil? Evil, I believed, was a concept we'd come up with because we couldn't face the sort of animal we were, the barbarians David had spoken about.

Even so, I had to acknowledge that on some level Flynn *seemed* evil. I sensed this mainly as an absence of feeling or remorse, an egotistical nihilism, a certain sociopathic emptiness of spirit. Like someone who might be capable of anything simply because to him, nothing really mattered but himself. When I spent time with David, his mind felt to me like a big, calm lake that reflected everything going on in the sky overhead—the grand tumult of wind and cloud, Sturm und Drang—without being ruffled by it in the slightest. Flynn's mind felt more like a crevasse, an icy chasm disappearing down into darkness. He'd lost a lot of men hunting me down and seemed not the least bit troubled by it. They had existed to serve him, as far as he was concerned. If they were dead and could no longer do so, they were best forgotten quickly, for who were weaker or stupider than the dead?

"How vain you are," Flynn said, startling me. I met his eyes again and was able to hold his gaze, which surprised me. "How much you love your notions of right and wrong. They're all inventions, you know."

The nihilist argument, not surprisingly. It seemed we were engaged in some kind of unnerving psychic dogfight.

"Inventions, maybe," I answered. "That doesn't mean the materials they're made from aren't real. You invent nothing from nothing and call it a life, but you have no idea what a real life is."

He laughed. "You think helping others makes a life," he said. "It's just a dishonest way of serving yourself, because power makes you uncomfortable. So you trust the universe's benevolence, and then it runs out."

"Power's overrated, don't you think?"

"I can kill you in five seconds if I decide to," he replied. "Nothing overrated about *that*."

"Then how will you get what you want?"

"I'll find a way."

"Or maybe you're just so starved for a little philosophical debate that you had to sacrifice eight of your men for it?"

"You kept count," he shot back.

"I kept count because I regret what happened to them, unlike you."

The other guys were paying attention now, I noticed.

"Let's try this again," Flynn said. I was trying to strategize the next gambit when he strode up and kicked me in the face.

My head snapped back into the tree and blood exploded from my nose. It was also running down my throat so fast I was choking on it. I gasped for air, sputtering crimson bubbles from my mouth. Flynn squatted down in front of me and grabbed me by the throat.

"What I *want*, you moron, is the *cure*," he said. "I know it has to get to California, and I know you're the mule. Now tell me where it is, so I can cut it out of you and go the fuck home."

And then I understood.

Disease X was almost infinitely mutable; paleness and whatever went with it constituted Flynn's version, but the endgame never varied. He was pushing forty, he would die soon, he saw it coming.

I could barely speak for all the blood, but I had to. "Go home with it and do *what?*" I said, spitting red. "California's the only place they know how to use it."

"First, I don't believe that, and second, there's a price on my head out there," he hissed. "If I can't find someone who knows, I can at least make sure *those* shits don't get it. Is that clear enough to you, mule?"

But something was off, it occurred to me. How, exactly, had he known I'd be at the Colorado hospital? He'd found and tracked me too easily. "You're working for someone, aren't you?" I rasped. "Who is it?"

Flynn stood and went over to the truck. He lifted the hood, found my toolbox, and came back with a screwdriver and a pair of pliers.

"Last chance," he said.

"Tell me the truth, Flynn."

"Here's the truth," he said, and he took hold of my left hand and shoved the screwdriver under the nail of my index finger, halfway through the quick. In that instant, the universe became bright, electric pain, as if he'd jammed a high-tension power line into me. I was screaming, still choking on the blood from my nose, and then he grabbed hold of the nail with the pliers and pulled it off.

I hadn't thought more pain was possible. I shrieked and just kept shrieking, as if I'd stopped being a human or even an animal and had simply become a being of pure, searing agony. Darkness formed at the edges of my vision and closed inward into a tunnel. Brief blackness, then oblivion. I awoke to Flynn slapping me; then one of his men poured a bucket of brown river water over my head. My bloody finger throbbed as if it had been set alight and would burn forever. I gasped from the cold water, now mixing with my copious blood. I tried to think what to do, frantic in the way of an animal that's been hit by a car and is scuttling around in the road, stunned and blind, searching for escape even as death takes hold of it. I was there and not there, half body and half empty space, a beast in agony, and I couldn't think of anything at all.

"Still worth it, this noble journey of yours?" Flynn asked.

I was suddenly dry-heaving, then, and that was all I could do for a little while. I needed to come up with some sort of answer or solution, but I simply couldn't process anything. I vomited a pint or so of my blood, and the heaves finally passed. I was exhausted, my body formed from incandescent lava, and I thought, Well, I was wrong, because Flynn was simply *evil*, and any other way of looking at him was naive.

I was slumped forward in my ropes, trembling, as the blood dripped, a little more slowly now, from my broken nose. I thought of his question—Still worth it?—and began to wonder if it was. But of course, I couldn't tell him where the ampoule was because I didn't know, so I didn't have a lot of options.

Then it dawned on me that I still had one left.

"Shave my head," I muttered. Or thought I'd muttered, but maybe I hadn't said it loud enough for him to hear.

"What?" he asked, leaning in, a new, avid interest blooming in his eyes.

"Straight razor, glove box," I whispered. "Shave my head."

They got the razor and the little sliver of soap I kept with it, and they brought another bucket of water and shaved my head, managing to cut me four or five times, which got me thinking about tetanus. But I probably wouldn't live long enough to develop tetanus, so why worry?

When they were done, Flynn stood back and whistled.

"What is it?" said one of the others.

"There's some paper and a pencil in my saddlebag," Flynn said, and the man went to get them. How interesting, I thought, that he could simply state a fact and his man would understand it as a command.

Flynn took his pencil and began copying down the chemical formula that had been tattooed onto the back of my scalp in the Crestone hospital. When he finished, he folded the paper and strode back to his horse. It was still early afternoon, and it was hard for me to believe that I existed in the same day as the one I'd started by feeding oatmeal to Sophie and talking to Cassie and Peau. Lifetimes seemed to have passed. Flynn would take the formula to Bruce Hannock, the chemist in Princely, and see if Hannock could make it. He gave instructions to his men about me, saying he'd be back in a day or two.

I stayed tied to the tree. Eventually, after an hour or so, my nose stopped bleeding. I was afraid that if I moved too much it would start again, but I felt as if most of the life had been kicked out of me, and I didn't really want to move anyway, so it didn't matter. The men ignored me, rooting through the truck to see if there was anything they wanted. They found the machetes and took some of the food. When they saw me dully watching them, they waved.

"Don't worry," said one cheerfully, the one who'd given me so much trouble back in town. I was really starting to hate him. "When he gets back, you won't be needing any of this."

In midafternoon they brought a bottle of whiskey out of a saddlebag and started passing it back and forth. By sundown, they were passed out cold. As darkness crept over the canyons, I saw something moving behind them, something shadowlike, but my eyes were swollen and bruised from the kick, and I couldn't make out what it was. It was as if the ground itself had come to life and discovered motion.

In another minute I realized what was happening. The ants had been driven from their nests by the flood. There were millions of them. They collected around the men almost as quickly and fluidly as water itself. It occurred to me, in a vague and hazy way, that I'd read a piece about them two or three decades before, when they were first discovered in the Amazon, before they found their way here.

They were specialized, these ants, like humans. Two or three of them gathered near each of the men's nostrils and near their ears. They inserted their abdomens and sprayed a tiny blast of something, a formic version of lidocaine. Then the sprayers retreated and were replaced by other ants sporting big, serrated jaws. When the orifices had been numbed, they crawled in, five or ten per nostril, same for the ears. I remembered that they'd be scything their way through sinuses and eardrums, directly into the brain. The men continued lying there; it looked as if they felt nothing at first, and they didn't awaken. Then, after half a minute or so, they experienced brief convulsions and their eyes popped opened. They lay still, conscious but paralyzed, and this sudden stillness was the calm before the storm, the signal for the rest. Thousands of ants attacked, entering through any available opening—noses, mouths, eyes, ears, anuses. I knew that the hollowing-out would happen so quickly that within a half hour the men would begin to cave in like jack-o'-lanterns a few days after Halloween. I wasn't sure how much they could feel, but it seemed probable they felt a lot, and it would be a truly horrible death.

But then, I realized, the rest of the colony was crossing the ground to me. I called out for Peau, but there was no answer. I called for Sophie. Nothing. And then I realized I'd probably only thought I was calling.

Just as the ants neared my feet, I heard footsteps, and for a moment I was afraid that Flynn had forgotten something and returned. But it was Sophie, come at last, and she quickly took in the situation and kicked the ants away. She untied and moved me, weak and stumbling, to safety. She went back for the men's horses and tied them to the back of the truck. We got in, she snapped the reins on the mules, and we went back upstream to the place we'd camped the night before. I knew I must look a sight, with my shaved, cut-up head and bloody face.

"God, Will," was all she could say. "God almighty."

She built a fire and boiled some of our water, then used my old bandanna to clean me up as best she could. It was delicate work. I couldn't stand for her to touch the raw, bloody finger, so she squeezed the cloth and dribbled water over it, then tore off a strip and wrapped it around. Peau and Cass came into the clearing and joined us.

"I snuck down to the rocks across the creek from where they had you," Sophie said, her voice trembling. "I could have shot them, Will. I didn't because you told me not to."

"Don't apologize."

"Where did Flynn go?"

My face throbbed and my finger still felt like it was on fire, but I did my best. "He thinks he has a cure," I mumbled.

"This tattoo?"

I smiled a little, as much as I dared without opening the bloody faucet in my nose again.

"A veterinary cousin of codeine," I said. "Put there for this sort of situation. If Hannock has what he needs to make it, Flynn's about to go to sleep for a couple of days."

IT WAS BRUTALLY DIFFICULT getting up the next morning. My eyes were swollen, bruised slits, and my face felt full of concrete, so I had to breathe through my mouth. My finger still smoldered, and accidentally touching it to anything instantly brought back bright, searing pain.

Sophie squatted by the fire, cooking the oatmeal. Cass sat nearby with what was left of a baby squirrel, finishing her breakfast. Cruel world. Oh well.

"I went down to look at the men," Sophie said quietly.

"And?"

"They're all bone, clean and white. With their clothes still on. Scarecrows, kind of."

"Speaking of, where's Peau?"

"He wanted more pine nuts, I think."

"How do you know that?"

She shrugged. "Just a sound he made. You look like shit. Come eat."

I sat down stiffly and did my best to spoon in some oatmeal, which was challenging, since I could barely open my mouth. I sprinkled some aspirin on the food, and we ate together in silence. One good thing: with all the stunning new pain, I barely noticed the toothache. Then Sophie mentioned that she'd made harnesses from some old rope I kept under the hood, literally doubling our horsepower. With four of them pulling, we'd be able to gear up to an occasional trot, do six or seven miles an hour. We could cover a lot more ground every day.

"Smart of you," I said. "I might have let them run off."

"I got our machetes back," she said. "And the men had AR-15s in their saddle holsters. Good news: we own them now. Bad news: there aren't any bullets."

"They were *bluffing*?"

"Seems so," she answered. "Can't speak for Flynn."

"Well done. How much of our conversation did you overhear?"

"I was too far away to catch much," she answered. "I kept him in my sights, though, and after he kicked you in the face, I almost dropped him. But Peau was with me, and he made a little croaking noise, and somehow I knew he meant *no*."

I laughed then, as much as I could anyway—more of a constricted chuckle. Peau fluttered in. I told him we had to find a safe place to spend a few days.

"Go on ahead," I said. "An old miner's cabin, a cave, whatever. Something out of sight where I can heal up and decide what to do next."

He said he'd put the word out, then flew off.

I heard some sort of whining and looked off to my right. The hounds had crept into camp, tails between their legs. They squatted down, heads lowered, submissive. They looked like they were used to being whacked, and they were hungry.

Cass's fur stood up, and she hopped into the back of the truck.

"What do we do?" Sophie asked. "If we leave them, Flynn will use them to find us again."

"Give them something to eat," I said. "They'll follow us then, and we can figure it out later."

8

Driving a truck pulled by four big equines might have made me feel like Odin or Hippolytus or some other godlike hero if I hadn't actually felt like a run-over turd in the road instead. The F-150 wasn't a celestial chariot, but at least it had a padded bench seat and a roof.

The horses quickly proved themselves a temperamental handful, as they were accustomed to being ridden but evidently not to being in harness. At first, when I put them in behind the mules, they lowered their heads sullenly and refused to budge, so I went back and, grumbling insults, shifted them up front. Once we got rolling, the buckskin gelding shied easily, pulling to the side and repeatedly breaking the rhythm of the other three. The big black mare, for her part, exploded into sudden bursts of frisky, gallant prancing, as if she'd once been a show horse. It was pretty to look at but a pain in the ass if you were trying to get somewhere. The mules, bless their hearts, endured it all with their usual stolid resignation until finally, after a few hours, the horses got the idea and settled down.

My nose throbbed and my finger still burned, of course. Cass snoozed in the back. The dogs, fortified by scraps, trotted happily along behind us. Sophie sat up front with me, reading from a 2020s film fanzine she'd brought from Serena's place. I glanced over from time to time and recognized most of the names—Meryl Streep, Viola Davis, Tom Hanks, Margot Robbie, Brad Pitt, Emily Blunt, Cate Blanchett, Denzel Washington—but there were a bunch of others I didn't know. People who were practically worshiped then but were largely forgotten now, twenty-five years later, in a world without movies or places to show them. The magazine was so old that the dry, yellowed pages kept falling out or tearing as Sophie turned them.

I was still breathing through my mouth, which made me feel like some sort of ape, and I expected it would be days before the pain and swelling left my face. All my snacks were taken with a sprinkling of aspirin now. I figured that we resembled those pathetic families of destitute misfits that wandered the dusty roads of the world after all the various Mayhems in history. As we ascended the grade into the mountains that had sent us the generous flood, and as the morning progressed and the air became cooler, I savored it because I knew that when we came down the other side it was going to get hot and grow hotter still as we crossed the desert in the days ahead.

"How did you know about *The Sound of Music* and all that other stuff?" I asked Sophie. My consonants weren't really working, and I sounded like I had a bad cold.

She seemed a little dreamy, alternating her gaze between the magazine and the scenery outside. I hadn't seen this side of her before, probably because we'd been in a state of constant emergency in the two days since she'd joined me. But we finally had a little time, and it was nice to see her space out a bit. The sweet luxury of inattention, so rarely afforded us.

"Oh, the old movies?" she said. "Tim, the guy who ran the Flagstaff orphanage. Gun nut, but also a film buff."

"Unusual combination."

"I know, right?" she said. "He had a bookshelf of DVDs. He was desperate to keep us entertained and teach us something about the way the world used to be, so twice a week it was movie night."

As the world disintegrated in the various stages of Mayhem, she told me, Flagstaff had managed to endure, more or less as an island, for maybe ten years. But finally, what was left of the university was abandoned, and the rest of the town had pretty much shut down, boarded up, burned to the ground, or died of TB. Leaving the house after dark became dangerous, and when one girl disappeared, Tim and his wife, Melissa, had instituted a strict curfew. By then the town contained maybe a couple of hundred souls, forlorn and heavily armed; a dirty three-room clinic staffed by a gaunt, authoritarian nurse who kept a Glock on her desk to fend off drug thieves; and a small grocery whose shelves were usually bare of everything but sprouting potatoes, soft old carrots, and flour a few years past its sell-by date.

So escaping into movies wasn't half bad. Watching Maria von Trapp and family fleeing the Nazis was something everyone could relate to. The girls had loved musicals generally and learned all the numbers from *West Side Story* and *Cats* and from Lin-Manuel Miranda's films. And darker stuff too: Nicholson in *One Flew Over the Cuckoo's Nest*, or Streep in pretty much anything from *The Deer Hunter* onward. Colin Firth and Emma Thompson and English accents generally. And of course they'd adored the *Star Wars* flicks. By the time the L.A. studios finally collapsed, there had been something like thirty of them, and Daisy Ridley was playing aging Jedi queens with magical powers and perfect teeth.

"How did you end up in the orphanage?" I asked.

She set the magazine aside and looked out the window. "I don't even know," she said. "Apparently, I just showed up at the door one day strapped into a TurboBooster kiddie seat, like I'd just driven it there without wheels or an engine. They said I kept blowing spit bubbles and making little flying motions with my arms, and seemed remarkably happy under the circumstances."

"So then what?" I asked. "You were there the whole time?"

"Yeah, I got there fourteen years ago, when things started falling apart," she said. "I learned to use what was left of the Internet and got through fourth grade before everything really imploded. Then it was homeschooling and movies, and then Tim got TB and Melissa got something really awful, fever and vomiting for days. She died, and Tim held on another year, but then he died too."

"Sounds like he did his best."

"He was a really good guy," she said. "By the last few years, there was no supervision from the state or anybody else, so the situation could have been a lot worse. He worked like a dog to keep us fed, especially after Melissa, when we were really down. After that it was all musicals. We couldn't stand sad movies anymore."

She brushed a tear from her cheek, then told me the rest. Afterward, they had no way to get food, and even Flagstaff, at elevation, was too hot part of the year without power for air conditioning. She'd heard Phoenix was routinely 140° by then, deserted by everything except nocturnals—cockroaches, rats, bats, and rattlers. She and three of the other girls found a small, abandoned flatbed trailer and a wandering mule and figured out how to hitch them together. They scavenged flexible PVC pipe from an old garden supply, then bent it to make hoops. They added sailcloth from some dead guy's backyard boat, and they had a Conestoga for the trip north.

"Where did you hope to get to?"

"We had no idea," she said. "We mainly wanted somewhere cooler. But then, as I guess Serena told you, the mule died in Princely. We were out of food and water and luck, so. Four teenage girls in a town of hungry men. Serena kept me out of it, but it was a rough road."

I didn't have any idea how to respond. "Sorry you had to go through it," I said. "That's stupid and insufficient, but I don't know what else to say."

"Do you mind if we don't talk about this anymore?" she asked.

"Of course."

She picked up the magazine again. We rode on in silence for maybe half an hour. It occurred to me that she was reading articles she'd probably read fifty times before, but it didn't matter. The point was soothing familiarity, not news.

Eventually she turned to me, showing me a photo that must have been from the 1970s. "Nicholson was pretty hot as a young dude, huh?" she said. "Ever see *Five Easy Pieces?*"

"It's one of my favorites."

We were moving at a good clip with all the horsepower, and around midday we crossed the range's divide and started down the long grade westward. We were in the basin and range country south of the Grand Canyon now. It was a glorious day, and when we reached a little shady spot under some junipers, I pulled on the reins and hit the brakes so we could stretch our legs and take in the view. The mountains pulled a surprising amount of rain out of those desert skies—hence yesterday's flood—and there was lush green grass here, not just sage and bitterbrush. Birds sang in the trees, and the horses and mules lowered their heads and began to graze. The dogs, which had been lagging, caught up with us, and I gave them water from one of the five-gallon buckets stored under the hood. We had four, and I hoped to find more water before we had to cross the Mojave.

The landscape spread out and flattened to the west, with great stately cloud shadows creeping slowly across forests under a cobalt sky. The breeze touched us, warm and brisk and fragrant, and it felt particularly refreshing on my newly bald head.

"Okay day to be out in the world, I guess," Sophie allowed, taking it all in. "Makes a person feel almost optimistic."

"Heavens forfend."

"Yeah, it scares me," she said. "As soon as things look promising, you can expect the next shitstorm."

"In the old days, therapists called that magical thinking," I said.

"In the new days, I call it reality."

"Anyway," I said, "for most of us, philosophy depends on age. When you're young, you're an optimist. When you're middle-aged, you're a realist. When you're old, you're a pessimist. Then, when you're *really* old, you become an optimist again, because you can't wait to get the hell out of here."

She smiled. Just then I heard a call and saw Peau flying in from the northwest. He spread his wings, sailed in, and landed on the rump of Mule One.

What ho, he said.

"What ho, my good lord. Any real estate to speak of?"

He rattled off a repetitive little ravenism that translated tolerably well as *Location, location, location.*

WE PASSED THROUGH THE TOWN of Paris, population 324, which was extinct and falling apart and now population zero. Peau led us off the highway, then down a series of winding dirt roads before we finally came out into a little hidden valley about a quarter of a mile long, surrounded by pale cliffs and boulder fields. Junipers and ponderosa pines ringed the valley, and meadows of wildflowers swayed in the breeze. There were birds everywhere—ravens, not surprisingly, as well as jays and songbirds and the occasional red-tailed hawk. Deer grazed in the meadows, which were fed by a couple of streams that cascaded down through the cliffs.

"Wow," said Sophie, and I nodded. A little secret paradise.

The deer raised their heads as we rumbled past, and a few of them trotted off a little way, but mainly they seemed unperturbed. I was pleasantly surprised that the dogs didn't give chase; whoever Flynn had taken them from had apparently trained them well.

Near the center of the valley, the road headed west toward a little stand of trees nestled into a tall granite outcrop. We came to a fence, passed through the gate, and I stopped our four-horsepower engine.

"Holy smokes," said Sophie. Spread out before us was a field full of watermelons. It seemed too early in the season and too high up, but with a broad southwestern exposure to the sun, apparently it worked. We got out of the truck and wandered down the rows.

"How do you know they're good?" she asked.

"Thump them with your knuckles," I said. "They should sound hollow and kind of resonant."

"Like your head, you mean?"

"Exactly."

She tried a couple and moved on. "Here's one," she said, finally.

We cut two off at the stem and carried them back to the truck. Peau circled in and landed.

"Is there a house or something?" I asked.

He said it was a little farther. We followed him down toward the outcrops, which were maybe thirty feet tall, smooth and shiny in the light, as if glaciers had once ground over them. Soon we came to another fence, so I halted the animals and got out.

It looked as if it had been built after things in the wider world had started to disintegrate. Steel poles ten feet high, spaced about a dozen feet apart and tied together with heavy metal mesh. Barbed wire on top. The gate was built of thick steel bars and looked stout enough to halt a tank. It was definitely somebody's idea of a last stand, which worried me. I'd hate to go ambling innocently toward some fortified bunker and end up with a bullet in me.

"There's no one here?" I asked him.

Used to be, he said simply.

I inspected the gate. I could use the torch to cut through, but then it would be open to anyone else who happened to find the place. It looked as if the fence surrounded the whole property.

I changed the dressing on my achy, weeping finger, then Sophie and I pulled the acetylene and oxygen tanks out from under the hood, along with the torch and the welding goggles. We took the machetes and started walking the perimeter. After about twenty yards, we had to detour around one of the granite outcrops. The rock was too sheer to climb, but we picked up the fence on the other side. We followed it until I found a spot I liked, where the fencing was partly hidden by rock and hemmed in with scrub oak. It was hard to reach, so we used the machetes to clear a little tunnel, then got all the brush out of the way so we wouldn't spark a fire. I put on the goggles, turned on the gas, and fired up the torch. The mesh was heavy-duty steel, but the torch cut through it quickly enough. I took out a piece roughly two feet square, then we pushed the tanks inside, hid the spot with some of the brush we'd cut, crawled through, and pulled the mesh back into place. A few spot welds and it was nearly as good as new.

We picked our way past more rocks and brush, then came into a clearing where the house stood. When I saw it, I almost fell over. It wasn't some prepper's bunker at all; it was an elegant two-story home, maybe three thousand square feet, nestled so perfectly in among the outcrops and trees that it would have been invisible from any angle except straight overhead. Which was, of course, how Peau had found it, guided by intelligence from his latest flock of friends.

Sophie and I whistled appreciatively at the exact same moment. We took a tour of the exterior, which was in remarkably good shape, probably because it was almost all shaded and the sun hadn't been able to destroy it. It was young for a house, probably not more than twenty years old, sided in lovely, broad clapboards and capped with a tile roof in a mix of greens and browns and grays, to augment its invisibility. It had big double-paned windows all around and a capacious front porch with a swing. A couple dozen chickens were scampering about, pecking at bugs, their ancestors evidently liberated from a coop at some point.

Around back we found said coop, in fact, where several hens continued to roost. We also discovered the power source for the place, a broad lawn, overgrown with weeds now, containing an array of fifty large solar panels raised up on platforms three or four feet tall.

Then, as we strolled up the slope to the back of the house, we came to a flat flagstone patio, in the middle of which was a sunken swimming pool with a camo-patterned cover floating on it. Of course, I expected to lift the cover and find a dark-green mat of algae, or a dead cow, or something else despoiling the water.

"Listen," said Sophie. I heard the low hum of a pump—a pump that would presumably be pulling in spring water and running everything through a filter. Amazing. It was all self-perpetuating, fed by the juice from the panels. I squatted down and pulled the cover back; the water was clear and cool, colored blue by the tile that lined the pool. Sophie whooped, then quickly caught herself and covered her mouth. Despite Peau's assurances, I expected somebody to come barreling out of the house with a shotgun any second.

We waited. Nothing. Just the sound of the pump and canyon wrens in the trees overhead. I noticed there were mourning doves too, which I'd always loved because they reminded me of home, of clear childhood mornings in Colorado.

A series of sliding glass-panel doors abutted the patio, built to accordion out of the way if you wanted to merge the inside of the house with the outdoors. I knew these things weighed a ton, and if they were locked, forget it. Half-heartedly, I gave a tug. The thing slid sideways as if it were as light as a shoji screen. Quality construction.

A gust of cool air hit us in the face. It was stale and a little funky, what you might expect if you opened a long-sealed tomb. And of course, I realized, that was possibly what we'd done. Why bother to lock up if you're sequestered in a hidden fortress in the middle of nowhere?

We eyed each other, then quietly crossed the threshold. I called out, to announce ourselves and be sure. No response. To our right lay the skeleton of a large dog, which pretty much told us what we needed to know. We found ourselves in a big rec room, with couches arranged in a square and, over to the side, a Ping-Pong table. One corner had been made into a screening area with a couple more couches and a huge flat-screen TV. A big rack held hundreds of DVDs, the movies ordered alphabetically by director—Allen and Altman, Bergman and Bertolucci, Capra and Coppola, Hitchcock and Huston, Kasdan and Kurosawa, and so on, all the way to Orson Welles and Billy Wilder, with Chloe Zhao at the end—and I began to get a sense of who had owned this place. If you were, say, a hyper-organized and risk-averse producer or director in L.A. and the shit hit the fan, you could get the hell out and be here in about ten hours. Just one or two recharges for most cars, a very doable situation.

"I thought *Tim* had a lot of movies," said Sophie. "This is unbelievable."

Adjacent to the screening area was a bar, with a refrigerator and bottles of liquor along the wall. Everything in the room was covered in a thin layer of dust but otherwise looked essentially pristine. I opened the fridge; rows of soft drinks and beer sat there in bottles and cans, awaiting a party. If we hadn't shown up, they might have waited a thousand years.

"Want a ginger beer?" I asked.

She took it wonderingly. "Is it good?"

"Try it and see, but expect to be sugar-buzzed for the next couple of hours."

She opened it and took a swig, then grinned. "It's so fizzy!" she said. "Let's go upstairs."

At the back of the room, a stairway built from fashionably thick, floating slabs of walnut led up to the main floor of the house. Walking up the stairs made my nose throb, but I was too excited to care.

We came into a small hallway adjacent to the kitchen. The closets were full of coats and boots. There was plenty of light in the house, but out of curiosity I hit a switch—a quality rocker switch with smooth action, of course. Some of the lights in the kitchen came on. I hit the switch beside it and more came on, over the sink. A system set up to be self-sustaining and maintenance-free, and it was.

"Unbelievable," said Sophie again.

The kitchen was huge, with granite countertops, a main sink under the window, and a secondary sink on an island. The cabinets were crafted from cherry, with glass fronts, and were full of painted ceramic dinner plates and salad plates and soup bowls and cereal bowls. There were coffee mugs, water glasses, wine glasses, champagne flutes. Copper sink, copper fixtures, a sprayer that pulled out from the head of the faucet. A shiny Bosch dishwasher. A small table and chairs, distressed as if shipped over from an old French farmhouse, sat by the corner windows, for breakfast and lunch.

I turned the left-hand faucet over the main sink. Hot water came out. I turned the right. Cold water. Twice in one week I'd experienced this miracle.

On the dark, gleaming corner of the granite that topped the island sat a stack of mail and a set of car keys. Everything in the house lay under the same thin blanket of dust. I picked up the letters and blew them clean. Michael O'Connell and Catherine Wylie, their names had been. They weren't producers, I realized; they'd been writers—film and television both—and successful ones. I'd seen an article once and vaguely remembered who they were. They'd written the whole *Guns and Butter* series, about a Mafia-like syndicate of renegade Mennonites who'd cornered the international market for high-end organic dairy products with startling violence. It had run for, like, four years. Oh, and *My Darling Cousin Mofo*, a lighthearted feature that interrogated seventeenth-century European royal incest; it had won the Buñuel Award and been released to great critical acclaim. I was also pretty sure they were the team behind *Deep Thoughts, Deep Pleasures*, a mockumentary miniseries that unpacked the tormented relationship between a penniless philosopher, D. P. McClune, and his wealthy nymphomaniac benefactress, Maude Bakelight—*Fifty Shades of Grey* meets *Critique of Pure Reason*, as best I could recall, and a smash hit at Toronto and Telluride.

I couldn't help myself. I picked up one of the letters, which was from WB Studios. It had already been opened, and tucked inside were a brief, fawning letter and a check for $1.6 million. Such were the perks of stardom; they could still insist on paper checks when everyone else had long since switched to electronic transfer. I understood, actually; it felt strangely wonderful to hold a check for $1.6 million, printed on thick, embossed stock, even if it was worthless and made out to someone I didn't know. I folded it and put it in my pocket.

There were pictures all over the fridge, so I went to have a look.

My heart sank then. I'd envisioned these two as fatuous nabobs, with stretched faces and filled lips and planted hairlines, but they actually appeared relatively normal: a middle-aged couple whose smiling faces evinced perhaps the slightest pain, whose eyes still looked warm and lively but also showed the beginnings of disillusionment and disbelief. People who had almost certainly wanted to write more prestigious stuff but could never quite make it work—who were doing their best, in other words, like the rest of us. Their son was about seven and looked bright and mischievous.

Suddenly I felt embarrassed to be in their house, as if they might unexpectedly come down the driveway, find us here, and politely request an explanation before just as politely asking us to leave. I took the check out of my pocket and slipped it back in the envelope. I noticed the date on it for the first time, then: fourteen years earlier. It was amazing that the house wasn't dustier, but again, it had been well sealed.

Big windows illuminated the living room. Couches and comfortable chairs were clustered together for intimate conversations. There was a working fireplace with wood piled beside it. Fine old litho prints of

birds as well as original paintings hung on the walls. Michael and
Catherine had had taste—not flashy, simply good. I began to like them.

Then, as I looked around, I kind of fell in love with them. There
were bookshelves everywhere—they had an actual library. I felt a little
giddy. It was madly, obsessively organized, of course, like the films
(and after seeing their photos I was pretty sure it was Michael who did
the organizing, and Catherine who gently suggested that it didn't really matter, in the grand scheme of things, if Soderbergh got re-shelved
to the left of Lynn Shelton). There was a nonfiction section emphasiz-
ing lay-sci explorations of the world (Abbey to McPhee to E. O. Wilson,
the original Ant Man himself, who had first written about the carnivorous Amazon variety that later overran the U.S.). Another section for
plays—Edward Albee to both August and Lanford Wilson, with the
prescient Tracy Letts ("Thank God we can't tell the future; we'd never
get out of bed") there in the middle, and, oh yes, Paul Zindel and his
man-in-the-moon marigolds tucked into the lower-right corner.

The biggest section of all was devoted to fiction, hundreds of hard-
back volumes covering most of a wall. I found many of my old favorites: Atwood and Austen; a hive of B's (Baldwin, Batuman, Bellow,
etc.); the complete boxed Chekhov stories in the Constance Garnett
translation; Conrad; Dostoevsky; Eisenberg; Erdrich; and on and on,
all the way through a middle section thick with M's—McBride,
Melville, Morrison, Munro, and Murakami, among others—to the
variously spelled wolves at the end, including Thomas, Tobias, and
Virginia. Oh, and there was Pirsig, one of my best old besties: *Zen and
the Art of Motorcycle Maintenance*. I'd been thinking about that book
lately; I pulled it out and put it on the table so I could look at it later.
I really wished Michael and Catherine were still alive, now, because I
wanted to embrace them and thank them for saving these books.

Sophie was in the pantry adjoining the kitchen, rifling through the
cabinets and emitting little squeals of delight and surprise. I walked
over to see what she'd found. Cookies and crackers and chips and

ramen and everything you needed to bake: white, wheat, barley, and buckwheat flour vacuum-sealed tight in glass, and baking soda and powder, and three different kinds of salt.

"I'm never leaving here," she said.

I knew that at least some of this food wouldn't be edible anymore. "Let's get the truck in before we make any life-altering decisions."

I opened the front door. The horses and mules stood in their traces fifty feet up the driveway, on the other side of the fortified gate. To my left, there was a little button by the light switch, so I pressed it. The gate made a clanking noise, then began to slide back. The horses shied and the mules stared unimpressed as the gate shuddered out of the way and stopped.

I walked up the drive, then led them inside the gate and parked the truck by the house. When the gate had closed itself, I let the animals out of their harnesses.

Peau glided in and said modestly that it was a decent poke nest, he thought.

I smiled. "You did *good*, honored bird."

I was curious, though. I knew ravens were territorial, like most animals, but Peau never seemed to encounter much hostility when he went out reconnoitering. When I asked him about it, he said it was partly because he quickly took on a time-honored role, that of the traveling storyteller. He told the ravens about places he'd been, usually with something thrown in about the stupidity of humans. They loved it, and soon they loved him. He told me that it was all about something—a Raven term I didn't know. Eventually I figured out that it was like a combination of "family" and "network" and "nesting tree," maybe closest of all to the Hawaiian "*ohana.*" He also said that this place was famous in local birdland because there was a big cornfield behind a line of nearby trees.

"It's still coming in as corn after all these years?"

The locals had told him it wasn't bad. Everyone flew in from miles around in the fall.

He shot up to the top of one of the outcrops, then let rip with a series of loud caws, which were answered by other caws from farther away. *Thanks* and *You're welcome*, I figured.

I took the watermelons out of the truck, got Cass, and went inside. The dogs, I'd decided, had best stay out. I placed the melons on the counter, then noticed Sophie waiting at the top of the stairs to the second floor, where the bedrooms were. She looked stricken and a little shaky, so I imagined it was bad. I climbed up to join her and said, "Show me."

The boy was down the hall in his own room, which had books on shelves and posters on the wall and an old iMac on an Ikea desk. He lay in dusty flannel pajamas on the bed, and on the bedside table sat a thermometer, a box of Kleenex, and an empty water glass. There was loose hair around the boy's skull, which matched that in the picture on the fridge, but other than that the skeleton was clean. In the water glass, the desiccated husk of a spider hung in its own web, where it had waited patiently for insects that never came.

We found Michael and Catherine in the main bedroom, a vast, light-filled space with its own bathroom and yet another big flat-screen. They lay side by side on the bed, holding hands, fingerbones interlaced, wedding rings hanging loosely on phalanges. He wore striped cotton pajama bottoms, she some kind of lightweight cotton nightgown. They'd all gotten sick at the same time, was my guess, then ants had found them later. It was hard to picture ants swarming this pristine house, but it didn't take much of a crack to admit a tiny army, and the stench of death was a powerful attractor even to the ordinary varieties.

I was still mouth-breathing, my poor nose clogged with clots. "Does it smell anymore?" I asked Sophie. She shook her head, but she was clearly upset.

"I just imagine that this is how my parents ended up," she said. "I think my mom died three or four months after I was born, and it would have been about the same time, right?"

"Probably."

I asked if she knew about the two pandemics. She knew a little, and at first I hesitated to get into it. But I figured she deserved the best explanation I could manage.

"The first time around was relatively mild," I said. "It unfolded in stages, caused by a coronavirus that spread from China and kept mutating through the 2020s. Deaths were in the one- to two-percent range—bad, but not even really enough to compensate for the birthrate. The second wave came in 2033, and it was much worse."

"What was it?"

"A bird flu that killed eighty percent of the people it infected, and it infected almost everyone. That was pretty much the end of civilization as we knew it. There was no one left to grow or haul food, no one to maintain the electrical grids, no doctors or nurses left to help anyone."

"Tim and Melissa told us about it," she said quietly. "Did you have it?"

"I was living an isolated life," I explained. "Someone had left packaged food for me, and I may have gotten it from that. But the food had been sitting in the sun and air for a few days, and my best guess is that it weakened the virus. I still got really sick, but I lived through it."

"Lucky you."

"Well, almost everyone I knew was dead within weeks, so not so much."

I decided not to tell her the rest; what would be the point in suggesting that her parents had more or less been murdered? There had been a lab in Zurich led by a notoriously egomaniacal microbiologist, a guy who'd been conducting gain-of-function studies on H5N1, a dangerous avian flu, and a couple of related H5 strains. He managed to produce a variety that passed easily between people but that lay dormant, more like a retrovirus, for up to eight weeks before symptoms appeared. This was idiotic enough, but then he'd done the stupidest thing of all: he published the genome, so that any nut on earth with a halfway decent lab could make the thing. To celebrate what they expected to be their newfound fame, he took his colleagues out for a beer.

The scientific world didn't react quite as he'd expected, however, and he soon found himself excoriated in the press as a mad scientist, which basically he was. I'd been one of the writers doing the excoriating, as it happened, with pieces in the *Times* and *Discover* and a couple of the virology journals. A lot of accusations were hurled back and forth. He and I ran into each other at a conference and almost came to blows—he called me a failed novelist and I called him a failed human being, and we were both right—but ultimately none of it mattered.

I was a little disgusted with scientists and their egos after that, so I quit writing about them for a while. I was trying to decide what to do next when I heard from David, so I moved to the dharma center, and things were quiet for a couple of years. There were further warning signs: a natural H5N1 pandemic in birds, an ominous spread into farmed minks and other mammals, the possible mixing of natural and lab-bred strains. Anyway, no one ever figured out where it started because when it finally came, nearly everyone on the planet was already infected before the index case got sick. Months later, after all the megadeath, the strain finally mutated into a more normal flu, in the sense that people became symptomatic within a few hours of exposure, and that helped stem the spread, even though it remained deadly once you *were* infected.

The other stages of Mayhem had fallen out more or less like dominoes from this signal event. Starvation; migration; a brief, limited nuclear exchange; then finally the return of endemic diseases like TB, diphtheria, typhoid, cholera, malaria, and plague to torment what scattered bands remained of the living. None of this explained Disease X, the one I was concerned about, the one that drove everyone mad before killing them in their late thirties or forties. But the avian flu had been the big bang that started it all, even though, after a couple of years, it apparently vanished.

I'd read about ordinary people's lives shortly before the big world wars—beekeepers in the Cotswolds contentedly tending their hives in 1913, or soccer players in the bloom of youth competing before crowds of thousands in 1935. Or the members of those crowds, who had finished their dinners and taken streetcars to the stadiums, enjoying their middle-class lives. How many of them would still be alive five years later? In hindsight we could see the shadow of the exterminating angel falling over them, a sudden cool darkness they mostly didn't notice. How could they not have seen it coming? What would they have done differently if they'd understood that the world they knew was about to change forever?

But of course it had been the same for us—business as usual, full throttle right over the cliff. People had been warning us for years, just as people had warned the world about Hitler, but civilization had its own momentum, and no one seemed capable of slowing it down or even turning it slightly away from its relentless trajectory of self-annihilation. In a hundred years, I suspected, people would look back at us, at the world of ease and plenty we'd enjoyed, and shake their heads in similar bewilderment: *How did they not see it coming? Surely they could at least have regulated experimentation and stopped breeding minks!*

As it turned out, we couldn't. Better to destroy the world than suggest that a virologist find a less lethal line of inquiry, or a mink farmer learn another trade.

I spared Sophie all of this, but she was still thinking about the little I *had* told her, and she had questions.

"What happened to the cities? Why are some of them gone and some not?"

"At one point during the pandemic, when everything was in chaos, there was a false alarm about a nuclear attack," I told her. "In the past, those had always been caught before anything bad happened, but things were so crazy that this time it wasn't. There couldn't be an all-out war because the people in the silos were dead from flu, and there was no one to turn the launch keys. But the submarine crews were all perfectly fine, and they fired off at least some of their missiles. The Russians hit America, the Americans hit Russia, and for about half an hour the Chinese thought it was their world until they got hit too. That's why some cities like Albuquerque survived, even though most of the people in them were already dead."

She had tears in her eyes. "It's horrible," she said. "What we've used our minds for is horrible."

"I know. We're a tribe of murderous thugs, and I'm sorry."

Which left us without a lot more to say, and with the problem of the family's bones still on our hands.

"What should we do with them?" Sophie asked.

"I suppose we could take them outside and bury them, but the ground's rocky," I said. "It would be hard work, I can still barely use my left hand, and we're both wiped out anyway."

"There's a little guest room down the hall," she suggested. "It's empty, there's no bed, so maybe we could set them on the floor in there for now?"

I nodded. "Let's put the boy with them, too. They'll be together, and you can have his room."

The remains safely stowed, we took the sheets and mattress toppers outside, since they'd been ruined by corpse muck. We put clean sheets on the beds and staked out our territory.

"You get your own room," I said. "But I get the big one."

She allowed herself a brief smile. "I've been waiting my whole life for this."

I was extremely pleased to discover, in the master bedroom closet, a new pair of leather hiking boots. Michael was also a size 10, bless his soles, and this was about the nicest gift he could have left me. I gladly took off my old ones, with their patches of worn-through leather and their almost-nonexistent treads. I'd forgotten what it felt like to wear new boots, to feel supported by the uppers and get spring from the shanks. They were still squeaky and stiff, but I knew they'd break in quickly.

I found scissors and a new safety razor in the bathroom, so I shaved off my beard. I'd gone from having hair and a beard to having neither. When I met Sophie in the kitchen a few minutes later, she jumped, startled, then laughed.

"You scared me," she said. "You look really different."

"Good different or bad different?"

"Younger, at least, that's for sure."

"I'll take it," I said.

We were both hungry. I made the mistake of opening the refrigerator, then swiftly closed it again. It didn't matter that it had remained cool; all the containers held variations of dead, brown fuzz, and I was glad I couldn't smell. I opened the freezer too, just to check: some old containers, ice cubes, the usual. Nothing needing immediate attention.

We found knives (excellent Wüsthof knives, naturally) and started by cutting up one of the watermelons. After I'd eaten a couple of slices, though, I looked through the cabinets and realized something wasn't right. There was enough food for two or three weeks—wonderful things like canned chili and high-end marinara sauce and six varieties of pasta—but this place was set up to survive the siege of Stalingrad. There had to be more food somewhere.

First, though, lunch. We mixed two cans of chili—one traditional, one vegetarian—and heated them up. We ate ravenously, barely stopping to speak, and polished it all off in about ten minutes. Newly energized, we set out to locate the other stuff we knew we'd missed.

And lo, the wonders that unfolded. I remembered the car keys, so I pressed the unlock button and heard a beep from behind a door that opened off the kitchen. I opened the door and found a garage, where two shiny electric SUVs, cords still attached, were trickle-charging away. It felt like discovering a pair of velociraptors in your garage; they should have been extinct, but there they lurked in all their glowering, fiendish glory. I briefly wondered if we could ditch the truck and drive one of these straight through to the California coast, but there were no more charging stations, and it wouldn't have had the range.

There were other things in the garage: camping gear, a battery-powered weed trimmer, rodent traps, a six-foot length of PVC pipe with a loop of clothesline through it, which I recognized as a rattle-snake catcher. Big bags of dog food and cat food in galvanized trash cans to keep rats out—those would come in handy. But no human food.

We went back downstairs. In the corner to the right of the bar we found a door I'd missed on the first pass. It led to a big storage room under the house, where lay the motherlode.

Steel racks, six feet high and twenty feet long, stacked with boxes full of canned goods and freeze-dried dinners and vacuum-sealed dried beans of all kinds. In a big walk-in cooler, I found five-gallon buckets of rice. We wandered down the rows, taking informal inventory.

"We could stay here forever," Sophie said, awestruck. "Seriously, Will, there's enough food for two people for thirty years, and neither of us is going to live that long."

"You may live longer than that if we get to California," I pointed out. "And don't forget Flynn."

She looked briefly deflated. "Fuck that asshole," she said. "I wish I'd shot him when I had the chance."

We found a huge freezer containing a dozen quarts of ice cream in different flavors, three dozen pizzas, and maybe thirty containers labeled with prepared meals—lasagna, spaghetti and meatballs, egg-plant parmesan, etc.

"We'll be coming back to this very soon," I said, closing the door.

By the door we found a few swimsuits hanging on a rack. We eyed each other.

"Let's go," she said.

I grabbed a pair of trunks and went to change in the other room. We met outside, me with my farmer's tan and decidedly non-ripped abs, she in an orange one-piece that fit well enough. We peeled the cover off the pool. I jumped in; the water was cold but refreshing. I didn't want to get my heart rate up too high for fear my nose would start bleeding again, and the water made my finger sting, but I didn't care. It was warm under the afternoon sun, and after I'd been lolling around a while, I noticed Sophie down in the shallow end, strolling about in water up to her chest.

I swam down and joined her. "Nobody ever taught you?"

"The Flagstaff pool was full of leaves," she said.

"Want to learn?"

She appeared skeptical. "Ever taught anyone before?"

"A niece and a nephew. No one's drowned on my watch."

She nodded a little nervously. Between the skeletons and this, I was starting to notice cracks in that formidable facade of hers.

"Water scares me a little," she said.

"I can tell. But if it knows you respect it, it's less likely to do you harm."

"You can be the weirdest dude, Will."

"Nobody's drowned *yet*," I said. "Mind your manners."

We did it the usual way. I held her as she stretched herself out in the water and figured out how to move her arms and legs and breathe at the same time. Occasionally I'd let her go and she'd start to flounder, so I'd catch her and lift her up again. Within a half hour, I could move along with her as she progressed—thrashing clumsily and laughing at her own lack of coordination—and take my hands away for a few seconds at a time. Within an hour I could stand off ten feet and she'd swim to me, a bit more gracefully now. In ninety minutes she was more or less good to go, but she was trembling and her lips were blue.

"Let's get out so you can warm up," I said.

. . .

WE WENT INSIDE, and she headed upstairs to take a hot bath. The horses and mules were grazing contentedly. Cass was out back, chasing chickens around as Peau observed from overhead, tut-tutting. The dogs wolfed down dog food from the big container in the garage, then had more, then more. Finally sated, they each drank a couple of bowls of water, then wandered off to sleep in the shade beside the house. All things were fine in the peaceable kingdom.

While Sophie bathed, I dusted and vacuumed the bedrooms and the main part of the house. I got my gloves, went down to the rec room, and carried the bones of the dog outside. Then I got onions and garlic from the truck and sautéed them on the six-burner Viking stove, with its flawless stainless-steel finish. Sophie appeared after a few minutes, flushed in the cheeks but still a little blue in the lips; I worried that she'd caught a chill. She opened a couple of jars of marinara sauce and a can of tomato paste. She scooped them into a saucepan and put them on a burner.

I'd noticed a little patch of basil beside the house, planted years before but evidently reseeding itself, so I picked some to add to the sauce. When it was all simmering, I opened a bottle of Napa Valley cabernet, and Sophie brought a couple of glasses from the cherry cabinets.

"Strictly speaking, you're too young," I pointed out.

"Strictly speaking, there are no laws anymore."

"Well, I suppose if we were in France, you could have half a glass."

"We're just outside Paris, Will. Did you forget?"

"Point taken." I poured her half a glass.

"And for the record, I'm pretty sure I'm emancipated," she added.

"Point taken again. If I keep taking all your points, you won't have any left."

"I doubt that very much."

The wine was good. I couldn't smell the sauce cooking but imagined it smelled wonderful, and with the imagining I almost *could* smell it. Golden evening light fell across the trees, illuminating their stirring leaves, and pressed warmly into the house. In the west, pink and purple clouds massed on the mountainous horizon like something enchanted from the Hudson River School. It was as if I'd awakened from a fourteen-year dream and found myself back in the world I grew up in, where everything was plentiful and easy and excellent. It hadn't really been like that, of course, but it seemed like it now.

We sat at the breakfast table with our wine, so I could stir the sauce from time to time. Sophie rested her forearms on the table, leaning forward over the wine glass and appearing thoughtful.

"You like it?" I asked.

"I don't have anything to compare it to," she said. "It seems a little bitter, but I think so."

We let the wine settle us. Outside the window, a chicken darted by, chased by Cass, and Sophie smiled.

"So why are you going through all this?" she asked. "Somebody named Lars?"

"Ah," I said. "A long story."

"Come on, don't be a dick."

So I told her. Lars was brilliant and magnanimous and had taken my side in the feud with the shithead from Zurich, which had helped me as my articles went from smaller publications to venues like the *Times*.

But as Eva had told me, he couldn't understand why I'd left it all behind, and he didn't make a secret of his disappointment in me. He considered anything that smacked of spirituality to be antiscientific and foolish, and he decided to outwait me, figuring that sooner or later I'd come to my senses and go to work for him.

The something better I was searching for turned out not to be books but rather meditation. I wasn't very good at it, admittedly. I spent a lot of time in "monkey mind," as my thoughts and attention flitted from one thing to another like a macaque swinging through the trees. All the usual distractions: sex, food, some stupid thing I'd said, the pain in my legs and back, sex again, more food, some stupid thing someone had said to *me*, and on and on through the vast, dreamlike phantasmagoria of the distracted mind.

But occasionally, the monkey would let go and fall, and I soon discovered that there was no ground to hit, just endless open space. On the rare occasions I could sustain this, there were long mornings sitting, gazing out over the Sangre de Cristo Mountains, when everything in me seemed to empty, when there was nothing left but open awareness and stunning beauty. I'd never experienced anything like it, and once I *had* experienced it, it was hard for me to imagine life without it.

"Anyway," I said. "That's where I was living when Eva came looking for me."

"This is the chick I remind you of?"

"In some ways," I said. "Not exactly a carbon copy."

"I don't even know what that is."

"Old tech," I said.

"As in, carbon-based life-form?"

I laughed. "I hadn't thought of that, but yeah, sure. *Really* old tech."

She considered this. "You loved her, though?"

"I did. She was smart, funny, beautiful. Everything."

Sophie smirked. "You're the worst kind of perv there is."

"Which is what?"

"A romantic."

"Eva said the same thing," I told her. "Though if being a romantic means the world constantly disappoints you and leaves you cynical and pissed off, then I guess I am."

She paused for a sip of wine. "I cringe to hear the rest, but go on."

"It went well for a while," I said. "We were both science nerds, and we had a way of loosening each other up."

"Sounds pretty good," she said. "Though it doesn't seem entirely healthy to me that you're still thinking about her so much, all these years later."

I sighed. "I can't stand not knowing what happened," I said. "That's partly what this trip is about."

"I guess I get that," she said. "Anyway, it's your business, not mine. What's for dessert?"

She did make me laugh, this kid. I went to the freezer in the basement and got us a couple of pints of ice cream—one chocolate, one vanilla. I opened them up, spooned a little of each into bowls for us, and carried them to the table. Sophie hadn't had ice cream since she was a child and barely remembered it. Heaven.

We were resting, sated, when Cass scratched at the back door. I went to let her in. Her face was all bloody.

"What happened to you?" I asked, and she hissed something about a rooster.

IT HAD BEEN A LONG DAY, so after dinner I sat by the pool to watch the sunset. I was thinking of an afternoon I'd spent with Eva in Colorado, as things between us first began to unravel.

We'd driven somewhere on an errand, then stopped for lunch in a little town southwest of Salida. It was a warm afternoon in late spring, and after a half hour of walking the streets, with their tidy houses and green lawns and gardens, we came to the edge of town. There was a brick elementary school with tall windows, and across the cracked macadam road, under tall oaks and maples, lay the town cemetery.

At the school, a couple of classes were out at recess, third or fourth graders, shrieking with delight and running around happily. We heard the airy elastic *whang* of red rubber dodgeballs hitting brick and blacktop and occasionally small screaming people. Overhead, big cumulus clouds were rolling in before an afternoon thunderstorm.

We walked among the graves. Some were so weathered we couldn't read the inscriptions. When we could make them out, we saw that many of these people had been dead for over a hundred years. Something about the permanence and weight of this rattled me.

There was a rundown gazebo in the middle of the graveyard, so we went inside and sat down.

"We think we have so much time," I said. "In the blink of an eye, those kids will be buried here too."

I was speaking generally, about the murderous velocity of time, but in hindsight it could have been a prediction of the coming pandemic. We didn't have that perspective then, but Eva understood me anyway.

"I never thought much about death when I was younger," she said. "I'm getting a little afraid of it now."

"It scares me every day," I admitted.

"Doesn't Buddhism offer you some sort of reassurance, though?"

"Certain practices supposedly help with the transition, but it takes time and effort to master them," I said. "If you don't, when this life ends, you may just get blown around by the winds of karma like anybody else. And then, of course, there's the possibility that there's *nothing* after death, but that's more my personal worry than a Buddhist position."

"Well, thanks for cheering me up."

"I figure it's better to know the truth, but it isn't always comforting."

We sat quietly, listening to the kids and to the rising wind in the trees.

"In some ways, I suppose death clarifies matters," Eva said, then.

"How so?"

"If you were immortal, you'd probably do whatever you wanted, literally forever," she said. "When you know you're going to die, you might pay more attention to what matters to you."

"True," I said, though I was often conflicted about that. Should I have a family? Should I try to get really good at something? Should I chuck it all and just get really good at meditating?

"My father gets most of his satisfaction from his work," Eva said, as if we were thinking along the same lines. "But it seems to me he's hollow, somehow. I don't know how to explain it."

I thought I knew what she meant, partly because I knew Lars. "You can become the best person in the world at what you do," I said. "But it won't necessarily make you happy, and it won't save you from death."

She smiled a little sadly, then leaned forward and rested her elbows on her knees. "I still think it's important to be engaged with the world," she said. "My research could save millions of lives. Don't you think that's important?"

"Of course it is."

She eyed me. "What aren't you saying?"

"It's important, but it doesn't necessarily affect your mind."

"Affect it in what sense?"

"The way meditation does," I said. "Scientists can be egotistical jerks like anybody else, even if their work helps people."

She huffed with irritation. "Maybe I should focus on psychiatric drugs instead of phages, then."

She'd grown impatient with me, and I couldn't really blame her. I wasn't explaining this very well, and I couldn't figure out how to put it without sounding dogmatic.

The sky had darkened. Cumulonimbus clouds had replaced the cumulus, and lightning burned through them. Thunder boomed, rattling the gazebo. The teachers quickly rounded up the kids and hustled them inside, and then it began to rain, lightly at first, then heavily, as the air cooled. We shivered and moved closer to each other on the bench. Sitting next to her like that, I could feel her resisting me, as if we were magnets that had been turned and were now pushing each other away.

"Here's the question," I said. "If existence is essentially illusory, then what is it?"

"Are you *saying* it's illusory? Seems like a dubious premise."

"Then you haven't talked to a quantum physicist."

She smiled, conceding the point. "Okay, go on."

"You can make a case that the universe is this fantastic display of energy and consciousness, and we're part of it," I said. "In that sense, it matters both how you live *and* how you train your mind, so that ideally you participate in that as fully as possible."

"Participate *how*? You're losing me."

"Sorry, it's really hard to explain," I said. The problem, of course, was that to really understand how meditation could affect your mind, you had to *meditate*.

"Look, you Buddhists are always talking about compassion," Eva said. "But you can be compassionate without all the religious trappings, right?"

"Sure. Some people are that way naturally."

She bristled. "But I'm not, you mean?"

"I meant that *I'm* not," I said. "I have to work at it. I can't speak for you."

It appeared we understood each other perfectly well in some ways, but in others we were trying to shout across a chasm.

"It can seem like we're in different worlds, I know." I meant this as a peace offering, but it seemed to irritate her even more.

"Well, in *my* world, the schoolyard sits next to the graveyard," she said. "There's always a terrible war somewhere, and most people's lives are bleak. For that matter, it's raining and I'm cold. I don't know how to reconcile all that with this fantastic universe you talk about. I don't even know what you *mean*."

I was trying to come up with some sort of clarifying response when she just got up and walked out into the downpour, headed for the car. By the time I caught up with her, we were both soaked and shivering, and I wondered whether anything I said would make a difference. So I said nothing, and we were silent for most of the long drive home.

• • •

AFTER THE SUN DROPPED BEHIND THE MOUNTAINS, I went inside and found Sophie up in the master bedroom, going through
Catherine's dresser. I lay down on the king bed a little gingerly, thinking of its previous occupants. But it was an excellent mattress, and
soon I forgot my qualms. Meanwhile, Sophie tossed aside Catherine's
jewelry and makeup without interest, then pulled out a few pair of
underwear and gave them a look. "These might come in handy," she
said, setting them aside, then rummaged further.

"Here we go," she said at last—flannel pajamas. She went into the
bathroom to change while I punched the buttons on the TV remotes.
All the batteries were dead, of course, but in the bedside table I found
packaged ones that had only expired a couple of years earlier and
turned out to be fine. There was nothing on any of the satellite chan-
nels, but the DVD player bleeped to life. They'd watched *Casablanca*
shortly before they'd died.

Cass wandered up and hopped into bed with me, then Sophie came
out of the bathroom and slid in on Cass's other side, wearing the baggy
pj's, which had some sort of green tartan print. *Casablanca* was new to
her, and she was crying by the end. It didn't escape her that this movie
and *The Sound of Music* were both about the same war. She said it must
have been a pretty big deal. I told her the world had never really recovered from it.

"No country ever trusted another one again," I said. "Which led to
more nukes and biological weapons and the whole situation that got
us where we are now."

"Weird how shit just goes on forever," she said. She lay down and
made a little noise of discomfort. She didn't look good, actually. A little
green around the gills. I worried that she'd caught something after getting chilled in the pool, or that we'd eaten too much, or both.

"You okay?" I asked.

"Not quite sure I am," she said. Given her general resistance to com-
plaint, this got my attention. I felt her forehead; she was burning up.

"Jesus, Sophie, how long have you been like this?"

"It started a few minutes ago," she said. "Wow, I really do *not* feel well."

There were various prescription drugs in the bathroom, but I didn't know what most of them were, and they were long expired anyway. My mind raced, exploring possibilities: She was a healthy kid; a little chill was unlikely to affect her much out in the middle of nowhere like this, where there were few viruses or other bugs to make her sick. And if she *was* sick, shouldn't I be too, with my middle-aged, diminished immune system?

But what if it was appendicitis? She was at that age. I went back into the bedroom and sat down beside her. "Let me check something," I said. I pressed on her lower-right belly, then suddenly released the pressure. "Did that hurt?"

"Not really," she said, then coughed.

Okay then. She coughed again, which made me wonder, but TB wouldn't have come on suddenly like this.

Typically, science writers know just enough about medicine to be dangerous. But even doctors, if there were any left, had few options anymore. You could have all the medical knowledge in the world, but if you had no blood tests, no diagnostic imaging, no anesthesia, and no drugs, you were back working with herbs and plasters like your great-aunt Gabija from Lithuania.

I went downstairs and fetched my little tin of Bruce Hannock's willow-bark aspirin, which I thought might be more potent than the old aspirin in the bathroom. Then I turned and saw it on the counter: the letter from WB with the big fat check. The last mail they'd opened before they got sick. A house tight with trapped air—that sealed-tomb *pfiss* I'd heard when I first opened the patio door. Dust that had settled on everything over the course of years. Three bags of bones we'd moved down the hall.

The motherfucking avian flu.

Was such a thing possible? If my food boxes sitting in sun and air for a few days had weakened the virus enough for me to live through it, shouldn't fourteen years in a closed-up house do the trick? Flu didn't live long, but smallpox could survive in a frozen vial for decades. And, of course, I'd opened the freezer and we'd had ice cream, potentially releasing God knew what. It seemed absurd, until I reconsidered how many questions remained about the pandemic's origin. After the megalomaniacal troglodyte from Zurich published the virus's genome, anyone with a CRISPR kit could have spliced in other genes—like, for example, the ones that gave smallpox its longevity.

I brought the aspirin powder back upstairs and gave Sophie some with crackers, but she was looking worse now. She was pallid, her eyes unfocused, her cough deepening and turning to a hack. All this had developed in, what, half an hour? I found alcohol and a thermometer in the bathroom, so I sterilized the thermometer and stuck it in her mouth. Half a minute later it beeped: 102°. Not good, but not terrible yet.

The boy's room had a vaporizer on a closet shelf, so I filled it in the bathroom and set it up on a table so we could try to keep her lungs from tightening up. Once that was done, I was pretty much out of ideas. It was the same situation as in the 1800s: you simply waited, then, to see whether the patient would survive.

It was seven thirty, and the sun had set a few minutes before. I collected pillows from the boy's room and piled them behind her, propping her up, thinking this might help keep her lungs clear. She soon lapsed into a kind of stupor, coughing from time to time, and I knew it was going to be a long night.

I went downstairs to find something to read. I picked up the Pirsig novel, then pulled down a couple of volumes from the Chekhov collection and brought them back up with me. Cass was still lying there beside Sophie, her eyes big; she was concerned.

I picked up one of the Chekhov books, but I was so exhausted that I'd barely started reading when I dozed off.

I woke at four, long before sunup. Cass was still there in protector mode, and Sophie was groaning softly in her sleep. I turned on the light and she stirred awake.

Her temperature was still 102°, but it was early. Afternoon would bring the test. She murmured something about water, so I went down to the kitchen and came back with a pitcher and a glass. I'd never been a father, and now I wondered how parents didn't all just disintegrate from terror.

I helped her sit up and drink. She looked terrible; her skin was the greenish white of a cadaver, and her lungs made deep, rattling noises whenever she breathed or coughed. After she'd had enough water, she lay back against the pillows.

Whenever I'd been sick, I'd always dreaded those hours before sunrise, which seemed frighteningly hopeless. You couldn't really sleep, but you couldn't quite awaken either. You entered an intermediate state of suffering, where you felt trapped and unable to escape, the body heavy and weak, the mind ablaze with fever and disorientation, as if everything you perceived moved around you in a blinding whirlwind while you remained bound in place, enervated and afraid.

Sophie had managed to fall back asleep. I turned out the light and settled in to wait for dawn. Finally, after what seemed a full lifetime lying there, I saw the lightening of the shades, the gentle blush of orange, that told me the sun would soon rise.

9

Sophie was wan and clammy, and she needed my help to get to the bathroom. I got her planted on the seat, waited outside while she peed, then hauled her back to bed.

"Feel like eating anything?" I asked, but she shook her head. Before I headed downstairs, I took her temperature again. It was 103° this time, and now that she was awake, her cough returned, violent and hacking.

Cass came downstairs with me, so I gave her some kibble, then went out to feed the dogs. Peau was waiting outside on a low branch. I told him the situation with Sophie and warned him that I had something in mind that he might not like.

There were fresh eggs in the chicken coop, so I brought in a few and fried two of them for breakfast, along with toast from bread that was downstairs in the chest freezer and that thawed out fine, all these years later. I'd noticed an apple tree behind the coop, and I'd been surprised to see fruit on it. As with the watermelons, there seemed something Edenic about the microclimate here. The apples looked small and hard, but otherwise okay, so I thought I'd pick a few later. Cassie and I sat down on the step of the back deck. With my swollen, bruised nose and her lacerated face, we made a fine pair. The hens were clucking, the roosters crowing, and except for the ambient, anxious misery, it would have been a fine morning. I did notice, though, that I could finally inhale a wisp of air through my nose, so at least there was progress in one tiny realm.

"Which one of the roosters did this to you?" I asked. Cassie studied the birds but confessed that they all looked alike to her.

"About the only thing I can think to do is make soup," I told her.

If *she* couldn't catch one, she wondered, how was I going to?

It wasn't a matter of speed, I explained, but rather of opposable thumbs. I walked over to the pool and came back with the long-handled skim net for scooping out leaves. It was exactly the right size.

I decided on a plump hen who seemed a little slower than the others, but it still wasn't easy. She was more agile than she looked and kept darting out of the way at the last second. Meanwhile, all the other chickens went berserk, flapping around and squawking. A couple of the roosters tried to attack me and had to be chased off by Cassie, who was careful to keep her face out of harm's way this time.

Finally I netted the hen. I reached under, grabbed her by the legs, and carried her to the chopping block. She flapped around so violently she nearly escaped. I waited till she'd tired herself out, then laid her down on the wood. She looked at me with her wet, frightened chicken eyes and I almost couldn't do it. I took a couple of breaths and tried to think of something soothing to say, but there was nothing soothing to say that wouldn't be a lie, so I just pulled out my hunting knife and cut off her head. Blood spurted everywhere, and there was another brief round of flapping, but after a few seconds it was over, and she lay still.

And that was how I broke my most important vow—to never intentionally take a life—and became, at least by Buddhist standards, a murderer.

I boiled water in a big pot, dipped in the hen for scalding, then brought her back outside to be plucked. All the other chickens hung back now, glaring at me in an aggrieved and accusatory way. I couldn't blame them; they'd had the place to themselves, without human interference, for many generations of chicken life, and I constituted a sudden and lethal invasion. It was a dramatically reenacted mini-history of the whole planet, in other words. All I needed to finish the show was to slaughter them all and burn down the house.

Cassie stared at me, looking alarmed.

"You're safe, Cass. Just remember those rooster spurs."

When I'd finished plucking the hen, I cut her from the breastbone to the vent, scooped out her innards, then brought her back inside. I filled the pot with fresh water, cut up carrots and onions and a couple of potatoes, plopped in the chicken and the vegetables, and brought it all to a boil. I added salt and cayenne and one or two other things, then turned the heat down to a simmer.

I went upstairs to check on Sophie. She was still bluish around the lips and lay almost motionless between fits of coughing. I sat down beside her on the bed and picked up her hand; it was limp as a fish. I didn't bother to take her temperature again; she was still burning up and there was no point.

Eventually she opened her eyes. She whispered for water again, so I held the glass to her lips while she drank. I told her about the soup, that it would be ready in a couple of hours, and she nodded.

"Ever been this sick before?" I asked, and she shook her head. "You'll get through it," I said.

She looked up at me with a disoriented gaze. "Not sure I want to," she whispered. She coughed violently for a few seconds, gasping for breath at the end, until the fit passed.

"Promise me you'll try."

"No promises I can't keep."

"Then keep it."

She coughed again. Cass came in and hopped back onto the bed.

Sophie put it together, then. "You killed a chicken?" she asked. "For me?"

I BROUGHT HER SOUP and helped her sit up so she could swallow it. At first, each swallow was followed by a coughing fit. Eventually, she was able to finish about a quarter of the bowl.

"It's good," she said. "Thanks."

And then she was asleep again.

I was outside pacing when Peau showed up, so I updated him. He made worried noises that sounded like a squeaky hinge, then soon took off again.

Later in the afternoon, Sophie was sweating profusely. I woke her and took her temperature: still 103°. Her pajamas were soaked, so I got her out of them and into a big clean T-shirt that must have belonged to Michael. I had her drink some water, then put the pajamas on the washing machine downstairs.

By sundown her fever was 104°, her breathing was raspy, and she couldn't keep anything down. I found a sponge and ran a pan full of cool water, then sponged water over her forehead and neck and throat. I don't know where I got this idea but had vague memories of my mother doing it when I'd been sick as a kid. After about twenty minutes her fever had dropped to 102°, but she was shivering and miserable. Forty minutes later she was up to 105°, into the range of organ failure and death.

I was more frightened than I'd been in a long time, more than when I'd been chased down the canyon by the flash flood, more than when I'd been tied up and tortured by Flynn. Fear had always been my nemesis. It pulled me from the world, shrank me to a tiny homunculus inside myself, made everything impossible. I tried to fight it with my mind, to reason my way around it, to find some ledge of logic to cling to over the great abyss. Such tactics never worked for long.

I had to do something, even so. I knew this was the sort of situation for which rituals were invented—when the universe is spinning out of control and you have to sit down on solid ground and do something with your hands, with your voice. To uncover a tiny green sprig of hope—no, not hope, but rather *trust*—in your pounding heart, then feed it and water it and nurse it to trembling life.

Sophie was fast asleep, so I gathered what I needed and went outside to the fire pit near the pool. I collected kindling and wood, piling it up for what I knew might be a long night.

I'd always wanted a daughter, even though I never really understood why. It just seemed that relationship would be fulfilling as few things could be, the chance to be a mentor and defender and goofball all rolled into one. I'd always assumed, somehow, that eventually I'd *have* a daughter, too; then one day, in my late thirties, with Eva gone and the world falling to pieces and zero romantic prospects available, it dawned on me that I likely wouldn't.

I barely knew Sophie, but she was smart and engaging and easy to like. I'd already begun to wonder if there might be a way to keep her around. It was absurd, I knew, projection and romanticism and all the things she scorned, but so what? With her and Peau and Cassie, I was starting to feel like a member of a family, fumbling our way through this perilous world, and I liked that feeling; it made everything seem more bearable.

I lit a small fire, then got out my text and my *tingshas*, small cymbals connected by a rawhide strip that rang lightly and elegantly when knocked together. I would do a *sur* offering, an old practice I'd learned at the gonpa. You offered smoke to ease the journey of the deceased, or to remove obstacles for the living. Severe illness was high on the list of such problems, and despite my natural skepticism, I'd seen it work. The smoke ultimately represented enlightened mind, the most profound of all offerings.

I opened my tin of barley flour and began making my way through the practice. As I proceeded, the fire burned down to glowing embers.

When I got to the right place in the text, I sprinkled some of the flour over the coals. The smoke sprang up, heavy and aromatic, as I made the offerings and recited the mantra, *Om Mani Padme Hung*. Which means, essentially, that by uniting wisdom and compassion in your heart, you can tap into your own Buddha nature and purify your own karma and that of others.

I thought of Sophie and prayed that she would survive. I thought of the men who had died chasing us, offered the smoke to them, and envisioned them as satisfied and moving on from this life. I also offered to the tiger and the crocodiles and the ants and to myself, because I had to admit that I'd been a little thrilled when the animals and the flash flood had laid waste to the men who meant us harm. I offered to Eva, as I always did during this ceremony. I offered to the poor beheaded chicken, and to Catherine and Michael and their son. Finally, I offered to all beings, human and otherwise, that they be satisfied and happy, that they escape the samsaric wheel of suffering. Then I offered to Sophie again at the end, just for good measure. The barley smoke filled the clearing and drifted slowly on the cool night air.

I went back to the beginning and made the offerings again and again for the next couple of hours, replenishing the fire as needed to keep the coals glowing. I was admittedly prone to second-guessing myself when it came to practices like this. Weren't aspirational prayers really a sort of game, another way to try to manipulate the universe into giving you what you wanted? And skepticism isn't a bad thing, after all, because when push comes to shove, if your faith is based on wishful thinking, when the shit hits the fan it's about as useful as a sailboat in the Sahara.

The irony with practices like this, however, was that even as you focused on the object of your desire, once in a while, instead of getting it, you just stopped wanting it because it no longer seemed necessary to your happiness. Or as an old lama named Patrul Rinpoche had put it in the 1800s, regarding possessions generally: "If you've got money, you've got money problems. If you have a house, you have house problems. If you have yaks, you have yak problems. If you have goats, you have *goat* problems!"

All of which was well and good, but sometimes it was perfectly appropriate to want something, and I did want Sophie to survive and live her life.

I took a break and went up to check on her. She was still asleep, her breathing ragged but steady. The moon had risen. I opened the bedroom window so I could hear her if she called me, then went back outside. I sat down by the fire and got out my pen and paper.

Dear Eva,

It's a clear night with a moon and much trouble in the land. I'm still traveling with the cat, the raven, and the mules, but we've been joined by a brace of stout horses, two hounds, and a girl. We're nearly a full-on circus—all we need is a big tent and a couple of acrobats in battered hats juggling bowling pins.

I think you'd like this girl. She has eyes like yours and a sense of humor that's maybe a little more acerbic than yours was, but she's been through a lot and it's understandable. She's smart far beyond her years, as I remember your father bragging you were at her age.

I saw David and Pelageya, from the gonpa. I think you'll remember him because he and I were friends, though she was a kid at the time. David told me he thought you were somehow getting these letters, and I have no reason to doubt his insight, so I'm encouraged to keep writing.

Sophie is extremely sick. I've done sur offerings for her, but the matter will likely be decided within the next day or so. I'm going to keep this short, but wherever you find yourself, if you have any influence over such matters, I beg you to wield it. She's a good kid, and she deserves to live.

You're in my poor, half-finished heart, as always.

—Will

I laid the paper on the coals and watched as it browned, then caught fire.

It had been a long day, and I was spent. I drifted off and dreamed, again, of the high mountain basin with the two lakes. Clear morning sunlight, crisp air, water and rock. I walked the path from the lower lake to the upper, following the trail between pale granite boulders. When I reached the higher lake, I looked across to the other side, maybe forty yards away. Eva stood there, her eyes resting on the water. I saw her reflection, very still, shimmering a little from the light movement of the air. Then, as I watched her, she sensed my presence, looked up, and met my eyes.

This had never happened before in my previous dreams, and the sudden shock of it jolted me awake.

Only a few minutes had passed. I was about to go back inside when Peau came sailing in with something in his beak. I reached out and he dropped leaves from a plant of some kind into my upturned palm. They were aromatic, a little sagey, but not sage.

"This is for her?" I asked, and he bobbed. "What is it?"

It grew around a seep in the mountains a couple of miles away, he said. His friends told him it could be helpful with an illness like this.

"Peau, if she has what I think she has, the best antivirals wouldn't help. I'm a little skeptical about some plant."

He emitted a little reproving clack. Had it occurred to me, he asked, that ravens might know something about bird flu?

I could be such a fucking idiot. I'd been sitting there for hours, praying for something to save Sophie, and when the possibility of just such deliverance came winging in from the heavens, carried by a messenger I trusted implicitly, my first reaction was disbelief rather than gratitude. In fact, I recalled that Jane Goodall had found African people who learned about dozens of medicinal plants by watching chimpanzees use them.

I thanked Peau, took the herb inside, and crushed some of it into a bowl of soup. I carried it up to Sophie, but it took some gentle nudging to wake her. She'd soaked the T-shirt with sweat and could barely hold up her head. I took her temperature: 104°.

"You have to eat this," I said.

"Can't . . . ," she whispered.

"Try." The good news, if you could call it that, was that she was too weak to push my hand away, so I just spooned it into her mouth. She gagged and spat some out, but then she swallowed.

"It's terrible . . . ," she said.

"A little more." I kept spooning, she kept swallowing, until the bowl was empty. Then I got the sponge and the basin and started in again.

Twenty minutes later, 102°. I got her into another clean T-shirt. Half an hour later: 103°. An hour after that: 103°. An hour after that: 102°. An hour after that: 101°.

By now it was past midnight, and I was exhausted. I trudged down to the kitchen to get some soup for myself, and Cass padded after me.

I fed her, then ate three bowls of the chicken soup. It wasn't half bad. I put a little of the herb on my tongue and saw why Sophie hated it: it was bitter and coppery and reminiscent of fermented fish. I spat it out and rinsed my mouth. I took another bowl of herbed soup back up to Sophie and made her finish the whole thing. When she was done, she fell back asleep, so I lay down beside her and waited.

Her coughing kept me awake most of the night, and then sometime before dawn I realized I'd drifted off because there was no coughing. I sat up, my heart pounding, but when I listened, I could hear her breath, moist and still raspy but regular. I got the thermometer and nudged her awake: 100.8°. Half an hour later: 100.4°.

I let myself drift off into a decent sleep, then.

•   •   •

IT WASN'T TO BE SO EASY, as it turned out. Later that morning she was back up to 102° and half out of it again. I brought her more of the bitter soup. I hoped the one batch would be enough, because if I so much as walked into the backyard now, the chickens went berserk and most of them flew up into the trees. I'd forgotten that wild chickens could actually fly, at least enough to save their skins from time to time. Peau considered their aerial skills laughable, of course; they could career around as long as they kept their wings beating, but forget about glide.

Near midday, Sophie seemed to rally again. Her fever dropped to 100.6° and she asked me to bring her fresh underwear. I handed them over and went back to the kitchen.

She had more soup for lunch, then slept a couple of hours. At two o'clock she hit 103° again, and I got the cold washcloth for her forehead. More soup, more sleep. Then, at four o'clock, when I would have expected her fever to peak, she'd dropped to 99.2°. I thought it was a mistake, but I took her temperature again and it was the same. Her color was better, and her eyes started losing their lost, distracted look and coming into focus. I tucked a lock of her greasy hair behind her ear, to get it out of her face.

She turned her head to the side and sniffed. "I reek."

"Maybe tomorrow you can shower."

She slept again, then I brought her more soup and some of the bread. After eating, she seemed more awake and asked me to read to her, so I picked up one of the Chekhov volumes. It had "Gooseberries" in it, the story with the original Pelageya, so I read that first. Then I read another favorite of mine, "Easter Eve."

"Those men were in love with each other?" she whispered, afterward.

"Yes," I said. "Everything had to be kind of coded in those days."

Then I read her "In the Ravine," which had always been my favorite of Chekhov's. I thought she might be a little young to get it, but as usual I'd underestimated her.

In the story, the peasant girl Lipa marries into a wealthy merchant family, though her new husband, one of the family's sons, shows no sexual interest in her and seems to be gay. She has a baby (fathered, apparently, by a local carpenter), but the child is "accidentally" killed by her sister-in-law Aksinya. Because Aksinya is indispensable to the family business, Lipa is blamed for failing to prevent the baby's death, then is essentially exiled. She wanders through the countryside, confused and bereft. Meanwhile, the family patriarch, a miserly old fool, is eventually marginalized and reduced to begging by Aksinya, who is as close to a true villain as the story contains. By the end, it is Lipa herself who offers the old man food, an astonishing turnabout in this world, where people are constantly cheating each other, frequently drunk or sick or starving, failing at illegal schemes, landing in hellish prisons, and so on.

"So beautiful," Sophie whispered when I'd read the last line.

"You think so?"

"It's like our lives now," she went on, quietly. "People at each other's throats, everyone dying of fevers or TB. Like the way we live isn't so new or unusual."

"But didn't Aksinya seem kind of ghastly to you?" I asked. "I mean, she'd sleep with anyone if they had something she wanted, and she was a baby-killer."

Sophie shrugged weakly. "Men use power to get sex," she said. "Women use sex to get power. Everyone wants the same things because then they're less afraid."

I reflected that if anyone would understand this, she would. "But still, you think it's beautiful?"

"It's Lipa," she said. "Everything terrible happens to her, but at the end she's happy anyway. I mean, she's *singing*, and she gives food to the old man who's responsible for a lot of her suffering. I just think that's cool."

. . .

AFTER A FEW MINUTES she was asleep again, so I took Pirsig's book downstairs with me.

Since my conversation with David about the language of birds, I'd been thinking about the intersections between insanity and spiritual life. There were the historical examples, of course, everyone from Joan of Arc to Drukpa Kunley and the other "crazy wisdom" teachers in the Eastern tradition. The physicist Karl Schwarzschild once said that you needed the vision of a saint, a madman, or a mystic to decipher the true nature of the universe. Lama Sonam used to tell us that there were many factors that could lead a seeker to the path: practice in past lifetimes, a sense of unhappiness or discontent with one's present circumstances, an unusually compassionate nature, or simple lunacy, which could shatter one's comfortable relationship with ordinary reality and open the mind to more profound understanding and wisdom. Not that he recommended madness or had any illusions about the suffering it entailed. But he did see clearly that it was one place from which a student could begin and, with proper training, turn the torments of the troubled mind toward useful and ultimately healing ends.

It had been a quarter century since I'd read Pirsig's book, and I was hazy on the details, but I did remember learning at one point that he had schizophrenia and realizing that this might explain a lot of what he experienced. *Zen and the Art of Motorcycle Maintenance* was sold as a novel, but it could as easily have been labeled a memoir.

I sat in one of the comfortable chairs and turned on a reading lamp on the table beside it. As I flipped through the book, rediscovering the story of his difficult motorcycle trip with his son, and the subnarrative of the resurgence of his former personality (called Phaedrus in the book, and supposedly obliterated in a mental hospital years before), I finally found the sections I was looking for. It all came down to this thing Pirsig called Quality. He wrote (italics his):

The past exists only in our memories, the future only in our plans. The present is our only reality. The tree that you are aware of intellectually, because of that small time lag, is always in the past and therefore is always unreal. *Any* intellectually conceived object is *always* in the past and therefore *unreal.* Reality is always the moment of vision *before* the intellectualization takes place. *There is no other reality.* This preintellectual reality is what Phaedrus felt he had properly identified as Quality. Since all intellectually identifiable things must emerge *from* this preintellectual reality, Quality is the *parent,* the *source* of all subjects and objects.

Then, a few pages later, as he read from the *Tao Te Ching,* he continued:

Line after line. Page after page. Not a discrepancy. What he had been talking about all the time as Quality was the Tao, the great central generating force of all religions, Oriental and Occidental, past and present, all knowledge, everything.

I reflected that in several Buddhist paths, students are led through a systematic deconstruction of the ordinary mind that may lead to a sudden experience of pure awareness, known in the Tibetan tradition as *rigpa.* I wondered if Pirsig, like other wild seers of history, had experienced that spontaneously. If so, his subsequent difficulty may have partly resulted from the lack of a qualified teacher. I knew this might be too facile an explanation, especially in the face of something as powerful as schizophrenia, but I wasn't willing to dismiss it. As David had pointed out, the line between the yogi's hut and the madhouse could be a fine one.

I returned the book to the shelf and noticed another volume lying there horizontally. There was nothing printed on the spine, so I opened it and found myself staring at about three hundred blank pages. It was one of those bound journals they used to make; I laughed because it seemed so much like an invitation. The word "journal" comes from the French *jour*, meaning "day," so I supposed this could become the book of my days, the story of this one journey (another form of *jour*) through the southwestern part of what had once been my country. A gift from my dead hosts to me, one that I could carry forward into whatever uncertain terrain lay ahead. I would have been an ingrate to refuse it.

BY THE FOLLOWING MORNING, Sophie's temperature was an even 99°, and by afternoon it was normal again. I realized I'd been holding my body rigid with tension for the past two days, and when I finally began to relax, I nearly melted. I went outside, sat down in the shade, and wept. This made my nose throb, but there wasn't much I could do about it. I felt immensely grateful; despite how sick she'd been, her illness had lasted only a couple of days. She hadn't needed a ventilator; she'd never fallen into a coma. It had been a relatively mild case, and I was pretty sure Peau's herb had something to do with it.

Sophie took a long, hot shower. When we met up later in the kitchen, she was wearing a clean T-shirt and a pair of sweatpants. She was hungry and a little wobbly on her feet. Her cough was still terrible, but she was young and tough, and I figured her lungs would clear in a couple of weeks.

"Do ravens become ravenous?" she asked hoarsely, after putting in an order for scrambled eggs, toast, and a couple of apples from the backyard tree.

"You'll have to ask Peau," I said as I headed out to get eggs and apples. "Oh, and by the way, you may want to thank him."

"Why?"

I explained about the herb, and she looked stricken.

"I didn't know," she said. "I just thought you were a shitty cook."

"That's a separate issue."

She followed me out the door. The chickens went bananas at the sight of us, of course, but once they'd flown the coop it made collecting the eggs easier. Sophie called Peau, and after a minute he winged in and landed on my shoulder.

Sophie reached out, tentatively, and stroked the soft, short feathers on top of his head. "Thanks," she said.

I DECIDED WE SHOULD CELEBRATE her recovery. I found a cake mix in the freezer downstairs that included everything but water, so I baked a chocolate cake to go with the last of the chicken soup and roasted potatoes. There was plenty of ice cream, of course.

After we'd feasted, I fed Cass, then called Peau in. We all trooped downstairs to the screening area with the big TV and looked through the films. Sophie loved *Cats* and had never seen *The Birds*, so those would be one and two on the bill.

Michael and Catherine had thought of everything: there was popcorn in a jar in the little fridge and a microwave on the counter. We popped the corn, added salt, then snuggled into the brown leather couch. Sophie still looked wan, but she was brightening up at the prospect of a little entertainment. Cass spread herself over our laps while Peau perched on the back of the couch.

Not surprisingly, Cass loved *Cats* at least as much as Sophie did. She watched every scene rapt, her ears up and her whiskers and tail twitching. During the song "Memory," she emitted a long, low moan, and I suspected that if cats could weep, she would have. Peau was less engaged—he seemed impatient, even—and appeared relieved when the credits finally rolled.

So good, said Cass, *so good.*

Quoth the raven: *What a bore!*

Cass batted at him, but gently and almost fondly. He simply bowed his head and took the blow, as if he understood. He emitted a little accepting cluck, and she made almost the same sound.

What to make of this odd thaw? Then it dawned on me; they'd each done their best to save Sophie, brought together by a common purpose. I felt a little emotional about this and wanted to say something appreciative, but then I worried that I'd merely embarrass everyone. Instead I gave each of them a pet and tousled Sophie's hair affectionately.

"What was *that* for?" she asked, bemused, as she combed it back down with her fingers.

"Just enjoying the company," I said and left it at that.

I got up and ejected the *Cats* DVD, then started *The Birds*.

Peau was immediately transfixed. He guffawed when Tippi Hedren drove to Bodega Bay, whipping her silver sports car around the curves, and the two caged lovebirds leaned into them. Later, he hooted when crazed crows attacked the kids' birthday party and broke a bunch of suspiciously phallic balloon arrangements. He hissed when enraged seagulls attacked a guy pumping gas, which led to a huge conflagration; then he muttered that seagulls were all like that, they were unbelievable. In the final scenes, when the family is boarded up in their house and the birds still manage to get inside and wreak havoc, he stared at the screen with increasingly fierce attention and started bobbing up and down as if someone were banging a drum.

"Easy, Peau," I said. "Don't go all Iron John on me."

But he was mesmerized. He emitted little cries of excitement—hilarious because he was usually so composed—and by the climax he was wild-eyed, hopping all over the back of the couch, including brief, startling moments on top of our heads that made Sophie shriek. At the end his feathers were all askew, and he looked exhausted and spent, panting through his big open beak as if he'd just had sex.

It was after midnight by now, so I let him out, then followed Cass and Sophie upstairs. Sophie went down the hall to finally claim her bedroom, and I put fresh sheets on the big bed and dozed off with Cass by my side.

Later, though, I was awakened by the sense that there was someone in the room. I started up, but it was only Sophie.

"It seems weird to sleep alone now," she said. "Can I have my usual spot?"

"Climb on in."

WHEN I AWAKENED THE NEXT MORNING, Cass was pacing the room in a strange, distracted way, emitting deep, guttural yowls, and Sophie lay curled in a fetal position on her side on the bed. What the hell was going on now?

"You okay?" I asked Sophie, suddenly frightened again.

"Cramps," she muttered. "I cannot get a fucking break."

"Ah," I said. "Cass?"

She shot me a tormented glare, and I understood: she was going into heat. Well Jesus Christ, I thought. I asked Sophie what she had for supplies, and she said there were clean rags in her bag. But something else occurred to me.

Sure enough, Catherine had a few boxes of tampons in the bathroom cabinet. I brought Sophie a box. Organic cotton, biodegradable applicator, recyclable wrapper; a real throwback to the good old days.

"Ever seen these?"

She took the box and examined it, then pulled one out. "Melissa told us about these, but there was no way to get any," she said.

"We'll see what's under the house; we may be able to keep you supplied for a while," I said. "Cass has to stay inside until this passes, so don't let her out. That kind of yowling draws all kinds of beasts that would rather eat her than mate with her."

Cass snarled that I was *not* keeping her in.

"I know, I know," I said. "They haven't built the jail that can hold you. Except they have, and this is it. Sorry, girl."

She hissed, then bolted from the room and trotted downstairs.

"There are two layers of fencing between us and the outside," Sophie pointed out.

"Yeah, but between her trying to climb out and the others trying to climb in, sooner or later one of them will succeed. It's better if they don't hear each other."

"How long will she be like this?"

"It can take a week or two. It's not ideal for tight quarters if you hope to get any sleep."

She smiled. "I guess we'll have to stay a while longer and suffer the hardships."

It was tempting, obviously, but I was getting anxious. The sudden *lack* of pursuit had made me almost as jittery as I'd felt while being hunted. I could almost sense Buck Flynn's agitated, hungry consciousness searching the land, trying to determine where we were and how we'd managed to slip through his fingers.

Peau and his flock of friends were flying vigilant reconnaissance and had seen nothing unusual, though. Was Flynn trying to recruit another platoon? It might be hard if word had gotten around about his attrition rate, which was considerably worse than that of Napoleon retreating from Moscow. Or was he simply waiting, like a cat by a mousehole, knowing that sooner or later we'd have to emerge from hiding? Or maybe he'd OD'd on the codeine cousin and put himself into a coma? Or—most worrying of all—had he made a better-than-average guess about where we'd cross into California and arranged to intercept us there? All these scenarios were plausible, alone or in some combination, but there was no reason to worry Sophie with them.

"Anything I can bring you?" I asked her.

"I think I'll just walk around a bit."

"One thing," I said. "I noticed there's an old computer in your room. Don't turn it on, okay?"

"Why not?"

"It's likely got a location tracker, and except for Princely, I don't imagine there's another working machine within a couple hundred miles. Someone might be paying attention."

WE WENT DOWNSTAIRS so I could make us breakfast and feed the animals. Sophie opened the door to go outside, then cried, "Shit!"

Cass had been lying in wait and seized the opportunity to escape. I gave chase, but by the time I was outside she was halfway up a tree. I realized that if she wanted to, she could follow the branches over the fence and drop to the ground on the other side. The second fence would pose less of a challenge because the posts were wooden, and she'd be able to climb right up them.

I sprinted for the pool net and came back with it, but she saw what I was up to and quickly scooted out of reach. She hissed that she was not a damn chicken, and if I got that thing near her, she'd tear it to pieces.

"Calm down," I said, laying down the net and raising my hands. "I come unarmed, I come in peace."

She shot back that I had clearly come to entrap her. She wanted a tomcat, and she wanted him *now*. That last word transformed into a god-awful yowl of carnal desire that echoed off the rocks and was likely audible nearly to Paris. I could sense feline ears of multiple species and sizes pricking up for miles around. The only way to keep her safe was to leave her alone; if I advanced, she'd be gone. After listening to a few minutes of her sluttish vocalizing, I'd had enough, so I gathered eggs and apples, then went back inside to cook.

After we'd eaten, Sophie went upstairs in search of a hot-water bottle, and I trooped outside again to keep track of what was happening. I

half expected to find a bobcat up the tree with Cass, but I was *not* prepared for what I actually saw. Cass lay on a wide branch, her haunches
raised and her tail laid coquettishly off to the side. Behind her, madly
flapping his wings and evidently doing his best to mount her, was Peau.

What the *fuck*? Interspecies sex, now? Was this connected to the
new warmth I'd noticed between them? Had we sunk into utter moral
depravity?

"Jesus, you two!"

But they ignored me; apparently it wasn't going well. Cass hissed
that he was in the wrong place. He expressed confusion, then adjusted
his position. That apparently did the trick; in a few seconds he seemed
to detonate, emitted a shrieking *awk*, then fell off the branch. He
caught himself in time to glide safely away, which was probably wise
because Cass was so agitated I thought she might whip around and
decapitate him like a praying mantis.

He headed in the general direction of the field where the horses and
mules grazed, so I left Cass looking crazed on the branch and went out
to check on him.

Peau was perched on the rump of Mule One, his head lowered,
quivering.

"You all right, my good lord?"

He emitted a few subdued croaks. He liked her but also kind of
hated her, he said. It was confusing.

"I noticed something's been going on lately," I said. "How does she
feel about you?"

More or less the same, he said, except she also wrestled with im-
pulses to kill and eat him.

"That's a lot more common than you'd think," I said.

He let out a rueful *awk*, then gazed skyward. He hadn't quite understood the configuration, he confessed; in birds, there was simply the
one vent. I pointed out that he'd gotten it there at the end, though,

right? He said he wasn't completely sure *where*; he might have polli-
nated the tree for all he knew.

It was warm with a cool mountain breeze. The horses and the
mules grazed and snorted, plumping up on all the good forage. I really
did wish we could stay here.

Peau asked if I found it difficult, being male. He'd never asked me
about something this personal; it was new territory, more than an exchange of information and inclined toward real conversation.

"Sure," I answered, hesitantly. "Men are expected to be tough and
stoic one second, then tender and sensitive the next, and it's not always
easy to switch gears. Other men are always jockeying to be the alpha,
like the guys in Princely, which is stupid and humiliating. And of course
you're always being sent off to slaughter each other in senseless wars."

He bobbed his head in comprehension.

"Women suffer just as much, but in different ways," I went on.
"Most of the time, nobody's really happy, men *or* women. Then, eventually, everybody gets sick and dies anyway."

He observed then that Sophie and I seemed to get along. He wondered how it worked with humans, whether she and I would become
mates now.

I smiled. "No, no," I said. "Things are complicated with people, all
kinds of unspoken rules and understandings. They get broken, of
course, but generally they hold."

He asked for examples.

"Well, there's a big age difference between Sophie and me," I explained. "So the relationship is more like father to daughter. I feed her
and protect her and try to answer her questions; in return, she does her
best to make me feel like an idiot."

He clacked and said raven chicks were like that too—they got
mouthy. I told him it was a sign of intelligence; insects and aardvarks
and smelt didn't have that problem.

He asked if I loved her, though; that's what he was really trying to understand.

"Ah," I said, surprised and a little touched by this. I considered how to put it. "I haven't really known her long enough to say that, but it does feel something like love. When you've helped each other survive terrible things along the way, it tends to have that effect."

He said he thought he understood that, and I could tell he did.

THE GOOD NEWS, we realized soon enough, was that against all odds, Peau had managed to trigger Cassie's ovulation, and (a) she soon came out of heat, and (b) she wouldn't be unloading a litter of kittens on us. So: Well done, bird.

I knew we should get moving soon, but Sophie wanted to stick around until her period was over, and she didn't get much resistance from me. When you've finally found what appears to be the last comfortable place on the continent, complete with a kitchen and toilets and a full freezer, a library, and an astonishing collection of films, it's a little hard to contemplate putting the mules back in their traces, climbing into the rusted-out pickup, and hitting the sweltering road.

But each week was a little hotter than the last, and I knew we shouldn't tarry. I could breathe through my battered nose more easily, and my finger was slowly healing. So after two more days of eating like hogs, lounging in the pool, and binge-watching movies—including a few shared faves like Past Lives and Seven Samurai—I discussed the situation with Sophie and she agreed.

"Also, there's something I didn't tell you," she admitted, averting her eyes in a way that screamed adolescent guilt.

"What's that?"

"You know the morning you told me not to use the computer? Well, the night before I went online. I couldn't sleep and wondered what was going on in the world."

This sent me reeling. "Sophie, you should have told me."

"I know, but I figured you'd make us leave right then, and I couldn't stand the thought. It's so sweet here."

"It won't be sweet for long if Buck Flynn shows up with another posse of goons."

She shrugged, as if the matter was out of her hands. "Anyway, now you know."

"I worry that you're getting a false sense of security," I said.

She laughed. "Is there any other kind?"

It was too late to get mad about it anyway. If Flynn, or whoever he worked for, had been monitoring the web that night at 2:00 a.m., they would likely have been here by now.

"How did you search, anyway?" I asked. "Google's kaput."

"Some kind of half-assed engine called Snail," she said. "It's about as fast as the name suggests and looks like it was created by ten-year-olds, but eventually it sort of works."

"So what *is* going on in the world?"

"There's basically nothing out there," she answered. "There are a few things from Brazil and Argentina and Australia, but about the only place left with any real presence on the web is New Zealand, where the news is shockingly normal. They still have grocery stores and real estate and horse racing. It's bizarre, like traveling back in time."

"Well, there's probably no way to get there, and we can't stay here."

"I'll sure remember it here, though," she said wistfully. "I guess we'll always have Paris."

PEAU ORGANIZED A FINAL SURVEILLANCE FLIGHT with several of his friends. They covered most of the country in a radius of thirty miles and saw nothing suggesting the presence of Buck Flynn, alone or with the assistance of additional thuggery. A handful of dusty wagon traders plied the roads, and the birds saw another tiger, dragging a dead deer by the throat, in a dry alpine forest a few miles away. There was also a herd of two or three hundred bison in a grassy valley to the northwest, but that was it. From what they could tell, the land was empty and the coast clear.

We decided to give up sleeping space to load the truck with some of the things we wanted from the house. We filled one box with books and another with miscellaneous supplies, including a couple of bath towels (I'd been down to using rags), soap and shampoo, a dozen rolls of toilet paper, and two of those old Costco packs of toothbrushes. Sophie took a case of tampons—twelve dozen boxes, which would last a while, and if nothing else could be sold to women along the way for roughly their weight in gold. We stowed four five-gallon buckets of water under the hood for the desert crossing, crammed in sacks of dog food and cat kibble, and put cartons of bagged rice and freeze-dried dinners along with the other stuff in the truck bed. We packed a dozen bottles of wine for ourselves or for trading. The truck was heavy, now, but we had sixteen hooves on the ground instead of eight.

The animals were looking good. The dogs had lost their big-ribbed, starving appearance, and the horses and mules had built muscle and fat during ten days of grazing and rest. It was hard to believe we'd been there that long; in one way it seemed we'd just arrived, and in another it felt like months.

We decided we should do something with the family's bones; it seemed vaguely disrespectful to leave them piled on sheets in the spare room. I also suspected that Sophie was thinking we might want to navigate our way back here someday (I know I was), and we'd rather not find them still in the house if we returned.

At first I thought we'd find a pretty spot to bury them, but the shovel I found in the garage had a cracked blade, and when I stepped on it and tried to push it into the rocky ground, it snapped off. We finally decided on a modest version of a sky burial. We dragged out the plastic-lattice recliners stowed in the rec room, then unfolded them and set them up by the pool, facing the western mountain range. We put one person on each recliner, Michael and Catherine side-by-side, the boy next to her.

Peau flew in, observing quietly.

I tried to think of something fitting to say. "Thanks for the hospitality, for preserving all the wonderful books," I said. "And for thinking to have chickens and so much food stored."

"And for the pool," Sophie added. "I feel safer knowing how to swim." She said it had meant a lot to her, too, seeing how the world used to be. "I wish I'd been born earlier, so I could have met you and shared a meal."

I touched her shoulder, and she smiled.

"The rings," she said then, pointing to the wedding bands that dangled from Michael and Catherine's fingerbones. "They're gold. What should we do with them?"

"Let's leave them," I said. "We owe them enough of a debt as it is."

Peau said his friends would have those rings off their fingers three minutes after we left. I told him they could have them; they'd done us a lot of favors. It did give me pause, thinking that if we *did* return someday, the skeletons might still be there. But we wouldn't be back anytime soon, and within a year or two they'd likely have been scattered by animals anyway. This was what a sky burial was supposed to be about, after all, and it seemed a more pleasant fate to me than being stuck in the ground. I hoped they'd agree.

It was late afternoon by now, so we decided to have a final swim, eat some dinner, polish off another quart of ice cream, then get on the road before dark. It was a full moon tonight; we'd find our way well enough. With our four-horsepower rig, I figured we could put in a good sixty miles before dawn, so that if Flynn did happen to be lurking about, he wouldn't realize we'd slipped the snare until it was too late.

10

The sun had set and the stars were out. Venus hung like a calm beacon in the west, and we were all stuffed with food. I locked the house's front door and stowed the key under a rock across the driveway, where I'd be able to find it if I ever came back. The horses and mules pulled us smoothly up the drive and through the gate, which, for good measure, I'd reprogrammed with a code I'd remember. The gate closed automatically after us.

Cass and Peau were resting in back, and Sophie sat up front with me, quietly sniffling.

"Hard to go, hmm?" I asked.

"That's maybe the happiest I've been in my whole life."

"Though you nearly died, of course."

"Not counting that."

"You'll be happy again," I said. "Maybe we'll go to New Zealand, and you can watch horse racing."

"Long swim for the mules, don't you think?"

"Don't underestimate them."

We traveled with the windows down, so we could hear anything approaching that we might not like. Occasionally I got out the night goggles and scanned the terrain around us, but it appeared to be safe. Mostly we heard crickets and the occasional whoop of a nighthawk, banking through a turn. Around midnight the dogs were lagging, so we moved Cass into the cab with us and put them in the back.

Sophie dozed off, and after another hour we came to a crossroads. I consulted my map and was able to guide us on a series of old state roads that led, before dawn, to a switchback slope down to the Colorado River. As best I could reckon, we were roughly twenty miles south of where Hoover Dam used to be. There was an old steel bridge across, then a road to the town of Opal. Once the sun rose, we had a good view from the top of the grade, and shade under a grove of piñon pine, so I thought it best to give the animals a rest. The dogs scarfed down some food, drank a half gallon of water each, and passed out under the trees. I fed the horses and mules, hobbled them, and let them out of harness so they could graze and sleep as they wished. Cass got kibble, Peau flew off to find pine nuts and whatever else he liked, and Sophie and I ate cereal and apples, with dried milk reconstituted with water. We'd crammed so much stuff into the truck bed that there wasn't room for both of us to sleep there anymore, so I gave it to her and found a spot under a tree.

I was too wired to drop off, though. I'd planned the best route I could to get us to the railway line, and that way we'd pass safely south of Death Valley. But "safely" is a relative term when you're talking about the Mojave in May. Not as bad as July, but routinely 140° at midday, an awfully easy way to die. Part of the problem was that it was nearly three hundred miles from the Sheep Mountain Pass to San Luis Obispo, where Lars and his colleagues had decamped after La Jolla largely went underwater. Until we got to the long tunnel between the Central Valley and the coast, it would all be shadeless and brutal, and God knew what we'd find in Bakersfield.

I figured the journey would take us three or four days. I had no idea if we'd be able to find shelter during daylight hours, and if we couldn't, we'd be cooked to desiccated jerky by the end of the second day. Such were my reassuring ruminations as I finally succumbed to the last cool mountain breeze I'd feel for a long time and dozed off.

SOPHIE NUDGED ME AWAKE in late afternoon. Our mountainside was facing the sun now. I struggled into muzzy wakefulness, feeling old and slow in the afternoon heat. I collected the horses and mules and got them into harness, then Sophie and I ate a quick lunch of canned tuna and bread.

Peau flew in. *People at the bridge*, he said. He added that they looked kind of mean, and they made you pay to cross over.

"Okay," I said, and we were off.

We reached the bridge a couple of hours before sundown. There were armed guards and a lift-gate at our end, shirts of raggedy old camo, AR-15s, the shit you'd expect from an ARM unit. It was one way to raise money if you were desperate enough, and who wasn't? This was a busy trade route, after all; a horse-drawn wagon or a hybrid rig like ours might cross over here three or four times a day, on the run between the California valleys and the deserts and mountains to the east. That would have been before California closed its borders, though, so who knew what the story was now? At the moment, there wasn't anybody but us waiting to cross in either direction.

I halted the mules, and a bristly-looking fellow in his mid-twenties peered into the cab. His hair was all crazy, and he had a wide-eyed, hyped look, as if he'd been smoking something heavy, the sort of look that would have been illustrated in the old animations by multicolored turning spirals. Another guy came to the passenger side and eyeballed Sophie, a little too approvingly for my taste.

"Gentlemen," I said, watchful now. These guys definitely weren't gentlemen, but it never hurt to suggest the idea.

"Trade to cross," said the guy on my side, whose camo shirt bore a red plastic name tag that read "Louise." I briefly wondered what had happened to her.

"What's it worth?" I asked.

"What you got?"

"Potatoes," I said. "Apples."

Louise and the other guy laughed.

"Tampons," I said, and they laughed harder. I shrugged, did my best to summon an easy smile, as if we were all in on the joke. "Okay, suppose you start."

"Let's start with the whore," said the guy on Sophie's side. He turned aside to spit, and Sophie reached smoothly into her pocket.

"Long bridge, lots of guns," I muttered. "Let's not escalate."

Her grip relaxed on whatever she had in there, presumably the shiv. But I could see she was scared.

"Listen, guys," I said. "She's my daughter. Maybe you have daughters of your own, or at least sisters or girlfriends. If so, I hope you'll understand that she's not really up for trade here."

They looked a little disappointed if not quite ashamed.

"We'd sure like to get across without any fuss," I went on, sounding like some folksy TV pitchman from the old days, selling waffle mix or bunion cream. The men eyed each other for a second, and there was a dead-eyed, half-lidded sadism in that look that filled me with dread.

"Maybe you're interested in armaments?" I suggested. Mercifully, this brightened them up.

In the end we traded them one of our AR-15s for a dozen cartridges to fit our other AR and safe passage. I was a little disappointed to learn that they actually had bullets but glad to leave them with a few less. We were kind of shockingly well-armed now, it occurred to me: the AR and the .22, each with a supply of ammunition.

They lifted the gate and waved a tattered flag so the guys on the other end of the bridge knew to let us through.

The bridge turned out to be devastatingly beautiful, the kind of elegant span that would have made an engineer proud when there were still engineers. All of it in deep-green steel, though the paint was flaking off and there was a little too much rust showing for my optimal comfort, given that the thing probably hadn't been inspected in decades and we were suspended a couple hundred feet above the river. But it was long and straight and supported by a huge arch that came up above the roadbed midway, with footings down below on each side of the canyon. The river churled beneath us as the faint susurration of rapids drifted up. The vast azure sky was patched with wooly white clouds. It had always seemed far-fetched to me that clouds were made of water, but there they were: the blank thought bubbles of the parched desert canyonlands.

Midway across the span, the manes of the mules and horses suddenly shot straight out to the left on the downriver jet stream, and the F-150 shuddered. Sophie's hair blew all around and she laughed.

"That's some fine air," she said. "*Dad.*"

"Hope you didn't mind."

"Not overly."

"I was wondering what you got ahold of in your pocket."

"Something from Catherine's dresser," she said. She pulled out a tidy little Glock.

I whistled. "Duly noted."

The wind began to rock the bridge, and soon we were riding the deck of a foundering ship. The thing kept swaying, the steel groaned and cracked, and the gale shrieked like tormented souls as it sandblasted its way between girders and cross-braces. My palms started sweating, I snapped the reins, and our sixteen-hooved engine revved and broke into a trot.

We made it across fairly quickly, then, and were met by the snide bully grins of the guards on the other side. I did my best to sound calm and confident, neither of which I felt.

"Every afternoon like this?" I asked.

"Pretty much," one replied, as if we were idiots.

I wasn't sorry to leave them in the rearview. The horses and mules hauled us up the grade, straining and panting. We reached the top as the sun was setting, so I halted them to take in the view and get our bearings. The sky turned from pink to purple, and a sweet, cool dampness condensed in the air. Below us, the bridge and the valley darkened, but we could still hear the river. It was hard to consider those deep layers of sedimentary striation, and the millions of years they represented, and not be reminded of how ludicrously short our lives were. It was humbling, this remembrance, but it held an uneasy peace too. Knowing that no matter what you did in life, or how well or badly you did it, sooner than you ever imagined, it would be over.

THE MOON WAS STILL NEARLY FULL, and we found our way through the open countryside easily enough in the hard blue light. We followed more state roads, west-northwest, until about 5:00 a.m., when we reached Opal. Here, supposedly, we'd connect with the rail line into California.

Opal was pretty much gone; from what I could tell, only a few burned-out storefronts remained. The rails ran right across Main Street, so we followed them west as the town diminished into a random array of defeated, shambling shanties roamed by skittish stray dogs. We finally came to a railyard where we could discern, in the moonlight, a big diesel locomotive and a few wrecked boxcars, among other detritus.

The California border lay about fifty yards west, so we strolled over there to stretch our legs. It took me a moment to understand what I was seeing. Lars was right in one way; there were no checkpoints, no guards. There was a big painted sign, though, so I aimed my dying flashlight at it:

SOVEREIGN REPUBLIC OF CALIFORNIA
BORDER CLOSED

It wouldn't have been a huge problem except that it was posted on a tubular steel barrier gate that had been erected right across the tracks and welded shut. Heavy-grade steel fencing extended on both sides for a couple hundred yards, and out there things got rocky. You could go around on foot, but not with any sort of vehicle.

"What are you thinking?" Sophie asked, as we walked back to the truck.

I decided to spare her the worst of my worries—namely, that regardless of whether Flynn had somehow read my email to Lars and headed south as a result, we still had big problems ahead. What came to mind was the symbol **M**—representing both "mass," as it would in physics, and also "Mojave." "Mass" was intimately associated with gravitation, of course, but so was "Mojave," in the sense that it would pull you down to the surface of the earth and then, given time, bury what was left of your bones beneath it.

The sun wouldn't rise for another half hour. I built us a fire and started cooking oatmeal, then let the horses and mules out of harness and fed them from the same big burlap sack of oats. The hounds crawled out, evidently well on the way to recovery. They allowed themselves to be petted now; with regular chow and a modicum of kindness they were becoming downright friendly. Cass awoke and emerged, blinking sleepily. She was still spooked by the dogs, so I lifted her up to the hood and fed her there. I didn't know where Peau was, but I figured he'd show up eventually.

After we finished the mush and had some bread, dawn brightened up the sky behind the mountains to the east. Sophie and I wandered around the yard. The first thing I noticed in the sharp slanting light of sunup was that there were fresh hoofprints everywhere. The horses had been here just a day or two before, then had headed off southward.

The second thing I checked out was the big diesel engine standing off at a siding. We climbed up the crew ladder and slid into the cab. It was filthy and smelled of ancient grease, the vinyl seat cracked with fluff coming out. All the instruments and controls were coated in thick, sticky dust, and there was rat shit all over the floor. I briefly mused about the risk of hantavirus, then decided I had enough to worry about.

"Ever drive one of these?" Sophie asked.

There were levers and switches and dials all over the place. "Wish I knew how," I told her. I pushed a big red START button. Nothing happened, of course, so we got out and climbed back down.

One spur rail ran into a capacious maintenance hangar, so we followed it in. Inside hunkered one of those mini-engines that crews would use to go fix track and signals. It was hitched to a small flatcar about fifteen feet long, which had a ramp at the back that would drop down so you could load on a backhoe or a small bulldozer.

Sophie looked at me, and I knew we were both thinking the same thing.

"Go ahead," I said.

She got up in the cab and started pushing buttons. "Nothing," she said.

I noticed a little office in the corner of the building, so I walked over. The door was locked, so I kicked it open.

I found about what you'd expect: a desk, a chair, a filing cabinet, some paperwork, everything under a quarter inch of dust. And a one-by-six plank screwed to the wall, with three things that resembled huge keys hanging on it. It was like a child's idea of what you'd need: giant vehicle, giant key. I took all three of them and walked back to the little engine that probably couldn't, wondering how long diesel fuel was good for. With stabilizers and biocides in it, it might go a couple

of years. Probably nothing here had been used in a dozen, so even if
the bones worked, good luck with the blood.

One of the giant keys fit an opening on the dash, if you could call it a
dash; mainly it was a steel console with a few gauges in front and a
painted Jesus glued on top. There were also two levers, in this case helpfully labeled THROTTLE and BRAKE I was initially surprised at the lack of
a steering wheel, but of course you were on rails, so why would you
need one?

Sophie turned the key and pushed the START button again. Still
nothing.

"Leave it on," I said. This was a much simpler instrument array, easy
enough to decipher.

"Fuel gauge says empty, so let's start with that," I said.

Given the hoofprints, I was a little nervous about spending all this
time on what would likely turn out to be a fool's errand. But since I
still hadn't come up with a viable plan, I figured we might as well try.

Inside the bay there was a fuel pump with a hose and a handle,
presumably leading to a buried tank of diesel. But the pump would be
electric, and there was no electricity. We walked out to the yard,
where all the randomly distributed rusted junk made the place look
like the site of a long-ago plane crash, and where a silver fuel tank
stood elevated on sturdy steel legs. But that was useless too; the fuel
had been baking in the desert sun for years and had probably turned
to goo.

We went back inside. Long wooden shelves lined one wall and held
all kinds of arcane tools, most of which looked heavy enough to stun
an ox, and which I didn't recognize anyway. Sophie walked down the
row, picking things up and putting them back, and then she stopped.

"What about this?" she asked.

It was a little hand pump, the kind where you simply turned a handle as if you were winding fishing line onto a reel. It was massively in-
efficient but better than trying to suck fetid, bacteria-laced old fuel

through a siphon hose. There was a male fitting on one end, and a little further rooting around in the general mess produced a coiled-up hose with a matching female coupler.

Set into the floor near the regular pump was a raised steel cap about six inches in diameter. The people who worked here must have tripped over it fifty times a day until they got its location hardwired into their hippocampus-based gray-matter GPS and started stepping around it. I suspected this because I'd only been in the room ten minutes, and I'd already tripped over the damn thing twice.

I found a length of pipe that fit a couple of raised arches on the cap, then leaned on it, pushing counterclockwise until it finally gave. I unscrewed it and set it aside, then peered down into blackness with my flashlight. I couldn't see anything, but the stink of long-buried diesel slipped upward like the hand of a ghost and slapped me in the face. This was the tank that fed the electric pump.

We fed the hose down this pipe, positioned the hand pump over a five-gallon bucket, and started reeling in the fish. Sure enough, after half a minute, thick gray diesel fuel spurted into the bucket. There was no way to get the bucket low enough to start a natural siphon, so we kept cranking, taking turns when one of us got tired and switching buckets when one was about three-quarters full. The stuff didn't look good, and it smelled more like rotting flesh than diesel, but it was our only chance.

While Sophie pumped, I searched the shelves and finally found what I was looking for among a bunch of old paint cans: a big round paint strainer that would work perfectly well for this too. When we had six five-gallon buckets filled and only one still empty, I stopped her.

"At this rate we'll be out of here well before New Year's," she said rather curtly.

I placed the strainer over the top of the empty bucket and poured the fuel through it. It caught a lot of gunk, so that the stuff in the bucket looked cleaner. I wiped off the strainer and did this twice more, and each time the fuel cleared up a little. Then I went searching again.

I broke the latch off a plywood cabinet and found the motherlode: two cases of fuel stabilizer in plastic quart bottles. Logically it was a little late to use it because the fuel had presumably long since *de*stabilized—but again, what did we have to lose?

So we arrived at a production line. We'd fill six buckets, strain them one at a time, clean the strainer and repeat, add half a quart of stabilizer, then carry them over and pour them into the fuel tank on the little engine. When we stopped for lunch, we noticed that there was a second tank on the other side, and we'd have to fill it too. It looked like each tank held about forty gallons. I briefly did the math: roughly three hundred miles at—well, I had no idea what sort of mileage the engine would get—say, four or five per gallon? Four, to be safe? We'd need seventy-five gallons, in other words, so if we filled both tanks we might barely have enough.

But I was getting ahead of myself. "Before we spend all day on this, let's see if it works," I said.

Sophie turned the giant key and pushed START.

Nothing. "Well, fuck," she said.

But I'd been watching the voltmeter when she pushed the button, and it hadn't budged. "The battery's dead."

More rooting. In yet another cabinet I found a huge, apparently unused lead-acid battery. There were three of them, but one would suffice. I couldn't lift it by myself, so Sophie located a hand truck, and we slid it onto that, then wheeled it over to the little engine.

"We need a name for this vehicle," I said. "It will respond better if it has a name."

"I was thinking that too," she replied. "Maybe Clementine."

"As in 'lost and gone forever'? You sure?"

She shrugged. "Lost from Buck Flynn. Gone forever from this fucking shithole."

"Clementine it is."

We lifted Clementine's skirt, which was steel and hinged on the side, so we could have a look at her equipment. Everything appeared to be there, though I knew basically nothing about diesel-engine anatomy. Together we pulled out the old battery, dropped in the new one, and connected the terminals. Then Sophie climbed up again and pushed START.

There were a couple of sparks, followed by a series of throaty shrieks, like what you might get if you tried to strangle an enraged camel. Then goddamn if Clementine didn't spring to stinky, rumbling, smoke-belching life. We were soon being asphyxiated, so Sophie shut her down.

We finished filling the tanks in late afternoon, exhausted and famished. We'd been awake for twenty-four hours, and it was time for food and a rest.

WE PREPARED AN EARLY DINNER for ourselves—rice, fried onions, some formerly frozen biscuits we'd pilfered from the Paris house and that had to be eaten before they spoiled. We even had butter and honey for them, so they more or less became dessert.

After we'd rested a while, I hitched up the mules and drove the truck out to the California gate. I didn't want to use a ton of acetylene, so I looked for the point of least resistance. The latching mechanism on the side away from the hinges appeared the obvious place to attack.

I attached the torch, turned on the acetylene and the oxygen, put on the goggles, and fell to. It took only about five minutes to cut through the weld. I pushed on the gate; it was heavy, and it took some force to swing it open. Once it reached a certain point, though, gravity took over—apparently the mounting pole wasn't quite plumb—and it swung the rest of the way on its own. It clanged into the steel fence behind it with a sound I hadn't thought about since Santa Fe, when I heard all the chains hitting flagpoles. That had been, what, three weeks ago? It seemed like a lifetime.

Peau had finally returned when I got back to the corporate yard.

"Where have you been? I was worried."

Following Flynn, he said. I guess he had a little Australian magpie in him, because his word for "Flynn" sounded almost exactly like "Flynn," despite his having no lips to make the *F* sound.

Shit, I thought. I asked where he was, and Peau said he'd been *here* a couple of days ago. It seemed I'd managed to confuse him.

"Last I checked he was out of men," I said. "He found more?"

Two more, Peau said.

"Where are they now?"

They'd had a big argument about what to do, Peau said, but Flynn finally decided to bring them back here. They were stopping for the night and would likely arrive tomorrow.

I petted his head. "Thanks, my good lord. Well done." Sophie asked what he'd said, so I filled her in.

"Oh God," she said. "I really need to sleep. You're not going to let me, are you?"

"Not quite yet."

CHIEF JOSEPH OF THE NEZ PERCÉ could have written his own version of *The Art of War*. Talk about using the terrain to your advantage; he'd led his U.S. Army pursuers on an astonishing chase of over a thousand miles, crossing mountain ranges, plunging down canyons, and enduring bitter cold and starvation in an effort to reach safety in Canada. It was one of the most brilliant tactical retreats in the history of warfare, but the end was dispiritingly predictable. He had women and children with him and not much in the way of weapons. Eventually the army cornered them, killed a few, and stuck the rest on a reservation. Joseph himself was shuttled between a series of army bases until he died years later.

I was no Chief Joseph—not in brains or strategic skills or stamina—so it was a sobering tale to recall. In some ways it seemed that big parts of my life had been spent in tactical retreat, though, so this was merely a particularly literal iteration of my usual m.o. If Flynn was losing support and patience, well, good. Maybe, if someone actually was paying him, they'd tired of his failures and started pinching pennies. Anyway, we were only one long sprint from the end of this, and I dared nurse a speck of hope that we might finally outwit the poor diseased lunatic once and for all. We couldn't wait, we couldn't sleep, but our deprivations were nothing compared to those suffered by Joseph and his tribe.

I tried a little inspirational speech along these lines, but Sophie was fourteen and exhausted and didn't respond with quite the level of enthusiasm I'd hoped. She was getting that look in her eye that made me wonder if it was a good idea to let her keep the Glock.

So I brewed coffee. Strong coffee.

The caffeine came banging into our veins after a few minutes. We began to lose our surliness and resurrect ourselves. We started up Clementine and drove her out to the yard. The noise and vibration in the cab rattled my teeth, which of course my poor bitching molar didn't like. We dropped the trailer ramps and drove the mules and horses up onto the flatbed. The trailer had a little metal retaining wall around the edges like a pickup, there were chains for holding down heavy equipment, and there was a plywood box full of shovels and sledges and pickaxes. I ran one of the tie-down chains through the rear axle of the Ford just in case. I took the animals out of harness so they could keep their balance, then tied them all to the front so they wouldn't panic and try to flee, breaking legs and necks in the process. The horses looked wide-eyed and spooked, the mules sour and resigned. Give me mules any day, I thought.

Amazingly, though, it seemed to work. I kept expecting the engine to die any second, but it kept thundering along, belching its awful black smoke and rattling our bones. A toast to you, Herr Diesel, and to whatever anonymous organic chemist invented fuel stabilizer. We rolled out past the gate, then I pulled back the throttle and eased on the brake, and everything came to a shivering stop.

"Are we there yet?" Sophie asked petulantly.

"If you want, you can go sleep in the back of the truck. I'll drive for the next few hours."

"You gave me *coffee*, Will. I weigh, like, a hundred pounds. I won't be able to sleep till midnight."

"Well, we'll keep each other company until neither of us can stay awake, and then we'll stop. Deal?"

"Like I have a choice."

I'd left the acetylene and oxygen tanks by the gate, so I went back, closed the gate, and welded it shut again. Flynn would probably see the weld, but if they didn't have gear, it would take them some time to go around. If they hadn't looked closely before, and didn't notice that this was a new weld, they'd be utterly flummoxed, and I had to admit I was pleased with the prospect. In any case, they'd never catch us on horseback.

I stowed the tanks and the goggles under the truck hood, climbed back into Clementine's cab, and eased the throttle forward. The fuel gauge read full. We shuddered and jolted and then things smoothed out as we got up to speed. The noise was deafening, but the little engine slid forward, westward down the tracks, toward the setting sun. It seemed like the RPMs settled in nicely when we hit about thirty miles an hour, so I figured that would offer the best fuel efficiency, and it was still a lot faster than I'd traveled in years. We'd cross the desert and emerge into the Central Valley by morning. By the time, that is, Buck Flynn wandered back into Opal with his men and realized he'd missed us yet again.

11

Sophie: "I don't care if it rains or freezes, long as I got my plastic Jesus, sittin' on the dashboard of my car!"

Me: "Doin' ninety, it ain't scary, long as I got my Virgin Mary, ridin' on the dashboard of my car!"

And on and on we sang. We didn't actually have a Virgin, and we weren't completely sure about the lyrics, but he had a nice paint job, this blond, blue-eyed, suspiciously Aryan Jesus, and we inhabited that time-bending state of wired exhaustion that people end up in when they've been awake for thirty hours and their bodies aren't used to caffeine. I felt jittery-jangly and on the verge of sudden slumber all at once. I showed Sophie how to run Clementine—it was pretty elementary, easier than driving a car—so she could take over if I conked out—which I did after a couple of hours, in fact, because riding a miniature train engine on straight tracks through a desert in the middle of the night turns out to be even more soporific than riding in a truck behind two mules. When the throttle was set, Clementine pretty much drove herself, and we were merely along for the ride. The noise and vibration were about all that kept us conscious, along with the knowledge that somewhere out there, at the far reaches of the headlight, the rails could have been undercut by flood or quake, and we'd require enough perspicacity to pull the brake before we went hurtling to our deaths in some godforsaken abyss.

One minute my eyes were drooping and the next thing I knew I was slumped sideways on the seat and Sophie was nudging me awake. It was after midnight, and she'd started dropping off too, so I rallied, and we did our best to keep each other talking. Smells of the desert night blew in through the windows—sage and bitterbrush and dry, desiccating heat.

"What kinds of things did you used to write about, when you wrote about science?" she asked.

I replied, groggily, that I didn't know she was interested in science.

"Yeah," she said. "After the Flagstaff high school was abandoned, I'd slip in through the window and bring home textbooks. I'd gotten up to calculus and some basic physics by the time Tim died."

This was startling news. *I* sure wasn't reading stuff like that at fourteen. "Could you talk to any of the other kids about it?"

She shook her head. "No one was really interested. I got along with most of them okay, but I pretty much felt like an alien all the time."

"I know that feeling."

She smiled. "Do you ever feel like you can't figure out how to be a human being?"

"Constantly. I'm completely clueless that way."

"I was hoping it would improve as I got older."

"It might for *you*, but don't bet the ranch."

We rode in silence a while. By moonlight, we could see the desert sliding by outside the open windows of the cab. I kept the headlight on its low setting because generating the juice to power it would require some fuel, and it was going to be down to the wire whether we had enough.

"I never answered your question," I said eventually.

"Which question?"

"My work," I said. We were definitely far gone.

"Oh, right."

"Probably the most interesting thing I ever wrote about was quantum mechanics."

"I read something about that, but I don't think I understood it."

"I understand it in the way of people who aren't good at math," I said. "Which means I don't really understand it at all."

"What is it, even?"

"It's a way of thinking about the universe, but in some ways it's totally crazy," I said. "It's like when you first learn the earth is round—it contradicts everything your senses tell you, but once you look at a globe it's obvious."

As an example, I told her about quantum entanglement. How if two photons are entangled, they can be separated by vast distances—millions of light years, even—but as soon as you measure one of them, it stops existing as a fuzzy potential energy and becomes a tangible thing, and at that moment, the other photon spontaneously exhibits the same properties but in reverse. Measuring one measures both instantaneously, and this had been proven in experiments involving telescopes, lasers, and a lot of math.

"That can't be true," she said.

"See what I mean? It's totally weird. It creates some tension with relativity, which is the other big theory of the universe."

"Why?"

I told her that relativity is based on the view that matter is really a form of energy, that the universe is made of space-time, that mass bends space-time, and that's what creates gravity. But the only way to explain quantum entanglement is if space itself is actually an illusion—that entanglement is the true fabric of the universe rather than space-time.

"So you're saying you can have one kind of universe or the other, but not both?"

"Except we *do* have both," I said. "Gravity exists, obviously, which is why the universe is full of spheres and when we jump off things we tend to fall."

"How did physicists reconcile all this?"

"They never did. It drove them batshit."

As I'd learned when I moved to the dharma center, entanglement happened to fit fairly comfortably with Buddhist cosmology, which posited that all things were interwoven in a great illusory fabric of experience. They called it "interdependent origination," meaning that the observing consciousness and the world observed arose in inseparable union. As it turned out, this was very much a quantum description of the universe as well.

Entanglement also partly explained my uncanny feeling that Eva and I hadn't really been separated by her death. I knew this could as easily have resulted from my inability to accept mortality in general and hers in particular—my own private Idaho of denial and insanity, in other words. Because if I was honest about my fear that I was losing my mind, it wasn't necessarily all about Disease X. It had to do not only with Eva's death but with the astonishing levels of physical destruction to which humankind had been subjected over the previous decade and a half. From a world population of 9 billion to, what, maybe 2 percent of that? That was still a lot of people—180 million, about the planet's population when Jesus was alive. But from what I'd gleaned, almost everyone left lived in the Southern Hemisphere. One of the most unsettling emotional effects of this is that when everyone you know has died, you begin to feel out of place in the world, as if you should be with them, on whatever distant shores they've landed, rather than here. My mind had strayed from physics now, but it didn't matter. If you already felt out of place, death made everything worse.

"Do you ever wonder who your parents were?" I asked Sophie.

"All the time."

"Whoever dropped you off in Flagstaff didn't leave any clues?"

"Nothing. But I have the weirdest feeling that they're actually not dead, even though they must be."

It kept striking me how our minds wandered in the same directions at the same time, as if we were weirdly entangled ourselves.

"I understand that feeling," I said.

"Well, I'll tell you this," she said. "If I find out they abandoned me and they *are* alive, I am going to be *pissed*."

We rumbled along through the night, maintaining the astonishing velocity of thirty miles an hour. By 2:00 a.m. we were two-thirds of the way through the desert, Sophie had curled up on the seat asleep, and I was doing my best to keep myself awake. I was thinking of Eva again, of how things had finally unraveled between us.

After she'd been at the gonpa a little over a year, she became increasingly restless and unhappy. She started skipping the scheduled pujas and would sometimes drive off to spend the day hiking instead. Occasionally, if I had time, I'd join her, but she was missing work shifts, too, and people had started to notice.

We'd been sharing one of the large double rooms in the residence hall for months by then. One afternoon, when I returned from my gardening, I found her sitting at the window as a cup of tea steamed on the little table in front of her. She sat very still, her eyes downcast, and I'd seen this before. I hung up my coat, poured myself a mug of hot water, squeezed in some lemon juice, and sat down in the chair opposite her.

I'd learned, by then, that it was best to be direct. "Tell me," I said.

She briefly brought her hands to her face, hiding her eyes as she composed herself. Then she lowered her hands and fidgeted with her teaspoon. "You know I appreciate this place, right?"

"I think so," I said evenly.

"It's peaceful here, and I like everyone," she went on. "Well, almost everyone."

I smiled.

"And I told you originally that I'd planned to take a year off before I started looking for a job?" she asked.

"Sure."

"I was already a month into that when I came here, and now I've been here fourteen months more," she said. "I think it might be time for me to leave."

I leaned back, doing my best to absorb this. "I wasn't sure you were still thinking about finding a job."

"I'm starting to feel like I'm wasting time," she went on. "I've tried, but I don't really get the meditation thing, and I'm not accomplishing anything in the world, either. I want to use my mind the way I think it should be used."

"I understand that," I said. I also wondered if I'd grow old and die at the gonpa without achieving anything worldly *or* spiritual. "It helps if you can be a little patient with the process," I added, feeling edgy now.

She huffed, exasperated. "I've been patient," she said. "I feel stifled. You're the only thing keeping me here."

I was quiet a moment as this sank in. "And it's not enough, you mean."

"Sometimes I think it is," she said. "Lately I think maybe it isn't."

I sat back, collecting myself. "When I was young, I thought there was a whole world of people out there I'd get to know and love," I said at last. "I don't think it's true anymore. It's important not to take it for granted."

"I don't," she said. She was frustrated now, and so was I. "I just feel like I'm compromising too much."

"That's how people keep relationships together," I said. "They compromise."

"By ignoring all the ways you're unhappy, you mean. You cut both your losses and your hopes."

"I didn't say that." Joan Didion had said something like that, as I recalled, but it didn't seem like the time to point it out. Since we were quoting people, I mentioned the old Rilke saying that in good marriages we're custodians of each other's solitude. She wasn't buying it.

"I can have all the solitude I want by *myself*, Will."

"Well, you certainly have plenty of it," I said. "You're gone half the time. It's not enough?"

"It's not," she said. "I didn't even know this about myself until recently, but I *need* that time. When I'm always around someone I start to feel like I'm being smothered."

"'Someone' meaning me?"

"You and everyone else here, yes."

"You're acting like a tourist," I said. "If you'd approached science the way you've approached meditation, you'd have ended up teaching junior high biology."

This was mean of me, I realized, but I'd meant it and I couldn't suck the words back in.

Eva was trembling now. "I think maybe we need a break," she said.

"Don't put it on me," I answered. "If *you* want a break, say so."

"*I* want a break, then, all right? I need a fucking *break*."

"Great," I said. "Fine. Great and fine. What do you plan to do?"

"What do you *think* I plan to do?" she asked. "I'll go to L.A., which is what I'd always *planned* to do. I'll get a job and find some grants, which is what I'd always *planned* to do. I'll spend a lot of time alone, which is what I'm definitely *planning* to do. Do you ever listen to what I say?"

I was shaking now, too, though as much from anxiety as anger. I loved her and wanted her to stay, but I couldn't say so. If I tried to bend her in that direction, she'd see it as an attempt at manipulation or coercion or maybe even incarceration, and she'd be right.

"You should do what you think is best, of course," I said, hating every word that came out of my mouth.

"As if I need your permission," she answered, and then she started to cry.

Neither of us spoke for a few minutes, which seemed the safest course. I got up and went to the other window. Turkey vultures were lazily spiraling upward in a thermal above the trees. Apparently something had died down there.

Eventually, Eva stopped crying. She took her teacup to the sink and poured out the dregs, then turned around and leaned on the little wooden counter that made up our kitchenette. She crossed her arms over her chest and studied her feet.

"What if I came to L.A.?" I asked. A brief, dark look crossed her face, like the shadow of a passing bird.

"I assumed you'd want to stay here and meditate." She said this quietly and carefully, as if she were figuring out how to dismantle some sort of explosive device.

"Theoretically, I can meditate anywhere."

"But this is your home."

"Actually, I think my home might be with you."

She smiled a little in spite of herself. Our eyes met for an instant, then we both looked away. "Maybe not right now," she said. "I need time."

"How much?"

"A few months? A year? What would you say to a year?"

I considered it. I'd always wanted to do a yearlong retreat. But I was usually too busy, it was a lot to take on, and it had never seemed like quite the right time. It occurred to me that perhaps *this* was the right time.

I told Eva that the gonpa maintained a couple of retreat cabins in isolated spots up the mountain, and that one of them happened to be unoccupied.

"Maybe I'll occupy it," I said. "I wouldn't mind spending a year up there."

"How would we communicate?" she asked.

"I like letters," I said. "But the cabins are in view of the main cell tower overlooking the valley, so we could actually talk on the phone if we felt like it."

"That's not against the rules?"

"Monks in Tibet have phones, so I think I'm allowed one," I said. "We could each have our year, then check in and see how we feel about things. If you hate L.A., you can come back here. If you love L.A., I can come there. Or we could go somewhere else that suits us both."

"What if we don't want to be together anymore?"

"Then we won't have to worry about where to settle, I guess."

She considered this, then finally nodded. "Okay," she said. "Okay, I can live with that."

She walked into my arms, and we held each other. A few days later she packed her car and left.

As the months passed, we talked occasionally on the phone and traded a few letters, but Eva seemed guarded about her life. I was meditating ten or twelve hours a day anyway, so I had plenty to do without feeling that I needed to pry; if there were things she didn't want to tell me, fair enough. Eventually, as we approached the anniversary of our parting, I assumed we'd talk and see where things stood.

Then, a few weeks before we reached that mark, the pandemic hit. I got extremely sick, with a high fever and what felt like pneumonia for two or three weeks. Eventually the fever broke and my lungs began to clear, but about that time, the hospital called and told me that Eva had died.

I didn't take this news stoically or philosophically or in any other manageable way. I was already weak from the illness and stayed in bed for the next week or two, raging, weeping, sleeping twelve hours at a stretch. Eventually, more or less broken by grief, I ran out of energy for any sort of emotion at all except a kind of listless, numb despondence.

After another several days—days lived as a desiccated husk, days I ate little and drank only the minimally necessary water—I began to understand a few things. I understood, not abstractly but viscerally, that sooner or later everyone who lives will be broken by grief. It was inevitable, inescapable, and in that experience I was not alone but in vast, good company. A week or two after that, practical matters began to assert themselves. I was nearly out of food, no one had come to re-supply me, and I had a pretty good idea what this meant. Winter was coming, and no matter how shut down and empty I felt inside, the state I was in was unsustainable. I had to find a way back to feeling and to life. Simply put, I had to get my act together or I'd starve.

I loaded my pack and walked the fire road down the mountain. When I saw the situation at the gonpa, I found a backhoe at a neigh-boring ranch and drove it over. I wrapped bodies in sheets and hauled them from sickbeds, dug seventeen graves six feet deep, and buried all my friends. I noticed that a few people were missing, including Pela and her parents, but I didn't know what had happened to them. I hoped that they had somehow fled to safety, but I had no idea where they would have found it.

I became the gonpa caretaker, then, the custodian of my own soli-tude, for fourteen years.

CLEMENTINE HESITATED AND COUGHED, then did it again. I checked my watch: 2:30 a.m. Fuck, I thought, please not here. Get us to Bakersfield, at least, where we won't die of heatstroke four hours after sunrise.

Another cough, then a kind of tripping hesitation, as if a drunk had lost his footing and begun to tumble down the stairs. Sophie woke up, disoriented, and asked what was going on.

"I don't know yet," I said.

In another minute the engine cut out entirely, and we glided to an agonizing metallic halt. I turned on the overhead light, and Sophie opened a little compartment in the console and dragged out a manual. It was well-thumbed and 327 pages long.

I frantically scanned my memory for a solution. My high school friend Steve, who'd driven an old VW diesel, was always having trouble with the fuel filter. What was true then would have been true fifty times over now, given the filthy crap we'd put in Clementine's tanks.

Sophie found the section about the filter, but we didn't have a spare. We did find a couple of crescent wrenches, though, and the diagram showed where the filter was mounted. "Easily accessible," it noted, "due to the requirement for frequent changes."

No shit. All we needed now was a handy train-parts store.

The light inside the cab was okay for reading, but it didn't illuminate the engine compartment, so I went back to the truck to get my flashlight. It took a little doing getting there, because the flatbed was covered with shit and piss from four confined equines and a couple of overfed dogs. Cass woke up with a start when I opened the truck door, and Peau was in there with her, nestled up. I explained the situation and got the light. Unfortunately, the truck wheels hadn't been turning, so the recharger wasn't working. The flashlight was dead.

I trudged back to Clementine's cab.

"I won't be able to see anything until sunup," I said. "We might as well get some sleep."

"How far have we come, do you think?"

"A hundred and fifty miles, roughly, maybe a little more. Flynn will be three or four days back, even if he starts at dawn, and then he still has a hellish furnace to cross on horseback."

"Can he even do it?"

"I don't see how, unless he found jerricans for water and parasols too."

• • •

WE AWOKE LATER to a stifling, cloudless dawn. When I'd been young, Colorado sometimes felt this hot a handful of mornings a year, in mid-August. But even then, it usually cooled down in the afternoon, when warm air flowed up the mountains, clouds formed, and the temperature in the valley dropped just before a rain. Recalling this, I realized it wasn't only the beautiful things I missed about the world. I missed some things I'd hated too—winter, traffic jams, deadlines, crowded supermarkets, online everything. A lost universe of hassle and pleasure. Did I actually want those things back, though? No, except maybe the supermarkets. Life was certainly quieter now, but it's hard to make the case that it's better when you're worried about survival all the time.

Sophie tore off some sagebrush branches, built a fire, and started fixing breakfast. Oatmeal and fried onions and the last of the eggs we'd purloined from Michael and Catherine's coop. I told her we'd better conserve the coffee in case of another long night.

I lifted Clementine's steel skirt again and poked around until I found the filter. It was a cylinder about six inches in diameter and ten inches long, and it came off easily with the larger wrench, which fit a nut-shaped casting on the end. I found a screwdriver, opened it up, and slid the element out of the casing.

The good news was that the problem was clear. That was also the bad news.

The filter element was choked with tar and water and some sort of foul, yellowish slime that smelled like dead skunk. It had done its job by collecting all this, but now that it was full, the stuff had been making its way to the engine.

I got a couple of rags and a wire brush from the toolbox on the trailer. After I'd gotten everything cleaned up as best I could, I reassembled it all, but I knew I'd be doing this every few hours from here on out, sun or moon.

Sophie had breakfast ready by the time I finished. It was seven thirty, the sun had been up for about an hour, and according to the thermometer inside Clementine's cab, it was already 97°. My watch had it a degree higher, but close enough; a normally lethal day for the Mojave in early May, in other words.

"It's good, Sophie, thanks," I said. I reflected that twenty or thirty years previously, this would have been a much less treacherous trip. In those days, desert temperatures got up to only about 115° this time of year, instead of the 140° they hit now.

When I was finished eating, I dragged one of the five-gallon buckets of water out from under the truck hood and poured some into bowls for Cass and the dogs, then let the horses and mules have what was left. Fifteen minutes later it was empty. We'd already used one bucketful getting here, so that left us two.

Clementine started right up, mercifully, and we were off. I figured we were about sixty miles from Bakersfield, where it might only top out at around 125° today.

By eight thirty it was 106°. We were drinking constantly and sweating it all out—in fact, I realized I hadn't peed since the day before, and I didn't think Sophie had either. The horses and mules looked miserable back there on their steel platform, and it occurred to me that they might actually perish before the day was over.

As we might too, for that matter. The sharp, dazzling light bounced all around on the salty earth surrounding us, sunlight so heavy it seemed to put enough pressure on my chest to crack ribs. Pale, shiny earth stretched to infinite horizons of dust in all directions. The stunted, desiccated sagebrush took on a shimmering purple aura, like the beginning of a migraine, and became nauseating to look at, especially since we were in motion. In the distance off to our right, a dust devil maybe three hundred feet high spun its coiled path across the flatlands, kicking up salt and sand, slipping along in no apparent hurry until, after a few minutes, it spun itself out into nothingness and all that salt began drifting back down to earth, a transient body of motion and air.

Clementine rumbled bravely on. By ten o'clock it was 118° and Sophie lay curled on the seat, barely able to move. I poured water over her, and it evaporated within minutes. I noticed with some alarm, then, that I was beginning to hallucinate. The usual stuff: water mirages beckoning from the horizon; dancing ghostly forms that might have been uprooted palm trees blown by the wind; what looked like heat lightning in the distance and may actually have been, for all I knew.

We came up over a low mountain range—the Tehachapis, I thought—maybe four thousand feet in elevation, and the heat became less murderous. Clementine slowed down to about eighteen miles an hour as the rails took us up through a series of long switchback valleys, and the temperature dropped to a moderate 105°. It required a couple of hours to cross over, then the engine picked back up to thirty as we started down the grade on the western side. Here, I noticed, the ground began to change from salt and sagebrush to something more like soil, and I saw tough, rangy weeds and wildflowers. We had left the Mojave behind and made the transition into the Central Valley.

By eleven thirty it was only 110°, but even so I hallucinated a low blue line of buildings in the distance. As we trundled on, though, the buildings didn't go away. I checked my watch and did the numbers as best I could, with salty sweat dripping into my eyes, and realized the buildings were probably Bakersfield, or whatever was left of it now. As we drew nearer, Sophie stirred.

"Where are we?" she asked, bleary-eyed.

"About ready for a rest stop," I said. "Another half hour and we'll find some shade and soak ourselves."

"Okay," she said. "Wake me." And then she was out again.

• • •

CLEMENTINE WAS STARTING TO SPUTTER and buck again by the time we reached the Bakersfield railyard. There was a shady spot near the western end under some trees, so I braked the little engine and shut her down. It took twenty minutes or so to take apart the fuel filter and clean it out again. When I was done, I saw seven or eight skinny kids watching me from the bushes that bordered the yard. They were deeply tanned, wide-eyed, long-haired, and feral looking.

"Hey," I said, and they came toward me. I figured we could offer them food, get some information about the local situation. Then I noticed they were carrying knives. They moved swiftly, and in a few seconds they had me surrounded. I did my best to stay calm.

"You guys are hungry, I'll bet," I said. "We have food."

The biggest kid, who looked about Sophie's age, shoved his knife a little closer to me than I liked. "Give us all the food," he said.

"I can't do that. We can give you enough for a few days, though." This was probably untrue, I realized, because there were so many of them. It didn't matter.

"*All of it!*" snarled the kid. He jabbed at me with the knife as I dodged aside.

"Look—" I said, but he wasn't interested in conversation. There was a brief, scary Texas two-step as he lunged and I evaded him a couple of times. Then a rifle shot rang out. The kid dropped the knife and started dancing around, yelling and squeezing his suddenly bloody hand. Part of a finger lay at my feet. The other kids scattered. I looked back and saw Sophie standing on the platform beside the engine's cab, holding the .22.

"You shot off half his finger, Sophie! What the hell?"

"We've got to go," she said. "They'll be back, and there will be more."

"Let me help him stop the blood, at least."

"Will—" she said.

But the kid was screaming, now, and he lunged for his knife. I stepped on it, and he responded by slugging me in the balls. I doubled over. His finger was spraying blood everywhere and he kept trying to grab the knife, and I knew there was a medical term for this, the kind of crazed fighting instinct that sometimes takes over after a serious wound. There was nothing else to do, so I just planted my feet and coldcocked the kid. He sprawled out on the hot tracks, unconscious, so I dragged him into Clementine's shadow and called for Sophie to bring me a rag.

She did, but she wasn't happy. "I've seen this shit before," she said. "We've got to get out of here *now*."

"Two minutes," I said. I got the kid's finger wrapped up tight and hoped that when he came to, he'd have sense enough not to pull off the bandage. The blood was already soaking through when we left him, but I assumed Sophie knew what she was talking about, so we got back into Clementine and started her up. I heard whistles in the bushes all along the tracks as I pushed forward on the throttle and the engine shuddered to life.

As we headed out, dozens of kids, ranging in age from roughly eight to fifteen, started sprinting along beside us, trying to pull themselves up onto the cab and the trailer. A couple of them made it onto the flatbed, but the dogs came out snarling and chased them off. By the time we hit twenty-five miles an hour, we had left them behind, but it was terrifying to see them all standing there on the track, carrying knives and clubs and machetes.

"What the *hell*?" I said, as we hit thirty and I started to calm down a little.

"Let's just get through town as fast as we can," Sophie said.

I checked the fuel gauge; we had about a quarter of a tank left. I pushed Clementine up to thirty-five.

We saw them on the overpasses, on side streets, running down ramps to gape at us. They were everywhere. There wasn't an adult in sight. As we headed toward an overpass on the western edge of town, one kid hoisted a brick over his head and heaved it at us. It bounced once on Clementine's steel hood, then jumped up and smashed into the windshield right in front of Sophie's face, spiderwebbing a big crack. She let out a yelp, her hands flying up to shield her, but then we were under the bridge and away, and Bakersfield receded behind us as we headed out into the valley.

Sophie sat there, her face pale and her arms wrapped around her middle, looking scared and furious all at once. "You're welcome, by the way," she said. *"Dad."*

"Don't call me that," I said. "You might have shot *me*, you know. You might have killed the kid, for that matter. Thank God you didn't use the AR."

"I used the .22 on purpose, and I hit exactly what I was trying to hit," she replied. "If I'd used the AR it would have blown his hand off, and he would have bled to death right in front of you."

"That doesn't change the fact—"

"I told you I can shoot, Will," she interrupted, glaring at me. "I sat by while your nose got broken, but you can't ask me to watch you get stabbed. I'm pretty sure I saved your life, so maybe you could swallow your pride for a second and thank me."

I sighed. She was right about the pride. "Thanks, Sophie."

She made a little *pfff* sound through her lips, the way the French do when they want to indicate that something is so obvious it's not even worth a word.

I thought of *Seven Samurai*, which we'd watched at the Paris house. How the village of peaceful farmers would have been wiped out by bandits if they hadn't hired the warriors to defend them, and how the town could go back to being peaceful again only after the samurai had finished their job. And I remembered the Shaolin monks, who'd been in pretty much the same boat and finally decided to train themselves instead of hiring someone else. *Fucking samsara*, I thought. But I was still upset, and I could tell Sophie was too, so another few minutes went by before I said anything.

"Look, you can call me Dad," I said at last.

"Forget it," she snapped. "I don't want to."

WE PRESSED ON WESTWARD, but we were both in a black mood, and neither of us spoke for a long time. After an hour or so we saw a huge dust cloud covering the valley in front of us, so I eased back on the throttle. Drawing closer, rumbling along at twenty miles an hour, we could make out a vast river of bison, migrating north with the hot weather. By the time I got us stopped we'd sailed right into the middle of the herd, nudging a bunch of them aside.

Sophie sat wide-eyed on the seat. There were thousands of them, and we'd become an island in the middle of the flow. The herd disappeared into distant dust on both the right and left of us, so we were going to be sitting here a while.

One way to make peace, I figured, was to segue into some semblance of normal conversation. "This is like it used to be in the 1800s, before the whites came and wiped them all out," I said. "They're *big*, huh?"

Sophie nodded and made a noncommittal noise. I gathered this was going to take some time.

It was still 110° and we were both hungry, so I got out of the cab and walked the gangway back to the flatbed. The horses and mules were miserable in the heat, their legs splayed and their heads down, and the dogs huddled abjectly in the shade under the truck. I pulled the third five-gallon bucket of water out from under the truck hood and poured half of it into a smaller bucket to take back to the cab. I watered the equines and the dogs with the rest, which left us five gallons with about 120 miles to go. Before making my way back I checked in on Cass and Peau.

"You two want to come hang out with us?"

Cass roused herself, said it couldn't be any worse than it was in the truck. I grabbed some food and kibble from the back, picked her up, and went to join Sophie for lunch. Peau flew off to see if he could find something to eat. The river of bison went on and on, headed north like the pigeons and nearly everything else. The beasts were moving fast enough that occasionally one collided with Clementine, who, despite weighing four tons, shuddered with the impacts.

After a few minutes, Peau flew in at the window. There was nothing around here for him, he said; it was mostly brush and grass. Sophie gave him part of her sandwich, and he thanked her.

"No worries," she said. "At least someone around here has manners."

We glanced at each other, then she blushed. "Whoa," she said. "I understood that."

WE WERE BUFFALO-STRANDED for the next two hours, so Sophie took advantage of the time to expand her vocabulary. She learned the terms for "hungry," "dangerous," "windy," "carve air" (my loose translation of a term similar to that once used by human snowboarders, which in this case described the wild aerobatics ravens would execute when playing), "calm" (weather), "calm" (temperament, a different word), "angry," and a few others, including "I'll fly over and see you there" (in Raven, a contracted construct of a couple of syllables, since they say it to each other all the time). Then they practiced.

"How's the weather?" she asked, and he said, *Calm.*

"How are you feeling?"

Angry and hungry, said Peau.

She offered him more of her sandwich, but he shook his head; he was fine, he'd just been giving her practice.

"I didn't get any of that," Sophie replied, so I translated, and they went over it again until she had it. Not surprisingly, she was a quick study.

Finally, as the afternoon wore on, both of us drinking water like crazy to stay hydrated, the bison herd began to thin out. As I watched the last of the stragglers, I saw something emerge from the blowing dust like dark wraiths in a dream: six or seven big, mangy wolves. They set upon one of the bison, dragged it down, and got ahold of its throat. Immediately there were more wolves, an army of them, chasing these last, weaker animals. Our horses and mules were sitting ducks, tied up on the trailer, so I started Clementine and hit the throttle. We lurched forward just as two wolves jumped onto the platform. Fortunately, the equines had their back legs free, and they sent the wolves flying with swift kicks. Even so, a small pack of ten or fifteen wolves began chasing us, seeing the possibilities in these non-horned, captive creatures. Our big, healthy hounds emerged from beneath the truck, faced down their voracious cousins when they jumped aboard, then chased them off. I goosed Clementine as fast as she'd go. Fortunately, after a few minutes of pursuing us at thirty-five, the wolves broke off the chase. They gazed longingly after us as I watched them recede in the rearview, their expressions almost innocent, as if they'd simply wanted to share a little nosh and conversation. They would have made excellent salesmen, or sociopaths. And that was the thing with animals, as David had pointed out. You couldn't really hold them to our standards, because they were just doing what they *do*.

We headed up the slope into the foothills as the afternoon rolled on, and I began to notice how many wildflowers were growing here. Poppies, lupine, and mustard, as well as dozens of others I didn't recognize, in a bountiful riot of colors. They'd taken over the abandoned farm fields and spread everywhere else too. No more herbicides or pesticides, and boom—they knew what to do. I remembered reading John Muir's journal of his long walk from Oakland across the Central Valley and into the Sierra. He'd described the valley as full of wildflowers, but it was hard to believe forty years ago, when I was young, because then it was all farms and feedlots and dust. Now, here it was again, a resurrected landscape Muir would have recognized and enjoyed.

Clementine rumbled slowly up the grade until the tall tunnel entrance loomed into view a quarter mile ahead. As we approached, I eased off the throttle and applied the brake. The tunnel had been built by the Works Progress Administration in the previous century, and the sculpted concrete facing boasted those old art deco sensibilities. Concrete had been cast to look like sunrays emanating out from the tunnel's dark mouth, and at the apex of the arch was a scorpion. It was perhaps four feet tall from venomous tail spike to pincers and had been rendered in exquisite detail, especially given the crudity of the medium, appearing more chiseled than cast.

Cass peered ahead. It was completely dark in there, she said. There could be bears or tigers or anything.

"What?" Sophie asked. "I'm starting to get Peau, but I still don't understand Cassie."

I translated. I noticed she was still a bit cool with me, but it wasn't carrying over to the animals. A good thing, I supposed.

"We're basically riding in a tank," Sophie said then. "You don't have to worry, Cass."

Peau asked how long the tunnel was. I checked my map. "Forty miles, give or take," I said. "There's a section where it comes out into a valley for a couple of miles before it goes back under. But it's going to take an hour and a half, probably, and almost all of it will be in the dark."

Peau said he wasn't doing it. It was a bit too something—he didn't know the word.

I suggested "afraid of the dark," but that wasn't it. "Claustrophobic? Like, scared of a confined space?"

He bobbed his head, and I realized that of course a bird who built open nests, who enjoyed the perfect freedom of the skies, wouldn't like a long, dark tunnel. He said he'd fly over and see us there.

"I got that!" said Sophie.

Peau took off. I let out the air brake and pushed forward on the throttle, then we lurched forward into darkness. Clementine's light had begun to fail and provided almost no illumination, so it was like entering an infinity of blackness or dark, heavy fog.

The bigger problem was that the engine exhaust was confined in the tunnel with us, and soon we were coughing and gagging. We reached to close the windows, but both hand cranks were broken off. Sophie and I put wet rags over our noses and mouths. It was awful, like being suffocated in a grave, and I envied Peau his escape.

"How could they build it like this?" Sophie asked.

"There are probably vent shafts overhead," I said. "But the fans would have been electric, so . . ."

I goosed the throttle and took us up to forty-five, which appeared to be Clementine's absolute top speed. She rattled violently and seemed on the verge of shaking us all to pieces, but we left more of the exhaust behind us that way, and we'd be through the tunnel faster.

And it was cooler, anyway, a great relief. Ten minutes inside the mountain, the temperature was down to 80°, and it stayed steady there. It was a surreal experience, though, hurtling forward into darkness like that, with no moon or landscape to provide a sense of space as the shiny rails unspooled themselves beneath us. As the time passed, I began to feel a little mesmerized, though this might have been the lack of oxygen.

After about twenty minutes, the headlight finally died, and we had no idea if we were about to hit something or go off the rails into a sinkhole. To be able to breathe, though, I had to keep our speed at forty-five, so we kept plunging onward. With no visual cues, I lost the sense of motion; the engine rattled and banged, and wind tousled our hair, but other than that we might as well have been standing still or flying through space. I could still see a little inside the cab, though, thanks to the glow from the instrument panel. Cass, oblivious, curled up and went to sleep, but Sophie sat petrified, her hands in her lap and her back rigid as her eyes gazed ahead into perfect blackness.

12

W hen we finally emerged from the first section of tunnel into the sunlight of a valley in the middle of the coast range, I felt I'd been resurrected. The light in the trees was dazzling, the sky stunningly bright. Sophie and I took off our damp masks, which had been blackened by diesel smoke, and gulped lungfuls of clean air. The disorienting sensation of stasis gave way to the clear perception that we were indeed moving, had been moving all this time. I saw a low bridge over a little stream ahead, so I brought Clementine to a halt.

We got out to check on the animals. The dogs were still hunkered under the truck, this time apparently from fear and disorientation. When I called them, they came out to be petted and reassured, but they kept their tails between their legs and peered around at the sunlit world uncertainly, as if they weren't sure they should trust it. The smell of the exhaust had been horrible enough for us, so it was hard to imagine how it must have been for them, with their hypersensitive noses. The horses, surprisingly, seemed calm—as did, less surprisingly, the mules. It occurred to me that maybe, for them, the tunnel wasn't so different from having blinders on.

Sophie and I walked the dogs down to the stream, which ran clear and cold under a riparian cover of cottonwoods and oaks. We washed our masks, cooled our feet, threw sticks for the dogs, made small talk about nothing. We seemed to be searching out ways to forgive each other for the earlier fight.

"We're getting close, now," I said. "We should be out of the tunnel within an hour, and from there it's only another few miles to San Luis Obispo."

She watched the water pensively. "You get that I didn't *want* to shoot that kid, right?" she asked at last.

"The whole situation took me by surprise," I said. "I was scared; I didn't mean to yell at you."

She nodded, accepting this. "It's hard to know what to do sometimes," she said.

"I'd say *all* the time. I constantly fuck things up."

She smiled a little, if grudgingly. "Like for example?"

"I was a second-rate writer," I said. "I read a stack of books every year by people who were better at it than I was. I basically failed at romance, and I'm not always that great at meditation either."

"How exactly does one fail at meditation?"

I thought of how to put it in a way that didn't seem too abstract. I explained that in Buddhism there was a concept, "carrying all things on the path," which meant simply that whatever arose, whether helpful or harmful—circumstances, thoughts, emotions, physical sensations—you recognized their inherent purity and emptiness. I knew it could be done because I'd seen both Lama Sonam and David do it, but I couldn't manage it at all. As soon as I was anxious, or angry, or my back was killing me, I lost all perspective and got waylaid by the apparent solidity of that experience.

"My temper's the worst thing," I added. "I get pissed off all the time, which is really idiotic at my age. I feel ashamed, but then I do it again."

She was quiet for a few moments. "Do you ever feel guilty when you're in a beautiful place like this?" she asked.

I puzzled over this. "Not sure," I admitted. "Say more."

"Like maybe I don't deserve it."

"Why wouldn't you?"

She thought about it. "When I went from Flagstaff to Princely with the other girls, we kept each other alive," she said. "In the desert, some days the only question was whether we'd find water in time. But we were a team, we joked around and kept each other going even when our throats were so dry we could hardly talk."

"Okay . . ."

"And then we ended up at Serena's, and they had to do stuff that I didn't have to do, because they were older. And suddenly we weren't really a team anymore."

"I see."

"After a few months we barely spoke," she continued. "The things they started joking about were the strange shape of some guy's dick, or how much gold he had, or what kinky thing got him off. Stuff I didn't know anything about and wasn't sure I wanted to know about."

"I'll bet."

"And they'd give me this look, like, *You're going to learn all about this, so don't think you're better.* I could see they were still my friends, somewhere in there, but they were different, too, and I didn't know what to do."

She paused, collecting herself, then went on. "Then one day I heard them talking, and I realized they were placing bets on how much somebody would pay for me when I turned fifteen," she said. "Which was going to be a guess anyway, since I don't even know exactly when my birthday *is.*"

I remembered what Serena had told me about her. "So you got mad?"

She considered it. "Not at *them,* exactly. Just *mad.*"

"That's why you feel guilty? Because they're unhappy, you think you should be too? That you're not allowed to enjoy simple beauty anymore?"

I understood this well, because it was similar to what I'd experienced when I found myself the sole survivor at the gonpa.

Sophie put her head in her hands. "When you put it that way, it does sound sort of fucked up."

I smiled. "You're okay with being mad, right?"

"In both senses of the word, I'm pretty sure."

"Well, start there," I said. "Be as pissed off and crazy as you want. It won't bother me because *I'm* pissed off and crazy."

"But like, for how long?"

"Until you get tired of it and don't need it anymore, I imagine."

"But you're fifty-two."

"Let's not go there."

One of the hounds brought her a slobbery stick. She took it from his mouth and heaved it off into the weeds, and the dog took off after it. Soon he was lost and wandering through the underbrush with a baffled expression.

"Over there!" Sophie said, pointing, but he didn't seem to register what she meant. "Are these the same dogs that just chased wolves off our trailer? What the hell?"

"Bravery and brains don't always keep the closest company," I said. "They're all heart, but they're no Einsteins."

Finally the dog found the stick. Instead of bringing it to Sophie, he carried it over to the stream, dropped it in, then pounced on it and splashed around happily. Sophie rolled her eyes.

"I don't know if I'll ever even *get* to fifty-two," she said. "In one way that scares me, but given how things are, sometimes dying sounds like kind of a relief."

I was less shocked to hear this than I might have been. "I understand that impulse," I said, eyeing her. "But it's a bad one, trust me."

"Why?"

"It's very hard to get a human body, Sophie."

"I don't even know what that means."

"The only life we know of for sure is here on earth, and for most of the past four billion years it's mainly been bacteria and viruses," I said. "Eventually there were plankton, fish, dinosaurs, then mammals and people. Of all of those trillions of living things over all those eons, we're the only ones who really wonder about it all and can figure things out."

"Animals aren't *that* dumb," she said. "Look at Peau."

I nodded. "Other animals are smart, and their emotional lives are like ours," I said. "But their minds can't quite do what ours do, as far as we know. Having a human body is a rare opportunity, especially now that there are so few of us left."

"It sure doesn't feel that way sometimes."

I told her that she'd helped me see that I tended to romanticize my past with Eva, and I was grateful for that. I suggested, in turn, that she not romanticize death. "When it comes, it comes," I said, "but it isn't an easy escape from anything."

"I'm a little sorry to hear it," she said. She shielded her eyes, then, and scanned the sky. "I thought Peau might have found us by now."

"Don't worry, he always does."

"So you named him after the poet?" Sophie asked.

I explained the spelling and how it had happened. Then something occurred to me that I thought she might like. "Do you know how Poe—the human, I mean—came to write that poem?"

She shook her head, so I told her that Dickens had kept ravens and brought one to the U.S. with him in the 1840s. He met Edgar Allan Poe on that trip, and Poe was so entranced by the bird that he went right home and got to work.

"I like it when things like that have stories behind them," she said.

We heard a flutter of wings, and she looked up again. "Hey, Peau!" she called, waving. He came circling in for a landing.

What ho, he croaked.

"What ho, my good lord."

He'd made a few friends when we were in Opal, he told us. This came as no surprise. He asked them to keep an eye out for Flynn and his men, and they'd set up a sort of relay.

"And?"

A few minutes ago another raven had found him. The big engine had crashed through the gate that morning and it was coming this way.

I got to my feet. "Where is it now?" I asked. He wasn't sure, but he knew it was moving fast. It got slowed down by the first range of mountains, but by now it might have passed the town.

"It's past *Bakersfield*?" I said. "Jesus, we have to go *now*. We'll see you on the other side of the mountains."

He had an idea about something, he said; he'd fly over and see us there.

We hustled back to Clementine with the dogs and got rolling immediately, breathing as deeply as we could while we still had sunlight and open air. I thought of all the delays—the fuel filter, the Bakersfield kids, the bison, even stopping to play with the dogs. Hours we'd lost that we'd never get back.

"How could this happen?" I asked, as I frantically goosed the throttle up to forty-five.

"We were exhausted and we didn't clean up," Sophie said. "We left the cap off the underground tank, we left the buckets, we left the hand pump and the other batteries and the stabilizer. We basically gave them a how-to manual on getting the thing up and running."

"I must have left that stupid giant key lying around too. All I had to do was slip it in my pocket and this wouldn't be happening. This is what I mean when I say I fuck things up."

The next section of tunnel loomed up ahead, so we put our masks back on as we plunged once again into darkness. And again, into utter disorientation. Now that we were on a subtle downslope out of the mountains, Clementine could be nudged up to a bone-rattling fifty miles an hour, but that was it, and I knew a big locomotive could easily do twice that. We settled in, bracing ourselves against the shock and vibration, and waited for daylight. Eighteen miles to go, then fourteen, then ten.

I looked behind us, then, and saw the light. Far away, more like a distant star in that long, straight tunnel, but there was no mistaking what it was. And like a supernova, it was growing brighter.

Clementine started choking and sputtering. She wanted her filter changed. "Come on, not now," I muttered, but over the next mile our speed dropped from fifty to forty to thirty. After another mile it finally held steady at twenty-three.

I waited as long as I could, but at two miles to the exit, the light behind us was bright enough that I knew we were nearly out of time. I throttled back and slammed on the brake, then we skidded to a stop, steel wheels shooting sparks on the rails. Sophie and I quickly got the horses and mules into harness, backed the rig off the flatbed, and drove them onto the little service path beside the tracks. I was thinking I could really use some plastic explosive when I realized that I had the next-best thing. I pulled the acetylene tank out from under the hood and told Sophie what to do. She grabbed a short shovel from the flatbed and rapidly dug a hole in the cinders under a section of rail, her arms moving so fast she looked like one of those blurred-action cartoon characters. We dropped the tank into the hole, its top still showing, and ran back to the truck. She got out the AR-15 and loaded a clip. The locomotive was storming closer, the headlight shining brighter, but at least it gave us a little light to see by. We could hear the deep rumble and feel the vibration in the rails.

We crouched down behind the truck so it and Clementine would shield us from the shock wave and the shrapnel. Sophie took aim at the acetylene tank, then fired and missed.

"Easy," I said. "Calm down."

"It kicks more than I'm used to."

She fired again and missed. "Christ!" she yelled. In maybe forty seconds, the locomotive would collide with the tank and then with Clementine, and I was pretty sure we wouldn't survive it.

"The tank is your asshole of a father, who abandoned you," I said. "He's an ugly fucker and he hates your guts."

Sophie squeezed the trigger a third time and the explosion from the tank knocked us both flat on our asses. Every window shattered in both Clementine and in the truck, and cinders flew everywhere and cut up our faces and hands. After a few seconds, when the dust had settled, I saw that the rail was torn from the ties, broken at a joint, and bent up and out over a length of about four feet. When the big diesel got here, it would be catapulted to the side and slammed into the tunnel wall, and then it would collide with Clementine, who had her air brakes set. We just had to get far enough away.

"Yo, mules!" I cried, snapping the reins, and we broke into a full sprint. I knew almost immediately that it wasn't going to be fast enough. I felt the whole tunnel rumbling now as the locomotive bore down on us, and in a few seconds Flynn apparently saw something in that big bright headlight of his. He blasted the air horn and pulled the brake, and the engine began to screech as the wheels locked up.

With all that mass in motion, the engine slid a long time down the rails before it got to the bent section. We were still running the animals at full speed, hoping against hope, but suddenly there was a change in the sound, from the screaming steel wheels to a torquing, shredding *Boom!*, and then more shrieking as the big engine slammed off the tunnel wall and hit Clementine. A shock wave hit us and hurled the truck forward, into the rear of the mules, who went down, and then we too came skidding to a stop in darkness, truck and mules and horses and dogs all tangled up together, and Cass I didn't even know where.

Then, fire. Bright yellow flames sprang up out of the crushed fuel tanks of the big engine and the little one, lying in a twisted heap of steel maybe thirty yards behind us. The fire grew, engulfed fuel lines and filters and soon anything that had diesel or grease on it. The tunnel was heating up, the mules were hurt, there was no way to untangle everything, and we had to get out.

I called for Cass and heard a terrified little meow, and it was only then that I realized I was *outside* the truck, lying in cinders with all of my clothes and a good bit of my skin torn up.

"Sophie?" I called, but there was no answer. "Sophie!"

I went to the cab. Inside were Sophie and Cass and the rifle. Sophie was out cold. I grabbed Cass and draped her around my neck, then lifted Sophie out and picked her up in my arms. The horses were still on their feet, saved by the concussion-absorbing mules, but they were spooked and whinnying and wouldn't let me near them. I suddenly felt woozy, so I set Sophie down and squatted against the tunnel wall until the dizziness passed and I could get my breath again.

Cass climbed down and was sitting at my feet. I pointed her toward the exit.

"Run!" I said. "We'll see you outside."

She bolted off; then the dogs materialized out of blackness and followed her. Sophie woke up and examined her cut-up hands abstractly, as if they belonged to someone else. We got up, went to the horses, spoke consolingly to them, then eased them out of their harnesses. We gently stroked their noses, patted their necks, and slipped on bareback. We grabbed fistfuls of mane and gave them a kick. The acceleration was instant, so sudden I almost fell off.

Behind us something blew up, and a couple of shards of glowing metal shot by with a little *fwoo* sound, missing us by inches. The horses upshifted from a gallop to a run. Something bigger blew, then, but now we were far enough away. For a second I was worried the horses would trample Cass, but then I saw her flash by as we passed her, safely out of the way and keeping up a decent head of steam herself, for someone with such short legs.

In a couple of minutes we saw sunlight, and soon we were in it, on a beautiful sloping hill. The horses slowed to a trot, then a walk. The blue Pacific sparkled calmly in the distance. Calm as in turbulence, or calm as in temperament, Peau would want to know.

Calm as in the ocean, another word entirely that meant both and neither. I pictured trying to explain this to him and suddenly felt such love: Just *calm*, you meathead, you featherbrain, you beautiful, brilliant bird.

CASS SHOWED UP A COUPLE OF MINUTES LATER, twice her normal size, her fur singed and standing on end. The dogs took one look at her and retreated behind our legs, whining. Thick black smoke poured out from beneath the tunnel's ceiling, as if a dragon lurked inside.

"Where's Peau?" Sophie asked.

"I thought he'd be here by now."

I noticed, then, that the rails ended at the tunnel exit. Someone had probably pulled them up to take the steel; after that it was plain dirt road. If we'd come barreling through in Clementine at forty, there would have been several seconds of extreme excitement followed by a tumbling world of pain and destruction that could easily have continued all the way over the cliff and down into the sea. I pointed this out to Sophie, and she made that irritatingly dismissive French *pfff* sound again.

We were sitting there, still more or less stunned, picking cinders out of our lacerated skin, when I heard hooves clopping through gravel. At first I was relieved that the mules had made it through okay, but when they emerged from the darkness, Buck Flynn was perched on the back of Mule One, followed sullenly by Mule Two. Flynn was soot-blackened. Most of his clothes and hair had burned off, he was bleeding badly from three or four wounds, and he carried a machete, loosely, in his bloody right hand. Sophie and I got to our feet.

She was shaking, and I wasn't all that steady myself. Every time I thought we'd finally rid ourselves of the guy, he kept popping back up. I knew he had to be mortal, but it was sure starting to seem like he wasn't.

He slipped down off the mule, landed heavily on his feet, then stumbled and nearly fell. He slapped the animal on the rump, and both mules limped off toward the sea. Flynn was ten yards from us and began advancing, slowly swinging the machete, cleaving air the way he evidently intended to cleave our flesh.

"Now," he said, his voice a scalded whisper. "No more tricks. Give me what I want, please."

"I can't, Flynn, you know that."

He shrugged. "I know they put it in you somewhere," he went on. "I just need you in small enough pieces to find it."

Sophie reached into her pocket and raised the Glock. "One more step," she said.

Flynn halted where he was, swaying on his feet, still lazily swinging the blade. The dogs began to growl, deep in their throats. I wasn't sure whether they were growling because they didn't recognize him or because they did.

He pondered his options. "One way it's hot, one way it's cold," he said. "One way it's slow, one way it's fast. And it's only fast if you have any bullets in that thing, which I doubt. Why do you torment me like this?"

I couldn't tell if he meant that we were tormenting him by refusing him what he wanted or by failing to kill him. "Flynn—"

He waved dismissively. "Don't try," he said. "Don't even . . ."

"They may be able to help you here."

"Nobody is going to help me."

"How do you know if you don't—"

"One way is slow, one way is fast," he said. "You really better have some bullets."

He started forward again, and then I heard something above and behind us. We fell into shadow, and Flynn peered upward and shielded his eyes. I thought a cloud had crossed the sun, but when I turned to look, the thing in the sky was darker than any cloud I'd ever seen. It descended on us with tremendous speed, and then I heard them calling to each other.

The ravens fell upon him in a great, black, feathery mass, beaks pecking and claws slashing, as Flynn swung the machete wildly and staggered backward. Within seconds they'd torn up his face and plucked out his eyes. He kept hacking at them, severing wings and heads, cleaving shiny black bodies in half, but there were too many and he couldn't see, and in ten or fifteen seconds he'd dropped the machete and fallen to his knees, covering his bloody face with his hands.

I'd been doing my best to channel Sun Tzu and Chief Joseph, but Peau had cut to the chase and channeled Hitchcock.

The ravens exploded away like a brilliant black supernova, then gathered together in the air and flew off as a dark, shape-shifting cloud. Flynn kneeled in the grass, his hands still shielding his face, as blood ran through his fingers and snaked in crimson rivulets down his arms. He began to weep.

On his knees, anguished and blind, Flynn suddenly didn't seem so evil anymore. Seeing him so abruptly and abjectly vanquished, I felt arise in myself a disquieting contention of triumph and pity. I wasn't quite certain which would prevail.

"I meant what I said," I told him guardedly. "They may know how to use what I've brought."

He was quiet for a few moments. "I don't want it," he said at last.

"What do you mean?" I asked, shocked. "You killed all your men to get it!"

"Think about it, Collins," he said. "If it works, I'll spend forty years blind, and probably behind bars."

He was likely right, I realized. "What *do* you want, then?"

"Take a guess. Consider it merciful."

I hissed in exasperation. "I can't do that, and you know it."

"What about the girl? Is she still there?"

"No bullets," said Sophie, sounding almost apologetic. "I never figured out where they were hidden."

The stupid irony of this wasn't lost on me. When all Flynn wanted was more life, I couldn't give it to him. Now he wanted death, and I couldn't give him that either. We seemed perfectly designed to madden and thwart each other.

He took hold of the machete and rose unsteadily to his feet. A nimbus of dead ravens lay around him. It seemed possible that Peau was among them.

"I hear the sea," Flynn said softly, now.

"Yes."

He turned and stumbled toward the cliff.

"Flynn—"

But he brandished the machete in warning, so I didn't follow him. He staggered forward and hesitated, feeling for the edge with his foot until he found it. He took four or five deep breaths.

"I've always loved that smell," he said. He hummed a little something to himself; I didn't know what it was. Then he leapt forward into nothingness and was gone.

SOPHIE STOOD WHERE SHE WAS, trembling. I put an arm around her, and we moved closer to the fallen ravens. "Is one of them Peau?" she asked unsteadily.

"I don't know."

She began to sob. But then a raven croaked above us. He came flying in, circled over the carnage, and landed on my shoulder. Sophie
emitted a little cry of relief, then folded her hands around him and
kissed him on the beak.

He'd surveyed the scene, though, and he was agitated. All these ravens, he said. He wasn't local, this was very bad, he had serious amends
to make. He launched himself from my shoulder and flew off in pursuit of the retreating flock.

Sophie and I walked to the edge of the cliff. Flynn's body lay in
rough surf forty feet below, tossed against rocks, his eyeless face relaxed now, washed nearly to innocence by the sea.

The dogs began to bark. Two young men in uniform came riding up
the road on horseback. They eyed us apprehensively—our shell-shocked
stares, our burns and wounds and tattered clothes. They nudged their
horses and came over to have a look down at Flynn. I figured we were
about to be arrested and suddenly felt extremely tired.

"We'll have Riggs get him if the sharks don't first," one remarked
nonchalantly. The other nodded, then they turned to us.

"Dr. Collins?"

"I'm not a doctor," I replied. "And call me Will."

"We've been wondering when you'd show up," he went on.
"Dr. Thönberg would like to see you."

"Lars," I said. "Of course. We'll do that right away, as soon as we've
eaten and slept and disinfected our wounds. Would that be all right
with you, officer?"

He didn't react to the impertinence. "You can do those things soon,"
he answered calmly. "But first, you need to see the dentist."

And then I understood. Weeks of toothache. Buck Flynn could have
sliced me to confetti and he still wouldn't have found the thing I was
carrying, because they'd slipped it inside my goddamn molar.

13

I awoke dreamily from the anesthetic haze and gazed around. The room was clean and white and modern, the sort of dental-surgery suite that didn't exist anymore, except that evidently it did. I briefly wondered whether I'd been able to maintain any sort of awareness during the anesthesia, but there was only the usual blank nothingness.

Lars stood off to one side, staring at me with a mixture of vexation and concern. The poor man was seventy years old, and it showed in every line on his worried, weather-beaten face. His hair had gone white since I'd last seen him, sixteen or seventeen years previously, and he still had the same thick, wire-rimmed glasses he'd worn then.

"Where *are* we?" I asked, but then the dentist picked the tiny ampoule out of a stainless-steel tray with a pair of tweezers and handed it to him. Lars put it in a little plastic box, then slid the box into his shirt pocket.

"Come with me, Will," he said. He and the dentist lifted me out of the chair and led me out of the room as I wobbled unsteadily along.

The hall was flanked by offices on one side, and on the other by floor-to-ceiling windows that streamed evening light. Outside, in a grassy courtyard, fifteen or twenty people sat at tables, eating dinner together under trees. California! The full, sweet panoply of humanity that I remembered from my time at Irvine, various races and ethnicities commingling congenially, talking and laughing as they ate.

The dentist peeled off down a side hallway. Lars and I walked on together, then came to a door marked "Laboratory," where I followed him inside. We entered a room full of computers and arcane-looking equipment, where people in white coats were waiting for us.

Lars pulled out the little plastic box and held it out to a young Asian woman, who scribbled something on a pad of paper, then took the box and handed it to someone else.

"How long will it take?" he asked.

"An hour or two."

"Thanks, Amy. Call me when you're done."

And then we were out walking the hallways again. I continued to wake up, gradually, and it occurred to me that I must look a sight among all these well-dressed, well-fed young people. But then I glanced downward and realized that I'd been scrubbed, disinfected, bandaged, and reconfigured in clean clothes. No shave, but they'd been otherwise occupied and it had been less than a week since we left the Paris house. I was relieved to discover that I still had my new boots on, and a good thing too; they would have had to pry them from my cold, dead feet.

"Hungry?" Lars asked, bringing me back.

"Where's Sophie? Where's the cat?"

"They're together," he said. "Sophie's seen a doctor and had everything tended to. They've both eaten. They're fine. It's you I'm worried about."

"Yes, I'm hungry," I said.

"It's linguine with meat sauce and garlic bread tonight," he continued. "Sound okay?"

I stared at him a second. "I don't know," I said. "How's the wine?"

·   ·   ·

WE SAT IN THE CORNER of the cafeteria, which had glass panels facing the courtyard. It was a warm, perfect evening. As with most places I'd been, almost everyone here was under forty.

We were on a satellite campus of Cal Poly, Lars told me, on a bluff overlooking the sea south of Morro Bay. The main campus buildings, a dozen miles east, still contained the skeletons of hundreds of students and faculty from all those years previously, since there had been little time to evacuate and nowhere safe to go. But enough people had gathered in the area that crews were finally clearing out the bones and hoping to bring some services back within a year or two. The living who remained were here, ensconced in a few older buildings that had been sparsely occupied when Mayhem hit. There were a couple of hundred students now, and the place served primarily as a research center. Los Angeles and San Francisco and Sacramento were gone, but we still had San Luis Obispo, and Monterey and Santa Cruz, and then Mendocino and Eureka and the whole north coast. Thousands of people were rebuilding their electrical grids and their lives, reestablishing farms, creating networks to deliver food and fuel.

"We've kept an extremely low profile," Lars explained. "We built our own closed intranet, and given that Snail is the only search engine left out there, we're pretty safe. We're working with people in Oregon, where a few towns like Ashland and Bend and Eugene still exist. Washington State is mostly gone, but there are ten or fifteen thousand people in Vancouver, BC. Also Hawaii. We're trying to create a functioning republic, and we don't want a bunch of ARMers showing up and trying to take over all our hard work by force."

"Bakersfield is full of starving kids. What about them?"

"The Central Valley is chaos," he said. "We haven't been able to do anything out there, but eventually we hope to."

"Who's the 'we' here? How are you involved?"

"I advise when they ask me to advise," he said. "Sometimes it's helpful. There aren't a lot of scientists left."

We ate as I considered all this. It struck me as ironic that the people who'd always advocated for open borders now felt compelled to close them, and that the people who'd always sought to close them might now be on the outside wanting in.

I was still hungry when I finished my plate, so I went back for seconds. There actually *was* wine, it turned out, and it was local and pretty good.

When I sat down again, Lars asked me about what I'd seen on my travels. "Is anything alive out there at all?"

"It's amazing," I replied. "We saw huge flocks of passenger pigeons. Herds of bison. Wolf packs, deer everywhere. Animals that escaped from old game farms and reserves—camels, tigers, crocodiles, God knows what else."

"I knew about the pigeons," he said. "A couple of friends of mine were involved in that. I had no idea about the rest."

I wasn't much in the mood for travelogue, though. "Lars, what exactly did the people in Colorado put in my tooth?"

He cleaned his plate with a crust of bread, then chewed it.

"A compound," he said. "They found it in a university lab in Boulder, but the researcher died before he could finish testing it. I thought we could complete that here, and you were the only person I knew who might be capable of such a journey."

"It's supposed to cure Disease X?"

"It's promising. That's all we know for sure."

"How the hell did Buck Flynn find out about it?"

"One thing I've always appreciated about you, Will, is that you make leaps of logic," Lars said. "Back in the old days, you used to see connections that people with better training didn't see, and when you interviewed folks at conferences, you were always pissing them off because you'd ask the most obvious and confounding questions. That's one reason I tried to mentor you."

This nonresponse was both evasive and flattering, which immediately put me on guard. "Thanks," I said. "Sorry that didn't turn out the way you wanted."

He waved it away. "We're both old men now," he said. "Here's what I'd like to ask you, though: What do you think Disease X actually *is?*"

I'd wondered about it, of course. Did it attack older people because it was like other opportunistic diseases that preyed on weakened immune systems? Or was it something that got into people young and then took a long time to develop? And how could it affect all the organs at once, and cross the blood-brain barrier, instead of specializing, the way most diseases did? There were a few conditions like that—mainly neurological ones—but they were rare, and it was hard to imagine how they'd spread enough to infect everyone in a population as soon as they got to a certain age.

"I could make a guess, but it would be a wild guess," I said quietly.

"Go on."

I considered how to frame it. "It behaves like TB in some ways," I said. "It can lie latent for a long time, it spreads through the body, and it's lethal. But there's a lot of TB out there again, and it's definitely a different disease."

He interlaced his fingers. "Yes."

"If I had to speculate, I'd guess it's a new kind of prion disease," I said. "Like Creutzfeldt-Jakob or mad cow, only widely epidemic, the way those illnesses are in elk and deer."

Lars beamed. "That's what I've been thinking," he said. "*Exactly.*"

"But almost nobody got prion diseases before," I said. "Everyone comes down with this. Why? What changed?"

"Not everyone," Lars replied. "Not me, and not you yet, either."

"Okay, maybe one person in a hundred turns out to be immune. So?"

"What do those people have in common?" he asked.

"No clue."

"When everyone was dying of avian flu, did you get it?"

I felt suddenly emotional, realizing that we were talking about the thing that had killed Eva. He saw the expression on my face and sat back.

"I'm sorry," he said. "That was insensitive of me. I should have thought . . ."

"It's all right. It's a fair question." I took a moment, then told him about my case.

"It was the same for me," he said. "That I survived relatively unscathed, I mean."

"So what's your theory?"

"I've been wondering if some people made special proteins to fight off that flu, and whether those proteins later morphed into prions that kicked off the whole cascade."

"But why wouldn't that apply to everyone who had the flu?"

He shrugged. "Something genetic, probably," he said. "Which means it might have responded to gene therapy, if we still had the equipment and the capability to do that."

"Then what's the use of the compound you had me bring?"

"The notes were cryptic," he admitted. "But it may imitate what happens in the body *after* gene therapy. Proof of concept or even a cure."

"Can you actually make drugs here?"

"In small batches, yes."

"You have a case?"

He glanced away a bit evasively, I thought. "We have a lot of cases, like anywhere."

"But why did you have me rush out here? Who is it for?"

His face fell into a look of such sudden and profound sorrow that it took me aback. "We have plenty of time before the lab calls," he said. "Why don't you come with me."

·   ·   ·

He led me down a series of hallways, his shoulders slumping under the weight of whatever he planned to show me. Finally, we came to a large, locked door. He pulled a card from his pocket, slid it through a reader, and the locks clicked and disengaged. He led me into an observation gallery that overlooked a smaller room below, enclosed in glass walls. A hospital bed sat in the middle of the floor, roughly ten feet below us, and on the bed lay a woman.

Eva.

Adrenaline shot through me so suddenly I thought my heart would burst. I gaped at Lars, speechless, to see if I should believe my eyes. He nodded.

"How do I get down?"

He pointed to a stairway.

I bolted down the stairs, pushed through a heavy glass door, then went to her bed. I sat, took her hand, and squeezed it. Her eyes opened for a moment, but there was no light in them, no recognition of any kind. I said her name. I told her it was me, told her that I hadn't known or I would have come long ago.

But none of it had any effect. I didn't know what else to do, so I simply sat there a few minutes. She had aged as any living person would age; when I'd known her, she was a young woman of thirty-two, and now she was a middle-aged woman of forty-seven. There were lines on her face, gray streaks in her hair. But she was still Eva.

Lars came down into the room and put a hand on my shoulder.

"You all right?" he asked.

"Not really," I managed to say. "She's not comatose, but she barely seems alive. What's going on?"

"We're not sure," he said. "She's been like this for fourteen years."

"But her color's good. She still has muscle on her."

He nodded solemnly. "Every couple of days, usually in midafternoon, her eyes open and she gets out of bed," he said. "She walks circles around the room like a robot. She eats and drinks and shits, and that's what's kept her alive. Then she gets back into bed and her eyes close again. She's like a sleepwalker. She doesn't interact with anyone, never appears to be aware of her surroundings. You've seen it yourself; nothing works. I've never heard of a syndrome like it."

"So it's brain damage?"

"Her EEG looks fine. It's similar to Disease X, except it's never progressed. We don't know what's happening."

"She had the flu right before this, right? The hospital told me she'd died."

"I'll explain about that later," he said. He started for the door.

I got up and followed him up the stairs.

"How can you just leave her like this?" I asked. "Wouldn't it have been better to let her go?"

He glared at me. "First, I'm her legal guardian, and she gets excellent care here," he said. "Second, there are no oversight or enforcement agencies anymore who might intervene. And what would they do? Tell us to stop feeding her? She eats on her own. It would be murder."

"Why did you get in touch with me now?"

"She's deteriorating," he said. "She used to get up and eat every day, but now it's every other day and often every third. Her bloodwork is worse and worse. She's been getting infections—pneumonia, other things—so we give her IV supplements and antibiotics when she needs them, but the trends aren't good."

"No, I mean why didn't you tell me *fourteen years ago*? I would have come right away if I'd known."

In response, he pulled an old, yellowed piece of notepaper from his pocket. "I expected you'd ask that, so I brought this along," he said as he handed it to me. "She wrote it in the hospital when she had the flu, half an hour before she lost consciousness and—as they thought—died."

I unfolded it, and there, in faded ink, in her handwriting, were the words:

Will Collins is to learn nothing of this situation. If I die, you can tell him so, but I've sent him a letter explaining the rest. I want him to hear it from me.

—*Eva Thönberg*

"What 'situation'?" I asked Lars. "What's 'the rest' that she's talking about?"

Lars took the note from me, folded it carefully, and slipped it back into his pocket. "I have no idea," he said. "What about the letter?"

"I never got any letter," I said. "This would have been about the time all the mail stopped, so if she sent one, it's probably in a bin with about a million others at a processing station somewhere."

As he was walking me out, the lab called, so we detoured there. He read the report, nodding, as the team waited in front of him.

"Good," he said at last. "I know it's late, but would a couple of you mind staying to make this? I'd like it in hundred-milligram capsules by tomorrow morning."

I FOUND SOPHIE AND CASS in the apartment Lars had arranged for us, a holdover from the old days when visiting professors needed housing. The sun had set, and the raucous birdsong had dwindled to the occasional tentative peep from the trees outside. It was an elegant Mission-style building, white stucco, arched windows, colorful tiles on the stairs. We were on the second floor, with a view of the sea. The windows were open, and the breeze billowed out the curtains.

"Jesus," said Sophie when I walked in. "You look terrible. What's happened?"

I sat down, feeling agitated and drained all at once, and told her what I'd seen. I was doing my best to keep it together, but my best wasn't good enough, and my eyes kept welling up. She sat beside me on the couch and put her arms around me. She held me a good long while as I wept, until eventually I stopped. She asked me what was going to happen next.

"Tomorrow morning they give her the drug," I said. "Then we wait."

"She might wake up?"

"That's the idea. No one knows."

"What if she doesn't?"

I shrugged. I suspected the compound was unlikely to work, in fact. Lars was too manic. He was acquiring that jittery, obsessed persona that I'd always associated with overly aggressive scientists like the guy from Zurich, and I thought maybe he'd become delusional.

It had been a long day. I felt exhaustion dropping over me as if I'd been standing at the edge of a stage, and the heavy black curtain had slipped its moorings and come cascading down.

"I'd better go to bed," I said. "Your room all right?"

"Wonderful," she said. "I'll be up a while, but I'll try to be quiet."

IN THE MORNING, an hour before dawn, I lay in bed and listened as the city of birds awoke outside and began to stir. There were a few low calls at first, like tentative notes from an oboe as the player prepared the reed; then higher-pitched cheeps and twitters, little territorial bursts of petulant violin; then the whole winged orchestra establishing itself in lively consciousness and swelling into harmony shortly before the sun rose. They had their own world and didn't much notice what had happened to ours, it seemed. I kept expecting Peau to show up, but there was still no sign of him.

In my twenties and thirties, I felt so infused with energy in the morning that I could barely contain myself. I'd spring from bed, dress, throw down some breakfast, get going on my day. Now, when I awoke,

I usually felt as if someone had driven a truck into the room in the middle of the night and run me over.

I got up and went to the bathroom. There was a new razor and cream, so I shaved. There was still the matter of my stubbly hair, of course. It would require patience, which had never been my strong suit.

In the kitchen, there was cereal and fruit and milk for us, and kibble for Cassie, so I fed her and let her out. Sophie appeared, so I got her some cereal too, and we sat down to eat. I'd decided it might be a good idea to go out to the tunnel and see if anything could be salvaged from the truck.

"If there is, how will we haul it back?" Sophie asked, sensibly. "It's three or four miles each way."

"No idea," I mumbled. Logistics of any kind had somehow become too much. I pondered the prospects while I did the dishes and Sophie got dressed. Then there was a knock at the door.

A gawky student stood there with a key and an envelope, as if the gods had heard my befuddlement and responded. "It's in the lot behind the building," he said, handing me the key.

Lars had written:

> In all the tumult I neglected to tell you how much I appreciate that you actually arrived here in one piece with the material we asked you to bring. I do not know how difficult it was, exactly, but given how you looked when you showed up it was clearly no picnic. So thank you, Will. I have managed to borrow a car from the university for as long as you want it, so any traveling you do around here should be made considerably easier. We will give Eva the first dose this morning, by the way. Maybe you can come over later and we shall see regarding response. I will be monitoring the situation closely, of course.
>
> —Lars

Dear Lars, whose written English was still awkward after fifty years here.

When Sophie emerged, wearing a cotton top and jeans they'd brought for her, I dangled the keys in front of her.

"New nation, no laws that I know of," I said. "I think you should drive."

She was terrifyingly bad at it, of course. The car was a little electric hatchback, one of the last built before Mayhem. She was way too quick on the acceleration for someone who'd never driven anything faster than a horse and didn't have a clue what she was doing, in other words. The road ran a bit too close to the edge of the coastal cliff for comfort, and guardrails had apparently been considered a capricious extravagance. But her reflexes were better than mine, and by the time my leaden foot reached the imaginary brake on the passenger side in a futile effort to save our lives, she'd long since found the real pedal on her side and brought us around the bends safely. Once she got the hang of it, I felt like one of the leaning lovebirds in Tippi Hedren's sports car.

We left the pavement where we actually intended to, followed the dirt road to the tunnel entrance, and parked on the grass. The horses and the mules grazed nearby, an apparently amiable herd. I'd promised the mules a happy, verdant place to retire, and amazingly enough I'd managed to keep the promise. I went over to give them a pat and say hello, but they all shied away and wouldn't let me near them. I couldn't blame them; they'd done most of the work, and nobody had given *them* a car.

We had decent flashlights and found our way to the wreckage. The two engines were twisted around each other in a peculiarly carnal embrace, as if mating whales had suddenly been incinerated, and the tunnel stank of diesel smoke and burned rubber. As for the truck, poor thing, it appeared that a burning stream of fuel had found its way down the tracks and ignited the tires. Everything in the bed had been torched, but I noticed my old daypack had survived behind the seat in the cab. Not much in it but a useless old wallet and some papers, but I dragged it out and slung it over my shoulder.

"All that wonderful food," said Sophie sadly. "We might as well have given it to the kids in Bakersfield."

"And the books."

"And the tampons and TP and toothbrushes. Fuck."

"It's possible they sell some of those things in town," I said. "And if nobody makes tampons anymore, you might have an entrepreneurial opportunity."

She snorted a laugh. "I'm fourteen, Will. Not quite ready for a life of industrial drudgery."

WE DROVE BACK TO CAMPUS, then walked over to Lars's building and had lunch in the cafeteria. Now, a day after I'd had a tiny vial removed from my tooth, I noticed for the first time in weeks that I could chew food without agony.

I was wondering what we were going to do about Eva. Stand around and watch her waste away and die? I was braced for discouraging news from Lars. Her first death had been hard enough; I wasn't keen on us all going through a second one.

Sophie was interested in what was taking place in the building, which seemed to her like some sort of spaceship from another civilization. After lunch we started wandering around. There was a science library with computers, there were classrooms, there were interesting-looking young people.

There were schools in nearby communities, including San Luis Obispo, and we came upon a small gaggle of teenagers touring the campus as future prospects. The utter normality of this was astounding; the place wasn't a spaceship, it was a *time*ship. Most of the kids were a couple of years older than Sophie, but one looked closer to her age, and there were only seven of them anyway. I spoke briefly to their guide, and she said Sophie was welcome to join them. Happiness bloomed in her face as she wandered off with them.

I went to find Lars. He was coming out of the observation area overlooking Eva's room when I got there. I could tell from his face that the news wasn't good.

"Let's walk," he said.

We left the building and wandered out across green lawns. The afternoon breeze was fresh off the sea. I gently suggested that it was unrealistic to expect results this fast; wouldn't it more likely take days or even weeks?

"Days maybe," he grumbled. "Weeks, no."

"Lars, what *happened* fourteen years ago?" I asked. "The hospital told me she was dead. How did we get from there to here?"

He said that after Eva left me and took the job in Los Angeles, she'd been busy and distracted and upset.

"I tried to see her, but she didn't seem to want to."

"Why not?"

"I don't know, but she was a grown woman, and I had a lot on my plate anyway," he said. "We talked on the phone every couple of weeks but never got together in person."

Then the flu hit, he explained, and everything was thrown into chaos. One night he got a call that Eva had been admitted to the UCLA hospital and was comatose. By the time he got there two hours later, a harried clerk checked paperwork and said she had died. That, apparently, was how I got notified, because I was in Eva's directive. But the hospital was so overwhelmed that patients were filling parking lots on cots, and most of them didn't have basic monitoring equipment. Eva wasn't even cold when Lars arrived, and when he felt her neck, he thought he detected a faint pulse. The place was pandemonium because so many doctors and nurses had died, and he couldn't even find anyone to check her again. So he'd picked her up, put her in the back of his car, and driven her to La Jolla, where he had friends at the hospital. Sure enough, she was still alive, though barely.

"And this is how she's been ever since," he told me. "I found the note I showed you, which is why I didn't call. And frankly, I wasn't even sure you were alive until you replied to my email a couple of months ago."

"Fair enough."

"Anyway, for the first few weeks, I expected she'd either die or eventually wake up," he continued. "But after a couple of months, I realized what I was dealing with. When we had to clear out of Scripps, I brought her along, because what else could I do? Then, as she was starting to deteriorate, I learned of the researcher in Boulder and the compound he'd made. It was a long shot but still worth a try."

"You've been a good father to her," I said.

"I'm just glad you were up for the trip. As I said, I know it can't have been easy."

"It would have been easier if I hadn't had Buck Flynn after me."

"Buck Flynn, Buck Flynn," scoffed Lars. "That ridiculous Twainian nom de guerre. The man's name was Cletus Groenfieler."

I stopped in my tracks, stared at him, and asked how he happened to know this.

"Because I hired him, Will."

"You *what*?"

"I mentioned an escort, did I not?"

"Lars, what the *hell*—"

"I've known you too long," he said. "You spent years sitting on your butt meditating, and when I asked you to come out here, I was worried you might have a tendency to dawdle."

"You told me it was urgent. I wasn't going to fucking *dawdle*, Lars."

"Really?" he asked. "You weren't ever tempted, say, to find a comfortable spot and a nice woman? Maybe take it easy for a month or two, until it became too hot to cross the desert, and then decide to wait it out till winter?"

"I was tempted, but I didn't," I said. "Your hired man broke my nose and pulled out one of my fingernails. And if *my* name was Cletus Groenfieler, I'd have gone with Buck Flynn too."

"He wasn't supposed to hurt you," Lars huffed. "He was supposed to catch up with you and spirit you out here as quickly as possible, under guard. But you kept losing him and getting his men killed."

"To be clear, *he* kept getting his men killed, not me."

"Anyway, I had no idea you'd turn out to be such a weasel! That damn tattoo! And you even threw *me* off with the email about going south. That cost us *days*."

"Flynn was sick, Lars. He had Disease X, and once he learned I might be carrying a cure, that was all he cared about. He didn't give a shit about getting me to California, and I'm pretty sure there are warrants out for him here."

Lars appeared stricken. "There are? For what?"

"How the hell should I know? The woman who stuck that thing in my tooth was a veterinarian! Flynn's 'guards' were ARM guys. For a professional researcher, you sure do shitty background checks."

"It's impossible to get good information anymore!" he said. He put his hands in his pockets and looked down at his feet, appearing chagrined. "I'll arrange for a surgeon to fix your nose, if you'd like."

"I think we have more important problems right now."

"Yes," he said bitterly, a tremor in his voice. "My brilliant daughter, the zombie."

And when he said that word, "zombie," I understood something about the situation that I hadn't quite grasped before.

Many spiritual traditions involve out-of-body experiences, of course. Western medicine is useless in this regard, because it doesn't concern itself with the spirit but rather with brain waves and arcane physiological definitions of when life officially ends.

In Tibet, I knew, a *delog* was an advanced practitioner who left the body in order to travel to other realms. This was a dangerous thing to do, since it was possible for the consciousness to become disoriented and unable to find its way back to its own body. The conditions had to be carefully controlled; usually the *delog* was sealed up in a cold room and left undisturbed for a period of days while the journey took place. If the *delog* wouldn't wake up when the room was unsealed, a lama would try to guide them back. Usually this worked, but sometimes it didn't. Certainly, no *delog* had managed to maintain that state for more than a few days at a time, let alone fourteen years. The more I considered Eva's situation, though, the more it seemed possible to me that she was somehow trapped that way, partly because modern medical technology had kept her body alive in a way no Himalayan monastery could have.

SOPHIE AND I SAT ON THE BEACH watching the sunset as I lit a fire, then tended it until it was burning well. I got out my new pad and pen, swag from the university. I was hoping David had been right about Eva getting my letters.

Dear Eva,

Your body is alive. It's waiting for you to return to it. I know you've had trouble finding it, but you've got to try a little harder.

I'm waiting too, with someone I'd like you to meet. I've mentioned her before, and I'm happy to report that she's recovered from her illness. You'd enjoy each other's company, I think.

I'm looking forward to introducing you.

—Will

I put the paper into the fire and watched as it burned and the smoke rose upward.

Sophie had been lying on the warm sand with her hands behind her head, watching the sky as the blue deepened and the stars came out. As the letter burned, she turned on her side and watched.

"Too weird for you?" I asked.

"Not sure anything is too weird for me at this point."

She sat up, then, and told me about her afternoon. I couldn't help smiling at how animated she became. Many of the kids she'd met were orphans—this was true everywhere—but families had been found for them, their situations were stable, they were going to school.

"So I might want to start classes in the fall, if that's okay," she said.

"Of course it's okay, it's exactly what you should do," I said. "Besides, you said it yourself: you're emancipated."

THE NEXT AFTERNOON, Sophie went with me to check on Eva. She was a little freaked out by the situation—the glassed-in room and the observation area all seemed cold and bizarre to her—but finally we went downstairs and sat beside Eva together.

"She's beautiful," she said, and I nodded.

I was deeply tired, and we just sat quietly. Lars was continuing to dose Eva with the compound, titrating carefully upward but so far without result. I'd hoped my letter might make a difference, but it seemed it was wishful thinking.

Sophie got restless after a while, so I told her she should go on. She put her hand on Eva's arm.

"Bye," she said. "Sorry we didn't get to meet."

I was so exhausted after she left that I fell asleep in the chair. I dreamed again of that place in the mountains, the little valley with two lakes. I was walking from the lower lake to the higher one, ascending the trail that wound its way among pale granite boulders. I came over a rise, and the upper lake appeared. I saw Eva there, on the far shore, her reflection in the water.

Our eyes met again, and for the first time I walked around the lake. I had the feeling she'd been waiting, and when I reached her, I held out my hand. She took it, then I turned and led her back. We slowly started making our way down the mountain.

When I awoke, Eva's eyes were open. At first, I thought it was the prelude to her occasional rise to eat and shamble robotically around the room. But then I saw that her eyes were *moving*. Her gaze found me, and she made a little noise in her throat. She reached out and seized my hand. She was awake.

I wasn't sure she'd recognize me, but apparently she did. Tears flooded her eyes then, and mine. We held each other's hands, neither of us speaking. I wasn't even sure she *could* speak, since she hadn't in so long.

"Welcome home," I managed to say, finally. "Welcome to the land of the living."

LARS CAME AT ONCE, and soon Eva began to speak a little in a rough, gravelly voice. They talked awhile, tearfully, then he went to find her some clothes.

Eventually she got up and shuffled to the bathroom. She was disoriented, and shocked to learn how much time had gone by. She thought she'd been unconscious for a few weeks at most and nearly fainted when she looked in the mirror.

Lars returned a half hour later with a pair of jeans, a couple of T-shirts, and an old fleece jacket, then thoughtfully left us to ourselves. I asked Eva what she wanted to do.

"Eat," she rasped.

"There's a cafeteria," I said. "Are you strong enough to walk there?"

"Let's try," she said. She looked down at herself, then whispered her first full sentence. "Help me out of these stupid pajamas, okay?"

We got her changed, then went up the stairs and made our way down the hall to the cafeteria. Her balance was off, and I had to steady her a couple of times, but she willed herself forward.

We loaded our plates and went out to the courtyard to eat. It was still early, about a quarter past five, and there were only a handful of others there. Eva ate a few bites, but once she'd taken the edge off her hunger, she put her hand on my arm.

"You haven't said anything about her," she said. "Is she with you, is she safe?"

"Who?"

"Lily. Is she here?"

"I don't know what you're talking about."

She cleared her throat, drank some water. "*Lily*," she repeated. "I wrote you!"

"The letter you sent when you got sick?" I asked, and she nodded. "I never got it—I just found out about it from Lars. Why didn't you call me?"

"Oh, no," she said. Tears slipped from her eyes and she wiped at them impatiently. "Two, three days after I sent it, I was on a cot in the hospital parking lot. I decided to call you then, but when I reached for my bag, someone had taken it. That's the last thing I remember."

"What was in the letter?"

"Are there computers here?" she asked.

"Sure," I said. "Finish your dinner and we'll go to the library."

"No," she said, heaving herself to her feet. "Now."

On the way, I asked again what was in the letter.

"Two months after I left," she replied, working to catch her breath. "Two months, I realized I was pregnant."

"Jesus, Eva," I said. Suddenly she was steadying *me*, or maybe we were steadying each other. "You're serious? Why didn't you tell me?"

She lurched onward. "I'll explain."

In the library, Eva tapped her foot impatiently while Snail reluctantly carried out her searches. The search for "Eva Thönberg" yielded a handful of her old academic papers; the search for "Lily Thönberg" yielded nothing at all. "Thönberg infant," nothing. "Thönberg child UCLA medical center," nothing; "Thönberg d.o.b. May 18, 2033," nothing. She tried various other permutations, but only Lars and his endless papers kept popping up. Finally she searched for "Danielle Lacuna" and found a brief death notice of the kind they'd issued during the pandemic fourteen years before.

"Oh no," she said. "No, it can't be."

"Tell me what's going on!"

She was sobbing wretchedly now. "Let's get out of here."

I HAD TO FIND HER A PAIR OF SUNGLASSES before we left the building, because even though it was early evening, her eyes weren't accustomed to so much light. She put them on, then we walked a hundred yards to a wooden bench that sat beneath a tall eucalyptus. She was tired by then, so we sat, but her voice was gaining strength.

"I tried to decide whether to tell you," she said. "But we weren't really together anymore. It seemed better to stick with the plan."

"I would have come."

"You were so happy to finally start your retreat," she said. "You would have resented it."

I shifted my weight. "It's possible," I admitted. "But I think it's also possible you didn't really want me there."

She sighed, rubbed at her reddened eyes. "It's true, I didn't," she said. "I loved being alone those months."

"We both did."

"Well, until I had this kid screaming at me all the time. *That* wasn't exactly relaxing."

"Her name was Lily?" I asked, and she nodded. "What was the plan, exactly?"

"I thought that if you and I got back together, then fine," Eva explained. "Or if we didn't, then a few years down the road I'd find a way to introduce you that didn't cramp anybody's style."

"I actually meant, what was the plan when you got sick?"

"Oh," she said. "Danielle was an old friend. She agreed to take Lily until I got well, or bring her to you if I died. You'd be expecting her because you would have gotten my goddamn letter."

"Why didn't you tell Lars about her?"

"He would have called you immediately and demanded that you come out here. It would have been a disaster."

"He'd have just been trying to protect you."

"I was thirty-two. I could protect myself."

"Danielle died on her way to find me?"

"The notice said she died in Arizona," she said. "Lily must have died too. I can't imagine how she would have survived."

My eyes welled. I pulled my old bandanna from my coat pocket and dabbed at the tears. Eva was weeping too, now. She patted her pockets but didn't find any tissues, so I handed her the bandanna.

She took off her sunglasses and unfolded the cloth to find a clean part, then blotted her eyes. "Paisley," she said, studying it. "I used to love paisley; it always looked to me like creatures in pond water under a microscope." She sniffled. "Do you mind?"

"Go ahead."

She blew her nose vigorously a couple of times, then refolded the cloth and held it out to me.

"Keep it," I said.

"You sure?"

"It's not that I'm so generous," I said gently.

She laughed softly in spite of herself. "You don't want my snot in your pocket, is that it?"

"That's it."

She put the bandanna aside and slid next to me. I put my arm around her, and she rested her head on my shoulder. We sat quietly together for a long time, listening to the waves breaking in the west.

"While I was unconscious, I think I still dreamed," she said, eventually. "There was a lake in the mountains. I waited for you there for what seemed like eons."

"I dreamed of that lake too."

"Really? I've wondered if I'm losing my mind."

"You're not."

"The light there was so lovely," she went on. "It always seemed to be morning. There were tall, rocky crags behind the lake, so I knew the water must be deep. It was clear and cool, the water."

"It was."

"And birds. There were birds in the sky."

"I don't remember birds, but I'm sure you're right."

"Can you explain this to me?" she asked. "Where is that lake? Is it a real place or not?"

"I don't know where it is, but it's as real as anything else. We've both seen it."

She considered this. "You once told me that we live in this fantastical, illusory universe," she said, finally. "I don't think I was very nice to you about that."

"It's all right. I didn't really know what I was talking about."

"And now you do?"

"I haven't a clue, in fact."

She smiled. "Well what, then? What happens next?"

"Lars has an apartment for you," I said. "Also, there's someone I'd like you to meet. Why don't you rest a bit, and I'll introduce you to her in a day or two."

14

I lay in bed the next morning, listening to the birds and rubbing my hand absently over my sprouting scalp. Sophie was banging around in the kitchen while she made her breakfast. She seemed incapable of doing anything quietly, but I was beginning to love all that noise.

I rolled out of bed, put on sweatpants and a T-shirt, and headed out there. I liked how cool and firm the apartment's terra-cotta tiles felt under my bare feet.

Sophie glanced up from her cereal. "Hello, dear," she said. "You're looking butt-ugly this morning."

I laughed, I couldn't help it. "You're extremely disrespectful of your elders, you know."

"An elder is a tree," she said. "I'm extremely respectful of all trees."

I sat down with her. She reached over and mussed my stubbly hair. "It's better now that it's growing in," she said. "You look less like a monk and more like a convict."

I asked what she had going on that day. She planned to be off with friends, as was increasingly her habit. It was good to see her happy.

"Eva woke up," I said.

"Really? The drug worked?"

"Well, *something* worked."

"Wow."

"I was thinking we should celebrate," I said. "How would you feel about a picnic?"

"Sure, just let me know."

She took her bowl to the sink and rinsed it out. Cassie came in and lay down in a patch of sun by the front door. Sophie went over, knelt down, and petted her. Soon Cass was snoring softly.

"Is she okay?" Sophie asked. "Ever since we got here, all she's done is sleep."

"There's a lot to recover from," I said. "She almost got burned up in the tunnel fire, and now she's in another new place she has to get used to."

"Is that all?"

I wasn't sure how much to say, but I wanted to be honest with her. "She's getting to be an older kitty," I said. "She may only have a year or two left."

Sophie was quiet for a moment. "I don't want her to die," she said.

"She'll have a good, safe life here. That's the best we can do for her."

"What a good girl, Cass," she said, but I heard a little waver in her voice. She petted the cat gently for a couple of minutes, then went and got her stuff together for the day. A few minutes later she was out the door.

I went outside to sit on the steps and finish my coffee. I was thinking about Cassie, and trying to figure out how looking like a convict was better than looking like a monk, when Peau came winging in with a little *awk* and landed on the railing beside me.

"Hi!" I said. I reached out and petted his head. "I've been worried about you. Is everything okay?"

He slumped a little, his feathers sagging. He was an outsider here, he said, and the first thing he'd done was get a bunch of birds killed.

He'd had fences to mend, and the flock was still wary. But he'd met someone, which helped.

"Someone as in *someone*?"

He bobbed his head. He was less lonely, he said, and now he had an advocate. He added that she was incredibly smart and that her primary feathers were like nothing he'd ever seen.

I thought it best not to mention that I had trouble telling one raven from another. "Does Cass know?" I asked.

He hadn't seen her yet. He was a little concerned that she might try to kill him.

"Let's go tell her," I said. "I'll hold her, just in case."

Cass woke up and took the news with equanimity. After all, they weren't even the same *species*, she pointed out. She wasn't interested in getting into some sort of competition over him; what would be the point? Peau admitted that that was kind of how he was thinking about it. Then he said he'd enjoyed traveling with us all.

This took me by surprise. "You're going away?"

He was, for a while. The local flock was big, and now that they were in the process of accepting him, he wanted to spend time with them. He asked if I minded.

"Of course I mind," I said. "I'll miss you."

He clacked the raven equivalent of "Well, ditto," which sounded like a one-second tap dance. I smiled, but my eyes were burning. I'd become absurdly emotional lately.

"I hope you'll visit."

He said he would, but I could tell it might be a long while before we saw him again. He said goodbye to Cass; she replied in kind, then lay back down and was quickly asleep again. Peau rubbed his beak against my cheek and made his little cooing noise. He took off, headed north over the treetops, and another couple of ravens swooped in and flanked him. In a few seconds they were gone.

•   •   •

I HADN'T HAD A CHANCE to meditate since doing the *sur* offering for Sophie at the Paris house, and I could tell I needed to. I was jittery and felt as if I wasn't grounded in my own body—a state Lama Sonam had referred to in his Tibetan-inflected English as *lung*-y, meaning that the person's essential energy—the *lung*—was out of balance.

I walked out to the edge of the bluff and sat, cross-legged, facing the sea. The sun was behind me, and the moisture in the air over the water filtered the morning light so that the world appeared soft, gentle, and luminous. I put my hands on my knees and let my eyes rest gently on the open horizon. The waves crashed a hundred feet below in a slow, regular pulse, three or four times a minute, like the roaring heartbeat of a whale. My breathing slowed, and I felt myself grow calmer. There would soon be matters that required planning, I knew, but I didn't need to plan them right now.

I let my thoughts arise like soft clouds in a clear sky, then watched them as they drifted and evaporated. It was helpful, I'd found, to pay attention to this dissipation. Then, after some time, I let that go and didn't think about anything at all, and I began to feel better. It was difficult to describe, a kind of healing or remembrance, a feeling almost of return. I'd told Eva once that I thought my home was with her, and while this was true in a way, I understood now that it didn't fully describe the situation. My place here, on this bluff by the sea, where I was sitting at this very moment, was also my home. As was the openness I'd begun to feel in my heart as I sat; that was a kind of home too. I had always known these things, I realized, though too often I lost sight of them.

I'd told Sophie about the idea of carrying all things on the path—making every experience part of one's meditation, regardless of whether it was wonderful or terrible or somewhere in between. This had mostly been an abstract and unattainable notion to me, I'd said.

But as I sat on the bluff, with the sun warming my back and the sea before me, I began to suspect that it wasn't quite as impossible as I'd always considered it to be. To some extent, I'd been doing it without realizing it, because I'd come to love Sophie so fiercely, so utterly. Carrying that feeling on the path wasn't some distant, idealistic goal, in fact. It was one of the easiest things I'd ever done in my life.

LATER I WENT OVER to find Eva. She was in a better mood and wanted exercise, so we took a walk on the open land adjacent to campus. As we passed through a eucalyptus grove, she told me a joke she'd made up, about a reincarnated Swedish Buddhist who was in a rut because he just kept being Bjorn again. She delivered the punch line and hooted with glee, and then a flock of crows exploded from the trees as if we'd shot off a cannon. It was a terrible joke, of course, just the sort of thing you'd expect from a microbiologist, but it pleased me immensely to hear it.

That afternoon Lars and I helped her move into the apartment, which wasn't particularly challenging since she owned almost nothing and the place was already furnished. After we'd put some food in the fridge, gotten her few spare clothes hung up, and made the bed, I put some water on. We all sat down to tea.

She chose this moment to let Lars know about Lily.

He stared at her, stunned. "Why didn't you tell me before?"

"Will and I had separated. I didn't want you to get involved."

"I would have too," he admitted.

"See?"

He nodded, then turned to me. "You didn't know either?"

I shook my head.

"God, what a situation," he said.

I'd wondered about that situation, of course. Danielle had died in Arizona. Sophie was the right age and had unusual blue-green eyes, like Eva's. They were both prodigiously smart and liked science. I debated whether or not to say anything.

"This girl Sophie I've been traveling with," I began, tentatively.

"Yes?" said Eva.

I told them how we'd met, the various horrors she'd endured. Then I explained about all the coincidences I'd noticed.

Eva sat forward, her eyes large. "Are you saying what I think you're saying?"

"There's a chance," I said. "It's unlikely, but we can't rule it out."

"Does she look like either of us?"

"She has your eyes," I said. "That's mainly it."

Eva seemed a little shaky. "What if she is, Will? Is there any way we can find out?"

"Is there, Lars?"

He sighed. "Our DNA machines are under four feet of saltwater in La Jolla," he said. "There's a lab in town that could draw blood from the three of you and tell you if you *might* be her parents, but not whether you definitely are."

I knew it would be improbable in any case, and ultimately what difference did it make? I was surprised to realize that it didn't make much difference at all to me.

"I'm not sure it's a good idea to put a lot of hope there," I said. "I mainly thought you should know."

"When can I meet her?" Eva asked.

"She's off hiking with friends today," I said. "How about tomorrow afternoon?"

I WALKED LARS HOME after that.

"Eva seems fine," I said. "I'd write it up as a case study if there was still anyplace to publish it."

He allowed himself a tired smile. "With the other patients we have, we'll have better evidence soon."

None of the others had a long-term case like Eva's, he went on. They all suffered from classic Disease X, which might make it more likely that the drug would help. Whatever the outcome, I supposed, there was always the chance that my connection to Eva had played a part in bringing her back. I didn't particularly care; I was just glad something had worked.

Lars asked me, then, about my financial prospects. "You'll need a way to support yourself here," he pointed out.

"Lars—" I began, but he put up a hand.

"I know you don't want to work for me," he said. "Eva can do that if she chooses, but you need to find *something* to do. They're basically founding a new country, and it turns out there's a fair amount of writing involved. I can put you in touch with the right people if you like."

For an aging science journalist with dim prospects, I had to admit it was a welcome opportunity. "Thanks," I said. "I appreciate it."

LATE THE NEXT AFTERNOON, I met Eva at her place, and we set out on foot to pick up food for the picnic.

"What are you going to do about her?" she asked.

I explained my idea, and she nodded. "Are you saying you want me in this with you?"

"It's up to you, obviously."

"I'll have a better sense after I've met her," she said. "And I'll have to keep searching even so. You understand?"

"Of course. You see what I'm asking, though."

"Yes," she said.

"Yes, you see? Or *yes*?"

"Oh, Will, I think so," she said. "I'm jittery, but I have to admit that solitude isn't nearly as interesting to me as it used to be."

"It isn't, is it? Fourteen years without much in the way of company will certainly change your perspective."

We walked on.

"I wonder if we should approach her as a team," she said. "Would she be more receptive?"

"Maybe." I told her what I knew about the process, and she mulled it over as we walked. I suggested that we keep things light. "Sophie won't take it well if it sounds heavy or scary in any way."

"Okay," Eva said.

I noticed her watching me, then.

"You've changed," she said. "I can see it. Or else I have."

"Both of us, I think."

"What happened to you? Something on the way here?"

Partly, I suspected, the constant terrifying proximity to death had left me less anxious about everything else, as if I'd burned out some neural circuitry, and anything this side of agony and annihilation was no longer worth worrying about. But there was more to it, of course, as I'd realized while sitting on the bluff the previous morning.

"Yes," I said, then. "Something on the way." I decided to leave it at that.

Eva smiled. "Well, maybe there's a shred of hope for us." She slipped her arm through mine, the way she had when we'd walked together that first evening in Colorado. "How do you feel about it?"

"I think you know how I feel."

WE ALL GATHERED TOGETHER on a blanket, on a shady bluff over-looking the sea, not far from the sitting spot I'd found. Light played in the leaves overhead. We'd stopped at the cafeteria and picked up some Greek food: grilled lamb, dolmas, spanakopita, hummus and flatbread, a few other things. It was all delicious.

Sophie and Eva both seemed shy and a little nervous about meeting. After we'd eaten a little, Sophie asked, "You were a scientist?"

"I was," said Eva. "I understand that interests you."

Sophie nodded. "What sort of things did you work on?"

Eva explained to her about phages, and Sophie shuddered a little.

"That was pretty much my reaction," I said.

"Well, what do *you* like?" Eva asked. "It's always best to start with that."

"I'm not sure yet," Sophie replied. "I might want to be a veterinarian, but I don't know if there are still any schools for that."

Eva smiled. "That's what I wanted to be when I was your age."

"Really?"

"I wanted to specialize in reptiles," Eva said. "I loved lizards and snakes."

"How come?"

"One day I was on a field trip to a swamp, and I saw a python climbing a tree," she explained, smiling at the memory. "Here was this animal six or seven feet long, as big around as my arm, with no hands or anything obvious to grip with, and it was *climbing a tree*. Then later I saw an even bigger snake swimming. They were *fast*, too, both of them. To me, it all seemed preposterous, as if it should have been physically impossible. Right then I was hooked."

"But it didn't work out?" Sophie asked.

Eva shook her head. "The only way to make a living as a herp vet was to work for a zoo, and I hated zoos."

"I thought I might specialize in cats and birds," Sophie said.

"Not sure that's practical," I interjected.

"Why not?"

"Think of the chaos in the waiting room."

"Don't listen to him," said Eva.

"It's all right; I don't."

I opened the cabernet and poured us all some.

"It's okay for you to drink?" Eva asked Sophie.

"Just a little wine once in a while," she answered, bristling a bit.

"I'm sorry," said Eva. "It wasn't my place to ask."

"We're in a lawless society," I said. "She drives now, too. It's crazy-town out there."

We ate and talked, and everyone seemed to relax. Eva was curious about my travels, so I told her what I'd seen, with an emphasis on megafauna. Camels and wolves; bison and tigers and bears, oh my.

"All those zoo animals you used to worry about are out devouring each other now," I added cheerfully, teasing her.

But of course she gave as good as she got. "Too bad they didn't eat *you*," she said, and Sophie laughed.

When we were nearly finished with the food, I turned to Sophie. "We might have a smallish proposal for you," I said.

She looked up warily. "Okay . . ."

"After Mayhem, there were so many orphans that they had to streamline the adoption laws around here, and it turns out they left a couple of loopholes."

"Such as?"

"Well, we were thinking you might not want us to formally adopt you, because then you'd have to do what we say."

"Good guess."

"It turns out they accidentally took out the age stipulations," Eva explained. "So we were wondering if you'd like to adopt *us* instead."

Sophie smiled. "Then you'd have to do what *I* say?"

"Yeah," I replied. "Though you'd have to go to work and support us. We'd need allowances."

"Fuck that," said Sophie, and I laughed. "Next idea?"

"Well, I suppose we could do it the usual way," I offered.

"It's very simple now," said Eva. "We all go down to the courthouse and have a brief interview, then we sign the papers and it's done."

"Uh-huh . . . ," said Sophie noncommittally.

I noticed Eva quietly collecting herself, and I figured a difficult question was coming.

"Do you happen to know your birthday?" she asked.

Sophie paused, registering the import of this, but then shook her head. "We were never really sure," she said. "Sometime between April and June of 2033."

"I see," said Eva. "So you'll be fifteen soon if you're not already." Our eyes met for a moment, but I couldn't tell what she was thinking. *I* was thinking that this didn't prove a thing, regardless of how much she might want it to.

"Look, Eva," said Sophie. "Will told me a little of your story, so I get why you want to know. To me it seems ridiculous that you might be adopting your own daughter, but mainly I wonder what happens if I'm *not*, and you find Lily someday."

"Then you'll have a sister your own age," said Eva.

Sophie studied her plate. "That doesn't sound completely terrible, I guess, as long as she's nice."

Eva regarded us with that astute, evaluative gaze of hers, then stood up and brushed the crumbs off her pants. "It's been a long day for me," she said. "Do you mind if I head home and leave you the clearing up?"

"Sure," I said, and Sophie nodded.

Eva gathered her things, told Sophie she'd enjoyed meeting her, and walked away. She gave me an opaque backward glance, and I could see that she didn't quite know what to think.

"She seems okay," Sophie said. She looked a little unsettled, though. "Can I tell you what bothers me about this?"

"Of course."

She took a breath. "Aren't you going to want to spend all your time with her now?" she asked. "I mean, I know how obsessed you've been all these years, and I worry that I'll never see you."

This caught me off guard. "Thanks, Sophie," I said. "But you're going to see plenty of me. You don't have to worry about that."

"I'm just not always great with change."

I explained that we'd likely be living together regardless, that the only difference was whether she wanted us to be officially responsible for her. Sometimes she'd have to do what we said, but I trusted her judgment.

"So if I agree, I'll get an actual allowance?"

"Ah, there it is," I said, chuckling. "I'm not sure what they use for money here, but yeah, we'll figure it out."

She began picking up the stuff from dinner and putting it in a bag. "Let me sleep on it, okay?"

"Sure."

We finished tidying up, then hung around to watch the sunset. A low gray cloud drifted across the sky, a half mile out to sea, dragging a light curtain of rain. The droplets, illuminated from behind by the sun, briefly appeared to be embers drifting down.

"That's what my life feels like," Sophie said quietly.

"Like what, exactly?"

"Like a raindrop that's left the cloud," she went on. "And then for a little while, as I'm falling, I'm transparent and full of light. Does that make any sense at all?"

She was such a surprise, this one. "Sure," I said, feeling moved. "An old guy named Shri Simha said something similar, a long time ago."

"Really?" she asked. "What did he say happens when the raindrop hits the water?"

"It dissolves, and then it knows everything the ocean knows."

"I like that," she said, and then she surprised me again by wiping away a tear. "I like that a *lot*, actually."

I put my arm around her as the sun slipped down behind garish clouds, all oranges and magentas and burgundies. A few minutes later, when the sun had set, the rain shone silver again, then eventually lightened into mist, drifting slowly upward until it vanished.

Sophie was warm beside me, leaning in.

Acknowledgments

My deepest thanks to Cindy Spiegel for her willingness to give this novel a read, and for being audacious enough to publish it. For any writer familiar with the world of contemporary publishing, working with Spiegel & Grau is like finding yourself in heaven without having to die first. Cindy is a prodigiously skilled editor whose astute observations and tactful suggestions have vastly improved the book.

I'm also grateful to her and to Julie Grau for the exceptional team they've put together, including Liza Wachter, Jacqueline Fischetti, Amy Metsch, Nicole Dewey, Barry Harbaugh, Joey McGarvey, Aaron Robertson, Andrew Tan-Delli Cicchi, Jess Bonet, Patsy Tucker, Nora Tomas, Lucia Gorman, and Natalie Wilson. Thanks, too, to Jamie Byng at Canongate, and to Susanna Lea of her eponymous literary agency, for their tremendous enthusiasm and support for the book in the U.K. and other overseas markets. My hawk-eyed copyeditor, Barrett Briske, did an excellent job spotting aspects of the book that were inconsistent, awkward, or otherwise distracting. I'm especially thrilled to have such an elegant, dynamic cover design by the talented Madeline Partner. I must also thank Hana Landes, who was an extremely helpful presence at S&G when they published my debut novel a dozen years ago; I'm embarrassed to say I forgot to thank her then.

My embryonic ideas about the natural landscape I wanted to create in this book were greatly clarified by Alan Weisman's brilliant thought experiment, *The World Without Us*, which made a compelling case for what planet earth might be like in the sudden absence of human beings. I'm greatly in his debt.

What modest knowledge I have of Buddhist philosophy and practices I credit to my superb teachers in the Tibetan tradition, most notably Chagdud Tulku Rinpoche, Khentrul Lodrö T'hayé Rinpoche, and Lama Padma Drimed Norbu. I owe them more than I can say for their immense kindness and patient instruction.

I was privileged to learn most of what I know about ravens by observing the large resident flock at Rigdzin Ling, a Buddhist retreat center in the Trinity Alps of Northern California, during the years I spent there in the early 2000s. Those smart, playful, and opportunistic birds were a marvel and an education. That said, I supplemented this experience with two secondary sources, *The Book of the Raven* by Caroline Roberts and Angus Hyland, and *Mind of the Raven* by Bernd Heinrich, both of which provided valuable insights into raven behavior and communication that I hadn't noticed.

I want to acknowledge my late older brother, Cam, for giving me a wisely curated plenitude of books when I was in college, longer ago than I'd now care to admit. These included two novels that ignited a slow-burning subterranean root fire that ultimately inspired this book: Robert Pirsig's *Zen and the Art of Motorcycle Maintenance* and Russell Hoban's *Riddley Walker*. Those books opened my mind to the possibilities of novels and changed me as a writer. Thanks, also, to my brother Chris, an excellent physician who's always game to shed light on the medical aspects of a narrative and help me avoid miscellaneous blunders.

This book wouldn't be what it is without a small circle of trusted readers who provided helpful insight into the weaknesses of my early drafts. These include the marvelous novelist Elizabeth Evans, my mentor in the MFA program at the University of Arizona and a dear friend to this day; and Tom Higgins, a gracious and careful reader who more than once kept the wolf from the door as my publisher during my years as a journalist. I'm particularly indebted to two of my former students, Chelsea Bowlby and Sachiko Ragosta, both profoundly gifted writers themselves. They usually understood what I was *trying* to do even when I was failing at it, and kindly let me know when I was being clueless about all kinds of things, as I so often am.

Finally, my deepest and most heartfelt thanks to my wife, Patti, who has been a kind, loving, and steadying presence in my life for more than thirty years. I'm a very lucky man.

About the Author

Cary Groner grew up in the Midwest and has lived primarily on the West Coast since finishing college. For many years, he has worked as a journalist covering medicine, healthcare, and the arts. He earned his MFA in fiction writing from the University of Arizona in 2009; since then, his short stories have won numerous awards and appeared in venues that include *Glimmer Train, American Fiction, Southern California Review, Salamander, Sycamore Review, Mississippi Review, Tampa Review,* and *Zymbol.* His debut novel, *Exiles,* was published by Spiegel & Grau (Random House) in 2011, and was a *Chicago Tribune* "favorite book" of that year. Cary has taught fiction writing at UA, UCLA online, and the Berkeley Writing Salon. He lives with his wife in the San Francisco Bay Area.